BAD SOLDIER

Also by Chris Ryan

CHRIS RYAN

BAD SOLDIER

Waterford City and County
Libraries

CORONET

First published in Great Britain in 2016 by Coronet
An imprint of Hodder & Stoughton
An Hachette UK company

1

A CIP catalogue record for this title is available from the British Library

Hardback ISBN: 978 1 444 78337 7
Trade Paperback ISBN: 978 1 444 78338 4
Ebook ISBN: 978 1 444 78335 3

Typeset in Bembo by Hewer Text UK Ltd, Edinburgh

Printed and bound by Clays Ltd, St Ives pl

Hodder & Stoughton policy is to use papers that are natural, renewable
and recyclable products and made from wood grown in sustainable forests.
The logging and manufacturing processes are expected to conform
to the environmental regulations of the country of origin.

Hodder & Stoughton Ltd
Carmelite House
50 Victoria Embankment
London EC4Y 0DZ

www.hodder.co.uk

PROLOGUE

Her people called themselves the Yazidi. Her captors called her a devil-worshipper. But really she was just a young girl.

Baba was sixteen and she had forgotten what it felt like not to be scared.

When the news had come that the fighters from Islamic State had surrounded her village in the shadow of Mount Sinjar in northern Iraq, the women started to scream, because they knew what it meant for their daughters. Baba's own mother did not survive the attack. Nor did her father. But they lived long enough to see what happened to their girls. In the one main room of their tiny house, the fighters had forced Baba's parents to their knees at gunpoint, then made the old couple watch as they beat and raped Baba's two younger sisters. They were twelve and fourteen.

The details of that afternoon would haunt Baba as long as she lived. She would remember the pitiful screaming of her mother and father, which the fighters turned into a muted whimpering by thrashing them hard round the side of their heads with the butts of their assault rifles, until they bled profusely. She would always remember her mother begging them to take her instead of the girls, and the way the fighters laughed and said they would rather plant themselves in a pig than in her wrinkled old body. She would remember one of them calmly explaining that, since Baba's family practised a religion other than Islam, the Qu'ran allowed true believers to rape them. It would draw the fighters, he said, closer to God.

But most of all, Baba would remember her sisters. They were too frightened to scream, and too young to understand what was

1

happening as the men bound their arms and gagged them, before prostrating themselves in prayer and then . . .

Baba tried not to picture what they had done to them next.

Several times a night, Baba's troubled sleep would be broken by the memory of the two gunshots that had killed her parents in front of their daughters. Each time she relived it, it felt as if the bullets had gone through Baba herself. And the image of her sisters being dragged, semi-clothed, out of the house with one last, tearful, uncomprehending look at Baba, was fixed in her mind.

'*Please* . . .' she had begged the one fighter who remained in the room with her. 'Please don't take my sisters from me. They are only babies . . .'

The man had surveyed her calmly. He wore black clothes and had a bandolier of ammunition over his shoulder. His open shirt revealed a horrific scar across the width of his neck. It was the same shape as a smile. He stood close enough to Baba that she could smell the sweat on his body. He traced that scar with his forefinger.

'You see this, devil girl?' he had whispered. 'This was given to me by an American soldier. He tried to cut my throat. I bled like a slaughtered goat, but I did not die. Allah protects those who do his work. Remember that, if you are thinking of doing anything stupid.'

'Please,' Baba had whispered in reply. 'My sisters . . .'

'Your sisters are to be given to my men,' the fighter had replied. 'They deserve it.'

'They are only children.'

'*Infidel* children. Each time my men have them, it will be *ibadah* . . . worship.' He stretched out one hand and caressed Baba's cheek. 'But for you, my pretty thing, greater honours await.'

The man with the throat scar had bound Baba's wrists behind her back and shoved a rag into her mouth to keep her quiet. Then he had forced her, at gunpoint, out of the house. Baba had looked desperately around, trying to find her younger sisters. They were nowhere to be seen. About twenty other men and women had been lined up in the shade of the acacia tree in the middle of the village, blindfolded and forced to their knees. Five fighters brandishing weapons were walking up and down the line, barking harsh obscenities at these people Baba had known all her life. Her best friend Parsa was there, and her uncle Labib. Baba had to avert her eyes when one of the fighters put his gun to Labib's head. She didn't see the gunshot that killed him, but she heard it.

The man with the throat scar threw her into the back of a vehicle. There were two other IS men in there. Before she knew what was happening, they were driving her out of the village where she had spent her entire life. Baba was numb. Too shocked to cry, too frightened to speak.

She didn't know how long they drove for. Perhaps four hours. It was dark by the time they pulled off the main highway and stopped. Her throat burned with thirst and her eyes stung. The driver killed the engine. Silence. The car's headlamps lit up the rough road ahead, but it seemed to Baba that they were in the middle of nowhere. She started to panic. Why had they stopped? Did these men want to do something so terrible to her that they needed to come far from civilisation to do it?

It was with a mixture of relief and dread that Baba saw a sudden burst of light. They were at some kind of checkpoint. The man with the throat scar opened the window. The guards clearly recognised him. They lowered their weapons and waved them on.

They came to a second checkpoint. It was in a high fence, with rolls of razor wire along the top. Again they were waved through. A minute later they stopped at a compound of buildings. They were by a body of water – maybe a reservoir.

The man with the throat scar pulled Baba from the car. She was dazzled by moving beams of torchlight, but still aware of there being many men in the compound – at least fifteen, all of them armed. Four or five of them had dogs on leashes: muscular, snarling beasts, straining to get at her. There was the occasional bark. Ferocious.

But not as ferocious as the men. They leered nastily at her. Baba could tell what they wanted.

'She belongs to Dhul Faqar,' the man with the throat scar shouted. That was enough to make them all step back, and disappear into the darkness, dragging their straining dogs with them.

Baba registered a little more about her surroundings. This was clearly a big compound. There were several buildings that she could see, and peeking up from behind one of them was the rim of a large white satellite dish. There were vehicles – open-topped trucks – all dusty and dented. Some of the buildings were covered with black graffiti, and there were a couple of flags hanging from them, showing the insignia of Islamic State.

Baba's captor pulled her towards the nearest building. There were two more armed men guarding this door, and they grinned as Baba was dragged towards them.

Her captor stopped. 'You are about to meet Dhul Faqar,' he said. 'If you look him straight in the eye, he will kill you.'

He didn't explain any further, but just knocked three times on the door. It opened. He pushed Baba across the threshold.

The room was warm, dimly lit and smelled of cinnamon. It was richly furnished, with sofas, embroidered cushions and patterned rugs on the floor. A fire was burning. There were two people in here, a man and a woman. The man was short and stout, with a long black beard greying at the tips. He wore white robes and white socks with leather sandals. His head was covered with a red and white *shemagh*. He was sitting on a comfortable low chair, and was nursing a glass of mint tea. His face was expressionless as he turned to look at Baba. She quickly averted her eyes.

The woman sat at the back of the room, next to another door, which was painted blue. She was very beautiful, with long dark hair and almond eyes. But she looked out of place, because she was dressed in Western clothes. A laptop computer sat on a small, ornate table next to her, and her face glowed in the light from its screen. She was applying nail varnish and she glanced up at Baba as she entered. There was something in her expression that chilled Baba to the core.

'Dhul Faqar,' Baba's captor said, bowing his head slightly. He was also avoiding eye contact.

'Mujahid,' the man replied. 'What is this you've brought us?'

'A gift. One of the Yazidi. I gave her sisters to my men, but I thought this one would please you.'

Dogs barked somewhere outside.

The woman walked up to Baba. Baba could smell her perfume, heavy and musky. It made her want to gag.

'We can't see her face properly,' she whispered. With a rough yank, she pulled the rag from Baba's mouth. Her long nails, glistened. Baba inhaled deeply, then tried to swallow, but her mouth was too dry and it hurt her throat.

The woman reached out her hand and brushed it against Baba's cheek, in almost exactly the same way that the man called Mujahid had done back in the village. Baba noticed that she wore several large rings on her fingers. 'She's a pretty one,' the woman purred. And when Baba yanked her face away from that horrible touch, she smiled. 'Are you a virgin?'

The question caught Baba by surprise. She nodded warily.

'You'll enjoy breaking this one in, my love,' the woman said. And she muttered, 'To the glory of Allah.'

'Get her cleaned up,' Dhul Faqar said. 'She stinks worse than a horse. Mujahid, you stay here. We have things to discuss.'

The woman turned. 'Follow me,' she said as she stepped towards the blue door at the far side of the room.

Mujahid pushed Baba in the same direction. She stumbled. The woman stopped and turned. When she saw that Baba had hesitated, she stepped back up to her again. Her eyes narrowed – she looked like she was sizing Baba up. With a sudden, brutal swipe, she hit Baba hard across her face. Baba gasped. The woman's long nails were viciously sharp. Baba felt blood trickling down her stinging cheek, but could not wipe it away because her hands were still tied behind her back. The woman stepped close to her again. She touched Baba's bleeding cheek, then showed her her fingertips. They were smeared with a mixture of deep-red blood and slightly lighter nail varnish. 'You are nothing,' she whispered. 'You are less important to me than an insect. I wouldn't think twice about treading on an insect, and I wouldn't think twice about treading on you. Every second that you stay alive, it is only because Dhul Faqar allows it. You are his to do with as he wants. If you deny him anything, you'll have me to answer to, and I'd rather see you dead. Do you understand?'

Baba managed to nod. When the woman continued across the room, she followed, only looking back over her shoulder when she heard the main door open again. She caught a quick glimpse of two more men. They were both unusually tall. One had very dark skin – he almost looked African, not Middle Eastern. The other had a milky patch of discoloured skin on the left-hand side of his face, as if he had been badly burned as a child. They were both averting their eyes from Dhul Faqar.

Baba didn't dare look at these newcomers any longer. The woman had opened the blue door and was disappearing through it. Baba followed. She found herself in a much less comfortable room. It had a stone floor, bare brick walls and a further door on the far wall. There was no furniture. Just a dim light bulb hanging from a single cord in the low ceiling. Baba had a sudden vision of herself hanging from that cord.

The woman closed and locked the door behind them. 'You will stay here,' she told Baba. 'You will be completely silent. If you disturb Dhul Faqar with your whimpering, I will cut out your tongue. If you don't believe me, I invite you to put me to the test. Do you understand?'

Baba nodded.

The woman left the room. Baba heard the sound of a lock clicking, and knew that there was no way she could escape.

Her knees would not support her. She collapsed, a shivering, bleeding, sobbing, terrified mess. As she lay crouched on the floor, she relived the monstrous events of that day – her parents, and her poor, poor sisters. She longed to be close to them. To hug them. To tell them everything would be alright, and hear the same reassurance in return. But deep down, she knew it would *not* be alright. Nothing would be alright ever again . . .

She heard dogs sniffing and growling by the far door. They

terrified her, so she crawled to the opposite end of the room, collapsing again right outside Dhul Faqar's door.

Baba didn't know how long she lay there, lost in that awful, waking nightmare. But gradually she became aware of voices on the other side of the door. She recognised Dhul Faqar, and Mujahid who had the scar on his throat. And although she couldn't work out what they were saying, she could hear certain words.

'Attack . . .'

She remembered how the IS fighters had attacked her own village that day. How they had killed people without seeming to think about it.

'Terror . . .'

She remembered the terror in her sisters' eyes. The way they had begged their rapists to stop, because it hurt so much.

'Jihad . . .'

It was a word all the Yazidi knew well. She knew the story of how, when she was just three years old, four suicide bombers had killed nearly 800 Yazidis. People said it was the second deadliest jihadi attack after the planes that had flown into tall buildings in America.

The room started to spin. Baba's exhaustion was catching up with her. She was desperate for a drink, but she dreaded asking that awful woman with the almond eyes.

'British . . .'

She had heard that word before. She knew there was a country called Britain, far away. Or was it part of America? Baba wasn't quite sure. Her face was throbbing badly. A curiously hopeful thought crossed her mind. Maybe, if the cut made her look ugly, Dhul Faqar would not touch her. But another thought followed quickly. *It's not your face he wants you for . . .*

'Westminster . . .'

The word meant nothing to Baba. She was hardly listening anyway. She started violently as she heard a key turn on the other side of the far door. Terrified, she lifted her head. The far door opened. The woman appeared. She looked calm, but somehow all the more terrifying for it.

'What do you think you're doing, devil girl?' she demanded. 'Eavesdropping?'

Baba shook her head. 'No ...' she whispered. 'I promise ... I was just—'

But the woman was storming towards her. She bent down, grabbed a clump of Baba's hair and pulled her harshly to her feet.

'I wasn't listening ...' Baba wailed. 'I didn't hear anything ...'

But she was silenced by another hard slap across her cheek. 'If you ever listen to things that do not concern you,' the woman breathed, 'I will throw you to the common soldiers, like your whore sisters. Do you understand?'

It was all Baba could do to nod.

The woman yanked her towards the open door. Baba didn't – couldn't – resist. But before she was dragged across the floor, she heard one more word from the adjoining room. Again, she had heard it before, but it meant very little to her.

The word was 'Christmas'.

DECEMBER 20

ONE

Sigonella NATO base, Sicily. Dusk.

The snow-capped peak of Mount Etna was lost in the dark clouds that boiled over the island of Sicily. Chief airman Romano Messi watched them through the windscreen of his olive-green Land Rover, whose wiper blades were clearing a thin drizzle from the glass. Romano was a young recruit to the Italian airforce, and had lived on the island all his life. He remembered his grandmother saying that when the sky went dark over Etna, trouble was round the corner. But she was just a superstitious old lady. In Sicily, with its gangs and its undercurrent of violence, trouble was *always* round the corner.

A fork of lightning split the sky, but the only thunder that followed it was artificial. It came from the four engines of a British Hercules C4 turboprop, as grey as the clouds from which it now emerged as it made its descent towards the runway. Romano had been waiting for this aircraft. They had all been waiting for it.

The runway was brightly lit. There was only another thirty minutes until sunset, but it was already half dark. Ground crew staff sat in stationary service vehicles, well clear of the runway itself, but with their engines ticking over. The word had come through two hours previously: this aircraft, and its four passengers, were high priority. The ATC operators knew to get the Hercules on the ground as quickly as possible – any other military aircraft wanting to land at the same time would have to circle. The passengers were to be ushered as quickly as possible to the nearby helicopter LZ. That was Romano's job. Get them to the chopper, and don't ask any questions. He knew that instructions like this could only mean one thing: a special forces unit was on its way.

It was an unusual situation. This was a British military plane. They often stopped here to refuel, but the passengers were generally not allowed to disembark. When they did, SF units were normally housed in the American sector of the NATO base. Italian squaddies like Romano were kept well away.

Romano blew a lock of his black hair off his forehead, then absent-mindedly brushed down his khaki camouflage gear. One day, he thought to himself, he would put himself up for selection to the *Stormo Incursori*. He and the guys he was about to meet were made from the same stuff. His eyes wandered to the tiny length of Christmas tinsel wrapped round the stem of the rear-view mirror. Deciding it didn't make him look hard enough, he tore it away and shoved it in the glove compartment.

The Hercules' engines screamed as the landing gear hit the runway in a cloud of spray. Romano knocked the Land Rover into first gear and screeched in the direction of the Hercules before it had even turned off the runway. Through the drizzle, he saw the aircraft come to a complete standstill. The tailgate opened immediately. By the time it was down, Romano had come to a halt twenty metres away. He saw four figures emerging from the dark belly of the aircraft. Two of them led the way. The other two, a few metres behind, were carrying a flight case between them. Romano squinted as he tried to make out their faces, but he couldn't, quite. All he could see was that they were all shouldering bergens, and one of them was slightly narrower about the shoulders than the others. He congratulated himself on his powers of observation – surveillance, he knew, would be an important skill when he became a special forces operator.

Romano got out of the car and jogged towards the aircraft, whose engines were still powering down. As he grew closer, the four figures became more distinct. Halfway towards them, he stopped for a moment. Was one of them a woman?

Romano wiped the rain from his face and looked again. He hadn't made a mistake. The figure with a slimmer frame was a stunning brunette, with grey eyes and clear, pale skin. Her hair was a tangled, rain-soaked mess, but to Romano's eyes that only made her look more attractive.

He started jogging towards them again, taking in the others. Standing next to the woman was a broad-shouldered man with thick blond hair and tanned, leathery skin. He was looking disdainfully across the airfield. Romano could immediately tell he had a bit of an attitude about him. The two guys carrying the flight case were both scowling. One of them was a little shorter than the others, with thinning hair, and the sight of him made Romano smile briefly. His dad had a penchant for Phil Collins, and the little guy looked just like him. Broader, stockier and a hell of a sight grumpier-looking, but otherwise the spitting image. His companion didn't look much more cheerful. With hair as dark as Romano's own, and a handsome face with several days' stubble, he looked like a statue, holding the flight case as the rain pelted against him.

Romano was a little out of breath when he reached them, but he did his best to hide it. 'Good evening, gentlemen,' he said in his very best English. The blond guy looked him up and down, and Romano could tell from his body language that he was in charge of this four-man unit. 'I am taking you to your helicopter.'

The unit leader looked over Romano's shoulder towards the distant Land Rover. 'Fuck's sake, Manuel,' he said with an unpleasant sneer. 'I know the I-tais are shit drivers, but couldn't you park a bit closer?'

Romano felt an embarrassed frown cross his forehead. 'No . . . I mean, I *could* . . .' He jabbed his thumb towards the vehicle.

'Forget it, shit-for-brains.' The man looked over his shoulder. 'Danny and Spud could use the workout, right lads? Especially Spud. Need to get him match fit. He's spent the last six months in hand to gland contact.'

Romano didn't know what he was talking about. The blond man pushed past him and started walking towards the Land Rover. The woman looked at the two guys – Danny and Spud, had he called them? – then she jogged after the blond man.

This really wasn't going the way Romano had wanted. He turned to Danny and Spud. 'I could maybe help you ...' he said. Neither man even glanced at him. They were watching the unit leader, with murder in their eyes. Romano jogged alongside them as they followed after the woman and the blond man. 'So guys,' he said, 'where are you headed?'

No response. Just dark scowls. As they approached the Land Rover, Romano saw that the blond man had already taken the front passenger seat. The woman was opening up the back of the vehicle ready to receive the flight case. The rain was falling more heavily now. Everyone was soaked.

Danny and Spud loaded up. Romano meekly took his place behind the wheel. When the others were installed in the back seat, he turned the ignition. The windscreen wipers flapped noisily as the vehicle trundled across the airfield.

'Fuckin' Sicily,' the blond man said. 'I thought it was meant to be all sunshine and sardines.'

'And organised crime,' Phil Collins said darkly. 'Right up your street, eh, Tony?'

Tony – that was obviously the blond man's name – looked in the rear-view mirror. 'Do us a solid, Caitlin love, stick a .762 in that bald cunt's skull, save me messing up my hands.'

Caitlin, the woman, smiled. 'Mind if I do it later?' she said in a very pronounced Australian accent. 'Don't want to mess up the upholstery for this two-pot screamer.' She jabbed Romano on the shoulder.

'Caitlin, Tony, cut it out,' said the man with dark hair.

'What's that?' Tony said in an exaggeratedly loud voice. 'Did Danny Black say something?' He smiled nastily. 'Last time I checked, Black, *I* was unit commander. So do us all a favour and keep your cakehole shut, eh?'

Romano looked in the rear-view mirror. If Danny Black looked annoyed, it was nothing compared to the expression on Spud's face, which was filled with undisguised hate. Tony looked over his shoulder at the same time. 'Spud, mate, relax. You should learn to enjoy yourself.' He sniffed and faced forward again. 'You could get run over by a bus tomorrow.' As he said this, he pulled a handgun from his ops waistcoat and ostentatiously started checking it over.

All of a sudden, Romano could barely breathe with the tension. He'd given up wanting to find out what these people were here for. He just wanted them out of his vehicle before the pot boiled over. He even twitched nervously when Tony said, 'How far to the chopper, Manuel?'

Romano pointed to his ten o'clock. The LZ was visible 100 metres away through the rainy twilight. A steel-grey RAF chopper – a Wildcat – was there, surrounded by three more military vehicles, the beams from their headlamps cutting through the rain.

'How about dropping us a little closer than half a mile to the LZ?' Tony said. 'Unlike you, we've got a bit more to do than chauffeur people round an airfield all night.' He frowned. 'Rear-echelon motherfucker,' he muttered under his breath.

It was a blowy night for a chopper ride. The Med was as rough as Danny had ever seen it. But it wasn't nearly as rough as the atmosphere inside the Wildcat.

Danny wanted to be anywhere else but here. Back home, his three-month-old daughter was waiting for him. Danny had wanted to name her Susan after his own mother. But the child's mother, Clara, had vetoed it and they'd named her Rose. Danny and Clara were together, but things were not good between them. It didn't seem to affect the baby, though. She was a good-natured kid, with a shock of black hair just like his own. Clara told Danny that babies were supposed to look like their dads because it stopped them from leaving mother and child after the birth. It had led to an argument, of course, with Danny trying to explain that his was not the kind of job that kept him safely behind a desk, and back home for bath time.

No. Danny's job was the kind that meant that on a blustery December night, five days before Christmas, he had to be cruising high above the choppy waves on his way to RV with HMS

Enterprise, a Royal Navy Echo-class survey vessel, currently on Mediterranean rescue deployment. The waters of the Med were awash with migrant boats, crammed full of frightened, impoverished refugees fleeing the battle zones of the Middle East. It was *Enterprise*'s job to help these people when their barely seaworthy boats fell apart in the middle of their crossing, as they almost inevitably would.

Danny glanced at Tony. The bastard had been insufferable since their OC had taken him to one side in Hereford and given him unit command. It was an obvious snub for Danny, who'd been i/c last time they'd done a job together. Since then, it had been no secret around RAF Credenhill that Danny and Tony were at each other's throats. The way Danny saw it, giving Tony the nod was a clear indication of which side of that particular fence the Ruperts had come down on.

But the bad blood between Danny and Tony wasn't the worst of it. It was an open secret that Tony was having a fling with Caitlin, the Aussie military intelligence operator currently sitting to his right. She'd more than proved her worth, but Danny didn't like it. It wasn't the fact that Tony was a married man that bugged him – what Tony did on his own time was none of Danny's concern. But having two members of the unit shagging each other was a liability. Their minds would be on something else, when they *should* be on the job in hand.

And then there was Spud. He and Tony had hated each other since the day they met. While Spud had been temporarily invalided out of the Regiment in the wake of a disastrous foray into the deserts of northern Yemen, it hadn't been a problem. But Spud had, against all the odds, regained his fitness and shown his mettle. Now he was under the command of the man he loathed the most.

Spud had his eyes closed as he sat against the webbing-clad side wall of the Wildcat. Tony was staring at him with a cold expression, like he was sizing him up. Danny had seen that look on Tony's face before. He had a bad feeling about the next few hours.

Danny had warned their ops officer, Ray Hammond, before they'd left base. 'It's a bad call, boss. Tony doesn't have the respect.'

Danny wasn't about to grass anybody up, but surely Hammond had heard enough of the whispers about Tony Wiseman – that his loyalty to the Regiment came a distant second to his lucrative contacts in organised crime. Spud's jibe had been bang on. And everyone had seen Tony's wife Frances around Hereford, with a split lip and a shiner on her left eye that she insisted had come from falling down the stairs.

'Just do your job, Black,' Hammond had said. 'And be thankful you've got one. There's more than one spook in Whitehall gunning for you. They look after their own. Take my advice and keep your head down.'

So Danny was doing just that.

It was grimy and noisy in the Wildcat. The flight crew had given them headsets but none of the unit were wearing them. Caitlin pulled out some A4 photographs from her bergen and handed them around, two for each person. Danny studied the pictures for what felt like the hundredth time in the last twenty-four hours.

The two photographs showed two different individuals. Danny knew that they were both Iraqi, although one of them had much darker skin than the other. The photograph showed this guy walking out from behind an open-topped technical, with the rubble of a demolished city building in the background. He was obviously very tall – maybe six foot six – and he had an AK-47 strapped to his chest.

The man in the second photograph looked very different. Shorter, for a start, and with a piebald white patch on his face, as though he had been burned as a kid. He also carried a rifle, but his surroundings were not urban. He was standing in front of an ancient desert ruin. Danny didn't know what it was, but he did know it was unlikely still to be standing, given IS's liking for blowing up anything of cultural importance in the badlands of Syria and Iraq.

'Fucking muppet,' Tony shouted over the noise of the chopper, holding his picture of the piebald militant in the air. 'Face like a robber's dog, too. They might as well send us a link to their fucking Facebook page.'

Danny didn't allow himself to show that he agreed with Tony. He examined the pictures again, ensuring that he'd committed them to memory. Because in approximately three hours, he'd need to identify these men in the flesh.

'Their names are Mahmod and Kasim,' the ops officer had told them in the briefing room back in Hereford. 'Codenamed Santa and Rudolph. Monsters of our own making.'

'What do you mean?' asked Danny.

'They both lost their parents during the Allied invasion of Iraq. Prime recruits for IS, but unknown to MI6 until the last couple of days. The Firm intercepted an NSA intelligence briefing about them which the Yanks have forgotten to share with us.'

'Friends like that,' muttered Spud, 'who needs enemies?'

'Quite. Seems like the CIA have evidence these two cunts are on their way to the UK. They're using a migrant boat as cover. It means they can get into Europe without the need for a passport. Just two more faces out of thousands. Nobody's going to ask any questions. The Yanks seem to think Santa and Rudolph might have terrorist intentions on UK soil, so why they haven't shared this with us is anyone's guess. Bottom line is, the Americans mustn't know that we're going after these suspects, because then they'll realise we're intercepting their intel. You'll forward-mount from the Italian section of Sigonella base, not the American section, and the ship's captain of HMS *Enterprise* has instructions to keep all non-essential crew below decks when the time comes – we don't want any loose tongues. We have local eyes on the ground in Libya that tell us the migrant boat is called the *Ocean Star*, and it will be setting sail from the north African coast at approximately midday tomorrow, heading for the southern tip of Greece. You can expect to RV with the ship approximately 200 nautical miles from the Sicilian coast. You're looking at about 100 personnel on the *Ocean Star*, all told. We'll be monitoring the currents and the sea state, so HMS *Enterprise* should have no trouble intercepting it. We're aiming for a midnight boarding. There's a Marine unit on board the ship. They'll surround the *Ocean Star* and offer fire support if you need it. You need to board the *Ocean*

Star, bring it alongside HMS *Enterprise*, cross-deck the migrants, identify the targets, get the migrants back on board and transport Santa and Rudolph to an interrogation centre for questioning.'

'Why not just drop us into Libya?' Spud had interrupted. 'We can pick the fuckers up before they set sail, instead of mucking around in the dark on a moving platform.' Danny had wanted to ask the same question. Was there was something about these instructions that didn't add up?

'Why not just keep your mouth shut and listen to your orders? Once you've isolated the targets, you'll await further instructions on the ship regarding transporting them to the interrogation centre. OK, you're dismissed. Tony, hang back a second. I need a word.'

None of the others had heard what Hammond had told Tony. Maybe he'd been warning the unit leader not to be an asshole. If so, he'd be wasting his breath.

'Fifteen minutes out!' the co-pilot shouted from the cockpit.

Spud opened his eyes. Danny leaned forward and unfastened the flight case that they'd carried on to the Wildcat. It contained their hardware: HK416s for the guys, and Caitlin's signature, harder-hitting HK417. Sig 225s, holstered up, for each of them. Their extra rounds were already stashed in their black ops waistcoats, along with their flashbang grenades and med kits. This was apparently a straightforward op – they were unlikely to put down a single round – but as Danny clipped on his Kevlar helmet and boom mike, he started mentally preparing himself for the job anyway. If he'd learned one thing during his time in the Regiment, it was that things often failed to go exactly as you planned. Now was the time to put aside any tension between them. They needed to work as a single unit, not as a collection of egos.

Danny sensed the others putting their heads in a similar place as they checked over their weapons and strapped them to their bodies. The Wildcat banked sharply. From the side window, Danny saw the lights of a naval ship glowing below them in the night. He felt a little surge in his stomach. He might be hundreds of miles from his baby daughter, the unit might be at each other's throats – but there was a buzz of excitement that preceded every op, and it was almost impossible to stamp it out. It was why you did the job in the first place.

The chopper lost height. A minute later, it was setting down on the landing deck of the ship. Proximity to the LZ made Danny realise how hard the wind was blowing – the helicopter was shaking badly as the landing gear connected with the ship. As soon as they had the thumbs-up from the co-pilot, however, the unit jumped out on to the deck and ran, shoulders bowed, away from the fierce downdraught of the rotors. Danny's ears were filled with the roar of the sea and the vast hum of the ship's engines. He felt salty spray stinging his face. The rough seas weren't a problem for the *Enterprise*, but anyone out there on a smaller vessel would be having a difficult time of it.

There was a greeting party waiting for them. The ship's captain was immediately identifiable. He had an aquiline nose and pinched lips, and was accompanied by a young leading rating. To his side there was a group of ten Royal Marines in camouflage gear and black boots, each sporting the distinctive commando and dagger flashes on their arms. Danny knew that they would be permanently stationed on the ship to support the crew should any of their encounters with the migrant boats turn ugly. A boat full of hundreds of exhausted refugees would definitely get nervous at the sight of a Royal Navy ship approaching, whatever its intentions. But tonight, they had a new remit: special forces support. The two guys the unit were intending to lift sure as hell wouldn't come quietly. And it wouldn't take much aggro for a boatload of edgy, frightened migrants to turn nasty. The support of the Marines could be crucial.

The captain cast his eye over the unit, and seemed to identify Danny as being the leader. He offered his hand, but Tony was there in an instant. He took the captain's hand, shook it cursorily and interrupted as the captain started to introduce himself. 'Do you have a fix on the migrant boat?'

The captain's eyes narrowed slightly. 'We picked it up on radar about three hours ago. We're tracking it from the horizon – they don't know we're here. We've got three rigid inflatables ready to launch. We can intercept as soon as you give the word.'

'Do it,' Tony said. 'You've cleared the deck of all non-essential personnel?'

'Yes,' the captain said, a definite edge in his voice.

'Make sure you keep it that way. Take us to our quarters.'

The captain looked like he was going to say something, but decided better of it. He turned to the rating by his side. 'You heard him,' he said.

'Aye Captain,' the young sailor replied. 'This way please.'

The rating led them into the ship, down a metal spiral staircase and up to a heavy grey door, which he opened for them. 'Alright, Popeye,' Tony told him, 'we'll take it from here.'

The unit's quarters were cramped, but perfectly serviceable. There were three bunks along one wall, and a flickering strip-light embedded in the ceiling. There had been a small attempt made to render the room a little more comfortable than it might otherwise have been; in one corner there was a water cooler – the surface of the water trembled with the vibrations of the ship, and on a table were a few out-of-date magazines and newspapers. Tony strolled over to the table and picked up one of the papers – a military news-letter of some sort. On the front was a picture of a wounded serviceman in a wheelchair. Tony tossed it casually back on to the table, then picked up a copy of the *Daily Mirror*. 'Last week's,' he said. And then, holding up the front cover: 'Look at this.'

Danny glanced at the newspaper. The picture on the front showed a young man with slick black hair on a golden beach, wearing shorts and sunglasses, with two bikini-clad women prac-tically draped over him. 'Look at him,' Tony said. 'What a cunt.'

The young man in question was a minor member of the royal family. To an SAS man, the royal family were known not by their names, but their codewords. Charles was Violet 1. Wills and Harry, Violet 2 and 3. The royals further from the throne had different colours and numbers. The lad on the beach was Yellow 7 – Duke of somewhere or other, Danny had forgotten – and a tabloid favourite.

'Still,' Tony continued, 'best job in the fucking world, eh. No chance of ever having to do any real graft, so you can spend your life chasing tail on the beaches of Dubai.'

'Thought you Pom boys did it all for Queen and country,' Caitlin said in her Aussie drawl.

'Queen and country my arse,' Tony said.

Danny dumped his bergen on the floor. 'He's alright by me,' Danny said, more to contradict Tony than for any other reason. 'At least he had the balls to go out to the Stan with Harry, get his hands dirty.'

'Oh yeah, and how many SF guys did it take to make sure *their* lily-white arses got home without a scratch?' Tony tossed the newspaper back on to the table, then joined the others in getting ready.

As Danny fitted his radio gear and attached a Surefire torch to the frame of his rifle, he noticed Tony taking a smaller black rucksack from his bergen and slinging it over his back.

'What's that?' Danny demanded.

'Packed lunch,' Tony replied. He looked around the room. 'Everyone ready?'

Without waiting for an answer, he strode out of the room. 'Your boyfriend's on good form,' Spud muttered to Caitlin as they approached the spiral staircase.

'Got a problem, Spud?' she said.

Spud shrugged.

'Good.' Caitlin clattered up the staircase after Tony.

Danny was on the point of following, but Spud grabbed him by the arm.

'You alright, mucker?' Danny asked.

Spud glanced around. He looked very shifty.

'Tony's just marking out his territory,' Danny said. 'Ignore him.'

'Maybe,' Spud said. He glanced at his shoes. 'Just watch my back, alright? When Tony's around, watch my back.'

He turned to climb up the stairs, but now it was Danny's turn to hold him back. 'What are you talking about?'

Tony looked up the staircase, clearly checking that they weren't overheard. 'Tony's missus,' he said quietly.

'Frances?'

Spud nodded.

'Mate, tell me you didn't—'

'Tony was out of town. One thing led to another.' He flashed Danny a quick grin. 'She's only human, after all.'

'Fuck's sake, Spud. There's a thousand squaddie mattresses in Hereford queuing up to put a Regiment notch on their bedstead. Why choose her of all people? Tony's a psycho. Do you think he knows?'

Spud's grin had disappeared. 'You've seen the state of Frances's face. I'm guessing she didn't get those bruises for not cleaning the toilet pan properly.' A shadow fell across his face. 'I should have a word with him about that. I bumped into her a couple of days ago. She couldn't get away fast enough. Started sweating like a blind lesbian in a fish factory . . .'

Danny swore under his breath. This should be a simple job, but there was already something going on that he didn't understand, too much tension among the team – and now this. 'Let's get moving,' he said. 'Get the op over and done with and get back to the UK. We can sort this shit out then.'

Spud nodded a bit sheepishly. He started to climb, but then looked back over his shoulder. 'Just watch my back, mucker,' he said quietly. And without waiting for an answer, he started clattering up the stairs.

TWO

The Marines were waiting for them up on deck. One of them – cropped hair and a flat nose – approached. 'Intercept in fifteen minutes,' he said.

Tony nodded curtly. 'I want two RIBs in the water, three-man Marine units in each. Any migrants try to jump ship, scoop them up and throw them straight back on. Once you've surrounded the *Ocean Star*, the four of us will board, subdue the passengers and manoeuvre the boat alongside the *Enterprise* so we can cross-deck them.' He turned to Danny and Caitlin. 'Get to the bridge,' he said. 'Tell the captain to lay down warning fire as we approach. I want the migrants to know we're not fucking around. Then get whatever joker's i/c of the *Ocean Star* to kill the engines and drop anchor. Spud, you stay with me.'

Spud and Danny exchanged a glance, but nobody argued. Danny and Caitlin turned their backs on the others and headed towards another metal staircase that Danny knew would take them to the bridge. Over his shoulder, he was aware of the two RIBs, each one manned by three Marines, being winched from the deck and lowered on to the rough sea.

'What's Tony got in his backpack?' Danny asked Caitlin as they hurried up the staircase.

'What am I?' Caitlin asked, her Aussie drawl very pronounced. 'His fucking mum?'

'No,' Danny shot back. 'Just his favourite sheila.'

Caitlin grabbed him by the arm. Her eyes were fiery, and for a moment Danny thought she was going to go for him. But a couple of seconds later she let go, made a noise of disgust and turned her back on him.

'Hey,' Danny said.

'What?'

'I don't care about you and Tony. Just so long as you keep your mind on the job.'

'Keep giving out orders like that, you're going to make yourself as popular as a rattlesnake in a lucky dip. Let's get to the bridge.'

Caitlin strode away. Danny followed.

The bridge was occupied by four naval personnel, plus the captain. They gave Danny and Caitlin a respectful nod as they approached. 'How long till we make contact?' Danny asked.

'Approximately nine minutes. We'll have a visual in two. We've got an open line to the MoD operations room. Sounds like quite a party there. Reps from the Home Office, Five, Six, Hereford.' He narrowed his eyes. 'Someone really wants to get their hands on your targets – whoever they are.'

Danny was well used to non-SF personnel trying to get information out of him. He quickly diverted the course of the conversation. 'You need to get the migrant ship's captain on the radio, tell them to drop anchor, then lay down warning fire.'

'Threat of force won't be necessary,' said the captain. 'Migrant boats in these waters know that a British naval vessel is a help to them . . .'

Danny's earpiece crackled and Tony's voice came over his personal radio. '*You sorted things with Captain Haddock yet?*'

Danny forced himself to keep cool. If Tony had his way, the relationship of mutual respect between the SAS unit and the naval crew would soon break down. 'Roger that,' he replied. He turned back to the captain. 'We need the option of that covering fire, Captain,' he insisted.

The captain hesitated for a moment, but then walked over to his crew to give them the orders. Danny's sense of unease grew stronger. Thanks to Tony, there was now bad blood between the unit and the naval crew. He glanced through the bridge window down on to the deck. Tony was directing the remaining Marines with aggressive hand gestures, while Spud stood quietly a couple of metres away, his hands on his assault rifle as if he'd like nothing better than to make sudden, unexpected use of it.

'We have a visual!' one of the naval crew called out. 'Two nautical miles.' Danny quickly altered his line of sight. He just caught sight of lights on the horizon to the ship's twelve o'clock. If that was the migrant boat, they were heading straight for it.

The ship's radio operator was a young lad with a bad dose of acne. At a short instruction from the captain, he started broadcasting. 'This is HMS *Enterprise*, broadcasting to *Ocean Star*. Do you copy, *Ocean Star*?'

A blast of white noise came over the radio. The operator repeated his message. 'This is HMS *Enterprise*, broadcasting to *Ocean Star*. Do you copy, *Ocean Star*?'

White noise again. Then, suddenly, an unnaturally loud voice burst over the airways. It was thickly accented, and spoke fragmented English. '*Yes, sir,* Ocean Star *sir. Boat in big trouble, sir. Sink very soon, sir.*'

The captain looked over his shoulder at Danny. 'They always say that. They know we'll offer aid to a vessel in distress.'

They were gaining very quickly on what was obviously a small boat. Distance, maybe 300 metres. 'Lay down warning fire,' Danny said.

The captain frowned. 'It's really not necessary. They won't—'

'Look, mate,' Danny interrupted him. 'You've got *your* orders, I've got *my* orders. Lay down warning fire, and instruct them to drop anchor.'

The captain considered it for a moment, then nodded to one of his crew. Twenty seconds later, a crack of gunfire echoed out over the noisy ocean.

There was a moment of silence. Then the radio burst into life. The radio operator was speaking much faster, and suddenly his English was a load better. He sounded panicked. '*This is* Ocean Star, *this is* Ocean Star, *hold your fire, we are dropping anchor now, repeat, we are dropping anchor now . . .*'

Through the window of the bridge, Danny could see the wake of the two RIBs containing the Marines, curling away from the *Enterprise*. Tony's voice crackled over Danny's earpiece. '*Get down here.*'

Danny turned to Caitlin. 'Let's go,' he said.

By the time they had rejoined Tony and Spud, the ship's crew was preparing a third RIB. 'Get a fucking move on,' Tony shouted at Danny as the unit jogged towards it. Another Marine was boarding the RIB and taking charge of the outboard motor, which was already turning over. The unit climbed in and the crane immediately winched them up over the side of the *Enterprise*, then lowered them seaward. As they passed over the railings of the ship, Tony shouted some last-minute instructions.

'I don't think our targets will risk doing anything to identify themselves once we board that boat. Most of the migrants fucking hate IS – it's them they're running from, and if they suspect they've got a couple among them, they'll most likely send them for a swim. But if our guys *do* make a move, we shoot to wound. You got that, Black?'

Danny gave him a dark look, then a curt nod. Tony liked to put it around that Danny was a loose cannon, but now wasn't the time to bite back ...

There was a noisy slap and a jolt as the RIB hit the water. They were hit with a cloud of spray, and the boat lurched forward immediately as the Marine lowered the outboard.

The rough sea state had barely affected the *Enterprise*, but the tiny RIB was immediately showered by the crest of a wave, before falling several feet into a valley of seawater. They were drenched in seconds. Danny gripped the side firmly, trusting that the Marine at the helm was well used to manoeuvring vessels in these conditions. He was right. The RIB didn't veer from its course. Each time the horizon bobbed into view, the lights of the migrant boat grew closer. In just a couple of minutes, it was fifty metres distant. The two RIBs with the Marine support unit were circling it.

'Approach the rear of the boat,' Tony shouted over the crashing of the waves. The Marine at the helm nodded, and they ploughed relentlessly through the rough seas towards the migrant ship.

Moments later, they were alongside it. It was being badly tossed and jolted by the waves, but Danny could see that it was massively overcrowded. At a glance, he estimated ninety to 100 migrants on an old tug that was no more than twenty metres in length. Its wheelhouse, painted in blue and white, seemed unnaturally tall and narrow. The name *Ocean Star* had been painted on the side, but most of the letters had eroded away. There was a boarding ladder at the rear, and the Marine manoeuvred the RIB towards it.

Spud grabbed the slats of the ladder. As he pulled himself out of the RIB and started to scramble up it, Danny engaged his weapon to offer covering fire if it turned out to be necessary. It didn't. Spud disappeared over the side of the migrant vessel, and over the noise of the sea Danny could hear him barking instructions, though he couldn't make out the individual words. Moments later, Tony was halfway up the ladder, followed closely by Caitlin. Only when they had safely boarded did Danny leave the RIB. The slats of the ladder were wet and slippery. The boat yawed with the movement of the sea. But his grip was firm. Seconds later he had boarded.

Narrow beams of light shone across the deck from the torches fitted to each unit member's rifle, illuminating the pelting rain, which had doubled in intensity in the last couple of minutes. By the light of those torches, Danny could see that in the few seconds they had been on the boat, Spud, Tony and Caitlin had been busy. Almost all the migrants on board had hit the deck. They were now lying on their fronts with their hands on the backs of their heads. They were all very poorly dressed in old shorts and tracksuit bottoms. A few lucky ones had hooded tops to keep them warm, but every garment was soaked by the rain. Many of the passengers had no shoes. The sea air was failing to blow away a nasty stench of unwashed bodies.

Three men on the steps that led up to the wheelhouse were still standing, but that was only because there was no room on deck for them to lie down. Tony was stalking towards them, weapon engaged, barking at them to get on their knees. They obviously didn't understand him, and looked confused and frightened. Towards the foredeck, fifteen metres from Danny's position, were five more migrants, also standing. To Danny's eye, they were more of a problem. They were talking quickly and looking out to sea, as though discussing whether or not to jump.

Danny surged forward. It was impossible not to step on the arms and legs of some of the crouching migrants, but none of them complained. As he moved, he saw that the central section of the boat, behind the wheelhouse, was not covered with bodies. There was a large rectangular hole cut out of the deck, leading down into the hull. Danny scanned the faces of the five men still standing. He didn't recognise any of them from the photos of the IS targets, but that wasn't a reason not to suspect them. 'Get to the ground!' he shouted at them, keeping the barrel of his weapon firmly fixed in their direction. 'Get on the ground – now!'

Three of the migrants fell to their knees. The remaining two still looked eager to jump, but their mates started yanking at their clothes. Seconds later they'd hit the deck too, but were still only kneeling. Danny got close, then forced a couple of them on to the ground with his foot. The remaining three followed suit.

He looked around the boat. Tony and Caitlin were by the wheelhouse, pointing their weapons up at two figures inside, controlling the boat. Spud was eight metres from Danny, on the edge of the open section at the centre of the boat. He also had his weapon engaged, pointing down into the hull.

'Someone's getting their fucking money's worth,' he called to Danny.

Danny checked the immediate vicinity to identify any particular threats. Now every migrant was cringing, terrified, on the floor. He stepped across the mass of bodies, towards Spud's position. As he drew within a metre of the open section, and the beam of his torch joined Spud's, he could see why his mate had such a disgusted look on his face. The hull of the boat was even more crowded than the deck. Danny estimated that there were another hundred people down here, and as he looked closer he could see that they were all …

'Kids,' Spud muttered.

The children's faces looked up, terrified, blinking against the torchlight. None of them spoke. They were pressed so closely together, it was impossible to see any of them below the shoulder. But what clothes Danny could make out were nothing but dirty old rags. A horrible stench of sweat and shit rose from the hull. Danny had to force himself not to gag. He caught sight of one kid with a nasty cut on the side of his face, which had obviously turned septic. For a moment, the image of his own child flashed in front of his eyes. He hardened himself against that thought. If he showed any sign of weakness, there would be men on this ship who would take advantage. And the brutal truth was that, even heavily armed, their four-man unit would struggle against so many people if they decided to riot.

'If we see anyone on their feet,' he shouted above the noise of the waves and the rain hitting the deck, 'we shoot.' He didn't know how many of them would understand English, but they'd sure as hell understand the intent behind his words.

He looked up to see that Tony had entered the wheelhouse and was in the process of forcibly ejecting the two men inside, who tumbled down the steps and landed in a heap on top of two other migrants. From the corner of his eye, he could see the two Marine RIBs circling. But the greater part of his attention was now on the *Enterprise*. It was very close now – thirty metres max – and facing into the wind to stabilise itself. It dwarfed the migrant boat entirely.

Tony's voice came across Danny's earpiece. '*Black, Spud, cover the migrants. Anyone kicks up a fuss, give them something to think about. Me and Caitlin will get the boat alongside the* Enterprise.'

'Roger that,' Danny replied. He turned to Spud. 'Stay here and cover the foredeck. I'll head aft.'

Spud nodded. He seemed to drag his gaze away from the kids in the hold as he moved his attention to the migrants on deck. He turned his body threateningly with the turn of his weapon and covered the teeming mass of desperate men and women.

Danny could hear the occasional sob as, rain dripping down his face, he moved aft along the deck. He cut them from his mind and focussed on what was important. Tony was in the wheelhouse and had already started to manoeuvre the boat alongside the *Enterprise*. Caitlin stood imperiously on the steps to the wheelhouse, covering the starboard side of the boat. As Danny continued aft, he found himself trying to pick out faces among the crouching migrants, the images from the photos they'd been studying clear in his mind. So far, he couldn't identify Santa or Rudolph. And nobody was acting particularly suspiciously. If the two IS suspects were on board, they were keeping a low profile, just as Tony had predicted.

Within two minutes, the *Ocean Star* was alongside the *Enterprise*, facing into the wind just as the larger ship was. The naval crew on the *Enterprise* threw ropes down on the smaller boat. Tony and Caitlin moved to the port side of the boat, grabbed the ropes and started tying them firmly to the railings. Danny sensed the migrants getting restless, so he barked out a further warning to be silent, and panned the barrel of his weapon threateningly over them. On the edge of his vision, he was aware of some safety netting being lowered from the *Enterprise*. Tony and Caitlin clipped it to the railings so it covered a five-metre-wide section, ready to catch anyone who should fall as the migrants cross-decked. The naval crew unfurled a rope ladder with wooden slats. Tony tugged hard on it to check it was secure. He nodded with satisfaction. They were ready to get the migrants on to the ship.

'*Black.*' Tony's voice came over the radio. '*Get on to the ship with Caitlin. Me and Spud will take care of things down here.*'

Danny caught a glance from Spud across the boat. Spud wiped the rain from his face, then nodded at Danny as if to say: 'It's OK.'

'*I said, get on to the ship, Black. Now!*'

Caitlin was already halfway up the ladder. Danny lowered his weapon and negotiated his path across the mass of drenched bodies on the deck. By the time he reached Tony, Caitlin had disappeared over the side of the *Enterprise*. Danny didn't wait for Tony to say anything else. He grabbed a slat on the rope ladder and started to climb. The ladder lurched slightly with the movement of the vessels. No problem for Danny, who'd encountered far worse, but he knew the migrants were going to be very frightened as Tony forced them up. Danny didn't mind that. Sometimes frightened people were easier to control. But he felt badly for the kids.

As soon as Danny hauled himself over the side of the naval vessel, he immediately saw that the remaining Marines had cordoned off a large area on the aft deck, ready to store the migrants as they embarked. Caitlin was standing at the top of the ladder, holding drenched pictures of the two targets. The ship's captain was striding towards them, his uniform soaked and his face a thundercloud.

'I've just had a communication from Whitehall,' he said. 'All migrants except the two you're looking for are to be returned to their boat as soon as you're done, no matter what state they're in.'

Danny immediately felt himself frowning. 'There's kids down there,' he said tersely. 'They need medical help.'

The captain drew himself up to his full height. 'You've got *your* orders,' he fired Danny's words back at him, 'I've got *mine*.' He looked over the side of the ship. Danny did the same. A thin, frightened young man was halfway up the ladder. He looked like he wanted to cry. 'I'm not saying I like it,' the captain added in a more conciliatory voice.

Me neither, Danny thought. And he muttered to himself: 'Something's not right.'

The migrant reached the top of the ladder. Danny firmly grabbed his forearm and helped him over the railings. He had dark skin, a hooked nose and the whites of his eyes had a yellow tint to them. He was looking around nervously. Caitlin grabbed him by the chin and examined his face. Clearly deciding that this was not one of the men they were looking for, she nodded at one of the Marines, who led him at gunpoint towards the far side of the cordoned-off holding area.

By now, a second migrant was cagily climbing up the rope. Moments later, having been checked by Caitlin, he was in the holding area too.

It was slow work. Thirty terrified migrants passed through Caitlin's checkpoint. Forty. None of them even remotely resembled the photographs of their targets. It started to rain even more heavily. Several migrants slipped as they climbed, but somehow didn't fall. The deck down below was half-empty. Danny was beginning to wonder if they were on a wild goose chase.

'Santa,' Caitlin said sharply.

Danny moved quickly and decisively. Without even looking at the face of the young man Caitlin had just identified, he hooked his left arm tightly round the suspect's neck and forced him hard to the ground, face down. The man tried to struggle, but he was no match for Danny, who pressed one knee hard into the small of the target's back, knocking the wind expertly from his lungs. The target went suddenly limp. Danny grabbed a sturdy plastic cable tie from his ops waistcoat and bound the man's wrists tightly together behind his back. The whole operation had taken less than five seconds. Danny rolled the guy over on to his front to examine his face for the first time. There was no doubt that Caitlin had made the right call. It was the tall guy, the one with the much darker skin who, in the photograph, had been standing by the open-topped technical. Santa had a sour, pained expression, but his attempts to wriggle away from Danny's firm grasp were pathetic.

Danny called one of the Marines over to him. 'Hood him, isolate him,' he said tersely. 'Keep the fucker quiet.' The Marine nodded. He was carrying a couple of yellow sponge earplugs, which he shoved into the ear canals of the struggling prisoner, before covering them with a set of sturdy ear defenders. He then pulled a dark hood with a drawstring at the open end from his pack. He pulled it over the target's head, yanked the drawstring tight and hauled him, staggering, to his feet. The target was now effectively blind, deaf and disorientated – in no position to struggle or run.

Danny spoke into the radio. 'Santa acquired, repeat, Santa acquired. Keep 'em coming.'

'*Roger that*,' Tony said, with the satisfied sound of a soldier whose op was going according to plan.

It took fifteen minutes to clear the rest of the deck. By now there were at least a hundred migrants in the holding area, but they were still one target down. '*We're going to start emptying the hull*,' Tony said over the radio. '*It's mostly kids down there. If we spot Rudolph, we'll send him over first.*'

'Best idea you've had all day,' Danny said under his breath. Over the side of the ship, he could see that Spud had lowered a ladder into the hull. He was standing by it, while a couple of kids scrambled up. Spud helped them over the top, then pointed them in the direction of Tony, who was standing by the larger ladder that scaled the side of the *Enterprise*.

'They're just children,' Caitlin muttered. 'They shouldn't be doing this.'

Danny agreed. He spoke into his radio. 'Let's just isolate the kids on the *Ocean Star*,' he said. 'We don't need to make them climb up here.'

'*Negative*,' came Tony's voice. '*Everybody leaves the boat. That's an order.*' He looked up as he spoke. Across the difference in height, and through the rain and the darkness, Danny caught Tony's scowl. It was full of contempt. And glancing at Caitlin, he saw an aggrieved look on her face as she stared down at her boyfriend.

The migrant kids were pitifully terrified as they scrambled, soaked, thin and dirty, over the railings of the *Enterprise*. Caitlin's face was unreadable as she gently helped them on to the ship and sent them to stand, shivering, in the isolation area. They were in a shit state. Shivering, emaciated, badly clothed. Half of them didn't even have shoes, and Danny could see that many of them were limping. As one of the limping kids passed him, Danny grabbed hold of him and checked out his feet. They hardly looked human – swollen in some places, practically rotting away in others. If they weren't already infected, they would be very soon. Without medicine, the kid would likely be dead in a few weeks. The child looked up at Danny, obviously very frightened. Danny winked at him and tried to look encouraging as he pointed the kid in the direction of the isolation zone.

As Danny counted more of the kids on to the ship – twenty, twenty-five – his loathing for whoever had crammed them like sardines into that small boat intensified. But then he told himself to stay detached. He was here to do a job, not to right wrongs ...

'*We've got an adult down here.*' Spud was speaking quietly, and there was an edge of tension to his voice.

Caitlin was carefully manoeuvring the twenty-sixth kid over. Danny looked down towards the *Ocean Star*. Spud was helping a hooded figure up from the hull. He had allowed his weapon to fall across his chest, obviously aware that Tony had his rifle engaged and was aiming it towards them, just in case the hooded migrant should get any stupid ideas.

Everything happened so quickly.

It was immediately obvious to Danny that Tony was about to fire. In a split second, he recognised the positioning of his body ... the way he set his frame against the recoil of his weapon ... the tiny adjustment he made to his aim as he prepared to release a round ...

Danny's eyes flickered towards Spud and the hooded target. The target had his head bowed and was just staggering off the hull ladder on to the deck of *Ocean Star*. There was no sign of a weapon, or any threatening behaviour.

Spud was a metre behind him, and fractionally to his left.

And Danny knew, instinctively, that Tony was aiming not at the hooded migrant, but at Spud.

'*HIT THE FLOOR! HIT THE FLOOR!*' Danny barked over his radio.

Spud's reaction was immediate. He dived heavily towards the wooden deck of the boat at the same instant that a shot rang out. Danny saw a muzzle flash from Tony's rifle, then a second spark as the round ricocheted off a railing at the stern. It took a full second for the hooded migrant – whose reactions were not so keen as Spud's – to hit the ground. By which time, Danny was shouting into his mouthpiece. '*HOLD YOUR FIRE! HOLD YOUR FIRE! WHAT THE HELL'S GOING ON?*'

Tony lowered his weapon. He stared towards Spud and the migrant, then glanced up towards Danny. '*Thought that cunt was pulling a weapon,*' he said calmly, as if he'd done nothing more serious than spill someone's pint. He strode over towards the two prostrate figures. Danny saw Spud jump to his feet. He could tell Spud was shouting something at Tony, but as it wasn't over the radio he couldn't hear what. As Tony approached, Spud bore down on him and yanked the heel of his hands against Tony's chest. Tony's body language was immediately offensive.

And they had both taken their eye off the hooded man.

He had jumped to his feet, and was running to the stern of the ship. Danny didn't know if he intended to hurl himself overboard, and he didn't intend to wait to find out. He followed the figure swiftly with his rifle. When the man was five metres from the stern railings, he released a round that exploded on to the deck a metre in front of him. The target hit the ground again, but Danny had already turned his attention to Spud and Tony. The noise of Danny's round had stopped them fronting up to each other. Tony had moved past Spud and was heading, weapon engaged, towards their target. He reached him in five seconds while Spud remained stationary, clutching his own weapon – and not, Danny surmised, because he was worried about the migrant.

Tony yanked the migrant up by his forearm, then pulled the hood back from over his head. '*It's Rudolph,*' he said curtly. '*Blotchy-faced cunt. Sending him up now.*'

Danny was aware of Tony dragging the target towards the ladder. But his mind was whirling. Rudolph *hadn't* been pulling a weapon. He hadn't even *looked* like he was pulling a weapon. And Tony – grizzled, experienced, untrustworthy Tony – wouldn't have made a mistake like that. And even if he *had* made that mistake, it was impossible that he would have missed his target from that range. If Tony had wanted to put a bullet in Rudolph, he'd have done it.

But if Danny hadn't warned Spud to hit the deck, what then?

There was no doubt in Danny's mind. Tony Wiseman had just tried to nail Spud. A tragic accident, but friendly fire, easily explained away in the heat of battle.

Except there hadn't been a battle. Just a disgruntled SAS trooper taking a potshot at a member of his team.

Spud looked up. He caught Danny's eye. It was clear from his expression that he knew exactly what had just happened.

THREE

Rudolph looked like he didn't know whether to run or jump. Neither was an option. He was halfway up the rope ladder, with Tony at its foot pointing his weapon up towards him. For thirty seconds he didn't move, but eventually he seemed to decide that the sight of Caitlin holding out one arm at the top of the ladder was the lesser of two evils. He ascended through the driving rain. As soon as he was in reach, Danny and Caitlin hauled him over the side of the ship. Danny bundled him roughly to the ground, rolled him over on to his back and yanked his right arm up into an armlock. Caitlin got to her knees, grabbed a clump of his hair, lifted his head back and stared at his frightened face.

'It's him,' she said.

Thirty seconds later, the second target was plasticuffed, deafened, hooded and being led roughly across the deck by two Marines. Danny and Caitlin got to their feet. They were drenched, and slightly out of breath.

'What the hell happened down there?' Caitlin demanded.

Danny was prevented from replying by the captain, who was striding officiously towards them. 'Get on the radio to HQ,' Danny told him. 'Tell them we've acquired both targets.'

'They're on the line now,' the captain said. 'They're still insisting that all migrants get returned to the boat as soon as your targets have been located.'

Danny looked over towards the frightened, huddled mass of people in the isolation zone. And especially the children. 'Get your ship's medics over to them,' he said. 'Provide what help they can.'

The captain shook his head. 'I'm not going to ignore a direct order,' he said.

As he spoke, Danny's earpiece crackled. Tony's voice: '*Approximately ten kids still in the hull. We're going to empty them out and keep them on the deck here. Then I'm going to search the hull, check we haven't missed anything. Spud can babysit. Poor fella looks a bit shaken up.*'

Danny looked over the side. As babysitters went, Spud looked the least maternal Danny had ever seen. He was standing aft, rain pelting on to him, the butt of his weapon pressed hard into his shoulder. He was covering the open area above the hull. But the beam of his torch was flickering around Tony. Spud was defending himself. No doubt.

Danny turned back to the captain. 'We can't send them back down for at least another fifteen minutes,' he said. 'Surely your medics can patch a few of those kids up. Depends how you want to sleep tonight.'

The captain's face was momentarily a picture of indecision. But then he turned to one of his crew and barked: 'Get the medics here. Now!' The crew member scurried away. 'I'll update Whitehall,' he said, before turning on his heel and marching back towards the bridge.

'You do that,' Danny muttered. He looked over the side. Spud hadn't moved. It was up to Tony to help the remaining kids out of the hull.

'We should check Santa and Rudolph are secure,' Caitlin said.

Danny didn't take his eyes off Spud and Tony. 'They're not going anywhere,' he said. 'The Marines can take care of them for a bit.' He raised his weapon and directed it down on to the *Ocean Star.* As he did so, he could feel Caitlin's eyes on him.

'It was just an accident,' she said, rather uncertainly. 'Tony wouldn't—'

'Tony wouldn't what? There's *nothing* Tony wouldn't do. You should remember that. And don't take your eyes off them, OK?'

Danny was only half aware of the movement of personnel behind him on deck. He trusted the Marines to keep the frightened migrants in order. He stood like a grim statue, looking down on to the *Ocean Star*, the beam of his Surefire torch diffusing into the rain-filled night. Caitlin was three metres to his left, doing the same. Down on the deck of the smaller boat, Spud had got the remaining children to sit cross-legged by the wheelhouse while he stood sentinel beside them, as motionless as Danny, his weapon pointed towards the open section into which Tony had disappeared.

Five minutes passed. There was no sign of Tony, and no word from him. The sea state was getting rougher. The rain harder. Danny couldn't have been wetter if he'd jumped into the ocean. But still he didn't move. What the hell was taking Tony so long? From his vantage point, Danny saw the occasional flicker of Tony's torch down in the hull. How long could it take him to search such a small area?

Tony suddenly appeared back on deck. The unit leader looked across at Spud, then up at Danny and Caitlin, who had their weapons trained on him. Danny couldn't see Tony's expression, but there was something in the way he hesitated for a moment that told him he knew he was being observed.

'*Smells worse than an anchovy's cunt down there*,' Tony's voice came over the radio, '*but it's clear. Start sending them back down.*'

Danny barely moved. He just turned his head to look at Caitlin. 'Do it,' he said. Then he went back to covering the *Ocean Star* in general, and Tony in particular. He didn't care if it looked suspicious that he had his rifle aimed at his unit leader. And he didn't care that Caitlin had to help the terrified migrants back down the precarious rope ladder by herself. Spud had asked him to watch his back, and he was going to do just that.

It took a full thirty minutes to cross-deck the migrants again. It was grim work. None of them wanted to get back on to the *Ocean Star*. Many were sobbing. Some implored Caitlin to let them stay on the naval vessel, but they had their orders from Whitehall: every last migrant was to return to the boat. It left a bad taste in Danny's mouth watching Tony force the kids back down into the dark, cramped hull. He wondered if Tony gave a shit, and as he kept his rifle trained on Tony's back, he found his forefinger twitching occasionally on the trigger . . .

'That's the last of them,' Caitlin said, as a tearful young woman made her way down the rope ladder. Danny glanced over to the isolation area. Sure enough, it was empty. Down on the *Ocean Star*, the crowd of migrants were face down on the deck again, being pelted by the rain. They were caught, surely, in the middle of their worst nightmare. Danny found himself hoping that they hit land safely, and soon. But he reckoned some of them wouldn't make it through another night.

It was time for Spud and Tony to get back on to the *Enterprise*. Spud climbed the ladder first. Tony stood at the bottom looking up at Danny, who made no attempt to hide that he was aiming his weapon directly at him. Once Spud was safely over the railings, Danny felt himself relax, just a little. His mate was out of Tony's reach, for now. Danny kept watching Tony, though, as he pulled a knife from his ops waistcoat and with several easy slashes cut the netting, then the ropes that bound the *Ocean Star* to the *Enterprise*. In the split second before the two vessels separated, he leapt from the smaller boat and caught hold of the rope ladder. He scaled it quickly and efficiently, and moments later he was hauling himself over the railings of the *Enterprise* and on to deck.

A fresh wave of driving rain lashed down on them. Danny stepped up to Tony, his chin jutting out. 'What the hell?' he hissed at him. From the corner of his eye he could see the *Ocean Star* drifting away surprisingly quickly. There were already fifty metres between them.

'What?' Tony's voice was aggressive, but he didn't seem to want to meet Danny's gaze.

'You know.'

'It was a successful op. Where are Santa and Rudolph?' He looked over Danny's shoulder, towards the far starboard side of the deck where three Marines were holding the two targets at gunpoint. 'Caitlin, come with me. We'll move them to the SF room, then get on the blower to base.'

He strode off, clipping Danny's shoulder with his own as he walked. Danny watched him go. Spud and Caitlin, standing just a couple of metres away, did the same.

'He tried to slot me,' Spud said. 'The cunt *actually* tried to slot me.'

Danny was still vaguely aware of the *Ocean Star* in his peripheral vision. It had drifted a hundred metres away now, and its lights were occasionally bobbing out of sight among the rough waves. But most of his attention was on Tony, who was striding towards the prisoners with his arrogant swagger, as if nothing untoward had happened.

'You joining your boyfriend?' Danny asked Caitlin.

'Either of you two call him that again,' Caitlin said, 'I'll slot you myself.'

'Just go with him. Watch the prisoners. We'll go to the bridge, get on the radio to HQ. Hammond needs to know what's—'

He was interrupted by the sound of an explosion. It was a distant sonic boom, coming from the port side of the ship, and almost drowned out by the competing noise of the rain, the waves and the hum of the engines. But Danny could instantly tell where its source was. He spun round to look out towards the *Ocean Star*. Spud and Caitlin did the same thing.

There was no sign of the light in the wheelhouse of the boat. Danny yanked a spotting scope from his ops waistcoat and quickly scanned along the horizon. At first his field of view was taken up by a dark, shadowy confusion of waves and dark, stormy sky. But after a few seconds he located the boat.

Or what was left of it.

'It's sinking,' he said tersely.

And it was sinking, rapidly. Its stern was completely submerged, and Danny estimated that no more than five metres of the aft deck were still peeking above the water.

'Those kids,' he heard Caitlin whisper. And by the time she'd said it, Danny had lost sight of the *Ocean Star* completely.

He lowered his scope, then turned to look across the deck towards Tony.

'What did Tony have in that rucksack?' Danny repeated the question that he knew none of them could answer. And before any of them could speak, he started sprinting across the deck to where Tony was in the middle of roughing up the two prisoners, while their Marine guards stood helplessly by. Danny grabbed him just as he was planting a fist into Rudolph's guts, and swung him round so that they were facing each other. He instantly saw something wild in Tony's face and he knew, without doubt, what was coming. Tony jabbed the heel of his hand up towards the centre of Danny's face, but Danny was fast enough to knock it out of the way. 'What did you plant on that boat?' Danny hissed.

Tony sneered. 'What are you talking about?'

Danny was about to reply, but realised that Spud, Caitlin and the captain had surrounded him. 'What was that explosion?' he barked. 'What the hell's going on?'

Tony had a maddeningly smug look on his face. 'Rudolph and Santa must have had explosives on board. Guess we missed them.'

He looked at Caitlin, clearly wanting backup. He didn't get it. Caitlin gave him a hard stare. For a moment, Tony's eyes tightened. He bore a fleeting look of genuine madness.

Caitlin took a step away from him, towards Danny and Spud. 'You're out of order, Tony,' she said.

Silence. Tony gave her a death stare, but she just jutted her chin out.

Then Tony shrugged. The death stare gave way to an expression of nonchalance. 'Those stinking migrants would have died a shitty death anyway. Rough seas like this, they wouldn't have made it through the night.'

'Is that all you've got to say about it?' Caitlin flared.

'Tony,' Danny cut in. 'Get the prisoners to the SF room. Caitlin, go with him.' And when Caitlin looked momentarily uncertain about being alone with Tony, he added: 'Take a couple of Marines with you.'

'*I'm* the one giving the instructions,' Tony spat back. But then he looked at Spud and Caitlin, who had flanked Danny and were mutinously staring him down. It was very obvious that the balance of power had just shifted.

There was a tense silence. Danny and Tony locked gazes. Tony broke away first. He grabbed Rudolph roughly and started dragging him across the deck. 'Make sure he doesn't do anything stupid,' Danny told Caitlin. She gave him a sour look, then grabbed Santa and followed Tony.

The ship's captain was storming down from the bridge through the rain towards them 'Did you sink that boat?' he demanded. 'It was full of children . . .'

Danny avoided the question. 'I need a secure line to Hereford. Private room. Can you sort it?'

The captain paused, his face livid. Then he nodded. 'There's a radio room off the bridge. Follow me.'

As they entered the bridge, Danny felt the hard stares of the ship's crew on them. The sinking of the *Ocean Star* had obviously shocked them, and Danny could tell they held the SAS crew responsible. Danny shut it out. He and Spud stood to one side of the bridge while the captain took his radio operator into an adjoining room. Two minutes later he reappeared and nodded at them.

'It's all set up,' he said tersely. His opinion of the Regiment unit was clearly in line with his crew's.

Danny and Spud strode into the adjoining room. It was small – five metres by five – with two chairs and a table for the comms equipment. Danny turned to the captain. 'Encrypted?'

The captain nodded.

'We'll call you if we need you,' Danny said. The captain's cheek twitched, but he took the hint and left the room. Danny turned to Spud. 'Guard the door,' he said. 'I'll make the call.'

Spud hesitated for a moment, but then left the room, closing the door behind him.

Danny grabbed the radio. 'This is unit Charlie Alpha Zero,' he said.

There was a hiss. '*Go ahead Charlie Alpha Zero. This is Hereford.*'

Danny recognised the voice of their ops officer, Ray Hammond. 'OK, boss,' he said. 'How about telling us what's going on?'

'*Have you acquired the targets?*'

'Roger that. We also seem to have sent a boatful of migrants to the bottom of the Med.'

A pause.

'*Is Tony there?*'

'Negative. He's watching Santa and Rudolph with Caitlin. Boss, we've got a situation—'

'*Are there any survivors on the* Ocean Star?'

Danny sniffed. 'No. Was it Tony?'

Another pause.

'*I don't know what you're talking about, Black. Ships sink. Happens every day.*'

'You think I wasn't up to carrying out an order?'

Danny fell silent. If his suspicions were correct, what he'd just witnessed was a borderline war crime. Sure, the Regiment was expected to carry out some dark operations. Danny had done it himself. But there were a hundred kids on that boat. *Would* he have carried out that order? Maybe not. Would Tony? Without question.

Did he want Tony on the team? No way.

Danny took a moment to gather his thoughts. 'We've got a problem.'

'*What?*'

'Spud and Tony. This is off the record, but I've just found out Spud's been nailing Tony's missus.'

Hammond swore. '*What is it with Spud? Can't he keep his fucking salami to himself?*'

'That's not all, boss. I think Tony just tried to whack Spud and pass it off as an accident.'

Silence. Danny found himself holding his breath. He knew that if he'd made that accusation of anyone else, nobody would believe him. But everyone knew about Tony Wiseman. 'I saw it happen,' he pressed when Hammond failed to reply. 'They're at each other's throats. And Caitlin looks like she wants to murder him too. The unit's not functioning.'

'*Alright, Black,*' Hammond retorted suddenly. '*I've got the message.*' There was another brief pause. '*You, Spud and Caitlin are to accompany Santa and Rudolph to the interrogation centre in Malta. We're sending instructions through to the Wildcat flight crew to get you there now. When you arrive, you're to stay in on the interrogation. I want you to hear what these fuckers have to say first-hand. And Black.'*

'What?'

'Keep a close eye on Spud. He's been at the receiving end of more than his fair share of field interrogations. The military shrink flagged it up before I put him back on ops. You're heading to a black camp in Malta. He won't like it.'

'Spud will be fine. What about Tony?'

'I'm going to reassign him.'

'Where?' Danny asked, a feeling of cold satisfaction creeping up on him. And even though he was soaking wet and more than a little pissed off, he couldn't help but allow himself a small smile when Hammond explained what was in store for Tony over the next few days.

Tony blinked at him. '*What?*' he demanded.

They were standing in the SF room. The two prisoners, still hooded and cable-tied, were lying face down on the floor, unable to see or hear anything that was going on. And Danny was relaying, practically verbatim, what Hammond had told him. 'Yellow Seven,' he said.

Tony stared at him.

'Hammond said the royals have been on at the MoD for days, trying to get a Regiment man out to Dubai to escort him back home for Christmas.' He turned to Caitlin. 'The royals are a bit like that about the SAS,' he said. 'Seem to think we're their personal bodyguards. Anyway, turns out Hereford kept stonewalling them, saying they didn't have a man spare.' He gave Tony a cool look. 'Looks like they've changed their minds. Unit command passes to me. You're to wait on board for a chopper to airlift you back to Sigonella. They'll fly you out to Dubai from there.'

Tony's neck had flushed red. He fronted up to Danny. 'You'll pay for this, Black.' For the briefest moment, he looked genuinely insane.

46

'Not my call,' Danny breathed. 'Blame the headshed, not me.'

Tony's eyes narrowed. He looked like he was about to say something, then thought better of it. He pushed past Danny and over towards Spud. 'Touch my missus again,' he breathed, 'you'll find yourself wishing I'd released that fucking round two seconds earlier.'

'Easy Tony,' Spud said. 'You're a royal flunky now.'

Tony turned to Danny, and pointed to Caitlin. 'I suppose you'll want to get stuck in with her, now I'm off the scene,' he said.

'Go to hell, Tony,' Caitlin spat.

Silence. Then Tony turned his back on them and headed to the exit of the SF room.

'Wait,' Danny instructed.

Tony stopped and turned slowly, his face filled with utter hate.

'Whitehall are spinning the *Enterprise* crew your little story that our two targets must have left bomb-making equipment on the boat. Trouble is, they're not stupid. Take my advice, Tony: don't wind them up. A few of the crew were looking like they wanted to send us the same way as the migrants. We'd all hate for anything bad to happen to you.'

'The hell you would,' Tony muttered. He strode up to Danny. 'You're going soft, Danny Black,' he said. 'Everyone knows it. It's that baby of yours. I've seen it happen a million times. You reckon anyone else in the Regiment would give a flying fuck about a boatload of ragheads?' He sneered, then turned his back on Danny and stormed out of the SF room, slamming the door behind him.

Caitlin was staring at Danny. 'Remind me never to get on your bad side,' she said.

'He had it coming,' Danny said.

'Did he sink that migrant boat?'

'I don't know. The headshed stonewalled me.'

'You want to watch him, Danny. I know what he's like. He'll go off like a frog in a sock next time he sees you.'

'I can deal with Tony,' Danny said. He looked over to where the two prisoners were laid out on the floor. 'Let's move them to the Wildcat,' he said. 'The headshed wants us off the ship as soon as.'

Spud and Caitlin did the honours, pulling the two targets up to their feet. One of them said something in muffled Arabic. Spud jabbed him in the stomach with his elbow, just hard enough to wind him. The man doubled over, but didn't speak again as Spud and Caitlin dragged them out of the room, following Danny towards, and then up, the metal staircase.

There was no sign of Tony on deck, which was still clear of regular naval crew. The lights of the Wildcat were beaming, and Danny could see the shapes of the flight crew in the cockpit, ready to leave. The captain was standing to one side of the landing deck, his wet hair blowing in the wind. Danny strode up to him. 'We're leaving one of our guys with you,' he shouted over the noise of the helicopter's rotors, which were just starting up.

The captain nodded. 'We've just had a communication to say there's a chopper on its way from Sigonella to pick him up.'

'A word of advice,' Danny shouted. 'Don't let any of your men rub him up the wrong way.'

'Noted,' the captain replied. He held out one hand. 'I owe you an apology. Whitehall explained what happened to that boat. Explosives on board. A bad business.' He looked across the deck to where Spud and Caitlin were bundling Santa and Rudolph into the Wildcat. 'I don't know where you're taking those two, but I hope they get what's coming to them.'

Danny gave the captain a dark look. 'I think I can guarantee that,' he said, before giving him a brief nod and running across the deck to join the others in the Wildcat.

FOUR

Calais, northern France, the same night.

A solitary figure stood twenty metres from the side of the main road into Calais. His eyes were half closed against the bright head-lamps of the lorries trundling into the port town, interspersed with the occasional smaller car. On the other side of the road was a high fence protecting the railway line. A heavy freight train was trundling noisily past. He wondered if the passengers in the road vehicles could see him standing here, alone. If so, he could well imagine what unfavourable things they would be thinking and saying about him. But he didn't care. He knew what he was running from, and that anyone would do the same in his circumstances.

His real name was Yusuf, but on his journey across Europe he had changed it so it sounded more Western: Joseph. Joe for short. He had first heard that name three months ago on the southern coast of Greece, fresh from the overcrowded old boat that had deposited him there – scared and hungry, but alive. It was amazing how much friendlier people were when you gave them a name that didn't sound Muslim. Now Yusuf was so used to it that he'd even started thinking of himself as Joe.

Joe was tall, thin and lanky. As boys, his friends had always prided themselves on being strong and tough. Joe never was. He had a pronounced Adam's apple and his dark hair fell in a centre parting. He wore an old pair of thick glasses that his mother had always said made him look very intelligent. He couldn't see with-out them, but they were scuffed, scratched and held together with bits of tape. He dreaded the day they broke. Joe could steal most things he needed, but a pair of prescription glasses would be impossible for a fifteen-year-old impoverished migrant to get hold of.

It was a cold night, and Joe shivered. He looked to his right. Thirty metres away, set back from the road, a glowing fire burned in an old metal dustbin, with flames licking up from the rim. The silhouettes of several other people were huddled round the fire, but Joe kept his distance, just as he had ever since arriving in Greece. He knew that most migrants making their way across Europe towards the UK preferred to travel in groups. It was safer, they said, and they had more chance of making it if they could help each other. But Joe didn't agree. He had seen the way people looked at these ragtag groups of foreigners, first in Greece, then in the Balkans, and all the way across northern Italy, Switzerland and now France. He had seen the hatred and mistrust in their eyes. By himself, he could be invisible. And he could move quickly, stowing away in the back of articulated lorries as they trundled across the continent and over borders. On his own, Joe had been able to move freely and easily.

This final border, however, between France and the UK, was more problematic. Hundreds of migrants had congregated here. High wire fences prevented them from accessing the railway lines that led under the sea – though they didn't stop people from trying. Armed police and soldiers patrolled the port, and lorries were meticulously searched. Joe knew it would take all his ingenuity to get into the UK.

'Hey!' one of the figures around the fire called. Joe started. 'It's OK, you can come and get warm.' The man spoke in English, but with an accent. Joe, who had learned the language with no trouble at school back in Syria before the war, looked nervously from left to right. He wanted to stay apart from the other migrants, but he *was* very cold. Reluctantly, he approached.

The people standing round the fire – four men, three women – were a mixture of nationalities. Middle Eastern and Eritrean, Joe thought. That seemed to be the mix here in Calais. One of them handed him a bottle of some clear liquid. Joe gingerly took a sip, then coughed violently as he handed it back. There were a few laughs as he screwed up his face in disgust. But then he felt the harsh alcohol warming him from within, and he muttered some words of thanks.

'Where are you from?' asked the man who had beckoned him over. He had reverted to Arabic now.

Joe hesitated. He hadn't discussed his journey with anyone, and he didn't want to. But the fire was warm, and he was afraid that if he didn't engage, they'd send him away. 'Syria,' he said. 'Aleppo.'

A few of the migrants made a clicking sound in the back of their throats: an acknowledgement that Aleppo was not a good place to be.

'How are you going to get across?' another man asked. He looked in the direction of the port.

'I don't know,' Joe said. This was not entirely true.

'You want to be careful,' said one of the women. She wore a red headscarf and her face was pinched and lined. She suddenly started coughing rather violently, and took a moment to get her breath back. 'Two of us have died in the last three days. One boy, about your age, from Afghanistan – he got on to the Eurotunnel yesterday, but was run over by a train. It dragged him along for 400 metres, ripped his body to shreds. They only knew who he was because he had his real name on a fake passport.'

A few of the others nodded their agreement that this was a true story.

'And two days before that,' said a second woman, 'an Eritrean man got into the back of a lorry. He must have dislodged some of the pallets inside, because when the lorry started off, they toppled over and crushed him to death.'

There was more muttering. The group huddled a little closer to the fire. The woman with the red headscarf was looking intently at Joe. There was an expression of pity in her eyes. 'Family?' she asked.

'Dead,' Joe said.

'In Syria? Because of the bombs?'

Joe looked at his feet. 'No,' he said quietly. 'Not because of the bombs.' He looked up again and stuck out his chin aggressively. 'Daesh,' he said.

As he uttered the word, he cursed inwardly. Daesh was a nickname for the group that called themselves Islamic State. It was a nickname they hated, and Joe didn't know where the sympathies of these migrants lay.

He needn't have worried. A couple of the migrants spat on the ground. Others muttered swear words. There was clearly no love for Daesh in this little group. Joe relaxed a little.

'What happened?' one of the women asked. Joe felt his expression hardening. He hadn't told anybody what had befallen his mum and dad. It seemed too private, somehow. Not that he hadn't relived that awful day a thousand times in his mind. Several times a day, he saw his father's body, hanging from a tree with a black hood over his head. And he saw his mother, bloodied and beaten, being forced to do obscene things with the Daesh fighters. The memory made Joe's stomach boil with nausea and impotent fury. He saw the face of a man who had stood nearby their apartment block. He had a scar running the entire width of his neck, as if his grin had slipped down his face. When his men were finished with Joe's mother, it had been he who had shot her in the head. And it had been under his command that Joe had been taken away, and put to work . . .

But that was not a story he was going to share here. 'It doesn't matter,' he said. He knew they wouldn't push him any further. Everyone who ended up here had horrors in their past that they didn't want to talk about.

The migrants fell silent for a couple of minutes and rubbed their hands warm by the fire. The woman with the headscarf started coughing again. It sounded very bad, as though she had an infection on her chest. 'Some of us were thinking of Finland,' she said breathlessly when the cough had subsided. 'If we can get there.' She stared at Joe again across the fire. 'You could come with us,' she said. 'It's safer in groups. And look, you're so thin, there's nothing to you . . .'

Joe shook his head. 'No thanks,' he said. 'I . . . I prefer to stay alone. And anyway, there is somebody in the UK that I need to see.'

'You have family there?' Everyone round the fire seemed suddenly much more interested in him.

'No,' Joe told them quickly. 'Not family. Just . . . just this guy.'

The interest waned as quickly as it had risen. But Joe felt like he'd said too much. In any case, he had just felt a few drops of rain. He had been expecting this, having seen a weather report in a discarded newspaper that morning that said that a front of low pressure would be moving north-west from the Mediterranean. He put his hands in his pockets, hunched his shoulders and stepped away from the fire. He started walking along the road. As a car passed, its headlamps cast not only Joe's shadow, but also a second one: somebody was following him. He stopped and turned. The woman with the red headscarf was a couple of metres behind him. She looked concerned.

'Where are you going to stay tonight?' she asked.

'It doesn't matter,' Joe said.

'You must be careful if you're thinking of trying to cross. I wasn't joking. People die trying to do it. And they're searching the back of every lorry . . .'

Joe smiled at her as the rain started to fall harder. 'I have a plan,' he said. 'I think it will work.' But he wasn't sure if she heard him, because as he spoke she started coughing again. A terrible, hacking sound. The woman needed medical care, but that was obviously impossible. Joe fished around in his pocket. He pulled out a small pack of paracetamol that he had stolen from a shop in northern Italy. There were only four tablets left, but they might make the woman feel a little bit better. He stepped up to her and pressed the packet into her hands. 'You should stay warm,' he said. 'Stay out of the rain. Go back to the fire at least. Don't worry about me. I won't do anything stupid.'

The woman looked up into his eyes, but didn't argue. With a slight bow, she clasped the tablets to her chest, then turned and started to walk back to the fire. Joe continued along the road, but stopped again when he heard the woman's voice calling. 'Young man!'

Joe turned. 'Yes?'

'I hope you find what you're looking for,' she said.

Joe inclined his head. 'Me too,' he said under his breath. 'Me too.'

Sending Santa and Rudolph back to the UK was out of the question. Everyone in the unit – or what remained of it – understood that. As soon as the prisoners set foot on British soil they'd be lawyered up, given medical care, fed, watered, the works. It would take the spooks weeks to get anything out of them. By which time, it could be too late. The headshed hadn't even instructed Danny and his unit to conduct the questioning. No. These two were about to be the recipients of what was delicately known in the trade as 'enhanced' interrogation.

Santa and Rudolph were in for a long night.

Whether they knew this or not, they were utterly compliant. Fear was a good motivator. Hooded, and with their wrists and ankles bound, they lay face down and silent on the floor of the Wildcat. A strong smell of urine wafted up from where they lay. One, or maybe both, had evidently pissed themselves.

The unit were silent too. The events of the night had obviously shaken them up. Danny found himself reliving certain moments. The kid with the rotting feet. Tony's near miss, Caitlin standing up to him, and the look of absolute hatred on his face when he heard that the headshed had reassigned him . . .

Flight time to Malta: fifty minutes. It was pitch black outside. The pilot was flying low over the waves, with no external lights but with the aid of a night-vision headset. The lights of the coast-line came into view through the window of the Wildcat, but quickly disappeared as the chopper headed further inland. Hammond had told them that they were delivering their targets to an interrogation centre. Such places were unlikely to be situated in built-up areas. Danny didn't know what kind of under-the-table dealings had been done between the British and the Maltese government to allow them to fly in under the radar like this, and he didn't much care. He wanted to be back home. The sooner they delivered the two scumbags in the hoods to the creeps who were going to torture the hell out of them for whatever intel they had, the better.

There were no lights or sign of habitation as the chopper finally started to lose height. The conditions outside hadn't improved much. The helicopter shakily set down in the middle of the darkness. Caitlin kicked open the door and a wave of rain hammered into the interior. It made no difference to Danny, who was still damp and cold after their stint on the ship. He cut the cable ties binding the prisoners' ankles, then grabbed one of them – he wasn't sure which was which – and pulled him roughly from the aircraft, leaving Spud to deal with his mate. The prisoner stumbled as Danny dragged him away from the downdraught, Caitlin at his side, Spud following.

Once they were twenty metres from the aircraft, Danny stopped and tried to get his bearings. They seemed to have landed on a flat patch of rough ground at the foot of a steep hill. He detached his torch from the rack of his rifle and shone it up the hillside. It lit up a high wire fence, with razor wire at the top and sturdy uprights every twenty feet. To his nine o'clock, also at the foot of the hill but further along, was a low building – single-storey, and small. Little more than a hut. As Danny shone his torch in that direction, a second flashlight appeared outside the building, and Danny could just make out the silhouette of the figure holding it.

The rain suddenly intensified. Still dragging his prisoner, Danny led the others towards the figure. When they were five metres away, the figure turned and walked through an open door into the building. They followed him in, out of the rain.

By the light of his torch, Danny saw that the inside of the building was empty, except for a staircase along the left-hand wall, leading downwards. He directed his torch towards the figure, who had now lowered his. He was wearing a hooded raincoat, which was dripping on to the stone floor. Danny couldn't see much of his face.

'Penfold,' the man introduced himself in a thin, reedy voice. 'MI6. Are these the prisoners?'

Danny resisted the urge to give a sarcastic response, and was glad that Spud managed to hold his tongue too. He just nodded.

'Follow me, please,' Penfold said. He walked across the room to the staircase and started walking down.

All of a sudden Danny's prisoner, who had been so accommodating up till now, started to struggle. Danny jabbed an elbow just below his ribs. He doubled over, coughing violently. Danny pulled him down the steps, making sure he didn't fall. No point in him breaking any bones just yet.

There was a steel door at the bottom of the stairs. The man who had introduced himself as Penfold unlocked it at three points before opening it up. Danny squinted. The corridor beyond was brightly lit by flickering, fluorescent strips along the ceiling. On either side were identical steel doors with rivets, and at the far end a further door, guarded by two men in civvies, but with handguns holstered to their hips. Penfold shuffled down the corridor in front of Danny and the others, dripping water from his raincoat as he went. 'Technically speaking,' he said, without looking back at them, 'this place doesn't exist. You'll need to forget about it once you've left.'

'What was it originally?' Danny asked. He sensed it was an old building that had been reassigned to its new purpose.

Penfold frowned, as if he didn't like being asked the question. 'Bomb shelter,' he said reluctantly. 'Second World War.' He reached the armed guards. 'It's OK, you can let our guests through.'

One of the guards unlocked the door. The sodden party shuffled through.

They found themselves in a large, hexagonal room. The ceiling and floor were constructed from grey, stained concrete. At regular intervals around the edge were six separate rooms, each of them a good fifteen metres deep. The rooms all had a sturdy door and a toughened glass window, about three metres by two, so that it was possible to see inside. Each room had a couple of industrial-looking spotlights set about three metres from the front, pointing towards the back walls. Danny understood why. With the spot-lights shining in the eyes of the room's occupants, anyone standing behind them would be unidentifiable.

One of the rooms contained what looked like a basic dentist's chair. A rubber hose was coiled snake-like next to it. Danny instantly knew that it was a waterboarding facility. The room next to it was empty, except for a three-metre length of chain attached to the far concrete wall, with what looked like a leather dog collar at the other end. A third room contained a chair similar to the waterboarding room, but instead of the hose there was a trolley laden with surgical instruments in sterilised, sealed packages. The remaining three rooms appeared to be empty, but Danny instantly observed that they all had a drain grate in the centre, and a tap on the far wall. There were dark stains on the floor of each room, and the whole area had a faint smell of antiseptic. A further door led out of the hexagonal room, and in the middle of the room was a table with four chairs. A set of headphones lay on the table, with a long lead plugged into an audio jack on the floor.

Penfold pulled back the hood of his raincoat and unzipped it. For the first time, Danny got a proper look at him. He was completely bald, but not old – mid-thirties, maybe. He wore a pair of round glasses and was very clean-shaven, although his skin was red and blotchy with razor burn. He reminded Danny of a tyrannical twat of a science teacher who'd made his life hell as a kid. Danny took an instant dislike to him. Penfold laid his wet coat on the table, then walked over to two of the empty rooms and opened them up. 'You can put them in here,' he said. 'This one's the cold room – we can get it down to just below freezing. This one's the noise room – sound-insulated, but bloody noisy inside. Soon gets them talking.'

'And if it doesn't?' Danny asked.

Penfold gave him a thin smile, and his eyes flickered over to the other rooms. 'Inside, please,' he said.

Danny and Spud dragged their guys to the open doors and pushed them carelessly inside. Both of them stumbled and tripped. Penfold had their doors closed and locked within seconds, then beckoned Danny, Spud and Caitlin to the far door. Danny glanced back at the prisoners. They were both on their knees, their hooded heads bowed.

'The doctors are on their way,' Penfold said as they left the hexagonal room and entered what was obviously a storage area with racks of shelves along the walls. 'They'll check them over in the next half hour.'

'What's the point?' Spud growled.

Penfold looked at him over his shoulder, obviously rather surprised at the question. 'To establish,' he said, 'how much interrogation they can take. I was told there would be four of you.'

'Change of plan,' Danny said.

Penfold inclined his head. 'Er, please don't touch anything,' he said. Spud had wandered over to one of the racks and was examining something closely. He turned round, holding it up. Danny's eyes widened. It looked like some kind of sex toy.

'Seriously?' Spud said. 'I know it must get lonely here, but—'

'It's not for *recreational* use,' Penfold said. His lips had gone rather thin, like a disapproving teacher. 'It's an interrogation tool . . .'

But Spud had already put the object back on the shelf and was now reading some sticky labels that had been attached to the shelves. 'Rectal feeding . . . rectal rehydration . . .' He turned back to look at Penfold with an expression of great distaste. 'What's wrong with just hitting the fuckers?'

'Different subjects react in different ways,' Penfold said prissily. 'It's important that we have a wide range of techniques available to us.'

'Including shoving dildos up their arses? Whatever floats your boat, mucker.'

'What are you?' Penfold asked. 'The terrorist's friend?'

A sudden, heavy silence. All three members of the unit gave Penfold a contemptuous stare. Spud started to pace towards him.

'Leave it, Spud,' Danny said quietly. Spud stopped and took a deep breath, clearly calming himself down.

The terrorist's friend. If only Penfold knew the truth. But Danny thought he understood why his mate was having a go.

Spud had seen the inside of one torture facility too many over the course of his career. It was hardly surprising that he had opinions about what was acceptable and what wasn't.

'You'll be wanting something to eat,' Penfold said abruptly as he led them out of the storage room and into a kitchen area. There was a sink, a fridge and a microwave. Penfold pointed at the fridge. 'There's food in there. Help yourselves. I've received instructions that you're to be present at the interrogation. It's not something I would usually recommend, but . . .' His voice trailed off. 'I'll return when we're ready for you.'

Penfold nodded at them, wiped a few beads of sweat from his forehead and left the room.

Joe was pleased that it was raining hard. True, he was soaked to the skin. True, he was shivering with the cold. But he had been waiting for the rain, because he knew this was his best time to strike.

And he knew this, because he had been watching.

In the five days he had been loitering around the outskirts of Calais, Joe had witnessed several attempts to get across the border. He had made two observations. Firstly, when his fellow migrants tried to get over the high wire fences on to the freight or passenger train lines, they always did so in groups of six or seven, sometimes more. It made it easy for the police and soldiers guarding the area to spot them. Once he had seen this happen a few times, Joe had decided that he would continue his strategy of remaining solitary. A single person attempting to breach the lines would be far less obvious.

His second observation was this: nobody ever tried to scale the fences when it was raining. The migrants and the authorities had fallen into a routine. If the weather was fine, they would engage in their little game of catch. When it was foul they would take shelter. Joe had spent many hours standing in the driving rain, watching the weak points of the fence. During those times he had not seen a single attempt, nor a single guard on patrol.

Joe knew that he was brighter than most people. But he was surprised that nobody else had put two and two together.

He was two miles from the centre of Paris, standing on the litter-strewn verge of the dual carriageway road, about 200 metres from a bleak Ibis hotel. On the other side of the road was the main freight train line. He found it hard to see, because droplets of rain were collecting on his damaged glasses. The vehicles on the road were blurs of light as they passed, but that was OK. All he had to do was wait for a gap, then scramble across to the central reservation. And he didn't have to wait long at this time of night: a couple of minutes and he was running across, keeping his head low and focussing hard on not tripping up, because he was the kind of kid who tripped when he ran. At the central reservation he waited another minute for a gap in the traffic, before sprinting to the far side.

Here he stopped and wiped his glasses. Rain trickled down the back of his neck, and he only had a few seconds of clear vision before the lenses were wet again. But it was enough to get the lie of the land between his position and the fence that marked the boundary of the railway track: fifty metres of rough grassland. He bowed his head again, and sprinted through the driving rain up to the fence.

He was out of breath by now, but he knew he couldn't stop. The fence was twenty feet high, and topped by razor wire. There was no way Joe could scale it. He had neither the skill nor the strength. But he *did* have in his rucksack a small pair of hand-held wire clippers, which he had stolen from the back of one of the lorries in which he'd hitched an unofficial lift in northern Greece. He lay flat on the sodden ground to keep a low profile, and got to work on the wire fence. The links were difficult to snip, and his hands slipped badly on the handle of the wire cutters, which dug painfully into his hands. But after five minutes of hard work, he had cut a line about half a metre in length along the bottom of the fence. He reckoned that would be enough.

He shoved his rucksack through the hole first, then wormed his body into the gap. The wire was sharp where he had cut it. It hurt the back of his head, and ripped his trousers slightly, but that was OK. He was through. And just in time, because a train was approaching, its headlamps blindingly bright as they cut through the thick, rain-filled air. Having watched this section of railway carefully, Joe knew that it would stop at this location, presumably while some signalling issue was dealt with up ahead. Sometimes it stayed a minute, sometimes five. And ordinarily there would be guards patrolling the track while the train was stationary.

But not tonight. Not in this rain.

The train was deafeningly loud as it approached. Joe would have known just from the sound that it was a freight train: that low, rumbling, relentlessly mechanical noise. He crouched low again, curled up in a ball, camouflaged – he hoped – amid the grass. He could sense the bright lights of the headlamps even with his eyes screwed shut, and as the train screeched to a high-pitched halt, the sound seemed to go right through him, leaving him breathless.

Silence. He wiped his glasses and looked up. The train was thirty metres from where he lay and the carriages – open-topped, skip-shaped freight units – looked much bigger now that he was closer up than they had done from the far side of the main road. He felt a moment of doubt, but quickly mastered it. Pushing himself up to his feet, and checking left and right to the best of his ability that nobody was patrolling, he sprinted across the open ground towards the freight train. It seemed to loom threateningly over him as he approached. As Joe drew up alongside one of the carriages, he wiped his glasses for a third time and examined the side. There was a metal ladder fixed to the carriage. Its bottom rung was three metres off the ground – higher than Joe had estimated from a distance. He felt himself panicking that he wouldn't be able to reach it. *Take deep breaths,* he told himself. *You haven't got time to panic. The train could leave any second . . .*

He moved along to the ladder, bent his knees and jumped. His fingertips just brushed the bottom rung, but slipped off it. He cursed under his breath and tried again. This time he didn't even reach the bottom rung, and he fell in a painful heap on the floor.

61

There was a great hissing sound from the freight train. Did that mean it was about to move? Joe stood up. He took a deep breath and jumped for a third time. His left hand slipped off the rung again, but he just managed to grab hold with his right hand. He felt his other three limbs flailing pathetically, but got control of himself and grabbed the rung with his left hand too.

Joe wasn't strong, and months of travel had weakened him further. It took everything he had to pull himself slowly up four rungs of the ladder until his feet were no longer hanging helplessly in mid-air. His muscles burned, and when the train hissed again his sense of panic went into overdrive. He scrambled quickly up the remainder of the ladder and peered nervously over the top edge of the freight carriage. The one thing he didn't know was what this train was carrying. Would it be safe for him to stow away among its contents?

He peered through the darkness, and a sense of relief swelled up over him. It was gravel. A great, coarse, wet pile of it, filled to about half a metre below the brim of the container. Joe swung his legs over the edge and landed inelegantly. His glasses fell from his face and he spent a few seconds scrabbling around in the gravel. When he found them, however, he didn't put them back on his face, but instead stowed them carefully inside his rucksack. Then he started scooping out a hollow in the gravel. It took him thirty seconds to make one deep enough to cover up his rucksack, before he started digging himself into the gravel. Just because there was nobody checking the train at this location, security might be tighter when they grew closer to the border. It was important that he stayed hidden.

Within seconds, Joe's clothes and skin were caked in wet gravel. It was much more difficult for him to cover himself than he had imagined, but at least he was semi-hidden. He just hoped it would be enough.

A third hiss from the freight train. Two seconds later, Joe felt it move. He shivered. The wet gravel was extracting any remnants of warmth from his body. His plan was far more gruelling and uncomfortable than he had thought it would be.

But as the train gathered speed, Joe consoled himself with one thought. It didn't matter how cold he was, nor how ill it made him. It didn't matter how dangerous his situation, or how likely it was that he would be captured. It didn't even matter if he was killed. Whatever the future brought, it would be better than what had happened in the past.

And when you have only one aim in life, as Joe did, there is nothing you won't suffer to make it happen.

FIVE

'I can't believe that fucker Tony tried to plug me.'

It was the third time Spud had said this in the past ten minutes. And as on each previous occasion, Danny and Caitlin said nothing, because there was nothing to say.

They sat with trays of heated microwave lasagne in front of them. Danny's was half-eaten. He didn't have the stomach for it. Spud had barely touched his food, but Caitlin had wolfed hers down.

'Hungry?' Spud said. He sounded slightly aggressive.

Caitlin gave him a cool look. 'I need some tucker. Got a problem with that?'

'Oh nothing. In fact, I'm really looking forward to witnessing a bit of . . . what was it? Rectal feeding? Whatever the fuck that is. Really sharpens the old appetite.'

'They'll cark it before morning anyway,' Caitlin said matter-of-factly. 'Nobody's going to let them live after going to the trouble of getting Tony to kill all those migrants.' She seemed quite sure that this was what had happened, and if she was upset at her sudden break-up with Tony, she didn't show it. 'They need to get the information out of them somehow.' She gave Spud a shrewd look. 'If you've got a problem with this kind of thing, get out of the game.'

Spud's cheek twitched awkwardly. 'I'm just saying,' he said, bristling like a child losing an argument, 'you've got to be pretty keen on your job to come and work in the arse end of nowhere like this for months on end. I don't mind a bit of interrogation. It's when the interrogators start to enjoy it that I get a bad taste in my mouth.'

What was it Hammond had said? *Keep a close eye on Spud. He's been at the receiving end of more than his fair share of field interrogations. The military shrink flagged it up before I put him back on ops.* Danny knew he had to watch his mate.

Caitlin, however, gave a callous little shrug. 'I just hope that Penfold drongo gets something worth knowing out of them,' she said. 'I'd hate to have gone through all this for chicken feed.'

Danny was about to reply, but the sound of someone clearing their throat at the doorway stopped him. Penfold was standing there, and clearly had been for a few seconds. Having heard what Caitlin had called him, his cheeks were slightly flushed. 'We're ready for you,' he said. 'Come this way.'

Caitlin showed no hint of embarrassment as she stood up and strode towards him. Danny and Spud followed. It was an indication of how shaken up he was that there was no sign of a smirk on Spud's face. The old Spud would have found a situation like that hilarious. 'You don't have to watch, mucker,' Danny said quietly.

Spud just gave him a dead-eyed look. 'What are you talking about?' he muttered. He followed Caitlin out of the room.

'Spud.'

Spud looked back at him.

'We leave them to it. Even if we don't like what we see.'

Spud sniffed. 'Course,' he said.

Danny watched him go, concern nagging at him. Spud was unfocussed, and had been ever since the incident on the ship. Danny didn't blame him, but he didn't like it either.

Penfold led them back into the hexagonal interrogation room. There were three more people in here now. One of them wore a white coat and carried a clipboard. A doctor, Danny surmised. A second man was very young – barely in his twenties – and looked Middle Eastern. Danny had him down as a translator. A third guy was broad-shouldered, with a shaved head and a cracked front tooth that gave him a brutish expression. The muscle. He looked at Danny, Spud and Caitlin with an undisguised frown as they entered.

'Put these on,' Penfold said, passing round a handful of black balaclavas to everyone in the room. They all pulled them on – even Penfold himself, whose glasses formed a slight bulge under the black material. The translator looked particularly uncomfortable as he pulled his balaclava on.

'Try not to get in the way, please,' Penfold told them. He received three flinty stares from the unit's eyeholes in return. 'OK, Birchill, bring him out.'

Danny, Spud and Caitlin moved to the edge of the room. The guy with the cracked tooth – Birchill was obviously his name, or anyway the name he preferred to use in this place – walked to the cell containing one of the targets, opened it up and disappeared inside. He emerged a few seconds later, dragging a thin, naked, shivering man with a bruised torso and shrunken genitals. Santa, the taller and darker of the two prisoners. He was still hooded but his ankles and wrists had been untied. His body was very lean. Small muscles, but well defined. A bit of a six-pack. Birchill removed the hood as a blast of cold air came from Santa's cell. Penfold and his team had obviously been making life as uncomfortable as possible for their guests.

Santa's dark face looked crazy with fear. All the arrogance visible in the photograph of him was now absent. His eyes were rolling in his head. His whole body was shaking. As Birchill dragged him by one arm towards one of the other chambers, Danny could see a stain of brown on the back of his thigh – a remnant of where his bowels had loosened out of terror. Santa was pathetically trying to cover his genitals with the palm of his free hand. He shouted a couple of words in Arabic that Danny didn't recognise. The translator stepped over to the man with the clipboard and muttered something. The man with the clipboard made a note, while Santa was bundled into the room that had the chain attached to the wall, and the dog collar at one end.

'Seriously?' Spud said quietly, his voice slightly muffled by the balaclava. 'Walling? Why not just waterboard him? Get it over with?'

Spud sounded disgusted, and Danny silently agreed with him. It wasn't that he felt a moment's real sympathy for the two IS suspects. It was just that there were more efficient ways to interrogate them, and he couldn't help feeling that what was about to happen had something to do with the sick enjoyment of Penfold and his team. He glanced at Spud. His mate's eyes were slightly narrowed. Even Caitlin, who had sounded so matter-of-fact in the other room, now looked a little doubtful.

'Our methods are effective,' Penfold stated. 'You don't need to worry about that.' He stepped into the chamber and switched on the spotlights. The prisoner squinted hard. 'Birchill,' Penfold told the broad-shouldered man, 'go ahead. You know the drill. Two minutes to start with.'

He looked over at the others and nodded at them to indicate that they could enter the interrogation room. They filed in, along with the translator and the guy in the white coat. They stood behind the spotlights, their arms crossed.

Santa was struggling violently – he had stopped trying to cover his genitals and was attempting to hit Birchill. It was futile. Birchill was easily strong enough to hold on to him with one hand and slip the dog collar over his neck with the other. He tightened it, like a belt. Santa's hands instantly shot up to his neck as he tried to rip the collar off. He started to shout loudly in Arabic. Birchill grabbed both his wrists, yanked them behind his back and bound them together again with a set of plasticuffs. The translator started speaking in a flat monotone. 'You've got the wrong guy . . . you've got the wrong guy . . . please . . . let me go . . . let me go . . . you've got the wrong guy . . .'

On the far side of the chamber Birchill had grabbed Santa's collared neck in one big hand. With a sudden, brutal thrust, he slammed the prisoner hard against the concrete wall. Santa's knees buckled with the impact. As he collapsed, the chain grew taut. His eyes bulged as his neck was throttled by the hanging, and he stuck his tongue gruesomely out.

Birchill let him hang like that for no more than a second before yanking him up again. The chain grew slack. The prisoner shouted something. The interpreter said, impassively: 'Not again.'

Santa's relief was only momentary. Almost immediately, his muscular tormentor battered him against the wall for a second time. There was a dull thud of impact. The prisoner's whole body seemed to go limp with the collision. He slid, dazed, down the wall. The chain tightened again. Danny saw a smattering of blood dripping down the side of Santa's face. Birchill shoved him up to his feet again so that he was no longer being throttled, but he was gasping noisily as he tried to swallow some air. Still holding him, Birchill looked over his shoulder, through the window at Penfold, with an enquiring expression on his face.

Penfold nodded abruptly. Birchill slammed the prisoner against the wall for a third time.

The man in the white coat had been scribbling notes while all this happened. Now he exchanged a look with Penfold, and inclined his head. Penfold raised one hand, palm outwards. A dreadful rasping noise came from the back of Santa's throat. It sounded like he was trying to say something, but couldn't formulate the words. The interpreter said nothing.

Penfold and the interpreter walked further into the room. They stood two metres back from the prisoner while Birchill continued to hold him up to keep the rope slack. 'You have information relating to an attack on British soil,' Penfold said. He waited for a moment while his colleague translated into Arabic.

Santa shook his head. His eyes were still rolling.

'You might as well tell me what it is,' Penfold said. 'It would be better for you, in the long run.'

The translator did his job. Again, Santa shook his head.

Penfold looked over his shoulder towards the man in the white coat. 'Would you join us?' he said.

The man in the white coat entered the chamber. While Birchill continued to hold the prisoner up, the doctor checked his pulse and pulled open his eyelids to examine his pupils. 'He's fine,' he said after half a minute.

'I think we'll move into the water chamber,' Penfold said, his eyes flickering over at Spud. 'Bring him please.'

Birchill undid the collar. The prisoner collapsed to the floor as Penfold and the doctor walked out into the main room. Danny looked at Spud again. 'Calm down, buddy,' he said quietly. 'This is their call, not ours.'

He instantly knew it was the wrong thing to say. Spud left the chamber. Birchill dragged the prisoner out of the walling chamber and into the waterboarding chamber. Penfold and the others were watching without any emotion. 'You know you're doing this all arse-about-tit, right?' Spud said, a hard edge to his voice.

Penfold shut the door to the waterboarding chamber, then slowly turned to look at Spud. 'I beg your pardon?' he said coolly.

'You heard me. You're screwing this up, big time.'

Penfold's gaze hardened. 'You'll forgive me if I trust to my own considerable experience,' he said.

Spud walked up towards him. Danny found himself holding his breath. He glanced at Caitlin, who nodded almost imperceptibly. They both took a couple of paces forward, ready to restrain Spud if he went for the spook.

Spud wasn't much taller than Penfold, but he was a hell of a sight more imposing. Penfold shrank back slightly as Spud fronted up to him. 'You want to talk about experience?' Spud breathed. 'You want to know what it's like to soak up everything the Syrian *mukhabarat* can throw at you?' He looked around the room with a sneer. 'Trust me, buddy, their set-up makes your little toys look like the fucking Early Learning Centre. Or maybe you want to know what an Eritrean jihadist can do to a man when he gets his talons stuck in?'

There was a silence. Nobody moved in the hexagonal room. In the waterboarding chamber, clearly oblivious to what was going on, Birchill was strapping a struggling Santa on to the reclining chair. The prisoner was clearly making a lot of noise, but they couldn't hear him with the door shut.

'Here's the problem,' Spud continued, his voice deadly quiet. 'If you go too hard and too quickly, they'll end up just telling you what you want to hear. He'll invent any sort of shit to make it stop. Trust me. I've been there. I know.'

As Spud spoke, Danny grew a little closer. By the time his mate had finished he was standing a metre behind him. He caught his own reflection in the window of the waterboarding chamber and saw that Spud was watching him. 'Any closer, Danny,' Spud breathed, 'and I might get nervous.'

Danny stopped. Penfold spoke. 'Thank you,' he whispered, 'for your input.' He turned his back on Spud and approached the water-boarding chamber. He opened the door, stepped inside and switched on the second set of spotlights. The others followed and took up their position behind the lights. Santa was strapped to the chair by now, and was struggling forcefully, straining against the restraints. He was shouting again. The interpreter didn't need to translate. Everyone understood that the prisoner was screaming 'No ... no ... no!'

Penfold nodded at Birchill, who conjured up a small towel from a box under the chair and laid it over his prisoner's face, with the strange care of a hotel maid folding back a freshly laundered bed sheet. He bent over and picked up the piece of rubber hose that was coiled on the floor, then fitted one end on to the nozzle of the tap on the back wall. He turned the tap and water started to sluice out of the hose.

The water spattered on to the floor and drained away. Santa's struggles against the restraints became more violent, his shouts more desperate. The interpreter continued talking in his flat, expressionless voice: 'No. Please. No. I don't know anything. You've got the wrong guy.'

Birchill approached the prisoner with the hose. Danny could see Penfold's eyes behind his balaclava. They were wide and bright. Like some sicko watching their favourite part of a video nasty. Danny felt his distaste for the man growing. What had Spud said? *It's when the interrogators start to enjoy it that I get a bad taste in my mouth.* Roger that, Danny thought. But it was still no reason to interfere. The interrogators had a job to do.

Birchill raised the hose and allowed the water to fall over the towel onto Santa's face.

The prisoner's voice fell silent. He arched his back and stayed in that position, rigid, while the water continued to sluice over the towel. Danny stared at the scene impassively and found himself counting up in seconds. Seven. Eight. Nine. Ten . . .

Birchill removed the hose and tore off the towel. Santa's back remained arched as he tried to get air into his lungs. Penfold stepped forward again. 'You have information relating to an attack on British soil,' he repeated.

Santa started gasping desperate words at him. They tumbled furiously out of his mouth, but the translator's version was as measured and monotone as ever. 'I don't know anything . . . I don't know anything . . . Please . . . Let me go . . .'

Penfold stood at the foot of the waterboarding chair. He was silent for ten seconds. Then he said: 'Do it again.'

The doctor stepped forward. 'I should check his pulse,' he announced. 'He took a couple of bad knocks to the head in the walling room. If he's concussed, the sudden oxygen starvation could—'

'I said, do it again.' Penfold's eyes were glinting sharply. He threw both the doctor and Spud a defiant look as he stepped out of the chamber and closed the door behind him. Danny could see Spud's fingers twitching. He half-expected his mate to go for Penfold, and knew he'd have to restrain him if he did. But Spud remained where he was. The doctor stepped back too, although Danny could see a vein in his neck going. Birchill laid the towel over Santa's face and started with the water again.

Danny didn't count this time, but he could tell that this second session with the hose was at least twice as long as the first. Santa's body arched again and his limbs trembled against the restraints.

'That's too long.' Danny looked to one side. To his surprise, it was Caitlin who had spoken. 'I said, that's too long. If you're too heavy-handed—'

'If you haven't got the stomach for it,' Penfold said, 'feel free to leave.'

Caitlin took a sudden step towards him. Danny moved to stop her, but suddenly there was a shout from the doctor. 'We've got a cardiac arrest!' Danny looked at the prisoner. Santa's body was no longer arched. He was slumped on the chair again, and twitching with short, violent movements. Penfold's eyes narrowed, but he said nothing and didn't move.

Danny turned to the doctor. 'Treat him!' he barked. 'If he dies, his intel dies with him . . .'

Both Danny and the doctor ran towards the prisoner. Birchill had removed the hose and stepped back, but the towel was still lying over the prisoner's face. Danny ripped it away. He instantly saw that the prisoner's eyes had rolled upwards. From the corner of his eye he could just see, behind the spotlights, that Caitlin was restraining Penfold, pulling him out into the main room. He left her to it while he grabbed Santa's wrist. 'No pulse,' he told the doctor, who had already got the palms of his hands over the prisoner's chest and had started regularly pumping the ribcage down a good couple of inches.

Thirty chest compressions. The doctor had a grim look on his face as he squeezed his patient's nose and bent over to give him two rescue breaths, before going back to the compressions. But Santa's dark face had developed a faintly chalky cast. He didn't need a doctor. He needed an undertaker.

Danny stormed back out into the main room. Caitlin was no longer restraining Penfold, but she and Spud were hulking over him, making sure he didn't move.

'Your man's dead,' Danny spat. 'If you'd known what had to happen to get him here, you wouldn't have let that happen.'

'Don't try to lord it over me,' Penfold spat. 'I know who you are. Are you trying to pretend you've never done this kind of work?'

'No,' Danny said flatly. 'But there's a difference. We do what's necessary. You're enjoying yourself.'

Penfold's eyes were darting left and right.

'You want to know what really gets people talking?' Spud said, his muffled voice suddenly very quiet.

'Pain,' Penfold spat back at him.

Spud inclined his head. 'Sometimes,' he said. 'But not always. But fear? Fear does the trick, pal. Trust me. Imagining what someone's going to do to you is always worse than the thing itself.' He looked over his shoulder towards the chamber that contained the second prisoner. 'Let's bring him out,' he said to Danny and Caitlin.

Danny had a call to make. Support Spud, or tell him to back down and let Penfold and his team do their job. Spud was on the edge, but he couldn't make a bigger hash of things than Penfold. Danny turned to Caitlin. 'Get him,' he said shortly.

She nodded and crossed over to get the prisoner.

'I would remind you,' Penfold said, 'that I am in charge of this—'

He didn't finish his sentence. Spud had grabbed him by the neck and thrust him up against the window of the walling chamber. He struggled slightly, but was clearly clever enough to realise that he had no chance of coming out best in a confrontation with Spud.

Caitlin dragged Rudolph out into the main room. He was naked too, and the piebald patch on his face extended over his torso. Like his mate, he was trying to cover his shrunken genitals, and he stank of urine. He was still hooded. Danny grabbed him, pulled his hands behind his back, removed his hood and turned him to face Caitlin. 'Pathetic, hey?' he growled.

Caitlin played her part well. She looked down at his genitals and narrowed her eyes in contempt. 'Pathetic,' she agreed, her female voice loud and clear. Danny knew from his own resistance to interrogation training that there were few things that weakened a man's resolve like humiliation. He felt him shiver, then spun him round and pushed him across the room to Spud.

If anyone really had thought that Spud was the terrorist's friend, the brutality with which he treated the prisoner would soon have disabused them of the notion. He grabbed a clump of Rudolph's hair and dragged him across the room to the waterboarding chamber. Danny turned to the interpreter. 'You,' he said. 'Get in.' The young man scurried into the chamber. Danny and Caitlin followed.

The balaclava'd doctor had stopped trying to revive his patient. The prisoner lay naked, limp and lifeless on the waterboarding chair, his limbs still strapped into their restraints. His eyes were open, and his lower jaw had slumped gruesomely on to his chin. Birchill stood at the back of the chamber. He was holding the hose, which was still spouting water. The floor was soaking wet.

Spud had positioned Rudolph right next to his dead mate. His eyes bulged as he looked up and down the naked corpse. He was still shivering violently, and as Danny watched with an impassive stare, he saw yellow liquid trickling down the prisoner's inner thigh. Spud looked over at the interpreter. 'Translate,' he said.

The interpreter nodded nervously.

'You're worried we're going to hurt you,' Spud growled. He paused to allow the interpreter to render his words into Arabic. 'You might be right. We can hurt you in ways you can't even begin to think about. We can start with your fingers – rip them out from the knuckles and if you're still not singing, go to work on your tiny, stinking dick.'

Rudolph's shaking grew more violent as the interpreter translated Spud's vicious threats.

'We can pull out your teeth, we can strip off your skin. Ever had a nightmare about being buried alive? We can do that too.'

Another pause while the interpreter caught up.

'See your mate here? We hardly got the chance to get started on him. And look at him now. You're probably wondering if he's dead. He's dead alright. And that's you, in half an hour, if you don't give us what we want. Nobody knows you're here. Nobody's coming to save you. So you want to know what the worst thing about your situation is?' He grabbed Rudolph's piebald face and twisted it round so the prisoner was looking directly at him. 'If you want to see the outside of this place, we're your best friends.'

Spud allowed the prisoner to look back at the corpse of his mate. 'Take a good look,' he breathed. 'That's the last time you're going to see him. We'll be burning his body just as soon as we've unstrapped him. Don't worry – we'll keep the fire going, just in case we need it for you.'

He let the interpreter catch up. Then he dragged Rudolph out of the room and back into his isolation chamber. The others followed. Spud ripped off his balaclava. 'Give him half an hour to sweat on that,' he said. He pointed towards the room that led to the kitchen. 'We'll be waiting for you in there.' He nodded towards Birchill. 'Don't let this klutz lay a finger on him. Our man will be singing before you know it.'

And without another word, Spud stormed out of the main room. Danny and Caitlin removed their own balaclavas and followed.

The atmosphere in the kitchen was tense. Spud was staring down Danny and Caitlin, as if daring them to criticise what he'd just done. Danny kept quiet. He'd made his decision to support Spud back in the chamber. Caitlin was less restrained. 'That was a right fucking cake and arse party,' she said. 'You should have just taken one of his fingers, told him you'd remove the others each time he told you a lie. It's textbook.'

'Maybe you should just go and join the freak show out there,' Spud spat back. 'Sounds like they're right up your street.'

Caitlin looked incredulously at him. 'What the hell's your problem? If you can't give a proper field interrogation, you shouldn't be here. These are IS suspects we're talking about. When the hell did you turn so bleeding-hearted?'

Spud's face was a riot of emotions. 'At least I didn't kill our one remaining prisoner,' he muttered, before stalking off to the other side of the room.

'We'll give it ten minutes,' Danny announced. 'Then we'll go back in. If he's not talking, we'll do it Caitlin's way.'

He took their silence as consent.

But they didn't need ten minutes. They didn't even need five. Barely a minute had passed before there was a diffident knock on the door. The interpreter appeared. His eyes flickered nervously at each of them. He spoke in a cracked voice.

'The prisoner's ready to speak,' he said.

SIX

Santa was no longer there. Nor was Birchill. Danny didn't need to ask what he was doing with the body.

Rudolph had taken his mate's place on the waterboarding chair. Penfold was standing by him, thin-lipped. He said nothing as the unit entered the chamber with the interpreter. Spud made to approach the prisoner, but Danny held him back. 'I'll do it, mucker,' he breathed. Spud looked like he was going to argue, but he held back.

Danny stepped up to the chair. 'Speak,' he said.

The interpreter didn't even need to translate Danny's instruction. Rudolph started gabbling breathlessly in Arabic, as if he couldn't get the words out fast enough. 'London,' the interpreter spoke over him, translating in real time. 'We were on our way to London . . . There is going to be a bomb . . . a big bomb . . . we were to wait for a phone call when we arrived in England, to tell us what to do . . .'

'Where will the bomb be?' Danny demanded.

The interpreter put the question. Rudolph hesitated. With a glance at Spud, Danny grabbed his left hand and, with a sudden yank, snapped back the little finger. Rudolph shrieked with pain. A weak smile crossed Penfold's lips. Danny leaned in closer. 'Where will the bomb be?' he demanded.

Rudolph spoke.

'Westminster Abbey,' the interpreter stated.

A sudden, heavy silence in the room. Even Penfold looked shocked.

'When?' Danny asked.

Rudolph's eyes bulged. Danny made to grab one of his good fingers. Rudolph shouted out again, his voice high-pitched and terrified.

'Christmas Day,' said the interpreter. 'Christmas Day.'

The silence fell again. Everyone in the room looked at the prisoner in disgust.

'We need to get on the line to Hereford,' Danny said. 'Now.'

Looking out from the corner-office briefing room on the seventh floor of the MI6 building in Vauxhall, it was clear that London was being battered by a rainstorm. The familiar sights of Parliament Square, the London Eye, St Paul's Cathedral and the bridges were glowing blurs in the night.

Inside the room was stifling. It bore all the traces of a long session. Empty pizza boxes were stacked in a wobbly pile – the residue of two meals taken on the hoof. The large table in the middle of the room was littered with polystyrene cups. There was a smell of body odour, and the men and women sitting round the table looked crumpled and drawn.

There was Guy Thackeray. The new director of MI6 had round glasses and an equally round face. His jovial demeanour masked a ruthless streak. Thackeray was the powerhouse behind recent legislation giving much wider powers of surveillance to the security services. It made him a bit of a hero in the corridors of MI6, and a despicable snooper in the eyes of the left-wing press. But he was the sort of man to wear that kind of criticism as a badge of honour.

There was George Chilvers, a surprise recent appointment to the position of Foreign Secretary. Plump, with floppy blond hair and a disarming schoolboy manner. But clearly ambitious for the top job. He'd arrived fifteen minutes ago, but he owned the room and seemed like he'd been there for hours.

There was Alice Cracknell, a security analyst in her mid-thirties, whose recent promotion to the inner sanctum of Thackeray's closest team – above the heads of many more experienced candidates – was rumoured to be because she and the director shared more than intelligence. Not that anyone doubted her ability to do the job. Alice was a very good intelligence officer.

And there was Ray Hammond, Regiment ops officer, in direct contact with the team currently on ops in the Med. His phone seemed to have been glued permanently to his ear over the past few hours as he kept the line open to the situation room at Hereford in order to update the assembled company in real time about the status of the operation. Hammond knew it was unusual for the head of MI6 to be taking such a hands-on role. It was even more unusual for the Foreign Secretary to be here. Thackeray was up to something. Hammond didn't know what.

'So this is it then?' Chilvers was saying. 'Proof positive that these IS chappies are using migrant boats to smuggle their operatives into Europe.'

'Yes, Foreign Secretary,' said Thackeray. 'We've had our suspicions before now, of course, but we've never actually had the smoking gun.'

Chilvers looked over at Hammond. 'I hope you have your best people on this,' he said.

'Of course,' Hammond said, his poker face not slipping for an instant. 'Good men. Good soldiers.' And when there was an awkward pause: 'The best.'

The Foreign Secretary shook his head. 'This migrant situation is getting out of hand. I had to talk very hard to get the PM to agree to up the UK's quota of refugees. We owe these people a second chance, damn it, since it was us that destabilised the Middle East in the first place. We've a proud tradition of providing political asylum to those in genuine need. But if it gets out that IS are using them as Trojan Horses, the border agency will go into lockdown.'

Thackeray settled his hands gently on his paunch. 'It's how they work,' he observed. 'The Taliban used to hide out in civilian areas so we couldn't bomb them without collateral damage. The mujahideen used to do the same. These IS thugs might have a different name, but they're the same people and they have the same tactics. They don't care about the lives of innocents.'

'I've got some intel coming through from our team in Malta,' Hammond interrupted. He listened for a moment, then reported the edited highlights.

'Christmas Day. Westminster Abbey. An IS bomb attack.'

Chilvers had turned slightly pale. Hammond had seen that look a hundred times. Give a politician a piece of bad news, chances are their first reaction will be to start calculating how it will affect them personally. He glanced out of the window, in the direction of Parliament Square. The roof of the abbey wasn't quite visible on account of the rain. 'They wouldn't dare,' he said.

Three cool glances made it clear what everyone else in the room thought of *that* statement.

Thackeray turned to Alice Cracknell. 'What's happening at Westminster Abbey on Christmas Day?'

Cracknell was examining some data on her laptop screen. 'Ten a.m. service,' she said. 'Normally a full house. We've got the PM attending, and his family.'

The Foreign Secretary gave her a sharp look. 'How do you know?' he demanded. 'I take it this isn't the sort of information you normally have at your fingertips?'

'This intelligence corroborates certain whispers we've been hearing from elsewhere,' Thackeray said.

'What do you mean? Why haven't I heard about this?'

Thackeray spread his hands apologetically. 'Foreign Secretary, if we informed you of every single lead we're obliged to follow up, there would be precious little time for you to do anything else.' He inclined his head. 'I will concede, however, that Westminster Abbey has been slightly higher on our radar than any of the other potential attacks. We already have – three, is it Alice? – independent sources suggesting some level of terrorist activity there around the Christmas period. Nothing quite as high grade as this, however – Internet chatter, Facebook comments, the usual stuff.' He looked at his assistant. 'I think we can consider it copper-bottomed, don't you, Alice?'

Alice nodded.

'Jesus wept,' the Foreign Secretary said. 'They're monsters.'

'Tell us something we don't know, George.'The director looked sharply at Hammond. 'Level one security,' he instructed.

Hammond stared at him. 'You're going to allow the service to go ahead?' He couldn't quite believe what he was hearing.

'I don't see that we have an option. Cancelling the thing would be a disaster from a PR perspective. Makes us look very weak. Gives IS the upper hand, publicity-wise. I'm sure the Foreign Secretary agrees.'

The Foreign Secretary hesitated, then turned to Hammond. 'It's up to you to stop this thing happening. What countermeasures can you put in place?'

Hammond was thinking on his feet now. 'Round-the-clock plain-clothes surveillance on all entrances by sunrise, obviously. We'll organise a full sweep of the interior and exterior, and we'll check for sniper positions in the surrounding area. We'll need military bomb disposal units. I also recommend full background checks into all ancillary cathedral staff. If someone's planting an explosive device, it's more likely to be a cleaner than a priest . . .'

'Of course,' the director said grimly. 'Alice, I want the Met's chief commissioner here immediately, and we need to put SCO19 specialist firearm command on standby. I'll need a full briefing with the directors of MI5 and GCHQ within the hour. And the Chief of the Defence Staff . . .'

'I need to inform the cabinet,' Chilvers said.

'Absolutely not,' the chief replied.

Chilvers blinked at him. 'Now look here—'

'If you imagine, George, that there are members of the wider cabinet who are not being actively monitored by the NSA, then you're badly mistaken.'

'I suppose you think the security services are impenetrable too,' the Foreign Secretary shot back.

'Certainly not. But we have to keep this tight. And it's not just to save face. If the Americans learn that we're intercepting their intelligence sources, they'll shut them down and use a different method of communication.'

'Why the bloody hell aren't they sharing this information with us in the first place? What about the special relationship?'

'Why our American cousins do anything is something of a mystery these days,' Thackeray said, with a meaningful look at Alice.

Hammond held up one finger. 'Updates from Malta,' he said. He listened to the voice at the other end of his mobile. 'Our team believes that their targets are being controlled by an IS commander based in northern Iraq by the name of Dhul Faqar.' He saw Thackeray and Cracknell exchange another look. 'I take it the name means something?'

'It most certainly does,' Thackeray said.

'*Well?*'

'Go ahead, Alice,' Thackeray said.

Alice cleared her throat. 'Dhul Faqar was a high-level member of the Ba'ath Party under the Saddam Hussein regime. He was also an excellent politician – you needed to be, if you were close to Saddam and wanted to stay alive. That said, there are rumours that he supplied Saddam and his sons with certain ...' she cleared her throat again '... playthings.'

'What do you mean?' Chilvers asked.

'Girls, Foreign Secretary,' Thackeray said. 'Slave girls. For sex. Uday, Saddam's eldest son, had some fairly exotic tastes, and the word is he inherited them from his father. Do carry on, Alice.'

'After the downfall of the Saddam regime, he disappeared from the radar. A lot of the people closest to Saddam did. Some of them never reappeared – we assume that the Iraqi people dealt with them in whatever way they saw fit. But some, the cleverer ones, popped up again with the emergence of the so-called Islamic State. They'd rebranded themselves, of course – spiritual leaders, fighters of Islam, all that stuff. But really it was just a way of regaining some of the power they'd grown used to having in the good old bad old days of Saddam. The emerging militants were just a bunch of disorganised thugs, and they needed people to orchestrate them. These are very clever men we're talking about. They understand the value of publicity. They understand that their battles are won on social media as well as by boots on the ground.'

'So, this Dhul Faqar character has no real religious affiliations?' the Foreign Secretary asked.

'Almost none of them do, George. The IS commanders, I mean. They pay lip service to the cause, of course, talk the jihadi talk, walk the jihadi walk. But in reality, their interests are the interests of powerful men the world over.' He looked at Chilvers, as if expecting him to know what he was talking about. When Chilvers's expression remained blank, he said, 'Sex and money, George. Sex and money.'

'I don't understand. How does this character get money and ...' Chilvers blushed slightly '... how does he get what he *wants*, by running a terrorist organisation?'

Thackeray smiled indulgently. 'The money is simple. Islamic State is well funded. They have rich backers – we're talking ultra-high-net-worth individuals – who pump substantial funds into the cause. IS militants are ruthless and expert looters – when they move into an area they strip its banks, businesses and military installations of whatever cash they're holding. They levy taxes on the areas they control. They smuggle antiques and artefacts on to the open market. They make millions from human trafficking, kidnapping and extortion. And then, of course, there's the oil. IS control vast swathes of northern Iraq and Syria. There are plentiful oilfields in this area, and many of them are under IS control.' He raised an eyebrow at the Foreign Secretary. 'You'll stop me if I'm teaching my grandmother to suck eggs, George?'

'What? No, no, do go on. It's always helpful to hear another perspective on the matter.' Chilvers failed to hold the chief's gaze, and his inexperience seemed to hang in the room like a cloud.

'Of course,' Thackeray said, and Hammond had the impression that he was choosing his words carefully, 'having control of the oilfields and actually being able to *sell* the oil are two different things, as I'm sure you can appreciate.' Chilvers gave no indication of whether he could appreciate this or not, so Thackeray continued. 'One doesn't simply walk into the head offices of BP and offer them millions of barrels of crude at a knock-down rate. IS are obliged to use more elliptical routes to get their product to market.'

'Go on.'

'There are certain middlemen who broker the oil for Islamic State on the open market. They launder it, if you will. Nation states who couldn't be seen to be dealing directly with IS can much more easily buy it from these middlemen – and they're happy to do so, because they offer the crude at a discount. It's simple economics, really. IS earn millions of dollars a day from selling the oil they control. They need to, of course – it's a big organisation with a lot of mouths to feed and salaries to pay. But it's straightforward for the people higher up the rung to cream a little off the top – backhanders from the middlemen, that kind of arrangement. A very tiny fraction of IS's daily income represents a substantial fortune for an individual like Dhul Faqar.

'The sex is more straightforward. IS routinely take girls hostage to use as sex slaves. Their commanders get the pick of the bunch. There have been a number of special forces raids – British and American – on the compounds these vermin use to keep their harems. We've managed to rescue some of the girls, and they've given us detailed information on how they are being used and abused. The reports make for . . .' Thackeray sniffed '. . . unedifying reading.'

'We should be bombing these IS strongholds – us and the Americans,' Chilvers said.

'I couldn't agree more, Foreign Secretary. There is some, how can I put it, frustration among the security services at the rationale behind which IS strongholds in northern Iraq and Syria are being targeted, and which aren't.'

'Your frustration is shared,' Chilvers replied darkly. 'But we don't have the mandate from the public to step up a bombing campaign in the Middle East. Not to mention that we don't have enough planes.'

Thackeray raised an eyebrow. 'Mandates can be doctored,' he said blithely. 'And resources can be made available. No, Foreign

Secretary, I think you and I both know that the Americans are running the show in the Middle East. We have a great deal to lose from falling out with the US, so there's no way we would bomb these targets independently without the Americans' say-so. And it appears the Americans have their reasons for holding back on these targets.' Thackeray got to his feet and started pacing round the room. 'Britain has its own little part to play in the conflict, Foreign Secretary, and we mustn't get ideas above our station.' He stopped and looked directly at Chilvers. 'Of course, there are those who think that Britain should not be playing the part of America's poodle. Whether you yourself are of that frame of mind, I couldn't possibly say.'

His comment seemed to hang between the two men. Hammond cleared his throat. 'Westminster Abbey?' he reminded them.

Thackeray sat down again. 'Westminster Abbey,' he repeated placidly.

'I have to warn you that we can put all the usual precautions in place, but—'

'—if a device has already been planted, we might not be able to locate it.'

'But how can that be possible?' Chilvers demanded. 'Don't you have resources for this kind of thing?'

'The kind of IEDs we're coming up against these days are incredibly sophisticated,' Hammond said. 'And the terrorists are fast learners. They're setting explosives into composite blocks, for example, then into concrete. When they do that, it's impossible for dogs to sniff them out. And they're getting skilled at making these things so that metal detectors can't pick them up – plastic components in the detonators, only tiny bits of metal.'

Chilvers scratched his blond hair. 'But ... in Westminster Abbey? How would they ...'

'The Brighton bomb that targeted Thatcher was in place months before it was detonated. With technology now, digital timers and the like, they can put IEDs in place *years* beforehand. A couple of rogue concrete slabs when they're doing restorations – the whole place could be an explosion waiting to happen.

Then, of course, there's the suicide bomber factor – if somebody wants to walk in there on the day wearing several kilos of C5, there's not a lot we can do . . .'

There was an ominous silence as the assembled personnel considered the implication of Hammond's words.

Eventually, Chilvers spoke again. 'This Dhul Faqar character,' he said. 'He would know the identity of whoever's in the UK orchestrating this attack, one presumes.'

Hammond had to hand it to Thackeray. He was playing Chilvers like an instrument. His reaction was subtle. An imperceptible widening of the eyes, as if he had not previously considered this option and was impressed at the Foreign Secretary's perceptiveness. 'One would assume so,' he said. 'As I'm sure you're aware, 9/11 was conceived and planned in Afghanistan. The Paris attacks were conceived and planned in Syria. The hard truth is that if you're trying to prevent these atrocities by targeting individuals in the UK, you're already too late.' He cleared his throat. 'If you're drinking water from a stream that's giving you stomachache, your best bet is to head upstream and remove the animal turd that's poisoning it, if you take my meaning.'

The Foreign Secretary blinked hard. 'Then we must apprehend him.'

Thackeray inclined his head. 'It's a possibility,' he said. 'But I should warn that the PM is unlikely to give his approval to our going in under the Americans' radar.'

'Bollocks to the PM,' Chilvers snapped. 'I'm the Foreign Secretary, this is within my authorisation.'

Thackeray nodded. 'A bold stance is needed,' he said approvingly. He turned to Alice Cracknell, but she seemed to be one step ahead of him and was already handing over a Manila folder. 'If that's your decision, George, there's a chance that we could kill two birds with one stone.' He gave a bleak smile. 'So to speak.'

'How so?'

'Our intelligence tells us that Dhul Faqar is hosting four of these middlemen we talked about, the ones who broker oil from the IS-controlled oilfields on to the wider market. I'm sure I hardly need to point out that the elimination of these individuals would be a serious blow to Islamic State. If they can't broker their oil, a substantial chunk of their funding will be cut off.'

'You're asking me to authorise an assassination attempt?' the Foreign Secretary said.

'It's your decision, of course, but such a course of action will require high-level approval. And like I say, I don't feel comfortable approaching the wider cabinet in case we inadvertently tip off the Americans that we're listening in on their intelligence sources. The PM would almost certainly veto the operation. It needs the authority of somebody with the ability to see the wider picture. And of course, the person who supported MI6 in this matter would be assured of our support in the future.' He sat back and let his words sink in.

The Foreign Secretary made a show of considering the matter, but Hammond could tell that Thackeray's wily flattery had already done its work. 'Let us speak plainly,' Chilvers said. 'You want me to authorise an operation to extract information from Dhul Faqar, and also to assassinate these four middlemen.'

Thackeray nodded slowly.

Chilvers sniffed. You could almost see the wheels turning in his mind. 'See that it's done,' he said finally. 'But I want your best people on it. There must be complete deniability. The Americans can't know and the PM can't know. Is that understood?'

'Perfectly,' Thackeray muttered.

The two men stood up and stiffly shook hands. 'I need to get back to my office,' Chilvers said. 'You'll keep me informed of any progress?'

'Of course, Foreign Secretary. You'll be the first to know.'

Chilvers gave Hammond and Alice Cracknell a cursory nod, then left the room, closing the door noisily behind him.

There was a moment's silence. Thackeray turned round to check that the door was indeed shut. Then he breathed out explosively. 'That man,' he announced, 'is a grasping, snivelling, self-absorbed little cunt. No wonder he's made such a name for himself in politics.' He turned to Hammond. 'I've had a whole team researching Dhul Faqar and his middlemen. It's taken me six months to get to this point. Alice will give you everything we have. And Chilvers might be an idiot but he was right about two things: complete deniability, and your best men. The team who lifted these two migrants in the Med – you said *they* were your best.'

Hammond nodded, trying hard not to let any expression of doubt show in his face.

'Do they have names, old boy?'

Hammond inclined his head and shuffled through the papers in front of him. He pulled out a file and handed three documents over to the chief. Thackeray glanced through them. 'Danny Black,' he murmured, 'Spud Glover, Caitlin Wallace. I wasn't aware you had females on the books, as it were.'

'Australian,' Hammond said. 'On secondment. I have every confidence in her.'

'Good,' Thackeray said, adding the documents to his own pile of papers. 'Assign them to the task. They're to take out the middlemen, apprehend Dhul Faqar and squeeze every last drop of information about this Westminster Abbey hit out of him.' He frowned. 'I've had my eye on that monster for a long time. We'll all sleep safer in our beds once Dhul Faqar's crossed off our to-do list.'

Hammond nodded. 'We need to make a decision about the remaining IS target in Malta.'

Thackeray gave him a sharp look. 'I understood there were two of them.'

'One didn't make it through the interrogation process.' And before Thackeray could ask the obvious question, he added: 'It happened under the authority of the MI6 team. The Regiment personnel took over and successfully extracted the intel from the second man. I suggest they accompany him out of Malta. I don't know who you've got running that place, but prisoners have a habit of ending up dead there.' Hammond knew he was overstepping the mark, but the MI6 chief didn't seem to mind. In fact, he appeared lost in thought. 'Sir?' Hammond nudged him.

Thackeray blinked. 'I'm afraid he can't leave the facility. We can't risk word getting back to Dhul Faqar that we abducted his men. Not to mention the Americans.' He sniffed. 'Your men will have to ... do what has to be done.'

Hammond inclined his head. He had noticed that when it came to ordering an execution, the spooks had an endless supply of euphemisms.

Thackeray neatened his papers, held them to his chest and headed to the door to follow Chilvers out of the room. But before leaving, he turned again, almost on an afterthought. 'Oh, and for God's sake, Hammond, *tell* me you've got someone on the way to Dubai to pick up that bloody liability Yellow Seven. I've got the palace on my back about it day and night – as if I don't have more important things to think about.'

Hammond took a deep breath, and forced himself not to give the answer he wanted to deliver.

'It's all under control,' he said. 'You can tell the palace that we've—'

'Got our best man on it?' Thackeray said with a faint smile. 'I think I will at that. I'll leave you in Alice's capable hands. Get the job done, Hammond. There's a lot riding on it. We can't stop these migrants coming in. The only thing we can do is weed out the bad eggs at source. Excuse me. I have a lot to organise.'

With that, he turned and finally left the room.

Hammond spoke into his mobile phone. 'Tell the Malta unit to eliminate the remaining prisoner, then get them back over to Sigonella military base, Italian section,' he said. 'I need to be on a plane to Sigonella as soon as possible to brief them. They'll need full gear and supplies. Inform them that they're heading east and I'll brief them further when I see them.' He killed the phone, then turned to Alice Cracknell, who was sitting primly, with a slightly superior look on her face. 'Alright, love,' Hammond said with a heavy sigh. 'Dhul Faqar. Sounds like a right charmer. Show us what you've got.'

★ ★ ★

Joe was shivering violently. He knew that he was dangerously cold. The wet gravel in which he was hiding was sucking every ounce of warmth from him. He was even beginning to feel sleepy, which he knew was the first sign of hypothermia. Time was running out.

The train had stopped moving an hour ago, but he knew that he was still on the French side of the English Channel because it had not travelled far enough to make the tunnel crossing. And in any case, the rain had been incessant. With only his face showing at the surface of the gravel, it kept washing pieces of grit into his mouth and eyes. At times, he felt like he was suffocating. If the train had gone under the tunnel, there would have been some respite. But there was none.

He didn't know what the delay was, but he didn't like it. The longer he remained in France, the greater the chance he would be discovered.

Voices. French. Joe felt himself go rigid. It was difficult to locate where they were coming from, not only because of the rain but also because they were down on the ground and he was much higher up. He tried to work out how many there were. Four? Perhaps five? Probably just railway staff, he told himself. Stay calm.

But it was difficult to stay calm when, thirty seconds later, he heard a needling, high-pitched whine. Like the buzzing of a giant insect, and it was getting closer . . .

Five seconds later he saw an object float up above the edge of the carriage. He knew instantly what it was: a small drone. No doubt it was fitted with a camera, and was here to search the carriages. He felt a moment of panic. Then he told himself there was no time for that.

There was no light coming from the drone, which meant that it had to be a night-vision camera. He quickly clamped his eyes shut, because he knew that an NV camera would pick up his retinas quite clearly. And he held his breath, because even the slightest movement could give him away. He concentrated hard on stopping the trembling, but that was more difficult. There was nothing he could do about it.

The whining grew louder. Joe couldn't see the drone, but he could sense it almost directly overhead. He had a horrible vision of it landing on his face. *Please don't see me,* he thought desperately. *After all this, please don't see me . . .*

There was a crack of thunder overhead. Rain lashed down. Joe felt it washing the gravel from his face. He cursed himself. Why had he thought nobody would guess there might be stowaways in these carriages? He had been so confident about his strategy before. Now he felt stupid.

The rain fell.

The drone hovered above his face.

He waited for the guards to start shouting. Or for the crunching sound of feet across the gravel load.

Neither came.

The whining grew softer. The drone was moving on.

Joe still didn't move. Didn't open his eyes. Barely breathed. His limbs were numb and heavy, and he felt the sharp nausea of fear. This *had* to work. He *had* to get across the border.

'*C'est bon!*' called a French voice from below. '*Allez!*'

There was a sudden, loud hiss. The freight train eased into motion.

Joe's pulse started to race. The train gathered speed and, a minute later, the sensation of hard rain across his face came to a halt. He opened his eyes. Total darkness.

He knew he was in the tunnel. He felt a sense of elation.

He forced himself to move. His body ached, and the inside of his mouth was caked with grit. He didn't know how high the roof of the tunnel was, so he kept low, hunched in a little ball as the wind and the noise rushed past his ears. He thought of how far he had come – the dangerous sea crossing on a tiny boat full of desperate migrants. The long journey through Europe, stowing away in the back of more lorries than he could remember. He ignored the hunger gnawing at his stomach, and the thirst that burned the back of his throat, and the pain in his muscles, and the piercing cold . . .

He was about to enter the UK, and that was all that mattered.

Lights. Rain. The train had suddenly emerged from the tunnel. Joe flung himself on to his back again, breathing heavily as the brakes gave a loud, ear-piercing squeak. Even up here, he could tell that the wheels were sparking against the rails, because there was a faintly blue light in the air. He uncovered his rucksack and pulled out his glasses. They were smeared from being stuffed in his rucksack, but he placed them carefully on his face. Smudged vision was better than blurred vision. He crawled to the edge of the carriage, and waited for the train to come to a halt.

Silence.

Joe put his hands up over his head and grabbed the edge of the carriage. The wet metal bit against his hands as he pulled himself up. The thin muscles in his arms burned.

He peered gingerly over the side of the carriage. The train had pulled in to a railway siding. In the distance he could see a network of wire fences, telegraph towers and solitary freight carriages. There was a road, maybe 150 metres away, with car headlamps burning through the torrential rain. Joe was breathing heavily. He had a call to make. Did he climb out of the train here, or wait for it to travel further into the UK?

He made his decision quickly. It was dangerous to be stowed away in a carriage full of gravel. He didn't know how it would be emptied out, but he had no desire to be inside when that happened. And it didn't matter *where* in the UK he alighted. As long as he was here, that was all that mattered.

He hauled himself over the side of the carriage, scrambling wetly to grab the rungs of the ladder on the outside. He descended slowly and carefully. His limbs were still trembling, and he wasn't at all sure that his fingers had the strength to grip the metal.

But they did. Thirty seconds later, Joe felt his feet crunch on to the ground. Not a moment too soon. The freight train suddenly hissed again, and began moving backwards out of the siding.

Joe watched it leave. Then he looked down at himself. His saturated clothes were covered in wet, gravelly mud. His jeans were ripped. One of his trainer soles had come loose. He removed his glasses and tried to wipe the rain from his face with his sleeve, but just winced as grit scraped across his skin.

He put his glasses back on – and his heart stopped. He could see many multiples of his shadow stretching out in front of him, fanned out along the train track. That meant there were several light sources behind him. They were moving.

'Hey! Hey you! What are you doing there? Get away from the side of the track!'

Joe spun round. He winced. There were three torches, very bright, about twenty metres away. He couldn't see the shapes of the people holding them.

'I said get away from the side of the track! We are armed. I repeat, we are armed.'

Joe stepped sideways, away from the track. At the same time, he raised his arms above his head.

It all happened so quickly. Before Joe even knew what was happening, the three men with torches were upon him. He caught a flash of camouflage gear and realised they were soldiers. Two of them stood to one side, holding their beams at head level and shining them directly at him. The third grabbed him roughly and forced him down, grinding Joe's cheek against the rough ground. 'What are you?' the soldier growled. 'One of those fucking migrants? Reckon you're going to be put up in some posh hotel, do you? Here for some handouts, are you?'

Joe felt the hinges on his glasses go. He tried not to panic. Instead, he twisted his head to look directly into the fierce stare of the soldier who had pinned him down to the floor.

'I want to claim political asylum,' he said.

DECEMBER 21

SEVEN

It had been two months since Baba had arrived at the compound of Dhul Faqar. The worst two months of her short life.

Baba had seen daylight three times. The first time had been three days after her arrival. Dhul Faqar's wife – Baba had learned that her name was Malinka – had made her scrub her skin so harshly that it was red and raw. It stung when she applied the pungent perfume with which she was obliged to douse herself. And the gossamer-thin, see-through gown she was forced to wear, although it looked soft and silky, was harsh and sore against her skin. When Malinka had taken her into Dhul Faqar's chamber, Baba had thought the sore skin was the worst of her problems. She had soon forgotten about it.

Malinka had whispered in her ear that if she did not perform properly, she could expect a harsh punishment. Then she had left them together.

Dhul Faqar had been strangely kittenish at first, as he approached her and tried to slip the gown from her shoulder, while Baba kept her eyes averted from his gaze. She had recoiled in instinctive horror at his touch. Dhul Faqar had instantly changed. He had called for his wife, who had entered so quickly that Baba knew she must have been waiting on the other side of the door. Malinka had dragged her out of the room by her hair and, blinking, into the midday sun. There, Malinka had ordered two of Dhul Faqar's men to flog Baba. They did it willingly, with vicious grins on their faces. Twenty lashes, each one leaving a snake of blood up Baba's naked back. They had taken three weeks to heal, but by that time Baba had learned not to flinch when Dhul Faqar approached her.

The second time she saw sunlight was a month into her incarceration. Dhul Faqar had called for her, and Malinka had brought her to his chamber. She didn't struggle – she had somehow found the ability to keep control. She cried, of course, when the act happened, but that seemed to increase Dhul Faqar's pleasure, not decrease it – even if her tears always earned her a few words of contempt from Malinka. On this occasion, it had been over more quickly than usual. The relief must have shown in Baba's face. Dhul Faqar had turned suddenly angry, as though his sexual humiliation was her fault. Malinka had dragged her outside again. On this occasion she had been spared a flogging. She was simply beaten and kicked until her breasts and stomach were bruised.

The third time she had seen sunlight was on the day she had tried to escape.

Baba hadn't been planning it. She was too numb to plan anything. Dhul Faqar had been particularly brutal in the preceding days. He had left her bleeding and unable to walk properly. When Malinka had inadvertently failed to lock the door of the dingy room in which she was forced to exist when she wasn't servicing Dhul Faqar's needs, Baba had simply made a run for it. To her astonishment, there were no guards outside. Baba had sprinted away from the buildings, and for a wild moment of exaltation she thought the nightmare was over.

But then she had heard the laughter behind her. She had turned round to see two of Dhul Faqar's guards – the two who had delivered the twenty lashes – watching from a distance of twenty metres. They each had a snarling black dog on a leash. The animals were straining to get at her. 'Go on then,' one of them shouted. 'Make a run for it. They could do with a meal.'

Baba had simply collapsed in fear.

Malinka's wrath had been truly terrifying. She had administered the punishments herself this time. Baba had two black eyes to show for it, a bleeding lip and more bruises to her body and cuts to her cheek from Malinka's perfectly manicured nails. There was a thin scab against her jugular where Malinka had held her evil knife and threatened to cut Baba's throat if she ever tried such a thing again.

Baba had hated the lonely cell in which she had been kept during the first six weeks of her incarceration. It contained nothing except a clay pot for her to use as a toilet. It stank, and was cold and uncomfortable. But after her escape attempt, she would have given almost anything to be returned to it. Because from that point on, she had been chained like an animal to a post in the room where Dhul Faqar spent his days. A thick metal collar was locked round her neck, with a chain leading from it to the post. Under the collar, her skin was sore, sweaty and spotty. And now she was no longer taken to Dhul Faqar's chamber when he wished to abuse her. Instead, on a daily basis, the room was cleared and the act would take place while she was chained up like a dog.

Now, Baba spent all day in the presence of the man whom she hated more than any other, always taking great care not to look him in the eye. She saw him at work. She witnessed his meetings with a wide variety of dead-eyed militants. Some of them she recognised. When Dhul Faqar was not around, they would leer unpleasantly at her. When he was there, however, they did not dare. It was clear to Baba that they feared him greatly. When she needed the toilet, or to be washed, Malinka would release her from her chain and accompany her, all the while whispering threats of great punishment if she did not remain utterly compliant. Then she would return her to the chain.

Baba was not without spirit. But that spirit was now completely broken. She knew that now Dhul Faqar had allowed her to hear his important, confidential business, she would never leave this compound. Which meant she would be killed when her usefulness came to an end.

In the meantime, she heard everything. She heard talk she did not understand of oil and of middlemen. She heard him discussing the wages his militants were to be paid, and planning the taxes that they would extort from ordinary people. With the taste of bile in the back of her throat, she heard him encourage his commanders – none of whom dared look him in the eye – to give young women to their men, as rewards for their loyalty, and as a means of spreading the fear that would keep the people under control.

And today, she heard him revealing the identity of one of his men in a far-off country.

'His name is Jacob Hakim,' Dhul Faqar told the fighter who was sitting opposite with his gaze averted. It was one of the men who had flogged Baba, and she noticed how his eyes kept flickering towards her. He was sitting at a low table with his boss, and they were drinking mint tea out of small handleless cups. 'He lives in London. We are sure that the British security services do not know his identity. He will be of great service to us in the events that are to come. I am telling you this because, when the time comes, he will need to leave the UK and come to live with us here. I will expect you to welcome him as a brother. But for now, you must keep this a secret, do you understand? Only you and I will know that we have spoken of this.'

The fighter nodded. 'Yes, Dhul Faqar,' he said, before taking a sip of his mint tea.

Dhul Faqar stood up. The fighter scrambled to his feet, clearly understanding that the interview was at an end. He bowed clumsily, his weapon clunking, then scurried out of the room.

Dhul Faqar had an oddly satisfied look on his face. He picked up the fighter's half-drunk mint tea and carried it over to Baba, who quickly averted her eyes. He handed it to her. Baba, who was very thirsty, gulped it down while he surveyed her quietly, his head cocked.

She handed the cup back to him as the door opened. Malinka appeared. She had a second man with her. She looked at Baba with suspicion as she handed back the teacup. An unusual thought crossed Baba's mind. It had never before occurred to her that Dhul Faqar's wife would be jealous of his sex slave – she seemed happy to be part of the whole sordid business. But maybe there was more to it than that. Maybe she treated Baba so badly because she was jealous of her. Or, maybe it made her feel powerful to be completely in control of Baba? Either way, Baba didn't like the way Malinka was looking at her as Dhul Faqar took the teacup and turned towards the newcomers.

'Sit down,' he said to the man, before nodding curtly at his wife. She inclined her head and left the room, but not before shooting Baba another poisonous glance. Baba dreaded the next time she was alone with that woman.

Baba didn't recognise this man. He was dressed in black like all the others. His eyebrows met in the middle, and his nose had once been broken. Even from the other side of the room, Baba could smell his pungent body odour. He sat down at the table, in the same place as his predecessor, his head bowed. Dhul Faqar poured him some tea. Baba saw that his hand was shaking as he accepted it.

'I am pleased with you,' Dhul Faqar told him.

'Thank you, Dhul Faqar,' the man muttered.

'I wish to share something with you. You must keep it a secret.'

'Of course.'

'There is a man in London. He is one of us. His name is Aslan Hossein. We are sure that the British security services do not know his identity. He will be of great service to us in the events that are to come. I am telling you this because, soon, he will need to leave the land of the infidel and come to live with us here. You must welcome him like a brother. But for now, only you and I will know that we have spoken of this. Do you understand?'

'Yes, Dhul Faqar.' The man's voice cracked. He sipped nervously from his tea, then put it down – spilling a little – as Dhul Faqar stood up. 'Thank you, Dhul Faqar,' he said, bowing slightly, before turning and scurrying out of the room.

Dhul Faqar took the teacup and once more brought it to Baba. He held it to her dry lips as she drank it down, taking great care not to look at him. When she had finished, he leaned in close to her ear. 'If you repeat anything you hear in this room to anyone,' he said, 'I will cut out your guts and spill them on the floor. Do you understand?'

Baba nodded as the door opened again. Malinka had returned, this time with a third man – the second of the two who had flogged her. She led him into the room, but as she turned to go Dhul Faqar said, 'Stay, my love.' Baba saw a small smile play across her lips. She crossed to the far side of the room and sat down in her usual place next to her laptop computer. Dhul Faqar indicated that the man should sit where the others had, and poured him some tea.

Baba didn't dare watch what was going on. She sat on the floor and bowed her head. But she was listening intently. What was Dhul Faqar doing? Was he going to repeat the same story to this third man, but with a different name?

Sure enough . . .

'There is something I must share with you. It will be a secret that must not leave this room. Do you understand?'

No reply. Just a nod.

'There is a man in the UK. In London. He is important to us. His name is Kailash McCaffrey.'

'That is a strange name. He does not sound like a Muslim.'

'And yet he is,' said Dhul Faqar. 'He will strike a blow at the very heart of the enemy. When his work is done he will come here to fight alongside us. You must prepare to welcome him like a brother. To teach him our ways and to fight alongside him. Is that understood?'

'Yes, Dhul Faqar.'

Once again, the interview ended abruptly. The man left the room – Baba got the impression that he couldn't get out of there quickly enough. Now it was just Dhul Faqar, Baba and Malinka. Malinka sashayed up to her husband. 'You're working too hard, my love,' she said softly. For such a vicious woman, she could certainly sound affectionate when she wanted to. 'You should relax a little.' She looked over to where Baba was crouched on the ground. 'Shall I prepare the girl for you?'

Dhul Faqar let his glance ride over Baba, who quickly lowered her eyes. 'No,' he said. 'I'm getting bored of that one anyway.'

'Shall I remove her?'

Baba's heart iced over with terror. She knew what Malinka meant by the word 'remove', and the cold smile with which she said it made Baba shiver.

'Not yet. I might change my mind.'

Relief crashed over her. She wanted to weep. But she didn't let it show. She knew that any sign of emotion could be punished. It was better to remain still, crouched on the floor, and hope they forgot about her for a while.

But Baba was unable to stop her mind from working. What had she just witnessed? Why had Dhul Faqar given slightly different information to three of his trusted lieutenants? Were there indeed three different individuals planning atrocities in that country so far away? Or was there some sleight of hand at play? Baba hated Dhul Faqar, but she knew he was a clever man. She thought he was preparing some kind of trap, like the hunters back in her village who would lay several snares at a time, in the hope that one of them would provide a meal . . .

That thought reminded Baba how hungry she was. She had eaten nothing but a few scraps that morning. She told herself to forget about Dhul Faqar's schemes. She needed to concentrate on herself, on her own safety and well-being. She needed to remain compliant. Uncomplaining. No trouble.

If, that was, she wanted to stay alive.

A grey, damp dawn crept slowly across the Med. And outside a faceless concrete facility on an uninhabited part of the island of Malta, three figures emerged into the half-light, their shoulders hunched, their bodies heavy with tiredness. It had been a long night.

The Wildcat helicopter that had deposited them outside this black camp had long since been deployed elsewhere. Danny doubted it had spent more than five minutes on the ground. The area where it had landed was empty. The rain had stopped, but a thick mist had descended, which seemed to cling to the soldiers and to the building.

Penfold appeared from inside the building. 'Do you want to see it happen?' he said.

Danny nodded. He turned to Spud and Caitlin. 'Make contact with the chopper,' he said. Then he followed Penfold back into the building, down the stairs and into the interrogation room. None of the others were there. Just Danny, Penfold and the prisoner.

Rudolph was strapped, still naked, to the waterboarding chair. He had a rag stuffed in his mouth to muffle his shouts, and was straining worse than ever against the restraints. On a small trolley next to him was a steel case with a hypodermic syringe full of a clear liquid. The prisoner was glancing, terrified, at that syringe. He clearly knew what it was.

Penfold licked his lips. He gently picked up the syringe, held it to the light and squirted a small amount of the liquid out of it. Rudolph suddenly fell silent. Then, just as suddenly, he started his muffled whimpering again.

With a glance at Danny, Penfold approached the prisoner.

He inserted the needle into Rudolph's straining right upper arm with practised ease. It took a few seconds to inject the liquid, but it had an immediate effect. Rudolph stopped straining. His body juddered involuntarily. His muffled shouts became slightly higher-pitched, more uncontrolled. Penfold laid the empty syringe back on its trolley, then stepped back to watch the lethal injection do its work.

It was not a quick death. Rudolph writhed in apparent agony for a full two minutes before the spasms stopped and the infrequent squeaks of pain finally fell silent. His eyes rolled up into his head.

Danny stepped forward and checked his pulse. Nothing. He let the wrist fall and looked at Penfold. The two men stared at each other, but were silent. Danny turned his back on the bald man and left him with his corpse.

Outside in the early morning there was the thunder of a helicopter rotor. A Sea Cat had touched down on the makeshift landing zone, the downdraught of its rotors making the surrounding mist swirl. Spud and Caitlin were already running towards it. Danny joined them. None of them looked back as the side door of the chopper opened up to reveal a loadie in standard camouflage gear beckoning them inside. They simply jogged up to the chopper and clambered in. Moments later they were back in the air again.

Danny glanced once out of the window. He saw the concrete entrance to the black camp, and the figure of Penfold standing outside, looking up at them. Then the chopper banked and eased up through the cloud line. Danny closed his eyes and pretended to be getting some shut-eye. In reality, he was avoiding the stares from Caitlin and Spud. There was tension in the team. Tony's departure hadn't entirely got rid of it.

Tony. Danny wondered where he was now. Hereford had told them to return to Sigonella airbase and await further instructions. It sounded very much to Danny as though their mission was not yet over. He was glad that Tony was no longer part of the team. He knew only too well that sometimes it was hard to tell the difference between your friends and your enemies. But as soon as that applied to your unit-mates, you were fighting a losing battle.

The chopper banked again. They headed north.

EIGHT

Tony Wiseman was the only passenger in the business class section of the Alitalia 747 who was not dressed in either a suit or a traditional Arab *dishdash*. He was also the only guy pissed at half past ten in the morning.

He had managed to change out of his stinking, wet gear at Sigonella base, where he had been dropped before dawn that morning. But there had been no time to clean up properly – another military chopper was already waiting to take him to Palermo airport. Obviously the desk jockeys back at Hereford had received the instruction to get Tony's arse out to Dubai as quickly as possible. Those motherfuckers hadn't been idle.

But Tony was too angry even to argue with the same Italian squaddie he'd been so rude to earlier that morning, whose unfortunate job it was to take possession of Tony's weapons – there was no way of smuggling them on to an Alitalia flight – and hassle him on to the transport to Palermo. So although his clothes were clean, his body wasn't. He stank of salt, cordite and sweat. And now booze. He'd been necking champagne from the breakfast menu ever since the flight to Dubai had taken off. And the more the prissy Italian air hostesses gave him dark looks and wrinkled their noses at his stink, the more he'd been inclined to keep necking it.

He stared out of the window. Thirty thousand feet up, they'd left the Med behind and were cruising over the southern tip of Syria. His mind wasn't on the shitstorm that he knew to be unfolding on the terrain beneath them. It was firmly on the faces of two men who he couldn't get out of his mind. Spud Glover, the fat little cunt who'd boned his missus, and who would – *definitely* – pay for it, even if he'd had a lucky escape that morning. And Danny Black, who had earned himself a place at the top of Tony's hit list.

'May I please take your rubbish, sir?' Tony glanced up to see one of the air hostesses – a pretty thing with an upturned nose and a decent rack, whose English wasn't bad – looking meaningfully at the three half-bottles of champagne and a half-empty glass on his table.

Tony grabbed the glass protectively, then nodded. 'And get me another one,' he said.

The air hostess pursed her lips. 'I think you've maybe had enough, sir,' she said as she picked up one of the empties.

Tony grabbed her wrist. 'Get me another one,' he repeated, his voice low and dangerous, but not without a slur.

The air hostess tensed up. She tried to pull her wrist away, but obviously it was a useless effort. 'Certainly, sir,' she said in a strained voice.

Tony let go of her. He watched her walk down the aisle towards the front of the plane, and confer with another member of the cabin crew – a mincing young guy with shiny skin and a Brylcreemed quiff. He frowned as he looked back at Tony, and for a moment the SAS man hoped he would come over and try to give him a hard time. 'Fuck it,' he muttered under his breath when it became obvious the boy didn't have the balls to do it. A fight with that perfumed faggot wouldn't last more than a couple of seconds anyway. The air hostess returned with another half-bottle, which she put on Tony's table without speaking.

'Wasn't too difficult, was it, darling?' he called out after her – obviously a bit too loudly, judging by the irritated glance he received from the Middle Eastern guy sitting in the adjacent seat, while Tony watched her arse wiggle back down the aisle. 'Got a problem, Abdul?' Tony demanded. The man's cheek twitched once. He glanced disapprovingly at Tony's drink, but then went back to reading the sheaf of papers in his hand.

Tony refreshed his glass, then stared out of the window again. He saw the burning chimneys of the oilfields below. His mind turned again to Danny Black, and once more his pulse quickened. No matter how much Black stuck to his story that it was the headshed who had reassigned Tony, Tony knew it wouldn't have happened without a bit of nudging. He felt another surge of anger. Tony Wiseman, off to babysit Yellow Seven, would be the laughing stock of Hereford. Every last member of the Regiment would be sniggering behind his back. And all thanks to Danny *fucking* Black. That boy was a bad soldier – a *shit* soldier – and now he was a fucking nark. He had it coming to him. No doubt. One day, when he was least expecting it . . . an accident on the range . . . a fragmentation grenade gone wrong . . . There were a thousand ways to hurt a man surrounded by ammo and explosives. It wouldn't take much.

He thought of Caitlin and his face soured a little more. She was a dumb bitch, but a good lay. Tony wasn't blind though. He'd seen the way she looked at Danny Black when she thought he, Tony, wasn't watching. Tony had already considered the possibility that she was shagging him just to make Black feel envious. It certainly wasn't a relationship based on enduring love and mutual respect. But the thought of her and Black on an op together made him even madder. Tony wasn't the type to let another man take his squeeze.

He took a long pull on his drink, then decided he needed a piss. He clambered out of his seat and walked unsteadily down the aisle to the bathroom. Once inside, he pissed thunderously into the tiny chemical toilet. He looked at himself in the mirror. He had a smudge of dirt on his face, and a streak of salt. He didn't bother to wipe them off.

As he left the bathroom, a man in Arabic dress was waiting outside. Tony gave him a death stare as he pushed past him. Back along the aisle, five seats from his own, the same air hostess was leaning towards another passenger. Tony caught the disapproving sidelong glance she gave him. It almost made him want to spit with laughter. He slapped one hand against her arse. 'Lighten up, love,' he said.

The air hostess spun round. She looked very angry. It just made Tony want to laugh. 'Please *don't* touch me, sir,' she said.

Tony sneered. He went for her arse again, but suddenly the guy she'd been dealing with was on his feet. He was older, in his sixties, with a neatly cut suit and a receding hairline. 'There's no need for—' he started to say in a pronounced Italian accent.

He didn't finish his sentence. Tony saw red. He didn't even bother to use his fists. He simply headbutted the guy squarely in the centre of his face. There was a cracking sound as the Italian man's nose went. He crumpled back down into his seat, clutching his nose to stem the sudden flow of blood. The air hostess gasped, but there was an acute silence from the other passengers – it was clear none of them wanted to get involved. Tony spat at the feet of the old Italian man, then wiped a smear of blood from his forehead. Staggering slightly from the booze, he started making his way back to his own seat. But he stopped before he reached it. Four air stewards were approaching, two from either end of the aisle. Tony found himself wanting to laugh again at these ponced-up pretty boys with their clean-cut collars and perfect haircuts. Did they really think that they would be able to restrain Tony? Didn't they know who the hell he was?

'Tossers,' he muttered under his breath. Then he looked up at them. 'Seriously, fellas,' he said. 'Don't even fucking go there . . .'

Tony took his seat. Two of the air stewards were standing right by him. They were glancing uncertainly at each other, as if this was a situation they'd never encountered, and they didn't know quite what to do.

Tony grabbed his drink, raised it to them in a toast, then downed it in one. He belched loudly. 'Wake me up when we get to raghead land,' he said, before reclining in his seat and closing his eyes. He knew the air stewards were still standing over him, and probably would be for the rest of the flight.

That was their problem, he thought. Tony had some booze to sleep off.

★　　★　　★

'Why the hell aren't we on a plane back home?' Spud demanded.

It was midday. The Italians at Sigonella base had given them a large Portakabin for their personal use, but it was hardly the lap of luxury: four chairs, no table, and a TV in one corner with an Italian football game, sound turned down low.

'You know as much as I do,' Danny said. 'We're heading east. Hammond's on his way. He'll brief us when he's here.' He kept his voice level, but he was just as peeved as Spud. And he found Hammond's insistence that they stay in situ just as mysterious. Surely the operation was over. He wanted to get back home. See the kid. Buy her a Christmas present. Not that he'd have admitted that to his unit-mates.

At least they'd had a chance to clean up and put on the dry camouflage gear supplied by the Italians. Apart from that, they'd stayed hidden in the Portakabin, out of sight of anyone else on the base, eating rations from their saturated packs. Grabbing what sleep they could, sitting on the hard chairs. And waiting.

There was a constant sound from the base of aircraft leaving and arriving. It was so regular that Danny barely noticed it as he stared unseeingly at the footie. It was 1230 hours precisely, however, when a sound shook him out of his trance. He'd heard a Hercules coming in to land often enough to recognise the distinctive roar of its engines. He walked to the window of the Portakabin, lifted the metal shutters and peered out. He just had line of sight towards the runway. Sure enough a C-130K was descending shakily towards the base. It could even have been the same aircraft that had dropped them at the base the previous night. Whatever, it was definitely a special forces flight, no doubt flown by the guys from 47 Squadron.

He let the blind fall and turned to the others. 'He's here,' he said.

Sure enough, ten minutes later the door to the Portakabin opened. Ray Hammond appeared.

It was a joke among the lads in the Regiment that the more stressed-out Ray Hammond was, the darker the rings under his eyes. Right now, he looked like he hadn't slept in days. He was a tough, grizzled soldier, a veteran of both Gulf Wars. Danny didn't think he'd ever seen him smile. He had a relentlessly hangdog expression that normally seemed to hide any emotion, whether positive or negative. Today, however, his frown was more pronounced than usual. It matched those rings under his eyes. There were no greetings. Just a curt: 'This way.' Danny, Spud and Caitlin grabbed their packs. 'Face like a dropped pie,' Caitlin muttered as they followed Hammond out on to the tarmac.

The rain had finally stopped, but the ground was still wet and the sky still boiled overhead. The peak of Mount Etna was still covered in cloud. The Hercules had come to a halt on the tarmac, and its tailgate was open. The team jogged towards it, led by Hammond. They ran up into its belly, their footsteps echoing against the tailgate's iron floor. The familiar stench of grease and aviation gas hit Danny's senses. Up ahead, dull strip-lighting illuminated the front end of the aircraft. He saw an RAF loadie and a couple of signallers moving about up there, but they showed no sign that they'd even noticed the team come aboard. There was also a woman – black hair cut into a bob, mid-thirties. She looked totally out of place, in what were obviously office clothes. Danny immediately knew she was a spook.

'We stay in here from now until it's time to leave,' Hammond told them over his shoulder as they continued up to the front of the aircraft.

'How long will that be?' Danny asked.

'As long as it takes to get permission from the Turkish authorities to fly a military aircraft through their airspace towards Armenia.'

'We're going to Armenia?' Caitlin said.

The woman with a black bob gave her a withering look. 'No,' she said. 'You're not going to Armenia. *We're* going to Armenia, but we're dropping you off on the way.' She sniffed. 'Literally.'

Caitlin gave her a look. 'Who's the wombat?' she asked.

'Alice Cracknell, MI6,' Hammond unenthusiastically introduced the bristling spook. 'Danny Black, Spud Glover, Caitlin

Wallace.' Caitlin gave the woman a faux-friendly smile. Danny left them to it. He looked to his right. There were a number of large, scuffed flight cases here. One of them had already been opened, revealing some of its contents. Danny immediately recognised freefall equipment, and the matt curve of a HALO helmet, with its glossy black visor attached. He knew what that meant: wherever they were headed, they could expect an airborne insertion. He turned to Caitlin. 'You OK jumping?' She didn't reply, but Danny thought he saw a flicker of anxiety in her face. He reminded himself that, good as she was, their Aussie colleague was not Regiment trained.

'Alright, listen up,' Hammond said. They had congregated around a single row of airline seats bolted to the floor. In front of them was a long metal table, also bolted, with signalling equipment, a couple of laptops and their attendant wires snaking all over the place. There was an unfolded military map of the Middle East, and several unopened files. It was clear that, for Hammond, this had been a working flight. 'It seems the target you picked up in the Med confirmed certain intelligence that the Firm have been collating over the past few weeks about a Christmas Day strike at Westminster Abbey. It goes without saying that if they manage it, it'll be the Islamists' biggest PR coup since 9/11. We're mobilising all our personnel into the capital, throwing everything we've got at it. But we've got no handle on the identity of the bombers. That's where you guys come in.'

All of a sudden, any tiredness Danny might have been feeling simply fell away. His mind was tuned in exactly, ready to receive every word Hammond had to say.

'I'm not going to bullshit you. This is one of the most sensitive ops I've been involved with. Perhaps the most dangerous, too. You know what the stakes are if things go tits up.' He paused. 'Your target Rudolph mentioned an IS commander by the name of Dhul Faqar. We already knew that this attack was being planned in Syria or northern Iraq, and we think he's the mastermind behind the operation. So we're going straight to the source. We think he's holed up in a compound to the north-west of Mosul. We also believe that he's expecting the arrival of four Turkish oil dealers at midnight tomorrow, that's the night of the twenty-second into the twenty-third. These are the guys who broker oil from IS-controlled oilfields on to the open market. Your principal objective is to lift Dhul Faqar, and get some names out of him. Your secondary objective is to eliminate the four oil dealers.'

'I thought the Yanks were supposed to be bombing these fuckers to kingdom come,' Spud cut in.

'Don't ask me about the politics,' Hammond said. 'All I know is the Americans are holding back from attacking certain targets. And as you know, GCHQ are hacking into certain American intelligence communications, and the Firm are paranoid about them finding that out.'

'It's not paranoia,' said Alice Cracknell. 'It's operational security.'

'You call it that if you want,' Hammond said. 'The bottom line is that we don't know the full story, so this whole op is strictly covert, strictly deniable. The Yanks *must not* find out what we're doing. What's the matter Spud?'

'I'm just trying to decide,' Spud muttered, 'if I'd rather go straight back on ops into northern Iraq, or drape my wet bollocks over an electric fence.'

'You want to be back in a desk job, just say the word.'

Spud's expression darkened as Hammond turned to the mapping that was spread out on the comms table. He traced his forefinger along the southern Turkish border, where it met Syria on the west and Iraq on the south. 'We can't fly in over Syrian or Iraqi airspace – the Yanks and the Russians are monitoring it too closely. They'd pick us up within minutes and start asking questions. That's why we're seeking permission from the Turkish authorities to enter their airspace. We'll drop you at a prearranged location close to the northern Iraqi border. Once you've inserted, we head north on a dummy errand into Armenia.'

'What's the plan for crossing into Iraq, boss?' Spud asked. 'That area's crawling with IS.'

'It is,' Hammond replied. 'But it's also crawling with Kurdish fighters – *peshmerga* – whose hobby is basically to kill as many IS militants as they can.'

'Good hobby,' Caitlin said.

'You might not like the way they play it,' Hammond said. 'They're easily as brutal as IS – beheadings, crucifixions, all the usual shit. MI6 have an open line of communication with them, but it's impossible to say where their real loyalties lie.'

'With themselves,' Danny muttered.

'We've made contact with one of these Kurdish groups in the past couple of hours,' Alice Cracknell said. 'They're expecting you at midnight tonight. They're very well acquainted with the border crossings. They'll get you into northern Iraq, and drive you to Dhul Faqar's expected location.'

Danny frowned. 'We make contact at midnight tonight, these oil middlemen arrive at midnight tomorrow. How far is it from the border to the contact point?'

'About seventy-five miles,' Cracknell said.

'That gives us hardly any time to put in an OP or conduct surveillance on the target.' Danny turned to Hammond. 'We need twenty-four hours' surveillance, minimum.'

'It is what it is,' Hammond said. 'If we give you another twenty-four hours, you won't lift Dhul Faqar until Christmas Eve itself. That's too late – it won't give us time to act on any intel you uncover. In any case, we're in the hands of these Kurds.'

'And are you seriously telling me that we're to expect a bunch of Kurdish militants to smuggle us over a heavily defended international border in a war zone out of the goodness of their hearts—'

'Of course not,' Hammond interrupted. He walked over to where all the flight cases were piled and banged his hand on the top of a cylindrical metal drum. 'Do the Kurds have Christmas?' he said. 'Well, you're taking them a present anyway.'

The unit walked over to Hammond and the drum. Danny twisted the top open and looked inside. It was tightly packed with five long items of weaponry. Danny instantly recognised them as surface to air missile launchers. 'Stingers?' he said.

'And up-to-date radio equipment,' Alice Cracknell said. 'Western governments have been trying to supply the Kurds with small arms ever since the ISIS offensive began. Hardly any of them get where they're supposed to – most go AWOL in Baghdad. They've been trying to get us and the Americans to put these sort of assets directly in their hands. They'll be very pleased to have them.'

These were big-boy toys – the sort of gear a loose band of badly funded Kurdish militants would go out of their way to get their hands on. They could cause a whole load of damage. But that still didn't make the Kurds trustworthy. Danny rapped on the side of the drum. 'So that ensures that they turn up. What makes us think they'll carry on helping us once we've handed over the hardware?'

'You'll just have to charm them, Black,' Hammond said, sarcasm dripping from his voice. Charm was seldom the first weapon in an SAS operative's arsenal.

'What about extraction?' Danny asked. 'How do we get out of the country when the op's complete?'

'As soon as you've gleaned any intel from Dhul Faqar, you radio it through to us. If possible, you extract Dhul Faqar himself, but his information is your primary priority. The Kurds will wait for you, then take you back across the Turkish border to a prear-ranged pick-up point. You'll have to dig in there until we can get transport to you. It could take a few days, so it's *critical* that you get that intel radioed through to us the *moment* you have it. You'll have a satphone for that purpose, but you need to keep all other transmissions to a minimum. The Yanks will be scanning the airways constantly. The Russkies too.'

The loadmaster stepped up to Hammond. 'We've just had word from the MoD,' he said. 'The Turkish authorities have given permission for us to enter their airspace. We can have wheels up whenever you give the word.'

Hammond nodded and turned back to the team. 'Your RV with the Kurds is at midnight,' he said. 'You need to be in position at least two hours before that, but you need night cover to HALO in. We're about three hours' flight time from the insertion point, so we'll leave here at 1800 hours. Everyone agreed?'

The team nodded.

'Operation call sign Delta Three Tango,' he said. 'We'll continue the briefing here while we wait for wheels up. We've got details of your Kurdish contacts, mapping of Dhul Faqar's compound – you'll need to commit it to memory by this evening. Dhul Faqar's a real piece of work, by the sound of it. Got a thing about people looking him in the eye. Anyone who does it gets strung up. Tosser. Intelligence suggests that he lets his men rape whichever captured women take their fancy, so long as they leave the choicest specimens for him. You can expect some pretty brutalised sex slaves in the stronghold. Don't start getting chivalrous. Nothing's more important than getting Dhul Faqar alive, and pumping him for intel.' Hammond looked over at Alice Cracknell, who was busying herself with piles of paper to continue the briefing. 'We're not going to stop this attack in London, we're going to stop it at source. *You're* going to stop it at source.'

He turned back to the briefing table. Danny, Spud and Caitlin exchanged a long glance, then joined him.

Tony had a splitting hangover as the Alitalia flight touched down at Dubai International airport.

He had woken up half an hour previously to see one of the pretty-boy air stewards still loitering in the aisle, eyeing him uncomfortably. He'd sneered unpleasantly at him, but now that the booze had worn off he'd decided not to give him any more aggro. There'd be enough of that when they landed. Instead, he stared out of the window, watching the scorched desert landscape become the glittering sea of buildings that was Dubai.

As the aircraft reached the end of the runway, and turned left on to the taxi route towards the terminal, he saw the flashing lights of two police cars waiting on the tarmac. He touched his hand to his forehead. There was still dried blood there, from where he'd headbutted the old guy. He didn't bother to wipe it off. The whole cabin had seen it happen, so there would be no point denying it.

As soon as the plane came to a halt, three members of the Dubai police force boarded. They had tan-coloured short-sleeved shirts, and aviator shades. Two were clean-shaven. One had a short-cropped beard. An air steward led them to Tony's seat and pointed him out. The stern Emirate cops didn't need to say a word. Their holstered guns were on full display, and it was obvious that they weren't going to take any shit. Tony, raised his hands to show that he wasn't going to cause any trouble, then stood up and allowed them to lead him off the aircraft.

He squinted as he emerged into the bright sunlight. It was warm enough to make him start sweating immediately.

He didn't speak until he was on the tarmac, being led towards the police cars. 'Speak any English, fellas?' he asked, keeping his voice calm and reasonable.

'You keep quiet,' said the police officer with the beard.

'You know you're dragging the wrong guy off the plane?'

'I said keep quiet.'

'That old guy they saw me go for, you want to know what he did?'

No reply. But the police officers glanced at each other. Tony could tell he had their interest. He stopped walking and they did the same. 'Touched my dick,' he said. 'Fucking faggot tried to feel me up. You should be leading him off the plane, not me.'

He watched the officers carefully. He could already see the disgust in their faces. Tony knew this was a country where such activities were harshly punished.

'Get to the car,' said the officer who had already spoken. But he sounded less aggressive now.

Tony nodded and started walking again. 'Seriously, fellas,' he said. 'You don't want dirty old guys like that wandering around Dubai, do you?'

'Do you know his name?' the officer asked.

'Didn't ask, mate. Didn't want to stay too close.' From the corner of his eye, he saw a black Mercedes screeching across the tarmac towards him.

Here comes the fucking cavalry, he thought to himself.

By the time they reached the police cars, the black Merc had screeched up alongside them. A Western man in his late fifties, wearing a charcoal-grey business suit, jumped out of the back. He looked very harassed as he strode up towards the three Emirate police officers, holding up an ID card. 'Dominic Copeland,' he wheezed. 'British Embassy. We have permission to accompany this gentleman off the premises.'

The officers looked warily at him. One of them got into his car. Tony saw him speaking into his radio while the rest of them stood awkwardly on the tarmac. He could sense that the cops didn't like this sudden change of authority, but their hostility was directed more towards the guy in the suit than to Tony himself. Their colleague emerged from the car a minute later and spoke a few short words in Arabic to them. They inclined their heads, then turned to Tony. 'You're free to go,' said the police officer with the beard.

Tony saw him glance back towards the plane. He leaned in towards him. 'You want to take that guy in,' he said. 'Ask him a few questions. Give him the old . . .' He made a gesture with his right hand to indicate someone being slapped around. And he could tell, by the stony expression on the officer's face, that he intended to do just that.

'Get in the car, please,' the embassy guy said in a not-too-friendly tone of voice. Tony gave him a pleasant smile and got into the back of the Merc. The embassy guy sat next to him. As they pulled away across the tarmac, Tony saw the three police officers heading back to the aircraft. He figured that the day of the old guy with the broken nose was about to get a whole lot worse. Served him right for getting involved.

The embassy guy was looking at him like he was a piece of shit on the sole of his shoe. He was wrinkling his nose. It was obvious that Tony stank. 'I don't know what the bloody hell you think you've been playing at,' the guy said. 'If you'd been anyone else, you'd be on your way to an Emirate holding cell by now.'

Tony stared out of his window. 'Maybe,' he said. 'Maybe not.'

'You should be grateful to the embassy for getting you out of this,' the man snapped. 'The phone lines between here and London have been red-hot. We're extremely busy, and we're not here to—'

'Do me a favour mate, and shut the fuck up. I've had a long twenty-four hours.'

Tony could sense the waves of outrage emanating from the embassy man, but he did at least keep quiet for the next couple of minutes, while the car was waved through an external passport control post on account of its diplomatic status. Soon enough, they were speeding along a raised section of highway, heading towards the heart of the Dubai metropolis. It occurred to Tony that the last time he had been in the region had been on a mission with Danny Black that had taken them into Doha, the capital of Oman. The two cities looked very similar – ostentatious displays of great wealth. Tony reckoned he could enjoy himself here, given the right company and a few grand in his back pocket.

But the thought of Danny Black put any idea of enjoyment from his mind. He felt a physical surge of intense dislike in his gut. He looked at his hands and saw they were shaking.

'You'll need to clean yourself up,' the embassy man said suddenly.

Tony snapped out of his thoughts and turned to him. 'What?'

'I said you'll need to clean up, man. You look and smell like a tramp. I'll be surprised if they let you into the hotel in that state.'

'Fancy one, is it?'

'We have a room set aside for you, and a change of clothes. But for heaven's sake have a wash first. The residents of Dubai are very particular about outward appearance. You're representing Her Majesty's government and I will not have you letting the side down.' He seemed almost to shudder at the thought. 'And besides, you're going to be in the company of royalty. It's not too much to ask that you look the part, is it?' And then, almost under his breath: 'Even if he is a damn liability to the rest of us.'

The ghost of a smile crossed Tony's lips as the black Mercedes turned on to a raised causeway heading out into the glittering sea, towards a tall skyscraper of a hotel, its mirrored windows glittering brightly in the sun.

NINE

Joe felt warm for the first time in days.

The soldiers who had found him on the railway track had been rough and unpleasant. One of them had called him a wog. Another had laughed when, as they led him from the track, he had fallen over and twisted his ankle. They had dragged him into the back of a military truck where he had crouched, huddled, his muscles aching with the cold and his skin sore from the abrasive grit in which he'd hidden himself. And yet, despite all this, he couldn't help but feel elated. He had made it into the UK. The first – and most difficult – stage of his objective was complete.

The remainder of that night and this morning was now a blur. Joe had been so exhausted he could barely keep track of what was happening. There had been a succession of abrupt officials who had asked him more questions than he could now even remember. They had taken him to a room where he was able to shower and put on clean clothes – a pair of jeans and a red hooded sweater. They had taken his photograph and recorded his fingerprints. They had given him lukewarm, sweet, milky tea in a plastic cup, which he had guzzled down as if it were the finest drink known to man.

Now, he was sitting in a stark, brightly lit room. It had windows on three sides that looked out into a busy open-plan office. Joe was reminded of the police stations in the American cop shows he used to watch back home in Syria when he was much younger, in the days when watching TV was an option. Those days seemed a long time ago now.

His new clothes were a little big for him, but he didn't care. He had been given a plastic chair to sit in as he waited. Although it was hardly the most comfortable seat in the world, he still found himself nodding off as he sat in it. In his drowsy state, the humming lights in the room somehow merged with the memory of the drone that had nearly picked him out as he hid in the train carriage. He relived the crushing claustrophobia of being hidden in the grit and started, suddenly, awake.

A woman had entered the room. She was tall and thin, with what seemed to Joe to be an abnormally long neck. Her lips were pursed, almost disapprovingly, as she pulled up another chair and sat opposite him, clipboard in hand. But when she spoke, it was not unkindly.

'I understand you speak some English, dear,' she said.

Joe nodded.

'I'll need your full name, please.'

Joe had lost count of the number of people he'd given this information to over the course of the morning. He recited his name again. The scratchy sound of writing filled the room as the woman carefully filled in her form.

'And what are your reasons for claiming asylum, dear?' she asked.

'I'm from Syria,' Joe said. 'From Aleppo.'

'I see,' said the woman. 'And are you saying that you can't stay safely in your home country?'

Joe blinked at her. He didn't quite know how to respond to such a stupid question.

'Young man, you are not the only Syrian refugee seeking political asylum in Britain. If you wish your application to be successful, you will need to convince us that it is valid.'

Joe nodded. 'I cannot safely return to my home country.'

'And why is that?'

Joe barely knew where to begin. Should he start at that moment, two years ago, when a bomb had hit the apartment block where he lived with his mother and father? Or the day, two weeks after that, when gunmen had burst into his school

119

while Joe was at his usual place at the computer? How they had killed thirteen of his friends? How a bullet had missed Joe by only an inch, and slammed into the computer screen, shattering it? How he had tried to keep his best friend Jamal alive by pumping his heart the way he had read about, but it had only seemed to force the blood more quickly from the wound in his throat in the moments before his death?

Or should he start with what happened next?

'I was abducted by Islamic State,' he said.

The woman's eyes widened. 'Go on,' she said.

'I was living in a small refugee camp on the outskirts of Aleppo with my mother and father. They came at sunset – five of them. They knew who they wanted and nobody dared stop them taking us.' Joe closed his eyes and swallowed hard. He had recounted this scene in his head every day since it had happened, but somehow saying it out loud was more difficult. 'They took us to the town of Raqqa. It was a very long drive – it took all night. When we got there the following morning, they made me and my mother watch while they dragged my father from the car. They stripped him naked and hung him from a tree with a hood over his head. They laughed as they did it.'

He was staring into the middle distance, and forcing himself to hold back the tears.

'They put me and my mother in a cell. Now and then they came in with their guns and made us get on our knees. They put their guns to our heads. Then they would laugh and leave us alone again. They did this for several hours. Then, near the end of the day . . .' Joe felt a hot ball of nausea in the pit of his stomach. 'They came into the cell. Four of them. They raped my mother in front of me. Then they killed her.'

He looked straight at the woman as he said this, and saw the horror in her face. But he didn't tell her everything. He didn't tell her that he knew the name of the leader of the four men – Mujahid, who had a scar carved into his throat in the shape of a smile. There were, after all, some things he needed to keep to himself.

120

'You poor boy,' the woman whispered. 'Why did they do this?'

'Because of me,' Joe said.

'What do you mean?'

'They wanted me to know what would happen if I didn't do what they said.'

'But why you?'

Joe managed a weak smile. 'Because they had heard that I was clever.'

'You certainly speak very good English . . .'

'It was not English they wanted me for. It was because I know about computers . . . electronics . . . coding . . . that kind of thing.'

'I'm not sure I understand,' the woman said.

'Could I have a glass of water?' Joe asked.

The woman nodded and left the room for a minute. Joe watched her through the window. She crossed the office to a water cooler. While she had her back to him, several people passed the office and glanced in at Joe. Without exception, they looked hostile. Joe didn't mind. He was used to it.

He drew a deep breath and organised his thoughts. It was important that he told her enough to gain her sympathy, but not so much that she might guess why he was really here. When she returned with a plastic cup of water, he drank it gratefully, then picked at the edge of the cup with his fingernails as he continued.

'Islamic State like publicity,' he said. 'They . . .' he searched around for the correct word '. . . they *thrive* on it. They *want* people in the West to see them beheading their hostages and shooting down their citizens in the street. Because then, the West are forced to bomb them – which is even more good publicity for their cause. Do you see?'

The woman nodded mutely.

'The best place to get publicity is on the Internet. Facebook, Twitter, the dark net. They are very active on all these networks. They need people who are skilled with computers to help them do all this. That's why they wanted me.'

He paused while the woman scribbled down some notes. When she looked up again, she was obviously about to speak, but

Joe got in there first. 'Then, of course,' he said, 'there's the communications.'

'What communications?'

'They are not as backwards as they like to pretend,' Joe said. 'They need to communicate with each other, and with their agents who are active all across the world. They know that people are trying to listen in – to hack their email accounts and do surveillance on their mobile phones. They need people like me to help them keep their communications secure – end-to-end encryption, OTR protocols, preventing external agents inserting malware on their systems. Cover their tracks. That's what I did for them. Every day they put a gun to my head and told me that if I failed in my duty, I would join my mother and father in the ground. What choice did I have?'

He hung his head and continued to pick at the edge of his cup, which was beginning to split.

'Why did they let you go?' the woman asked.

Joe couldn't help looking astonished at the question. 'Let me go?' he said. 'They *didn't* let me go. Why would they do that?' He sniffed. 'I escaped.'

The woman was staring at him in astonishment. She scribbled a few more notes. '*How* did you escape?' she asked finally. But before Joe could answer, she held up one finger. 'Just a minute,' she said. 'Are you telling me that you were party to Islamic State communications into and out of Syria?'

Joe fixed her with a calm stare. Then he nodded.

The woman scraped back her chair and stood up. 'Excuse me for a moment,' she said. 'Please wait here.'

Joe sat still as she left the room for a second time. He noticed that his hands were trembling. He crushed the plastic cup in an attempt to stop it happening. Looking through the window, he saw the woman approach one of her colleagues – an older man in a slightly crumpled suit who was sitting on the edge of a desk reading a piece of paper. He looked over at Joe as she spoke. When she had finished, he seemed to think about what she'd said for a moment. Then he nodded and picked up the phone on the desk behind him.

The woman hurried back to the interview room. She was slightly breathless.

'Is everything alright?' Joe asked.

'Fine,' the woman said. 'Absolutely fine. I'd just like you to speak to . . .' She hesitated. 'To some of my colleagues, that's all. I hope they'll be here as soon as possible. Can I get you another glass of water?'

Joe shook his head. He could sense that, all of a sudden, the woman's attitude had changed. He wondered if she had just called the police.

'Right,' the woman said. 'Good. Well, if I could just ask you to wait here . . .' She edged back towards the door, gave him a nervous smile and left the room. For a moment, he thought she was looking back in at him. Then he heard the sound of a key turning.

Joe was locked in. He supposed it was only to be expected. A wave of tiredness crashed over him. He got up from the plastic seat and walked to the corner of the room. There, he huddled down on the ground, cocooned into a little ball. It didn't matter that the floor was hard. He'd slept in far less comfortable places than this. And it didn't matter that he was locked in – he'd been in far more frightening jails.

For now, he was safe and warm. It meant that sleep came quickly.

The tailgate of the Hercules was closing. Danny Black stood in the belly of the aircraft, watching the wet Mediterranean night disappear. His mind was burning with the details of the operation they were embarking upon. He had memorised locations and terrain. Satellite mapping had shown them the area around Dhul Faqar's compound. It was located on the banks of a large reservoir fifty miles outside the city of Mosul. A main supply route cut north–south to its eastern side. Mountainous region to the north. But there was only so much a satellite image could tell you. They needed to get eyes on the stronghold before they could make a plan to assault it. All Danny knew was this: it would be a hell of a sight easier with a full squadron and a handful of Black Hawks. But they weren't an option. Not if they were going in under the radar.

As well as map work, Danny had learned identification code-words, and had a few words of Sorani Kurdish at his disposal. He knew there would be a mutual lack of trust between his team and their contacts on the ground. A few words of a foreigner's language was a good way of breaking the ice.

The aircraft started to throb and hum as its engines started up. Hammond joined him. 'You realise,' he said quietly, 'that you won't be the only SF team on the ground in northern Iraq.'

'I guess that figures,' Danny replied.

'You can expect Russians, Americans. And I don't have to tell you what's riding on this back home?' Hammond said.

Danny looked over his shoulder. Spud and Caitlin were still at the briefing table, poring over Alice Cracknell's maps.

'It'll be a gangfuck in London if you don't get to this Dhul Faqar character.'

'We're under-strength without Tony,' Danny said. 'You know that.'

Hammond nodded. 'I've seen what you can do, Black. Other people might think you're a liability. Make an effort to prove me right and them wrong, eh?'

It was the closest Hammond had ever come to giving him a compliment. Danny appreciated it. Kind of.

'We'll have to hit these oil middlemen *before* they arrive at Dhul Faqar's compound. We don't have the numbers to do it any other way. If we get delayed crossing the border, the op's screwed.'

Hammond gave him a look that said: you know what that will mean. 'Is Spud OK?' he asked.

Danny knew what he was driving at.

'Spud's fine. It would help if Caitlin knew how to HALO.'

'You can take her in tandem. She'll be fine.'

'She's a good operator,' Danny said. 'I just hope these Kurdish guys don't take a liking to her.'

'She might be your best asset. The Kurdish *peshmerga* have a lot of women fighting on the front line. Talking of which . . .'

'What?'

'You know Duncan Barker, right?'

Barker was a Regiment-mate of Danny's back at Hereford. He nodded.

'I've asked him to go speak to your missus. Tell her your op's been extended, not to expect you home for a few days.'

Danny gave him a sharp look.

'I want your mind to be on the job,' Hammond said by way of explanation. 'Not on any problems you might be having back home.'

'Who told you I'm having problems?'

'Nobody.' Hammond hesitated. 'I've got kids too, Black. I know it can change the way you think about the work, when they come along.'

But before Danny could ask Hammond what he meant, the aircraft moved forward. The loadmaster called to them to take their seats. Danny and Hammond headed back up to the front of the plane and strapped themselves in. Two minutes later, they were surging down the runway. Then they were airborne.

Danny didn't bother waiting for the loadie's go-ahead. As soon as he felt the aircraft straightening up, he unclipped his belt and headed over to where their hardware was stashed. They had weapons to check over and HALO gear to don. They needed to be briefed on up-to-date weather conditions at the insertion point. And they needed a final run-through of their security codes and mission objectives.

The three-hour flight time to the Turkish border would pass quickly. Danny got to work.

Duncan Barker considered himself a good mate of Danny Black's. That didn't stop him cursing his mate as he drove his motorbike through the Hereford rain towards Danny's flat. RAF Credenhill was all but empty. Three-quarters of the Regiment were abroad. Those that remained in the UK on standby had been called into camp and given their marching orders down to London. Barker himself was heading to the Smoke that evening. Something big was going down. Why, then, was it so important that Barker should be knocking on the door of Danny's flat to give his bird a message? What was wrong with the fucking telephone?

Rain was streaming off him as he rang the bell to the ground-floor flat. As he stood, waiting for an answer, he could hear the faint wail of a baby from inside. Through the glass of the front door he watched someone approach. When the door opened, and the someone became a real face, he found himself talking to a woman who looked like she hadn't slept for forty-eight hours.

'Are you Clara?' he asked.

'Who's asking?'

'My name's Barker. Mate of Danny's from . . . you know . . . work.'

She stared at him.

'Yeah, so . . . the headshed asked me to come round, let you know that Danny's not going to be back for a few days.'

Nothing registered on her face. It was only when Barker was about to excuse himself that she spoke. 'Will you come in?'

'Nah, you're OK, I'd better . . .' But Clara looked so crestfallen that he changed direction mid-sentence. 'Yeah, alright then, for a minute.'

Barker was a big guy. It was awkward for him to manoeuvre past the pram that was blocking the hallway. He knocked a colourful soft toy from the handle, and Clara immediately scrambled to pick it up and tie it back on to the pram. 'Danny bought it.' She smiled apologetically. 'From Mothercare. You should have seen him . . .'

Barker didn't know what to say. His boots left a line of wet footprints all the way down the hallway and into the front room. Clara didn't seem to care. Her baby was here, lying in a wicker Moses basket, bawling her eyes out. Her mother lifted her from the basket and she immediately stopped crying. Barker wasn't really a baby person, but even he had to admit the girl was a cute little kid. A shock of dark hair – like a mini version of Danny Black.

'Why is he delayed?' Clara asked.

Barker gave her an apologetic look. 'Sorry, love,' he said. 'Can't really—'

'—talk about it. I know.' She started rocking the baby, and humming very gently.

Thirty seconds passed. Barker started to feel awkward. 'Right,' he said. 'Well, I'd better . . .'

'Is he safe?' Clara asked.

Barker smiled. 'Danny? Don't worry about him, love. He can take care of himself.' He paused. 'You know, he's the guy that everyone in the Regiment looks up to.' He narrowed his eyes. 'Me included. I wish I had half Danny Black's skills. He's a good soldier. A *born* soldier. Danny'll be fine.' He sniffed. 'It's the rest of us that need to worry.'

'What do you mean?' she asked quickly.

'You've not got any plans to go to London?'

'No.'

'Keep it that way. Take my advice and stay home. It's the safest place right now.'

She blinked, then carefully laid the baby back into her Moses basket.

'Look . . . I've got to go,' he said. Which was true. He nodded at Clara, then turned and left, closing the front door behind him. And as he started up his motorbike in the street outside the flat, he looked back through the thin curtains into the front room. He could see Clara in silhouette. He had the impression that she was holding the baby to her chest once more and was pacing up and down the room.

As he drove away, Barker couldn't shake the suspicion that she'd still be pacing when Danny returned home. Whenever that might be.

Tony's hotel room was bigger than most people's apartments, and unbelievably opulent. It was littered with comfortable armchairs and rich, embroidered soft furnishings. It had a massive vista, looking out on to the Gulf, where the lights of countless yachts glittered like jewels in the night. His bathroom was marble-clad, with gold-leaf taps, two sinks and a separate jacuzzi. He'd spent the best part of forty-five minutes under the shower. Once he'd got changed into the clean clothes that had been provided for him, leaving the bathroom blood- and dirt-stained, he'd ordered the most expensive meal available on the room service menu, and wolfed it down in the separate dining room suite. He spared a thought for Black, that bitch Caitlin and that fat bastard Spud who was lucky not to have had his bollocks shot off. He didn't know what shitty little quarters they'd be slumming it in now, but it sure as hell wouldn't match this.

There was a knock on the door. Tony pushed his plate away, belched loudly, then slowly sauntered over to open it. A thin, pasty-faced man in a black suit was standing there. 'Are you Tony Wiseman?' he asked.

Tony looked over his shoulder. 'Guess I must be,' he said, 'as there's nobody else in here.'

The man offered his hand. 'Good to meet you, old chap. My name's Hughes. His Grace is ready for you.'

'I'll be out in a minute.'

The flunky blinked at him in astonishment. 'I'm afraid that when his Grace says he's ready, you . . .'

Tony didn't hear the rest of the sentence. He slammed the door in the man's face and wandered into the bathroom again, treading over the old clothes he'd left on the floor and leaving footprints across the marble. He took a long, leisurely piss, then wandered back out and opened the door again. Hughes – was that his name? – was still there. 'I'm ready,' Tony told him.

It was clear that the flunky didn't quite know how to respond. He turned on his heel and started walking down the plush, carpeted corridor. 'He's in the penthouse suite,' he said. 'When you first meet him, you should address him as "Your Grace". After that, a simple "sir" will suffice. Is that clear?'

Tony didn't reply.

'A small bow from the neck would be appropriate, but a hand-shake will do just as well. My advice is to take your lead from him.'

Tony still didn't reply.

They entered a large, mirrored lift. The flunky had a key card that allowed them to direct it to the penthouse. They stood in silence as the elevator took them up. As the door hissed open on to a large, impressive anteroom with a similar view over the Gulf to Tony's own room, he clocked two young guys who he immediately identified as Yellow Seven's CP – probably from SO14, royal protection. They were dressed in casual clothes but Tony noted the bulges in their jackets where they were undoubtedly carrying firearms. They watched him with unconcealed aggression. Typical coppers, hanging round like they're pop stars or something. They'd have been happy enough to come down to Hereford, spend some time on the range with SAS guys who really knew how to handle a firearm. But as soon as a Regiment man trod on their turf, they bristled at the presence of someone with superior skills.

One of the coppers walked up to Tony. 'I'll need to frisk you, mate,' he said. East End accent. Stupid swagger.

Tony smiled. 'I don't think so.'

The copper looked over to his mate. 'Looks like we've got a troublemaker.'

The flunky stepped nervously to one side. 'Now, look here, gentlemen—'

But Tony interrupted him. 'Thing is, fellas,' he said, 'I don't want to be here any more than you want me here. But someone in London's decided there's a threat level here that you boys can't handle. You want to get on the blower to them, talk it through, be my guest. But if you lay a fucking finger on me, you'll be getting first-hand experience of the Dubai medical system.'

The police officer looked a little less sure of himself.

'Let's not go down this route, hey lads? Let's all be friends.' Tony looked over at the flunky and nodded. Then with a glance at the police officers, he muttered under his breath: 'Knobs.'

The flunky obviously wanted out of the situation. He knocked on a door at the far side of the room. A muffled voice shouted: 'Come!' The flunky entered. Tony stood silently, ignoring the waves of unfriendliness coming at him from the CP guys. The flunky reappeared thirty seconds later. 'He's ready for you,' he said, holding the door open for Tony.

Yellow Seven's suite made Tony feel like he was slumming it. He found himself in a plush living room, all sofas and fresh-cut flowers. There was a fully stocked cocktail bar on one side, and a TV on the far wall the size of a small cinema screen. But there was no Yellow Seven. A door at the far side was open. Tony wondered if he should go through. He looked over his shoulder towards the flunky for guidance, but there was no sign of him. He'd shut the door.

Tony moved over to the cocktail bar. There were maybe a hundred bottles neatly arranged against a gleaming mirror. The bar itself was made of burnished oak. Tony immediately saw the remnants of a white powder. He dabbed his finger on it, then touched the powder to the tip of his tongue. He immediately felt the familiar numbness, and smiled. Looked like his Grace was living up to his reputation.

He heard footsteps and turned round. A figure appeared in the open doorway. Yellow Seven was wearing a white towelling robe. His black hair was dishevelled and he had bags under his eyes. It was very obvious that he'd only just got up. He peered at Tony with a frown. 'Who are you again?' he asked in a cracked voice.

'Tony Wiseman. From Hereford. I'm with 22.'

Yellow Seven rolled his eyes. 'My babysitter,' he muttered. He looked across the room. 'Where's that tit Hughes?'

Tony couldn't stop himself from smiling. 'Outside,' he said.

'Best bloody place for him.' Yellow Seven pointed to the mini-bar. 'Get yourself a drink. I'll be out in a bit.' He disappeared back into what Tony assumed was his bedroom.

Tony sauntered back to the bar. He grabbed himself a glass and selected the most expensive-looking bottle of whisky he could find. He poured himself a couple of inches, knocked it back, then replenished his glass, before taking a seat at the bar. Looking back towards Yellow Seven's room, he saw a quick glimpse of a naked female body passing the doorway. He smiled to himself again. He was warming to this rich bastard. At least he knew how to have a good time. He glanced out of the window over the Gulf, and his mind turned again to Danny Black and the others. Fuck them, he thought. They reckoned they could make him the laughing stock of the Regiment? Well, Tony was going to take a leaf out of the royal family's book. He was going to enjoy himself.

Yellow Seven appeared ten minutes later, showered and dressed. He was a good-looking bastard, and the Middle Eastern bird tottering along behind him wasn't too shabby either. She had on heavy make-up, and her tits were almost spilling out of her tight dress. She obviously noticed Tony giving her the once-over, but didn't seem to mind.

Yellow Seven checked out the bottle of whisky that Tony had left open on the bar. 'Sweet,' he said, pouring himself a glass. He looked over at the woman. 'You can probably run along now,' he said. 'Hughes will . . . sort you out.'

The woman gave him a disconsolate pout, but she didn't argue. Her arse wiggled outrageously as she left the room. Neither Tony nor his companion took their eyes off her until she was gone. 'Dynamite in the sack,' Yellow Seven said when the door was closed again. 'Bloody well should be, the price she charges.' He took a mouthful of whisky. 'So,' he said, 'you're here to make sure I get to Sandringham safely in time for Christmas. You ever been to Sandringham?'

'Can't say I have.'

'It's the most boring place in the fucking universe.' He knocked back the rest of his whisky, then poured himself and Tony another. 'I was in Afghanistan, you know.'

'I heard.'

'I didn't leave because I wanted to,' he said earnestly, as though he really wanted Tony to understand this. 'They said I was a liability to the other troops out there. Too much of a target.'

'Give me this over the Stan any day,' Tony said.

Yellow Seven looked round the room as though seeing it for the first time. 'Novelty wears off after a while.'

Tony pressed his fingertip into the remnants of white powder on the bar. 'Not much of this behind enemy lines,' he said.

Yellow Seven's eyes narrowed.

'You want to be careful,' Tony continued. 'They come down hard on the old marching powder in these parts.'

Yellow Seven gave a dismissive little laugh. 'Not if you're me they don't.' He watched as Tony tasted the powder again. 'Do you partake?' he asked.

'It's been known.'

His eyes lit up. 'Lock the door then. Those close protection idiots are such nobbers . . .'

Tony eyed him for a moment. Then he shrugged. Fuck it, he thought. He walked over to the main door and locked it from the inside. When he turned to walk back to the cocktail bar, his Grace had already emptied the contents of a small sachet on to the bar. 'Do the honours,' he said. 'I'm afraid I don't carry credit cards.'

Tony took his military ID card from his wallet and approached the counter, ready to chop.

TEN

2147 hours.

'This is Turkish airspace, about ten miles north of the Syrian border, approximately 200 miles from the northern Iraqi border. That puts us about thirty minutes out. Repeat, thirty minutes out. Plug in to the aircraft's oxygen systems, we'll be decompressing in five minutes.' The loadie's voice was hoarse as he shouted above the persistent grind of the aircraft's engines.

Danny gave him a thumbs-up. He and Spud both had their freefall rigs attached to their bodies. On their left arm, each had a glowing altimeter. On their right arms, a GPS device. They both had a bottle of compressed oxygen strapped to their chest, and an oxygen mask, although these were not yet fitted to their faces. They wore the matt-black HALO helmets, visors up.

Caitlin also wore the oxygen bottle, mask and helmet, but no freefall rig. Instead, she had a full harness, since she would be falling in tandem with Danny. Now wasn't the time for a rookie to perform their first HALO jump. There were too many variables. Too many things that could go wrong. Caitlin was keeping a lid on her nerves. Danny respected her for that.

'We need to get on to the aircraft's oxygen system,' he shouted at her over the noise of the aircraft. 'We have to breathe pure oxygen for a while before we jump. Prevents hypoxia. Helps us to avoid losing consciousness before we deploy the chute.'

She gave him a sick look. 'How likely is that?'

'I've seen it happen, but normally only when someone loses their oxygen mask in freefall.'

'What happens then?'

'You'll probably lose consciousness. Then you'll have to rely on the automatic chute deployment.'

'Anything else you want to tell me?'

'It's important to fall stable. We need to be careful none of our equipment shifts. If we start spinning, we'll have problems. I've seen guys get to the ground with burst blood capillaries in their eyes because of it. Not pretty. And if there's a packing error, and the chute doesn't deploy properly, I'll need to cut it away before deploying the emergency chute.' He winked at her. 'Don't worry. It's only ever happened once.'

They moved to a bench along the side of the aircraft where the oxygen masks were hanging, and where their bergens and weapons were waiting on the floor. From the corner of his eye he could see Hammond manoeuvring what resembled a 45-gallon drum. In fact it was a freefall container, made of heavy-duty compressed cardboard. It contained the weapons and radio equipment that they would be offering up to the Kurds as a gesture of goodwill. It had its own freefall rig attached. The unit sat on the bench and started strapping their bergens and weapons to the backs of their legs.

'It'll be very cold when we leave the aircraft,' Danny continued explaining. 'But we'll be falling very fast and we'll get to a more comfortable altitude in less than a minute. We're aiming to fall in formation with Spud and the drum of weapons, but the wind speeds can be quite high up here and you need to be prepared for buffeting. Do everything you can to keep your body rigid. I'll deploy a little drone chute as soon as we're out of the aircraft – it'll slow us down a little and help us keep steady.' He tapped the altimeter on his wrist. 'We're currently cruising at about 32,000 feet – that's about the altitude of a commercial airliner. You can expect me to deploy the main chute at 4,000 feet. I'll tap you on the shoulder before I do that – it'll be too noisy for us to speak. If anything goes wrong and I lose consciousness, I've got the automatic chute deployment system set to engage at 3,500 feet. Is that clear?'

'Clear,' Caitlin said.

'Once we're under canopy, we'll orientate ourselves using the GPS. With a bit of luck, we'll have eyes on the storage drum's chute and we can follow it down.'

'One minute to decompression,' the loadie shouted. 'Let's get those oxygen masks on.'

Danny, Spud and Caitlin grabbed the aircraft oxygen masks and fitted them to their faces. Hammond sat with the rest of the crew on the opposite side of the aircraft. They also had their masks fitted as the aircraft decompressed. Danny put his head back against the side of the aircraft and concentrated on breathing normally. He was nervous about the jump. He knew that Caitlin was extremely capable, and he'd done enough freefalling himself for it to be second nature. But one of the main reasons for performing a HALO jump was to reduce the window of time during which any enemy forces on the ground could spot you under canopy. There was still, however, a short period of time when you were an easy target, unable to defend yourself effectively or put in any kind of countermeasure against enemy fire. It was a prospect that always sharpened Danny's senses in the moments before an operational HALO insertion. He found that his best strategy was to clear his mind and focus carefully on getting safely to the ground.

Twenty-five minutes passed quickly. The turbulence was bad enough for his head to jolt solidly against the side of the aircraft. Suddenly, there was a rush of deafening noise. Danny looked right and saw that the aircraft's tailgate was lowering. The lower it got, the louder the noise. Speech was now impossible. But that was OK. They knew what they needed to do. Each member of the unit disconnected themselves from the aircraft's oxygen system, before placing their freefall masks over their faces and engaging their oxygen tanks. They breathed normally for thirty seconds to verify that their breathing apparatus was working correctly, then stood up. Danny approached Caitlin and carefully attached himself to the back of her harness using a series of sturdy metal clips fitted to the front of his own freefall rig. Now that he was close to her, he could feel her deep, careful breathing, which told him that despite her outward appearance, she was nervous about the jump. A couple of loadies approached them. They each wore thick web belts with lanyards connected to the side of the aircraft to stop them falling out. They positioned themselves on either side of Danny and Caitlin – for whom walking was difficult as they were strapped together and over-laden with kit – and ushered them towards the open tailgate. Spud positioned himself alongside them, next to the freefall container. Outside, in the middle of a turbulence bump, Danny caught a brief glimpse of a crescent moon.

A red light appeared at the back of the plane, above the tail-gate – the pilot's signal that they were to get ready to jump. They shuffled forward, closer to the edge of the tailgate. Danny caught another glimpse of moon, and gradually became aware of stars in the night sky. As he peered downwards, however, he saw nothing but blackness. No lights on the ground. No topographical features. It meant there was cloud cover, which they'd have to penetrate.

A minute passed. Then, suddenly, the green light came on. Danny heard a loadie screaming at the top of his voice: '*GREEN ON! GO!*' There was no hesitation. There couldn't be, since a delay of just a few seconds could mean missing their landing zone by a substantial distance. Spud pushed the freefall container out of the aircraft before immediately following it. At the same time, Danny and Caitlin tumbled out.

The rush of wind against Danny's face was sudden and intense. The cold was shocking. It almost knocked the breath from his lungs. He concentrated hard on breathing steadily, sucking down the oxygen from the canister at his chest. At the same time, he pulled one of his two ripcords. He didn't see the drone chute engaging, but he felt a slight upward force as it slowed their rate of acceleration. He arched his body firmly against the strong air currents that were buffeting them around. Caitlin did the same. He had to hand it to her. She was a natural.

The scream of the wind grew louder as their speed increased. Danny could make out Spud. He was about twenty feet below them. From the shape of his body, he could tell that his mate was trying to de-arch a little bit in order to slow down his rate of descent and keep close to Danny and Caitlin. And a little below him, little more than a smudge against the sky, was the weapons canister, hurtling down to earth.

Suddenly everything went black. They were in the clouds. They were no longer accelerating – they'd hit terminal velocity, the point at which they'd reached their maximum speed – and the shockingly icy temperature had eased a little. But now the moisture of the clouds seemed to saturate every part of him. His clothes were soggy. He almost felt like he was inhaling water, not oxygen. The altimeter on his left arm was only a faint glow in the thick mist.

As quickly as it had arrived, the blackness disappeared. For the first time since they'd jumped, Danny saw the terrain below.

He knew that their LZ was a long way from any built-up areas, and his vista confirmed this. There were barely any ground lights for miles in any direction. To the north, on the horizon, he saw a glow that he took to be the Turkish town of Silopi. Elsewhere, he saw the occasional line of an arterial road, and here and there the headlamps of a car. But in the immediate vicinity, nothing.

It was much warmer now. He checked his altimeter. Six thousand feet.

Five thousand feet.

Below, he saw the sudden eruption of the weapons canister's rectangular chute. It had obviously hit the 3.5k altitude. At the same time, he saw that his own altimeter was about to hit 4,000 feet. He tapped Caitlin on the shoulder in the prearranged signal. He felt her tensing up slightly as he pulled the ripcord for his main chute. He felt the familiar sensation of his chute opening, then the sudden upward jolt as their velocity dramatically reduced. The rush of wind in their ears disappeared. Danny grabbed the brake lines and checked for Spud's position. He was close – about twenty metres to the west, and at approximately the same altitude. Danny could tell that he was positioning himself to follow the weapons canister down. Danny did the same.

Forty-five seconds passed. The weapons canister hit the ground – Danny could see its chute starting to deflate. 'Loosen your pack,' he shouted at Caitlin, while releasing the strap that bound his own bergen to his legs. Both packs fell, suspending in the air beneath them for a moment, before hitting the earth. Seconds later, Danny and Caitlin made landfall, running in tandem as they touched the earth.

As the chute deflated behind them, Danny quickly unclipped his rig from Caitlin's harness. He spun round and started dragging his chute towards him as quickly as possible, aware that Spud was doing the same thing twenty metres to his nine o'clock. HALO jumps were dangerous, but this was by far the riskiest moment. They needed to collect up their gear quickly so it couldn't be seen. And they needed to scan the immediate area for threats. Danny saw, from the corner of his eye, that Caitlin had thrown herself on to the ground in the firing position, weapon engaged, as she did just that.

Within thirty seconds, Danny and Spud were in exactly the same position, their chutes bundled up beside them, their masks and visors disengaged. Each of them were pointing out in a different direction, covering the three vertices of a triangle. There was complete silence. Danny could feel his heart thumping behind his ribs as he took in the terrain.

It was hard, rocky ground. Desert-like, though it was clear that it had rained lately, because there was a slight moistness to the earth. The air was chilly – five degrees C, perhaps, though the slight breeze made it feel colder. The ground itself undulated quite heavily, so it would have been difficult to see more than about twenty metres in any direction even during the day. Danny remained completely still for a full minute, scrutinising the landscape and listening hard for any sight or sound of movement. There was none.

'Where's the weapons drum?' he heard Spud hissing.

Danny allowed himself to look around. Spud was right. There was no sign of it. 'Stay put,' he said. 'I'll look for it.' He slowly pushed himself to his feet, orientating himself and trying to fit their position to the mental image he had of the mapping they had been studying for the past twelve hours. Off to his three o'clock, there was a rough road. Danny thought this must be the track that would lead them to the RV point. He'd double-check that in a minute, but for now he needed to locate the weapons drum. At first glance, he couldn't.

It didn't take him more than a few seconds to see what had happened. Thirty paces to his seven o'clock – a quick glance at the compass on his wrist told him this was a south-westerly direction – the terrain fell away over a kind of cliff. Danny ran towards it, got to the ground again and carefully peered over. The canister was five metres below him, completely covered by its chute. He spent a moment checking for threats or other movement again – nothing – then hurried back to Spud and Caitlin. 'This way,' he hissed.

They followed him back to the cliff, each of them now carrying their packs on their backs, Danny and Spud with armfuls of bundled-up chute and para cord. The cliff was not entirely sheer – a moment's examination and they located a narrow gulley that they could scramble down. They lowered their gear over the cliff, then climbed down it and hurried towards the weapons container.

'We lucked out,' Caitlin whispered. She pointed to the base of the cliff. There was a cave here – a narrow entrance about two metres wide. It was cold inside the cave, and there was a horrible smell, like something was rotting inside. 'We can stash our freefall rigs in there.'

Danny shone his flashlight into the cave. It was deep – at least ten metres, although parts of the back were still hidden in shadow. They didn't, however, seem to have disturbed anything or anyone.

'We'll store the weapons canister too,' Danny added. He stepped back outside the cave and checked his GPS device. 'We're approximately two klicks east of the RV location. We can't move covertly across this terrain if we're carrying that.' He looked at his watch. 2203 hours. The RV was at midnight and they wanted to be in position well before then. They were behind schedule already, and needed to move fast.

139

Danny turned to Caitlin. 'Wait here with the drum. We'll make the RV, then get them to drive here and pick it up.'

A shadow crossed Caitlin's face. She obviously didn't like the idea of staying back to babysit the hardware, but she didn't complain. She quickly went about the business of stashing the freefall rigs far into the back of the cave – by the time anyone found them there, the unit would be long gone. Danny and Spud removed the remainder of their HALO gear and stashed it with the chutes, before manoeuvring the weapons drum quickly into the cave.

Caitlin took up position inside the cave mouth. She was clutching her rifle, which was strapped across her body, and had an unflinching, resolute look on her face that for the briefest moment reminded Danny of Clara back home. He pushed that thought from his mind. 'We RV at midnight, expect us back here at approximately 0030 hours, assuming there's no delays. If anyone else passes this way, stay hidden as far as possible. We don't want things to go noisy on us.'

Caitlin gave him a withering look. 'And if I want to kill someone, which end of the gun do I use again?'

Danny ignored that. 'We'll be in radio contact. We'll check in every thirty minutes, on zero hundred and zero thirty. Otherwise keep transmissions to a minimum.' He turned to Spud. 'Let's go,' he said.

They shouldered their bergens, checked that their personal weapons were cocked and locked and engaged their radio equipment. Spud took a moment to check over his 66 Law, and they both fitted their regular Kevlar helmets with NV goggles fixed to the top. Danny dropped a pin on his GPS unit so that they could quickly locate Caitlin's position when they returned. Then they moved silently away from the cave mouth. It was very dark – cloud cover obscured the moon and stars. That suited them fine – it made it easier for them to cross this rough, rocky terrain without being seen. Danny knew, from his examination of the GPS device and the mental image he had of the maps they'd been studying, that if they travelled approximately 500 metres at a bearing of thirty degrees, they would hit a small road. Two klicks further along, the road hit a T-junction. Their RV point was 500 metres directly north of this junction – the kind of location where it was extremely unlikely that anyone would randomly show up.

They would not, however, be following the road itself towards the junction. If the Kurds, or anyone else, had eyes on it, they'd spot Danny and Spud immediately. And while Alice Cracknell, safe in the belly of a C-130, might be calmly confident that these Kurds were on the level, Danny knew they'd be making a massive strategic error if they trusted them blindly. Just because they were enemies of Islamic State, it didn't mean they were friends of the SAS.

Instead, they kept a good 350 metres to the west of the road. They travelled side by side, with a gap of approximately ten metres between them, in order not to present a bunched-up target to any potential shooters. They jogged, clutching their personal weapons across their chests, but scanning for movement all the while. Every couple of minutes they came to a halt, went to ground and listened hard. But so far as they could tell, the area was deserted.

After twenty minutes of jogging, Danny checked his GPS unit again. They were seventy-five metres from the road junction. They went to ground and waited for a couple of minutes, watching and listening. There was no sight or sound of any traffic, so they continued to the junction itself.

Danny examined the road surface. Old, cracked tarmac. No road markings. There was wet mud at one edge, with a fragment of tyre markings. A vehicle had passed this way recently. They needed to get off the road, quickly. Danny jabbed a forefinger in a northerly direction. Spud nodded.

The RV point was a featureless patch of open ground. But it was surrounded by undulating terrain that meant it was unobservable from the road. Danny and Spud avoided the RV point itself. Instead, they started looking for suitable OPs. They couldn't both lie up in the same place. When – if – the Kurds arrived, their strategy was clear. If everything seemed OK, Danny would approach by himself, while Spud covered the Kurds and their vehicle. For that to work, they needed to be facing the RV at a forty-five-degree angle to each other, at least.

He and Spud identified the best locations immediately. They were two small hills – little more than mounds, really – one of them situated fifty metres north-west of the RV point, the other about sixty metres south-west. Danny headed to the northernmost OP point, Spud to the southernmost. When Danny reached his mound, he crouched down at its base and opened his bergen.

Each man, at the top of their pack, had what looked like a camouflage-patterned blanket. Back in Hereford, they'd dubbed these things 'combat burkas'. They were fitted with electronic anti-surveillance devices. It was new technology, capable of disrupting radar and infrared signals, which the guys knew were often used to scan wide-open desert areas in a search for human signatures. It was unlikely the Kurds would have such sophisticated surveillance systems – but it wasn't just the Kurds they had to worry about. This was Turkish territory, and although the Turks had given permission for a British aircraft to enter their airspace, there had been no mention of men on the ground. Hammond had warned of Russian and American SF in the region. And then, of course, there was IS.

Danny donned his combat burka, knowing that Spud would be doing the same at his OP. His radio earpiece crackled. Caitlin's voice. A single word: '*Clear.*'

Spud responded: '*Clear.*'

Then Danny: '*Clear.*'

He carefully carried his pack and weapon on to the brow of the hill. He lay on his front, completely covered, with his weapon alongside him, clutching a small night scope. Danny focussed in on the RV. It was simply a bleak, empty, windswept patch of open ground.

Time check: 2232 hours. An hour and twenty-eight minutes till RV. Time was important. As soon as they made contact, they needed to advance to target, because the longer they could put in surveillance on Dhul Faqar's compound – to work out the lie of the land and establish the regular movements of his men – the better their chance of success.

Danny lay there, totally silent, every sense on high alert, as he waited for their contacts to arrive.

'Sandringham tomorrow,' Yellow Seven had said. 'Tonight, we party.'

That had been two hours ago. It had briefly crossed Tony's mind that he should be staying sober. He was on duty, after all. But Yellow Seven had been quite insistent that they get pissed together. And who am I, Tony thought, to disobey a royal command? The guy had seemed so genuinely delighted that he'd found somebody to join him in his recreations, he appeared to be redoubling his efforts to have a good time.

They had remained in the penthouse suite of the hotel for an hour, hoovering up Yellow Seven's stash of marching powder like it was going out of fashion, and necking shots of single malt. It didn't take long for Tony to start feeling disjointed from his own body. Every time he turned his head, the lights in the room cast a trail across his vision. When Yellow Seven had called in his royal flunky and told him that he wanted to go to a club called Mahoka in downtown Dubai, Hughes had looked daggers at Tony, as if Tony himself had suddenly pushed the young man off the rails. Not that Tony gave a shit. He was happy to go along for the ride. And when his Grace had reminded him that there was no booze served in these places, so they'd better take advantage of the bar while they could, Tony had been happy to oblige.

Now he was sitting in the back of a black Mercedes. Tinted windows, suited chauffeur. The regular close protection guys were in a vehicle behind them. They too had given Tony the deadeye as he'd accompanied their charge out of the penthouse, through the lobby of the hotel and into their waiting vehicle. He'd been aware of a couple of people holding up their smartphones to snap a picture, and idly wondered if his own pupils were as dilated as Yellow Seven's.

'You'll like this place,' his royal companion said as their Merc swept across the short causeway that linked their hotel to the Dubai mainland. He was talking quickly, and had a slightly high-pitched edge to his voice. 'It's where all the best chicks hang out.' He grinned. 'We could have a competition. See which is the best fanny magnet – the royal family or SAS.'

'That's not a fair fight,' Tony said. 'A Regiment man never lets on in public that he's SAS.'

Yellow Seven's grin grew broader. 'Bad luck,' he said.

Tony raised an eyebrow at him. 'Maybe I don't need any extra help to score,' he said.

His companion doubled over with laughter, as if that was the funniest thing he'd ever heard. 'You're fucking hilarious,' he bellowed. 'I'm telling Hughes to get you along every time I need close protection. You're a hell of a sight more fun than Dick and Dom in the other car.' He jabbed his thumb over his shoulder to indicate the CP guys' vehicle behind them.

Tony sniffed. The charlie had numbed his nose and he found himself craving a little more. Not a problem, he thought, glancing at Yellow Seven, who was still giggling to himself. Plenty where that came from. He caught sight of himself in the rear-view mirror and realised he was smiling. Looked like he was landing on his feet after his summary dismissal from the Mediterranean op.

The bright lights of central Dubai flashed past his peripheral vision. He realised that the coke had screwed up his sense of spatial awareness, and even of the passing of time. Before he knew it, he was walking alongside his new companion into the VIP entrance of an impossibly swanky club. Fawning staff bowed as they opened doors for them, while the two CP guys kept a respectful distance of several metres. They walked into a warm, neon-lit room with softly thudding dance music. There were private booths along the left-hand side, and the whole place was decked out like a rainforest, although whoever had designed these sparkling indoor waterfalls and beautiful, verdant plants draped everywhere had obviously never spent much time in thick, stink-ing, primary jungle.

They walked up to a long, neon-lit bar, the music growing

louder the further into the club they went. Tony felt all eyes on them, and his senses weren't so far gone that he didn't notice that most of those eyes belonged to young women who made the hooker back at the hotel look like Susan Boyle. When they reached the bar, there were already two drinks waiting for them – fruit cocktails of some kind. Tony took his and raised a glass to the two CP guys, who were now loitering by the entrance, looking like a couple of spare parts. They scowled back at him, but Tony had already turned his attention to the rest of the guests. Like Yellow Seven, he had his back to the bar and was scanning the club, blatantly trying to pick out faces among the heavily made-up women on offer, as the dance music continued to throb through him. He caught the eye of several of them. They gave him smiles that left him in no doubt that they were unlikely to put up any resistance, if he were to approach them.

He turned to his companion, whose pupils were even more dilated now than they had been in the car. Yellow Seven gave him a lascivious grin. 'May the best man win,' he shouted over the noise of the music, before heading into the heart of the club towards a table where four chicks wearing not a great deal almost seemed to be waiting for him to join them.

He was a smooth bastard. Tony would give him that. He watched him suavely introducing himself for a moment, then turned his attention to his own prey. There were a couple of girls at a nearby table – one blonde, one brunette, sequinned tops and plenty of make-up, the way Tony liked it – who were casting him a coy look.

Tony took a gulp from his cocktail and cast another sneering glance at the CP guys, who returned it. Then he moved in for the kill.

ELEVEN

Danny's hands were numb with cold. The combat burka went some way to keeping the wind off him, but the ground itself sapped all the warmth from his body. He'd endured worse, though – and it wasn't like they would be dug in for much longer. He hoped.

Three vehicles had passed since they'd been there. He hadn't seen them, but he'd heard them – just – and seen the faint glow of their headlamps passing. Danny counted them all as suspicious. Who the hell would be driving here, miles from any town, so close to the Iraqi border, when they knew there was a chance of meeting militants of all persuasions?

2337 hours. Danny heard a noise. Very distant, but getting louder very quickly. Seconds later there was a sonic boom as an aircraft, unseen above the cloud cover, burst overhead and then disappeared into the distance. It was definitely some kind of fighter plane. Danny consulted his internal compass. The aircraft had approached from the east. Was it Russian, off to bomb rebel targets in Syria? If so, it was playing a dangerous game. The Turkish military had form when it came to shooting down Russian bombers when they strayed into their airspace.

0000 hours.

Caitlin: '*Clear.*'

Spud: '*Clear.*'

Danny: 'Clear.'

There was a moment's complete silence. Then Spud spoke over the radio for the first time since they'd dug in. '*Fuckers are late,*' he said. '*How are we supposed to trust them to get us across the Iraqi border when they can't even show up on time for the first RV . . .*'

'Keep in position,' Danny replied.

Time passed. At 0030 hours, each member of the unit checked in. 0100 same deal. But still no sign of the Kurds. Danny was acutely aware that the temperature was dropping. It was uncomfortable, but there was a way to go before it started having a negative effect on his body or his decision-making. He still had a creeping anxiety in his gut. Their contacts were an hour late. It was suspicious. Not to mention that they had limited time to get across the border and to the stronghold. He focussed on his surveillance of the RV point. There was no sign of anything. No movement. No traffic passing on the road.

By 0125 hours they were almost an hour and a half late, and Danny was getting properly worried. They were relying on these guys. Without them, the op was a non-starter. And what if there was a sinister reason for the Kurds being delayed? What if someone had got to them? What if they'd forced the details of the RV out of them? That would mean Danny and Spud were severely compromised.

0130 hours. Spud was the first to check in. '*Clear.*'

Danny: 'Clear.'

Silence.

Danny gave it fifteen seconds. 'Caitlin, do you copy?'

Nothing.

Danny felt a knot in his stomach. Why the hell was Caitlin not responding?

Danny ran through their options. If they left their positions now, they risked missing the RV. He was sure these Kurds wouldn't want to hang around. But there was a good chance they weren't going to show anyway, and what if Caitlin was in trouble?

'*Situation normal, all fucked up.*' Spud's voice on the radio sounded tense. '*Something's happening. We need to abort, get back to the LZ, phone in for a pick-up—*'

'Quiet,' Danny interrupted him. He'd seen something. A flash of light coming from the road to the south. It was only momentary, but that made sense. The ground was undulating. If it was the headlamps of a vehicle, they'd only see it when they were pointing upwards.

The decision was made for them. They couldn't risk showing themselves yet. They had company.

Danny engaged the NV goggles fitted to the top of his helmet. Ten seconds passed. Another flash of light. Danny found himself clutching his weapon with a little more purpose. He squinted as a vehicle came into view, trundling heavily off-road over the undulating ground towards the RV point. Danny tried to work out what kind of vehicle it was, but the headlamps were too bright for him to see. He looked to one side as it continued to approach. Twenty seconds later it reached the RV point. The headlamps faded. A moment's silence. Then the headlamps gave three short flashes.

'*That's the signal,*' Spud breathed.

'It's one of the signals,' Danny said. 'But I don't like that they're so late.' And he thought to himself: what if someone's got to Caitlin, and through Caitlin got to us? 'We'll give it two minutes,' he said, 'check they haven't brought any friends with them.'

'*Mucker, this is—*'

'I know.'

They lay in complete silence. Nobody exited the vehicle, and there was no movement from anywhere else. Not that it put Danny any less on edge. In a situation like this, there was always a point where you had to make the call to break cover. It was natural to be shitting yourself when that moment happened. As his eyes recovered from the glare of the vehicle's headlamps, he found that he was able to discern it in more detail. It was a pickup truck of some description, and there was nothing subtle about it – Danny could see the outline of some kind of heavy weaponry mounted to the back. A fifty-cal, maybe. Enough to mow down a couple of guys on foot in a matter of seconds.

'You got eyes on?'

'*Roger that.*'

'You clocked the hardware on the back of the pickup?'

148

'*Hard to miss it. I'm covering the vehicle with the 66. Any shit from these guys, I'll blow the living fuck out of it.*'

Danny paused. Time to make the call.

'I'll approach,' he breathed into his radio. 'Don't show yourself until I give you the sign.'

'*Roger that.*'

Danny rose from the ground, still hooded and wrapped in his combat burka. It took every ounce of self-restraint not to sprint towards them. He wanted to get back to Caitlin's position, check she was OK. In truth, however, his first duty to Caitlin was to stay alive. He couldn't help her if he'd been mown down by a fifty-cal. He had to play a bit smarter than that.

He had the butt of his weapon pressed hard into his shoulder. As he stepped carefully forward, he kept the vehicle's windscreen firmly in his sights. He could make out the silhouettes of two figures in the front and passenger seats. His field of view wobbled a little as he picked his way across the rocky desert earth, but he kept the cross hairs firmly on the windscreen until he was twenty metres out.

Then he stopped.

He stood, statue still, with his weapon engaged and the wind blowing his combat burka. The newcomers would soon realise that they had to make the next move.

The passenger door opened. A figure emerged, and slammed the door shut. The noise echoed across the open ground, carried on the wind. Danny realigned his sights on to the face of the figure. Only he couldn't *see* a face. The militant's whole head was wrapped in a black and white *shemagh*, with just a tiny slit for his eyes. He had an AK-47 hanging across his front by a neck sling. Camouflage jacket. Jeans. There was no way of identifying him as a Kurd. He moved to the front of the vehicle.

'Stop there,' Danny called in Kurdish.

The figure halted.

'Three,' Danny shouted out.

It was the prearranged call-and-response code Hammond and Alice Cracknell had given them. Danny was to call out a number.

The Kurd had to respond with a number that added up to ten. Any other response meant that he'd failed the test.

There was no reply. The militant stood very still.

Danny suddenly realised he could hear his own heart beating. He adjusted the trajectory of his weapon so the sights were firmly planted on the militant's forehead.

Five seconds passed.

Ten. Danny realised the militant was counting on his fingers. He obviously knew the consequences of making a mistake. Slowly, he raised his hands. On one hand he had five fingers showing. On the other, two.

Seven.

Danny allowed himself to breathe again.

'Do you speak English?' he called.

'Of course.' The man's voice was muffled by the *shemagh* covering his mouth. 'That's why they sent me.'

'Let's lose the headgear.' The militant inclined his head, clearly not understanding. 'The *shemagh*,' Danny called. 'Take it off. I want to see your face.'

There was a moment's hesitation. But then the militant did as he was told, slowly unwrapping the black and white *shemagh*. It took about fifteen seconds to unfurl, revealing a sharp chin and a hooked angular nose. And then the eyes.

Or rather, the eye.

The left eye was closed up. A vertical scar crossed the lids, with very clear horizontal stitching marks. Even in the darkness, Danny could tell that the area around it was swollen and puffy. He had the distinct impression that this was a recent wound. The militant's hair was black and close-cropped. He stood with his chin jutting out proudly, as though daring Danny to make a comment about the state of his face. He was in his mid-twenties.

'Get your friend out of the car,' Danny said.

The man turned wordlessly and nodded towards the windscreen. A second figure emerged – no *shemagh*, but a carbon copy of the first in terms of weaponry. With two distinct differences: the face was intact, and she was female. Her brown hair was pinned tightly to her scalp. Almond eyes. Dark skin. Spots. She was very young. Fourteen, max. She wore a baggy pair of sand-coloured trousers and a khaki jacket a little too big for her. She looked towards Danny with the same jutting arrogance.

'What the fuck?' Danny muttered. 'What time were you supposed to be here?' he demanded more loudly.

The man sniffed. 'Midnight,' he said lazily.

'Why are you so late?'

The man sneered. 'Not easy to move around,' he said. 'Heavy presence of Daesh. We had to wait for a roadblock to finish.'

'We should have just killed them,' the girl spat.

'My sister,' said the man. 'She hasn't killed *any* Daesh yet. This is her first mission.'

Jesus, Danny thought. *Are we a fucking kindergarten now?*

At least their use of the word 'Daesh' sounded plausible. It was a term the Islamists hated. But it could still be a ruse.

Danny slowly lowered his weapon. There was a fine line, he decided, between defending himself from a sudden attack by these two, and offending them to such an extent that they refused to help. Some sixth sense told him he was erring on the wrong side of that line at the moment. But he knew Spud had his back. One word from Danny and there would be fireworks.

He approached. Five metres out, he stopped. 'What's your name?'

'Rojan,' said the man.

'And you?' Danny asked the girl.

'You speak to me, man,' Rojan said, 'not her.'

Danny shook his head. 'I need a name, buddy.'

A pause.

'I am called Naza,' said the girl. She had a dry, throaty voice.

'You are alone?' Rojan said.

Danny didn't reply. He simply raised one hand. For a moment, it was clear that Rojan and Naza didn't know why. But after a few seconds, they looked over their shoulders and saw Spud emerging from the darkness. He looked askance at Danny. He clearly wanted to know what their strategy was with regard to Caitlin.

'You have something for us, man?' Rojan said, his gaze flickering between Danny and the approaching Spud.

Danny nodded.

'Where is it?'

'Nearby. What happened to your eye?'

Rojan frowned. 'Daesh happened to it,' he said. He turned to Naza. 'Show him.'

With obvious reluctance, Naza removed a chunky smartphone from her camouflage jacket. She swiped the screen, then held it up for Danny to see. There was video footage. It was blurred and shaky, with no sound. Danny could make out a crowd of people. The crowd had parted in the middle. A line of vans drove through the centre. Attached to the back of each van was a cage. In each cage was a man, dressed in an orange jumpsuit, cuffed to the bars. Outside each cage, hanging on to the back of the van with their rifles pointing into the air, was an IS militant. Black clothes. Black balaclava. Black flag with the IS symbol. The mob seemed to be cheering, and as the convoy passed through them, the camera focussed in on one of the caged men. It was Rojan. His eye was freshly wounded, a weeping, bleeding socket of red. Gore dripped down his cheek.

'What is this? Movie time?' Spud had reached them.

The video footage finished. Naza lowered the phone. 'This was two weeks ago. My brother escaped. I'm going to kill the people who did this to them.'

'You reckon?' Danny said, just as Spud drew him to one side.

'These two are a fucking joke,' he said. 'He's only got one eye, and what the hell's he doing bringing a fucking kid along? What kind of wanker does that?'

'All they have to do is get us to the border,' Danny said.

'I wouldn't trust these two not to wet the fucking bed,' Spud muttered as Danny tuned back in to the Kurds.

'We need to get back to the road,' Danny said. 'We have one more person to pick up. She's waiting near here with your weapons.' No point telling them of their concerns just yet – it might frighten them off.

'She?' Naza said sharply.

'Yeah,' Danny said. 'She. I reckon you'll get on like a house on fire.' Naza's expression told him she didn't understand what he'd said. 'Never mind,' he told her. 'Let's go.'

He and Spud took a moment to remove their combat burkas and pack them back into their bergens, while Rojan and Naza returned to the vehicle. Danny recognised it now as an old Toyota Hilux pickup. Front seats, rear seats and an open section at the back where the weaponry was mounted – a fifty-cal machine gun, as Danny had expected, fitted to a sturdy tripod and with the barrel pointing to the front of the pickup. The vehicle was white, but very dirty, with large off-road tyres caked in mud and sand, spatters stretching up the side and large patches of rust everywhere. A greasy stink of diesel hung around it. It had seen better days, no doubt, but if this was the vehicle in which they were going to try to get over the border into Iraq, they had to make the most of it.

Naza had the keys and made her way to the driver's door, but Danny blocked her way. She looked like she was going to argue, but thought better of it. Danny took the wheel. He drove slowly, keeping engine noise to a minimum, across the rough ground and then back along the track that led to Caitlin's vicinity. He stopped after four minutes and checked his GPS. The pin he'd dropped to mark Caitlin's position was 500 metres to their west. He killed the engine. 'We'll leave the vehicle here,' he said.

Naza shook her head. 'It is too valuable. If someone takes it—'

'Your brother can stay here. Man the machine gun.'

'We will both stay here,' Naza said.

Danny shook his head. There was no way he was leaving them together. If they got cold feet about the operation, the unit wouldn't see them for dust. 'You're coming with us.' She opened her mouth to object, but Danny interrupted her. 'If you want your weapons, little girl, you're coming with us.'

There was a limit to how many times he could use that threat, but for now there was no further argument. All four of them alighted. Danny made one more attempt to raise Caitlin on the radio. Nothing doing. Rojan climbed into the back of the pickup and manoeuvred the machine gun so that it was pointing towards the rear of the vehicle, back in the direction from which they'd come. 'I am a very good shot,' he boasted.

'Yeah, I bet you are, cowboy,' Danny muttered. He scoped the ground towards Caitlin's location. There was no movement. He turned to the others. 'Order of march, me, Naza, Spud. Make no noise – you understand, Naza? *No noise.* Let's go.'

They moved in single file, halfway between a jog and a run, five metres between each of them. It took a little over a minute to negotiate the rocky ground and get to the small cliff over the cave where they'd left Caitlin. Ten metres from the cliff, Danny raised one hand. Looking over his shoulder, he was pleased to see that Naza had stopped. Danny approached the edge of the cliff carefully, got down on one knee with his weapon ready, and looked over.

Distance to the ground, six metres. No sound. No evidence of a threat. But that didn't mean there wasn't one. The cave mouth, directly below him, was out of sight.

Danny jabbed one finger forward to indicate that the others should approach. They joined him silently. Spud got down into the same position and covered the brow of the cliff with his weapon, with Naza just behind him. Danny moved over to the gully they'd used to descend, and started to manoeuvre himself down it, as quietly as possible.

Halfway down, he double-checked that Spud was still covering him. The silhouette of his mate, gun barrel protruding from his chest area, was still there.

It was too awkward to hold his rifle usefully as he continued to descend. Instead, he pulled his handgun from his holster and unlocked it, while his rifle swung from his neck. Every sense was on high alert, finely tuned to the smallest movement or sound. He looked back up. Spud was still effectively covering the ground in front of the cave, so Danny continued his descent. Bit by bit. Rock by rock.

He reached the bottom of the cliff, holstered his Sig and returned to his rifle. Distance to the cave mouth: seven metres.

He flicked down his NV goggles, engaged his weapon and advanced.

Five metres. Pause. Listen. Nothing.

Three metres.

With his weapon still covering the cave mouth, he looked up and raised one hand at Spud, before turning his attention back to the cave. On the edge of his vision he could see Spud retreating from the top of the cliff. A few seconds later he sensed movement behind him. He knew that this was Spud leading Naza down the gulley.

Sixty seconds passed. Danny looked to his right. Naza was lying on the ground, Spud on one knee, covering the mouth of the cave.

Danny stepped forward. He was now just one metre from the opening. He could see about halfway into it. Green NV haze. No movement. The temperature, already low, dropped a little more in the vicinity of the cave mouth. Despite that, Danny was sweating. The unpleasant stench hit his nostrils again. Somehow, it seemed even stronger this time. More sinister.

He moved forward, covering the cave mouth with his weapon. This was where they had last seen Caitlin. Now there was no sign of her.

He inched into the cave. He knew he was in a dangerous position. Anyone could be hiding in there and he was an easy target.

He took two more steps inside . . .

Movement. Danny twisted towards it, but suddenly felt the cold steel of a gun barrel against his right cheek.

He froze. Without moving his head, he glanced right.

'What's wrong with your radio?' he said.

The gun barrel fell away. Caitlin stepped into his line of vision. 'Dud battery, I reckon,' she said shortly. 'Spud going to plug me if I step outside?'

Danny engaged his radio, his tension easing. 'Stand down,' he instructed. He nodded at Caitlin, who moved out of the darkness of the cave into the relative light of the desert night. Danny flicked up his NV and joined her. Spud engaged the safety catch on his

155

weapon and let it hang across his chest. Danny could see the relief in his face.

'Who's the sheila?' Caitlin asked quietly, so the girl wouldn't hear their conversation.

'Her name's Naza.'

'She's just a kid. What idiot brought her?'

'Her brother. Thinks a lot of himself.'

Caitlin ignored him and stepped towards the Kurdish girl. 'How old are you?' she asked.

'Eighteen.'

'The hell you are,' Caitlin said. She turned to the others. 'We should get away from here,' she said. 'There's been movement out there. Wild animals. Dogs, I think. How far's the vehicle?'

'Five hundred metres.' Danny looked back to the cave. 'Let's get our stuff and go.'

They left the HALO gear where it was. Danny and Spud carried the freefall container between them. Caitlin strode up to Naza. 'Stay close to me,' she said.

Naza didn't argue. She couldn't take her eyes off Caitlin, and the arrogance seemed to have left her.

The weapons container was heavy, but Danny and Spud were equal to the task of transporting it across the undulating terrain towards the Hilux, even if it meant they were sweating heavily by the time they reached it. Rojan was still in position at the fifty-cal. 'We are safe,' he called when he saw them approach. 'I have kept us safe.' He had removed his *shemagh* again to reveal his sewn-up eye, and seemed very relieved to see them. He jumped down from the back of the pickup, then staggered back when he saw Caitlin bearing down on him. 'What the hell are you think-ing,' Caitlin hissed, 'bringing her along? What is she, fourteen?'

'Don't talk to me like that, woman,' Rojan said, but he looked a little less sure of himself.

Caitlin was about to go for him, but Danny got between them. 'Leave it,' he instructed. 'I mean it.'

Caitlin spat. The Kurd ran over to his little sister. 'We need them,' Danny warned her.

'Happy to have fourteen-year-old girls on the team now, are you?'

'Not really. But we still need them.'

He looked over to where Rojan was putting a solicitous arm round Naza's shoulders, but she shrugged him away and turned to Spud. 'Open it,' she said, pointing at the freefall container.

Spud had a faint smile in his eyes, as though there was entertainment value to be gleaned from taking orders from this kid. He unsealed the canister and pulled out one of the Stingers. He handed it to Rojan, who made a show of checking it over, before nodding and handing it back. 'What else?' he said.

'Radio packs,' Spud told him. 'Only we need one of them now.' He removed one of the packs and threw it to Caitlin, so that she could scavenge the battery. He looked around. 'How far to the Iraqi border?'

'About two hours,' Rojan said, as if it was nothing. He looked at his watch. 'If we leave now, we'll get there just before dawn. That's a good time to cross. Most patrols change over then. We have friends on the other side of the border. They have been driving around for the last few hours, looking for Daesh patrols. It is safer to travel in convoy when we reach Iraqi territory.'

Spud and Danny lifted the canister up into the back of the pickup. Caitlin removed her med pack from her bergen, before stowing the bag into the rear of the Hilux with the rest of the gear.

'I'm driving,' Danny said.

Naza stepped forward, obviously about to argue. Caitlin put one hand on her shoulder. 'It's OK, honey,' she said. 'You sit in the back with me.' The girl sniffed, but she did as she was told. Danny took the wheel with Rojan beside him. Spud and Caitlin were either side of the back seat, with Naza in the middle. Danny turned the engine over, performed a three-point turn and started heading back to the T-junction.

'If anyone stops us,' he told Rojan, 'you do exactly what we tell you. Understood?'

Rojan frowned. He obviously didn't like the instruction. Danny stopped the vehicle. 'Understood?' A pause. Rojan nodded. They started up again. Danny glanced in the rear-view mirror as the vehicle trundled along the rough road. Caitlin was staring in contempt at the back of Rojan's head. Naza was watching her with rapt attention. Like a kid watching her big sister.

Caitlin caught Danny looking at her. Their eyes locked and the flicker of a smile crossed her lips. There was a time, on a previous op, when Caitlin had made it pretty clear she was interested in Danny. He'd made it just as clear that was never going to happen, but he also knew Caitlin wasn't the type to take no for an answer. She held his gaze as she replaced her jacket. Danny locked his back on to the road.

'You OK?' he said.

Caitlin looked straight ahead. 'Just drive the car, Danny Black,' she said, before turning her attention to the radio pack that needed fixing.

DECEMBER 22

TWELVE

Dawn broke over the Dubai skyline, the reflection of a blood-red sun glittering off the acres of mirrored glass. A black Mercedes with tinted windows was parked outside the front of the hotel. It had done the rounds of every exclusive club in the city, before returning here two hours ago. The driver was tired, but he knew he couldn't sleep. Just because his royal passenger had returned to his hotel, it didn't mean the party was over.

Far from it.

In the penthouse suite, the main room was a mess. There were two empty bottles of booze on the cocktail bar, one of them lying on its side. Anyone inspecting the counter a little more closely would easily discover a dusting of white powder. There were several drinks glasses dotted around the room, some empty, some half-full. And there were clothes strewn across the floor. Women's clothes. Four sets. Not much to them.

Two of the women to whom the clothes belonged were in one of the bedrooms that led off the main room. They were hot Eastern Europeans with creamy skin and jet-black hair who had worked out the preferences of certain rich visitors to Dubai. They were naked apart from their jewellery, kneeling together on the bed with their bodies pressed close, kissing. Now and then one of them would moan, then glance towards the man splayed out in the comfortable armchair on the far side of the room, watching them. Tony Wiseman had a chunky tumbler of Scotch in one hand, and he watched the show these two girls were putting on for him. He knew their sound effects were entirely for his benefit, but he didn't care. All in all, his evening had turned out better than he'd expected. He'd ended up inside his own personal porn movie. It sure beat slumming it on some ship with a bunch of stinking Marines and those cunts Danny Black and Spud Glover.

The thought of them made him take another pull of his drink. He must have frowned involuntarily because one of the girls – Tony couldn't remember their names – looked suddenly worried. She disentangled herself from her friend and walked over to him, her naked hips sashaying seductively. 'What's the matter, honey?' she said. 'We not doing what you like?'

'You're doing fine,' Tony told her. He put one hand on her naked arse as she bent over and started to unbutton his shirt.

'Why not come and join us,' she whispered.

Yeah, Tony thought. Maybe I will. He downed the rest of his drink, let the empty glass drop on to the carpet and pushed himself up out of his chair, with the girl still semi-draped over him. He stroked the curve of her hips and allowed himself to stare greedily at her breasts.

'Get back to the bed,' he told her.

The girl did as she was told. But halfway there, she stopped. A noise had come from an adjoining room. A woman's scream. Half scared, half pained.

The two girls exchanged a worried look, but Tony was already striding towards the door, buttoning up his shirt. Any sensation of drunkenness had disappeared. 'Stay there,' he told the girls, before exiting the bedroom.

There was nobody in the main room of the suite. It was exactly as Tony had left it. There was another scream. Panicked, this time. It came directly from the room Tony knew to be Yellow Seven's bedroom, where he'd disappeared with two girls of his own twenty minutes ago.

Tony hesitated for a moment. Then, instead of entering that bedroom, he moved swiftly over to the main entrance to the suite. He knew the CP guys would be manning the door. Clearly they hadn't heard the screams – they'd have barged in at the slightest hint of trouble. Something told Tony he didn't want that to happen, so he locked the door from the inside before running back across the room and bursting into his new mate's bedroom.

It was carnage in here. Bedclothes were strewn all over the floor. A bottle had smashed on the carpet. Of the two girls Yellow Seven had taken to bed, one was in the corner of the room, a large white bath sheet pulled up to cover her naked body. The other was standing naked between the bed and the door. She had a swollen eye and a bleeding lip. Her hair was badly messed up, as though she'd been in a struggle. Yellow Seven was standing in front of her wearing a white robe. He had red eyes, and a spaced-out expression. The girl was staring at him in utter terror. There was no doubt in Tony's mind as to who had roughed her up.

Self-preservation was second nature to Tony Wiseman. He knew, immediately, that this scenario could end up very badly for him. Yellow Seven, fuelled up on booze and coke, slapping some bird around on Tony's watch. He knew how the world worked. Only one person was going to get the blame for this – and it wasn't the guy standing in front of him in a dressing gown. He had to make some decisions, and fast.

Tony strode up to him. 'Get in the bathroom,' he said. Yellow Seven looked like he was going to argue. '*Do it!*' Tony pushed him in the right direction. He stumbled out of the bedroom and slammed the door behind him. Tony hurried over to where the girl was cowering in the corner. He grabbed her arm and pulled her across the room to where the girl with the mashed-up face was standing. He spoke in a low, aggressive voice. 'This is what happened,' he said. 'You were invited back here for a drink. You accepted. While you were here, I saw you sneak into our friend's bedroom and try to steal from him. I confronted you and you went at me with a knife. I retaliated.'

The girls looked at him in horror. 'He got angry because we refused to—'

'I don't want to hear it, love. Trust me, if it comes to it, it'll be the word of a couple of hookers against a member of the British royal family. Who do *you* think the Dubai authorities are going to

163

side with? You ladies will be in one of their shithole prisons before you fucking know it. No one will believe you.'

The girl with the bruises started to cry. The other one just blinked at him, uncomprehendingly.

'Get your clothes on,' Tony told her with a sneer, 'and get out. *Now!*'

The two girls scrambled out of the bedroom. Tony followed. Less than an hour ago, he'd been watching appreciatively as they undressed. Now he barely looked at them as they put their clothes back on. Instead, he walked into the bedroom he'd been using. The two girls had put on towelling robes. They were sitting on the edge of the bed, clearly anxious. 'Time to go home,' Tony told them.

One of them started to ask a question. She didn't get the chance. 'Out!' Tony shouted. 'Now.'

He could tell they had suddenly become frightened of him. Good. He followed them out into the main room. The other two girls were dressed, but they looked a mess, their make-up tear-stained and streaming. One of them moved towards the main door, but tripped in her high heels as she went.

'Wait,' Tony told her. 'You all leave together.'

It took the two remaining girls less than thirty seconds to dress. Nobody spoke. The girl with the split lip looked fucking awful. If anyone saw her, they'd ask questions. Tony moved to the front door and opened it. The two CP guys were there. They looked knackered and pissed off, but clearly knew something was going down – maybe they'd heard the door locking.

'Is there a back way out of here?' Tony demanded.

One of them nodded.

Tony looked over his shoulder. 'These four are leaving. Make sure nobody sees them. Take each one home. Make sure you see their front doors close behind them.'

'We'll take our instructions from his—'

He didn't finish the sentence. Tony grabbed him by the collar and pushed him hard up against the wall. 'You'll do what I fucking say,' he breathed, 'unless you want to end up on the front page of the *Sun*, and out of a job. Got it?'

He didn't wait for the answer. He just strode back into the room where the girls, fully dressed and terrified, were waiting. 'Any of you sluts mention a word of this, you'll be screwed, your family will be screwed,' he said. He strode up to the girl who'd been roughed up. 'And if you think you look bad now, wait till I have a go at you. Now get out of here.'

They couldn't wait to leave. Ten seconds later, Tony was alone in the room. He gathered his thoughts, then headed back into the royal bedroom. No sign of him, so he rapped hard on the bathroom door. No answer. He tried the handle. The door opened.

Yellow Seven was sitting on the edge of the bath. He was still wearing his robe, and he had the bright-eyed, slightly wild expression of someone dosed up with marching powder. He sniffed, and licked his lips rather fast. 'Are they gone?' he asked.

'Gone,' Tony said.

'Got a bit carried away. Hope they don't mention it to—'

'They won't. I saw to it.'

Yellow Seven smiled. 'Sweet,' he said, his eyes going slightly out of focus. 'It's, er . . . it's good to have you on board.' He stood up rather uncertainly. 'We'll find a job for you. With the family. If you're interested . . .'

Tony walked over to the shower and switched it on. 'Get cleaned up,' he said. 'We need to leave Dubai this morning.'

Yellow Seven blinked. 'Why?' he said. 'I thought we were having a blast—'

'This morning,' Tony repeated.

A pause.

'Right,' Yellow Seven said. 'Sweet.'

Tony left, closing the bathroom door behind him. He scanned the room, immediately picking out a couple of glasses dotted around the place. He gathered them up and looked at the rims. Lipstick. He rummaged in a wardrobe and found a sturdy bag intended for dirty linen. He dumped the glasses into it, then examined the bedclothes. There was a smear of blood on one of the pillowcases. He stuffed that into the bag too.

He could hear the shower still running, and he took a moment to pause. What had the twat said? *We'll find a job for you. With the family.* Part of him recoiled at the thought. He'd be the laughing stock of Hereford. But another part of his brain was coldly calculating the potential benefit to him. It was well known that the SAS gave the royals a bit of a hard-on. Now and then they took a Regiment guy – usually a Rupert – under their wing. The chosen one would be in attendance at every royal event. He'd appear in the background of every royal photo. He'd have unprecedented access. And he'd be made for life.

There was no doubt about it. If that jumped-up little turd, with his penchant for nose candy and slapping around hookers, was in Tony's debt, he, Tony, could work it to his advantage. Big time.

He looked down at the bag of incriminating evidence in his fist. That stupid bitch sure chose the wrong party to join. But it wasn't Tony's problem. He just needed to get rid of the evidence, then get his Grace on a plane back to London before anybody started sniffing around. If he did that right, things could be looking up for him. And Tony couldn't help but enjoy the thought that it would have Danny Black laughing on the other side of his stupid, smug face.

Danny drove east. He knew, from his mental snapshot of the terrain, that the road was following the Syrian border, a couple of klicks to its north. They'd been travelling for half an hour, mostly in silence, apart from the occasional one-word direction from Rojan. They'd seen nobody on these rough, unpopulated roads. Hereford had chosen their insertion point well, but Danny was very aware that anyone they encountered would be a potential threat. Nobody would be driving round these parts if they didn't have a good reason to be here. And the only good reason to be here was military. All Danny's senses were on high alert.

'Describe the border crossing to me,' he said.

'It is a river crossing,' Rojan replied. 'Dry in the summer, flowing in the winter. But shallow, if you know the right place, which I do. This vehicle can cross it easily.'

166

Almost as if in response to Rojan's words, big droplets of rain spattered hard against the windscreen. A minute later it was raining ferociously. The Hilux's headlamps cut through the rain, but their visibility was reduced to ten metres, max, with the wipers squeaking ineffectively.

'How far is the crossing from the nearest official border checkpoint?' Danny asked above the noise of the water hammering on the top of the vehicle.

'Thirty miles in either direction. I told you, it's a good place.'

They fell silent again. Danny could sense the tension emanating from Caitlin and Spud in the back.

'Your friends on the Iraqi side of the border,' Danny said. 'How many?'

'Four, maybe five.'

'How many vehicles?'

'One. Maybe two.'

'Which?' Danny asked peevishly. 'One or two?' Rojan pulled out a mobile phone and started to dial a number. 'What are you doing?'

'Calling them.'

'Put the phone down. I said, *put the fucking phone down*.' He grabbed it from Rojan's fist and threw it to the floor.

'What are you doing?' Rojan demanded angrily. 'Daesh are not listening in to our phones, we know that.'

'They're not the only people we have to worry about,' Danny snapped. And he meant it. It was inconceivable that GCHQ weren't hacking every communication they could pick up along this border. If GCHQ were doing it, you could bet your bottom dollar that the Yanks were doing the same. The unit's orders were very clear: do nothing to alert the Americans to their presence. That meant keeping mobile communications to an absolute minimum.

He didn't explain all that to the Kurds. Rojan's irritation was palpable. Danny didn't care. He just kept driving.

Time check. 0415 hours. Sixty minutes till dawn. The rain hadn't let up. The inside of the windscreen kept fogging from the

167

breath of so many people in the vehicle. The tyres felt sluggish on the ground. It was difficult driving, but that was OK by Danny. The rain kept them camouflaged, to an extent.

'Go right at the junction up ahead,' Rojan said, 'off the road.' These were the first words he'd spoken since their argument about the phone, and he had a sulky tone of voice.

Danny nodded. After 300 metres they came to an unmarked T-junction. The terrain to the right was marshy. Danny slowed down and knocked the vehicle into first gear to avoid wheelspin, then he killed the headlamps.

'What are you doing?' Rohan asked. 'You won't be able to see.'

Danny lowered his NV goggles from the top of his helmet. 'I'll be able to see just fine,' he said. The world outside turned into a green haze, with every bump and undulation of the terrain ahead clearly defined, despite the darkness and the rain. 'Distance to the border crossing?'

'About two kilometres,' Rojan said. Danny nodded. He manoeuvred the vehicle slowly and carefully through the driving rain. He didn't even need to look in the rear-view mirror to check that Spud and Caitlin had engaged their own NV. He could sense their tension in the air. 'You come to a hill in 1,500 metres,' Rojan said. 'Once you go over the hill, you can see it in the distance. There is a barbed wire fence on the other side of the river.'

'Do you have any cutting tools?' Spud asked from the back of the vehicle.

'You won't need them,' Naza piped up. 'We already cut a section out of the fence.'

There was a pause. 'When did you cut it?' Spud asked.

'Does it matter?' Rojan said.

'*When did you cut it?*'

'About twelve hours ago.'

There was a pause. It was as if none of the unit wanted to ask the question that they all had in their head.

'This section you cut out of the fence,' Spud said finally. 'You replaced it, right? It doesn't *look* like you cut anything out?'

Silence.

Danny braked. He turned to Rojan. 'Answer him,' he said.

'No,' Rojan said defensively. 'Of course not. What's the point? It's just a small gap. A few metres.'

Danny swore under his breath, and he heard a restrained 'For fuck's sake' from Spud. The Kurds had made an elementary error. A hole in the border fence, no matter how small, would be a beacon to anyone patrolling the area. It didn't matter who – Iraqi or Turkish authorities, IS patrols, border guards. Anyone who saw it would know that someone had got, or was planning to get, a vehicle through there. And that meant there was a high probability that someone would be watching the crossing point.

'Don't worry about it,' Rojan said, though his voice quavered slightly. 'We cross this border all the time. It will be fine.'

None of the unit answered. Danny knocked the vehicle back into first gear and continued to trundle south towards the border, his mind turning over. What should they do? Abort? Try to find another border crossing? That could take days. They only had hours.

Five slow, tense minutes passed. There was no let-up in the rain. Through the green haze of his NV, and by the feel of the engine's traction on the wet ground, Danny could tell that the gradient of the terrain had started to increase. This must be the hill Rojan had mentioned. Danny stopped the vehicle, engaged the hand-brake and killed the engine.

'What are you doing?' Rojan asked. 'We're not there yet.'

'We need to check the border crossing. Make sure there are no threats waiting for us.'

'There won't be,' Rojan said. 'There never are.'

'That doesn't mean there never will be,' Danny replied. 'Especially if you've left a signal for everyone, like a section of missing fencing. You and Naza stay here.' He looked at Spud and Caitlin. 'Get out,' he said.

They were drenched the moment they stepped outside. They stood in a huddle in front of the car. 'Caitlin, I want you to stay with them while me and Spud do a recce. And before you argue,

169

it's only because the girl seems to trust you.' He looked up the hill. 'We'll get eyes on the border crossing from the rise, see if there's anything suspicious. Then we'll make a call whether or not to cross.'

Caitlin frowned. She obviously wasn't happy at being excluded for a second time, but she didn't argue. She returned to the car, leaving Danny and Spud in the downpour, NV engaged, the world around them a teeming green haze.

Wordlessly, they jogged up the hill. Distance to the rise: twenty metres. They went to ground five metres short of it. Danny removed his night-sight. Then they crawled the remaining distance through the wet, muddy earth, before carefully edging to the vantage point and looking down towards the Iraqi border.

He didn't need the night-sight to realise they had a problem.

There was a vehicle. All Danny could see of it was red lights, which told him that it was facing away from them. He quickly disengaged his NV goggles and scanned the area with his night-sight. A couple of seconds' observation revealed the river itself – it was about fifty metres from their position, and 100 metres in width, with high reeds along either bank. The border fencing was on the far side of the river, just as Rojan had said. It was about six metres high, with upright posts every five metres, joined by rolls of razor wire. The gap that Rojan had cut in the fence was almost directly in front of them. The vehicle was driving away from the gap. With the benefit of the night-sight, Danny could see that it was a four-by-four of some description, not unlike their own Hilux.

Danny and Spud watched it leave. It took less than a minute for the red lights to disappear into the drenched darkness. They retreated back behind the rise. 'The border crossing's compromised,' Spud said. 'That fucking Kurdish tosspot's screwed up the whole op.'

Danny gave it a moment's thought. 'We need to find another crossing point.'

'Mucker, it's not going to happen,' Spud said. 'We need to get the hell out of here. It's eighty–twenty someone *knows* there's going to be a covert border crossing. They'll be fucking *waiting* for us.'

Danny knew he was right. 'Let's get back down to the others,' he said.

They slid back down the slope. By the time they reached the Hilux again, they were truly soaked through and covered in sticky, wet mud. Not that it mattered. They got back into the car and explained what they'd seen. Caitlin swore viciously.

'You're worrying too much,' Rojan said. 'It was probably just our friends on the other side of the border. They're expecting us, remember?'

'We can't be sure of that,' Danny said. 'Is there any other crossing point?'

'No,' Rojan said. 'Not for miles, and they'll be manned. This is the only place. Trust me.'

Silence in the car. The rain hammered noisily.

'We abort,' Danny said. 'Get on to Hereford, request a pick-up, dig in for the day and return to our LZ under cover of night.'

'Roger that,' Spud growled. Caitlin nodded. Full agreement. Trying to drive through a compromised crossing point broke every SOP in the book. It was potential suicide.

Rojan suddenly slammed one hand on the dashboard. 'You see what they did to me?' he spat. He pointed at his wounded face. 'Don't you see what they *did* to me? And you're going to give up now, because you're too scared to cross the border?'

'Get used to it,' Danny said. 'Because that's what's happening.'

'Fine,' Rojan said. 'Get out of the car. *We'll* cross the river, Naza and me. When we're on the other side, you can walk across. I'll cover you with my gun.' He jabbed his thumb backwards to indicate the fifty-cal on the back of the Hilux.

Danny thought about it. It was hardly ideal. Rojan would be putting himself right in the firing line. But if he was willing to do it, they could, maybe, make this work. Because if there was a vehicle fording the river, it would hold the attention of anyone watching it. Which meant that any other activity on the river might go unnoticed . . .

171

He turned to the other members of his team. Spud nodded, almost imperceptibly. He clearly knew the risk the Kurd was taking, and what Danny was thinking.

'Naza stays with us,' Caitlin says.

'No way,' said Rojan. 'She's my sister, she stays with me—'

'No,' Danny interrupted. 'She's just a kid. I'm not letting you put her in the firing line.'

'But—'

'Forget it,' Caitlin cut in. 'You do it alone, or we turn back now.' She looked so fiercely at Rojan that he instantly backed down.

Naza being a kid was only half the reason for holding her back, of course. They needed at least one of them alive, if they were to hook up with their Kurdish mates on the Iraqi side of the border.

'Do you know how deep the water gets on either side of the ford?' Danny said.

Rojan, still sulking, put his right hand at the level of his chest. 'Maybe a bit higher,' he said, 'in this weather.'

Danny sniffed, and wiped a drop of rain from his eyes. 'OK. You take the vehicle. The rest of us will wade through the river on foot. We'll be behind you and to your left. If you get into trouble, we can supply fire support.'

'There won't be any trouble,' Rojan said confidently.

'We'll see,' Danny murmured. 'We need to unload our gear.'

'The weapons container stays with me,' Rojan replied.

That was fine by Danny. He got back out into the pouring rain, along with Spud, Caitlin and Naza. They grabbed their bergens from the back of the Hilux. Before they slung them over their shoulders, however, they silently went about the business of preparing their packs for the river crossing. Each bergen had a waterproof lining, with a ziplock-type seal at the top. Danny checked the seal was firmly closed. This would not only keep the contents watertight; the air trapped inside would turn the bergen into a makeshift flotation device – very hard to sink, and useful to hold on to if they found themselves getting washed away. He had two full water canteens in the side of the bergen, which he emptied out before returning them to the side pockets. The empty bottles would add to the bergen's buoyancy.

Spud and Caitlin were finishing the same operation while Danny moved to the driver's window, where Rojan had taken his place behind the wheel and was scratching his closed-up eye socket. 'Wait ten minutes,' he said. 'That should give us enough time to get to the water's edge. When you move, keep your head-lamps off. And drive slowly – it'll keep the engine noise down. Do you understand?'

Rojan faced forward and nodded curtly. He clearly didn't like taking instructions.

'When you get to the other side, point your machine gun to the south-east. That's the direction we saw the vehicle leaving.'

'I know that,' Rojan said. 'I'm not stupid. Just go. It will be dawn soon.' He wound up his window without looking at Danny.

Danny swore under his breath. He didn't have time to argue. He estimated that they'd lose the cover of darkness in twenty-five minutes.

If they were going to cross the border, it had to be now.

THIRTEEN

'Do you understand what we're doing?' Caitlin asked Naza.

The girl looked unsure. She didn't answer.

'There's the river,' Caitlin said. 'On the other side of the river is the border fence. Your brother cut a hole in it, which means people on the other side might be expecting us to cross. So your brother is taking the vehicle across by himself. While he does that, we're going to wade through the river, out of sight. It's our best chance of keeping safe.'

'What if Daesh shoot at him?' Naza asked.

'Then we'll shoot back.'

Naza looked across at her brother, who was still sitting behind the wheel, scratching his eye.

'He's very brave,' Naza said.

'Yeah,' Caitlin muttered. 'He's a regular Ned Kelly.'

Danny walked up to them. 'Stick close to her,' Danny told Naza, pointing at Caitlin. 'When I raise my hand like this, get to the ground immediately. You understand?'

Naza nodded.

Caitlin took Danny to one side. She spoke quietly so Naza couldn't hear them. 'If the crossing is compromised, Rojan's a dead man.'

'I know,' Danny said, glancing at the kid.

The three unit members engaged their NV goggles. Danny jogged over to Rojan's vehicle. The Kurd lowered his window. 'Give us ten minutes to get to the river,' Danny said. 'Then make the crossing.'

Rojan nodded wordlessly, then shut his window. Danny

returned to the others. 'Let's go,' he said. He led them back up the slope, with Caitlin directly behind him, then Naza, then Spud. As before, they stopped short of the brow of the hill and Danny carefully scanned the area beyond the border fence. There was no sign of any movement or threat. Maybe Rojan was right. Maybe this was a safe crossing.

But Danny was not about to risk the safety of his team on the back of a maybe.

Crouching low, they crested the top of the hill and hurried back down below the ridge where they would be less visible. They struck off at a bearing of thirty degrees anticlockwise, so that when they hit the river they would be well clear of the shallow ford where Rojan would be crossing. Advancing carefully, it took five minutes for them to hit the water's edge 100 metres east of the ford. Here it was marshy underfoot, and difficult to walk among the waist-high reeds that lined the river, and which were battered by the heavy rain. Spud stood four metres to Danny's left. Caitlin and Naza stood an equivalent distance to his right. This was the correct positioning. Danny could see there was a reasonably fast current, flowing from right to left. Danny and Spud would be able to withstand it, and so would Caitlin if she was on her own. But with Naza clinging on to her, there was a chance of them being knocked downstream. Danny and Spud would be there to catch her if necessary.

Danny looked over his right shoulder. In the green haze of his NV, he could see the Hilux slowly cresting the hill towards the crossing point. He loosened his bergen so that it was hanging over just one shoulder. He held his weapon, cocked and locked, horizontally in front of him. Then he waded out, through the reeds, into the river. He was entirely soaked already, so the river water did not make his shoes or clothes any wetter. But he could instantly tell that the running water was several degrees colder than the air. The current was also a little faster than he'd anticipated. He hoped Caitlin would be able to hold on to Naza.

The unit waded forward in a flat line. The river bed was soft, and Danny's boots sank a good couple of inches into the mud.

Eight metres out, he checked on the position of the Hilux again. It had only just reached the bottom of the hill. It looked like Rojan was taking Danny's advice about driving slowly. Good.

The river became suddenly, unexpectedly deeper. Danny sank up to his chest and almost lost his footing. He felt his bergen floating obstinately behind him. The noise of the rain fizzed on the surface of the water, but he could still hear Naza gasp. He looked to his left, ready to catch her if necessary, but Caitlin had one arm round the girl, and she looked rock solid against the current.

Thirty metres in. Seventy metres to the far side. The river depth had remained constant. The current, if anything, was a little weaker here, making it easier for them to wade across. Over his shoulder, Danny saw that the Hilux had reached the water's edge. It stopped for a few seconds, then moved slowly into the river.

The unit continued moving forward. They were halfway across now, and Danny thought he could maybe feel the water becoming an inch or two shallower. Looking to his right, he could see that Naza was shivering badly. They needed to get her out of the water as quickly as possible—

'Shit.' Spud's voice to Danny's left. 'What the hell's he *doing*?'

Danny looked again. Now it was his turn to swear. The Hilux was halfway across the river, 100 metres due west of their position. It had picked up speed. Plumes of churned-up water were spewing from its wheel arches. And even over the noise of the rain, Danny could now hear the vehicle's engine – a high-pitched scream as it revved its way through the water.

The unit instinctively lowered themselves so the water lapped over their shoulders. Danny kept eyes on the Hilux. It was only thirty metres from the far side of the river now. Twenty metres. Ten.

He looked beyond, desperately scanning the Iraqi side for threats.

Nothing.

Rojan was going to make it.

He was emerging from the river and heading towards the gap in the fence—

Danny saw the explosion before he heard it. In an instant, the Hilux transformed into a massive fireball. A split second later, the roar of the explosion hit their ears. It was massively loud, even from this distance across the water. Danny knew for a certainty that it would have been heard for a radius of at least a mile. Burning debris shot up into the air, and there were a number of secondary explosions – probably the ammunition in the weapons canister detonating.

A scream from Naza. Blood-curdling. '*MY BROTHER!*'

'*Get under the water!*' Danny shouted. But Spud had already done that, and Caitlin was in the process of dragging Naza under to protect them from any flying debris. Danny struggled out of his bergen, took a deep breath and then pushed himself under the floating pack.

Ten seconds. Twenty. He remerged, knowing that any shrapnel would now have fallen. The Hilux was a flaming shell. But even worse, he could see the headlamps of a vehicle beyond it, on the other side of the broken border fence. Impossible to tell its distance under these conditions. Maybe 500 metres? Maybe less. But definitely approaching. Fast.

'*Get back to the Turkish side!*' he yelled. But a moment later, he realised that wouldn't be possible. Naza was no longer with Caitlin. They'd become separated. The Kurdish girl was now moving downstream, all arms and legs, a riot of splashes. She was at least twenty metres away, out of control, and the current was pushing her towards the Iraqi side.

Even worse, Caitlin was following her.

The headlamps were getting closer to the burning Hilux. Less than 400 metres, at an estimate. Spud was next to Danny. '*We can't get separated!*' he shouted.

He was right. They were more effective as a unit of three. It meant following Caitlin. '*Go!*' he said, before launching himself after the women. He felt himself having to restrain a surge of panic. It would only take the headlamps of that vehicle to fall in the wrong direction and they'd be lit up like a Christmas tree. They needed cover, fast. That meant getting to the reeds on the

Iraqi side as quickly as possible. Danny half-ran, half-swam, surging through the water that suddenly felt as thick as molasses. Up ahead, he saw Caitlin grab Naza, who was shivering and clearly in a state of great panic.

The water was only waist-deep now, the far side fifteen metres away. Danny checked on the approaching vehicle. It was 100 metres from the blazing Hilux, which put it about 170 metres from the unit's position, and approaching the gap in the border fence. Close enough for them to be seen if they were unlucky. '*Move!*' he hissed at the others. They surged forward towards the bank, covering the final ten metres in less than ten seconds. The border fence was twenty metres away. As soon as they reached the reeds, they flung themselves down into them, half submerged in the marshy ground. Spud was within earshot, about three metres to his left, while Caitlin and Naza were ten metres behind him. He could hear Naza crying and struggling. 'Caitlin, keep her quiet,' Danny hissed into his radio. He slung his wet rucksack in front of him, used it to rest his weapon on, raised his NV goggles and surveyed the scene through the sight on his weapon. '*No one move,*' he whispered.

His field of view was somewhat obscured by the reeds, but he could make out the bare bones of what was unfolding ahead of him. The vehicle had reached the remains of the Hilux, from which thick smoke was now billowing as the rain hit the flames. Whatever had destroyed it was no makeshift IED. Danny's money was on an anti-tank mine. But who the hell would be laying serious explosives like that? Danny flicked through the possibilities in his mind. IS militants? Turkish border guards? He didn't think so.

He remembered Hammond's warning before they deployed. '*You realise that you won't be the only SF team on the ground in northern Iraq ...*'

Men emerged from the new vehicle. At least seven, maybe eight. They were armed and possibly dressed in camouflage gear, though it was difficult to see through the rain. He couldn't make out their faces. But he *could* tell, by the way they surrounded the Hilux with their weapons prepared, that they weren't idiots. They were taking the time to double-check that there was no chance of any threat coming from the smouldering shell of the vehicle.

Fifteen seconds later, the group of men split up. Danny could tell now that there were eight of them. Three disappeared out of sight beyond the Hilux. They were obviously going to comb the riverbank in that direction.

Two stayed by the Hilux. The remaining three were heading the unit's way.

Each man had a torch fitted to their rifle. They moved slowly and carefully, scanning the area ahead of them, paying particular attention to the reed beds. Distance: fifty metres, and closing.

'Do we engage them?' Spud hissed.

Danny paused. A firefight was the last thing they wanted. It put them at risk, and a noise could alert other people to their presence. Much better to stay hidden here in the tall reeds if possible.

But that might *not* be possible. The three armed men were doing a thorough job. If they got too close, the unit might not have any alternative. Sometimes, the only option was to shoot first.

And they were now only forty metres away.

Thirty.

They were walking in a flat line, about three metres apart. Danny directed his sights to the guy on his right. He knew, without having to ask, that as Spud was on his left, he'd have the guy on the left lined up.

'Hold your fire,' Danny breathed.

There was a sudden surge of more powerful rain. The three guys looked up, and for a hopeful moment Danny thought it would make them retreat. It didn't. They just started moving more quickly, as if they wanted to get the job done sooner.

Twenty metres.

What if these were the Kurds? Danny cursed himself for not thinking of that before. He spoke very quietly into his radio. 'Caitlin, do you copy?'

'*Roger that.*'

'Can Naza identify them?'

A pause. Then Caitlin said: '*Negative. She says they're not our contacts.*'

That was all Danny needed to know.

Fifteen metres.

He squinted suddenly. One of the torch beams had shone directly into his sight, dazzling him. When he regained his vision a few seconds later, he knew immediately that something was wrong. The three men had stopped, and one of them was shining his torch directly at Spud. Even if he couldn't see Spud himself, he had surely noticed the impression he was making on the reed bed.

Which meant there was only one call to make.

'Take the shot,' Danny said.

Chances were that the two guys on either side of the trio never even knew what happened. Danny and Spud fired at exactly the same moment – the two reports of their weapons sounded like one – and the rounds found their targets in the men's chests with deadly, unswerving accuracy. They collapsed immediately, but Danny had already turned his attention to the third man. At the sound of the weapons, he had dropped to the ground, so quickly that Danny had insufficient time to engage him. Alarm bells rang immediately – whoever this was, his reflexes were instant and he wasn't panicking. This was not some IS shitkicker. This was a pro.

It wouldn't save him though. Danny and Spud both knew where he had fallen. Danny altered the trajectory of his weapon just a few degrees. He clicked the safety switch to semi-automatic. Then he fired a substantial burst of rounds towards where the target lay. Spud did the same. The resulting thunder of gunfire lasted only a few seconds, but it was deafening. There was no doubt that it could be heard from a substantial distance. The other gunmen – whose vehicle was by the blazing Hilux, 150 metres away – now surely knew they were there.

As their weapons fell silent, Danny heard screaming from the guy they'd just hit. It didn't last long, fading seconds later into a long, gurgling sigh. Danny's attention was already elsewhere. Five enemy remaining. Well trained, well armed. He could see, through his sights, the silhouettes of the other three men running back up to their vehicle next to the burning Hilux. For a split second, he considered trying to take one of them out, but he knew it was a risky shot, and there was a chance of giving away their position, if they hadn't already done so.

And then the moment was gone. Their enemy had taken cover behind their vehicle.

'These are trained soldiers.' Spud confirmed Danny's intuition. There was a tense edge to his voice. 'They had white skin. Not Iraqi or Turkish. Who the hell are they?'

Danny didn't have an answer. Just more questions. 'And why did they booby-trap the border crossing?' But they couldn't waste time figuring these things out. They were still in the heart of a firefight. 'We need to keep our positions,' he said. 'If we show ourselves, they'll be on to—'

He didn't finish. There was a sudden burst of automatic fire from the direction of the vehicle: a dull, clunking heavy sound that told Danny this was more than an assault rifle. More like a machine gun. Rounds whizzed over their heads, and exploded on the riverbank all around them. As the ammunition flew, and just before he pressed his body hard into the ground to protect himself from the incoming, he caught sight of two figures heading towards them in a pincer movement, protected by the covering fire.

And then, from the vehicle, another burst of movement.

One of the armed personnel had pulled down the rear panel of the Hilux. Something smaller than a human, and much faster, darted out.

'*Attack dog!*' Danny shouted.

The dog was unbelievably quick. It shot towards them, barely visible through the reeds, eating up the 150 metres between them so speedily that it was simply impossible for Danny to track it through the sight of his rifle. With his naked eye, he saw it cross the open ground in seconds and hurtle between the two approaching armed personnel, and when there was a momentary lull in the covering fire, he heard the animal bark twice.

Danny was a dog man. He could hear the aggression in that bark.

He lost sight of the animal, but knew it was less than fifty metres away. He grabbed the handgun holstered in his ops waist-coat as he said into his radio: 'Put the dog down if you can ...'

The covering fire started up again. The pincer movement guys continued advancing.

'*Where the hell is it?*' Spud hissed.

Another bark. Somehow, the dog was to their left. 'Caitlin!' he shouted. 'It's going for you and Naza! Put it down! Put it down!'

Seconds later, his warning was met by a scream. Naza.

Danny rolled on to his back so he could see what was happening behind him. Caitlin and Naza were lying on their fronts ten metres away. Just as he turned, Danny saw the dog hit hard and fast. As it leapt through the reeds towards them, he immediately identified the dog as a Malinois. Lean. Hungry. Like a skinny Alsatian, it was all bones and muscle. It was going for Naza, leaping through the air in a perfect trajectory towards the girl.

Caitlin's reaction was instinctive and lightning-fast. She hurled herself towards Naza, covering the girl's body with her own to protect her. A fraction of a second later the dog thumped against Caitlin, landing directly on her back.

Naza screamed. Caitlin squirmed and tried to roll over, but the dog instantly clamped its jaws into Caitlin's upper arm and started shaking its head violently.

The pain had to be bad, because the screams that followed didn't come from Naza but from Caitlin, who was tussling and rolling with the dog. There was an aggressive, low growling and snarling. Danny aimed his handgun in their direction, trying to line it up with the dog. But it was impossible. The movement was too fierce and frenzied. He risked shooting Caitlin instead.

Suddenly there were three muffled gunshots. The attack dog whimpered momentarily, then fell away from Caitlin. She'd obviously managed to get some rounds into the Malinois's guts to put it down, but even from this distance Danny could hear her heavy breathing, stuttering and painful, and small, terrified whimpers from Naza. He could tell the girl was frightened but unhurt. The same was not true of Caitlin. An attack dog like that could easily kill a man. Caitlin could be in a very bad way—

'Danny!' Spud's voice was tense. Danny rolled over to his front again. The attack dog was dead, but it had done its job of identifying their position. The enemy personnel knew where they were now. Danny surveyed the open ground between them and the vehicle. The two advancing men had gone to ground. Danny did not doubt that they had their position in their sights. If the unit tried to move, they were dead.

More gunfire, low across the reeds. Assault rifles – 7.62s. It came from the two advancing men. They were covering the remaining three men, enabling them to move forward from the vehicle. *Jesus.* These fuckers were really after them. Danny suppressed a surge of panic in his gut. They were truly pinned down, by professional guys with excellent combat skills. It wouldn't surprise him if these were special forces soldiers. In a corner of his brain he started cursing himself for going with Rojan's plan. But he quickly cut off that line of thought. He needed to focus entirely on the present.

Which wasn't looking good.

Silence.

Time seemed to slow down. He heard Spud hiss: 'Frag?' He had only half a second to consider whether a grenade would be a good idea – there was a good chance it would wound one of the men, but again the movement involved in throwing it might give away their *exact* position – before the enemy gunfire started up again. Short, coughing barks of automatic fire that told Danny without even having to look that the enemy were advancing again.

He tried to evaluate their options. Should they get back into the river, allow the current to pull them downstream? No. Caitlin was wounded. They'd be dead the moment they emerged from the reeds. There was nowhere else they could take cover here. It meant their only option was to engage the shooters. But that meant three against five, with no cover . . .

The gunfire fell silent again. Danny estimated that the five targets were twenty-five metres away. They had to do something. He slowly felt in his ops waistcoat for a fragmentation grenade. They'd run out of options. 'Frags on three,' he whispered to Spud. 'Ready?'

'Ready.'

'One ... Two ...'

The enemy fire started up again. Deafening. At least two weapons, their rounds falling even closer ...

Danny was about to shout 'three' and pull the pin on his frag when something stopped him. A new burst of gunfire. Heavy weaponry – at least a fifty-cal, by the sound of it – from a distance of maybe 100 metres. It completely dominated the relatively puny bark of the enemies' rifles, and it chugged on, relentlessly – ten seconds, fifteen seconds – before stopping as suddenly as it had begun.

When it finished, it was replaced by the sound of agonised screams. Three voices, maybe four. The unmistakeable shrieks of men who would be dead in a matter of seconds.

Danny was breathing heavily, his heart pumping fast. He looked gingerly through the sights of his rifle. Perched on the horizon, 100 metres to his eleven o'clock, just beyond the gap in the border fence, was a second pickup truck, much like the Hilux that was now no longer even smouldering. And like the Hilux it had, mounted on the back, a fifty-cal machine gun, pointing directly at them.

The pickup started moving towards them, trundling slowly. The screaming had stopped. That didn't mean all the enemy targets were dead, but they were severely weakened. 'Everyone stay down,' Danny hissed into his radio. He could see that the fifty-cal was manned by a single gunner, and while he had his suspicions about who these people were, he sure as hell didn't want them to make a mistake and start firing on the unit.

Twenty seconds passed. For the first time in what seemed like hours, the rain suddenly subsided a little. Danny could hear the low growl of the pickup's engine now. He found himself holding his breath as the vehicle drew closer. It stopped about thirty metres away. A voice called out. Male. Harsh. Danny didn't understand it.

A pause. Then Caitlin's voice came across his radio earpiece. Strained. Tense with pain. But audible. *'The girl says it's the Kurds. They're telling anyone in the vicinity to show themselves with their hands in the air, or they'll fire again.'*

Danny hesitated. This went against every instinct he had. They would be putting themselves at the mercy of people they didn't know, who had substantial firepower.

But they couldn't fight back, and if these were the Kurds they were supposed to be meeting, they didn't even want to.

'Get Naza to shout back. Tell them she's with three others, one female, two male. If we see any potential threats apart from her friends, we're going to fire on them.'

A pause. Then Naza's panicked voice drifted over the reeds towards the pickup. The male Kurdish voice barked again.

'He says OK,' Caitlin translated. *'He recognises Naza's voice.'*

Danny loosened his pistol in its holster. 'On three,' he said. 'One, two, three . . .'

He pushed himself up from the ground, one hand above his head, the other slightly lower – closer to his pistol – carefully scanning the ground between himself and the pickup.

He saw it immediately – movement in the reeds fifteen metres from his position. He went for his pistol, but Spud, three metres to Danny's left, was already there, pumping three rounds directly into the enemy target's body. The movement stopped.

The Kurd yelled something.

Caitlin's voice: *'Spud, drop your gun!'*

Spud had already done it.

They stood there, not moving. The Kurd at the machine gun shouted again. This time Naza called back. A short conversation followed. Two men emerged from the pickup. That made three guys in all. One had a mobile phone to his ear and was talking into it. He was young – early twenties – and even though it was still dark he had a pair of aviator shades propped on his forehead.

The other was older. Early fifties, maybe. He carried an assault rifle and he strode straight up to them. Scraggly goatee beard flecked with grey. Camouflage fatigues. Black and white *shemagh* round his neck. Sturdy, muddy boots. Dark, weathered skin. He looked tough and battle-hardened. 'Where's Rojan?' he asked, in a very good English accent.

Danny nodded towards the burned-out Hilux.

'You killed him?' the Kurd asked aggressively.

'He killed himself,' Danny replied. 'He insisted on driving over. We were trying to cover him.' He nodded at the dead soldier on the ground. 'These guys booby-trapped the crossing. Don't ask me why.'

The Kurd looked suspicious.

'Tell him, Naza,' Danny said. 'Tell him how brave your brother was.'

Naza looked terrible, like her eyes were burning. She spoke quickly and in Kurdish. A gabbling child. The man's face was expressionless as he listened. Danny held his breath and kept his eyes on the three Kurds in front of him, ready for any sudden sign of danger.

Naza stopped talking. There was a momentary silence. Then the Kurd lowered his assault rifle. He nodded at the unit to indicate they could lower their hands. Then he turned his attention to the dead soldier on the ground. The corpse was lying on its front. The Kurd rolled him on to his back. Danny approached. Close up, it was almost like looking in the mirror. The dead guy wore a Kevlar helmet with a boom mike attached. No NV, but an ops waistcoat over his camouflage gear. 'Special forces,' he muttered.

'Yeah,' said Spud, who was standing alongside him. 'But whose?'

The older Kurd had seen something. He bent over the body and pulled up the corpse's right sleeve. There was a tattoo on his forearm. A double-headed eagle and, surrounding it, seven red dots.

'Russian double-headed eagle,' Caitlin said. She was clutching her right arm, and blood was seeping between her fingers.

'What are those dots?' Danny asked.

'They represent drops of blood. Russian criminals use them to represent how many murders they've committed,' Caitlin said.

'This isn't some Russian inmate,' Danny said.

Caitlin shook her head. 'The habit's overflowed into the Russian military. He's a Russian soldier, and he's proud of his seven kills.'

'Spetznaz?' Spud suggested.

'Maybe,' Danny said.

'Fuck,' Spud muttered. He looked around nervously, as though half-expecting another SF force to be on the point of attack.

Danny looked towards the Russians' vehicle, parked next to the burned-out Hilux. 'What would they be doing here?'

'They've been patrolling the area ever since Turkey shot down that Russian jet,' the Kurd said. 'They know Turkish forces are crossing the border into Iraq and Syria. They want to kill as many as possible. Revenge.' He sniffed. 'You brought us weapons?'

Danny nodded, then pointed to the Hilux. 'They've gone the same way as your mate.'

A shadow crossed the Kurd's face. 'Unfortunate for you,' he said. 'Driving into IS territory is dangerous. We don't work for nothing. The deal's off.' He looked over at Naza and spoke to her in Kurdish again. Danny knew he was telling her it was time to leave.

'Wait,' Danny said.

The tough, battle-hardened Kurd turned to look at him. 'What?'

'You hate Daesh, right?'

'Of course.'

'We're going to hit them hard. And we're going to take out one of their main commanders. Trust me, we're going to get them where it hurts.'

The Kurd's eyes narrowed. He was clearly tempted. But then he shook his head. 'We have our own ways of fighting,' he said. He started to turn away from Danny. 'I recommend you get back across the river.'

'You still want weapons?'

The Kurd stopped turning. He nodded.

'We're taking out one of their camps. We'll bring you every damn gun in the place, if you get us there in one piece.'

This time the Kurd did not turn away.

'How do we trust you?'

Danny looked towards Caitlin. She was sweating badly and her face was pale. The wound was still seeping blood. 'See that injury? She got it protecting Naza.'

The Kurd considered that for a moment. Then he walked up to Naza herself. He spoke to her in Kurdish. The conversation lasted for thirty seconds, and involved a lot of nodding from the kid.

Finally, the Kurdish leader sniffed again and walked back to Danny. His body language was suddenly less aggressive. 'Every weapon?' he said.

'And every last bullet.'

The Kurd nodded. 'The place you want to get to is a day's drive. Very dangerous.'

'What's your name?' Danny asked.

'Pallav,' the older, battle-hardened man said. Danny looked him up and down.

'Do your friends speak English?' Danny indicated the other two Kurds.

Pallav shook his head. 'Only me and Naza.' He sniffed again. 'And Rojan,' he added. He looked around. 'It is getting light,' he said. 'We must only travel at night. We must find somewhere to hide during the day.'

Danny shook his head. 'No,' he said. 'We move now.'

'Mucker, they're right,' Spud said. 'We can't travel during the day.'

'We don't have a choice.' He walked over to the dead Russian soldier and prodded him with his foot. 'You know what the Russians are like. When they realise their guys have been hit, they'll be all over this place like a rash. Give it an hour, we'll have satellites, drones, the works. We need to get the hell out of this area. And anyway, our middlemen arrive at midnight. Much easier to hit them before they get inside the IS stronghold.' He turned to the Kurds. 'You know where we're going,' he said. 'Can you get us there without using any main supply routes?'

The Kurds exchanged an anxious look.

'If you want those weapons,' Danny said, 'you've got to do this my way.'

'It will be slow,' Pallav said. 'We will have to go off-road. There will be villages to avoid, maybe water we have to cross.' He looked over at the wounded Caitlin. 'And her—'

'Don't worry about her. Can you do it?'

The Kurd nodded. 'We have Daesh flags. It would be best to put them on our vehicle. That way, if Daesh see us from a distance, we have a chance of getting through.'

'No,' Danny told him. 'If the Russians are putting in surveillance, they might go for IS targets. We only put the flags out at the very last minute. If IS stop us before then, we can deal with it.'

The Kurd's eyes narrowed. 'We'll take the Russians' vehicle as well. Two vehicles are harder to hit than one.'

Danny liked the strategy. And he liked Pallav. He thought like a proper soldier. He turned to Spud. 'Get over there,' he said. 'Check it over. They probably picked the vehicle up in country, but I want to be sure there are no tracking devices on the engine block or the undercarriage. Dump all their packs out of the vehicle too.'

Spud nodded and started jogging over to the grey Hilux. Danny turned to the Kurds. 'You can help yourself to their weapons, ammo, clothes and any rations in their packs. Nothing else.'

'What about their radio equipment?' Pallav said.

'Absolutely not. It might be fitted with tracking devices. Don't take anything electrical, and tell your mate to switch his mobile phone off and remove the battery. Now get everything together. We leave in ten minutes. People might have heard the noise from that contact. We don't want to be here if they come looking.'

'I agree,' Pallav said. He turned his back on them and started giving orders to his men in Kurdish.

Danny looked at Caitlin. 'Let me see it,' he said.

She looked for a moment like she was going to argue. But then she lowered the shoulder of her camo jacket, wincing as she did so and looking down at the bare skin of her upper arm.

It was very clear where the attack dog had sunk its teeth into her flesh. There were three v-shaped punctures on the top side of her arm, and two on the underside. The skin around them was swollen and bloodied, and the wounds themselves were still oozing blood. It looked bad.

Caitlin covered it up before Danny could say anything. 'I'll bandage it as we're travelling,' she said, jutting out her chin defiantly. 'I'll give myself an antibiotic jab. It'll be fine.'

Danny glanced back across the river. He had a call to make. Allow Caitlin to stick with them, and run the risk that if the wound got infected, or deteriorated badly, she would be more of a hindrance to the operation than a help. Or force her to dig in somewhere, self-medicate the wound and wait it out until such a point that they could scoop her up and get the hell out of there.

'You need me,' Caitlin said. 'You're already undermanned.' She turned and went to retrieve her pack from next to the dead body of the attack dog. But Danny noticed that her eyes flickered in the direction of Naza too.

'Caitlin,' Danny said.

She looked at him.

'If it starts getting bad, you tell me. No heroics. Not if you want to stay on the op.'

They locked stares. 'No heroics,' Caitlin said quietly.

The two of them grabbed their soaking packs and their weapons. Ten seconds later, they were jogging towards the vehicles.

FOURTEEN

Joe woke up.

At first, he didn't know where he was. It didn't worry him. He'd been sleeping on the floor, which was hard and a bit uncomfortable. But he was warm and dry, which was more than he normally hoped for these days.

Then he remembered. The interview with the asylum official. The way she'd locked him in the room when he had told her his story. He sat up and wondered how long he had been asleep. An hour or two? He stood up, walked to the edge of the room and looked through the glass window towards the open-plan office beyond. When he'd last looked, it had been full of people. Now there were only a few. One guy, obviously a security guard, was sitting on a chair just outside the room. When he saw Joe at the window, he sat up a bit straighter, but didn't make eye contact. Joe saw that the screensaver on one of the computers had been set to tell the time in large digits. 0615. He realised he'd been asleep all night.

He was about to sit down when he saw two men striding across the office in his direction. Their eyes were fixed on the interview room. They were a mismatched pair – one very tall, with a bushy moustache and thinning hair, the other short and dumpy, with a very full head of black hair and a crumpled suit and tie. Joe could tell these were the people he'd been waiting for.

The security guard obviously had the same intuition. Either that, Joe thought, or he'd seen them before. He stood up, almost to attention, and when the tall man gave him a nod, he unlocked the door to the room. The two guys entered and closed the door behind them. During his time with Daesh, Joe had grown sensitive to the presence of weapons. He immediately noticed the bulges under these guys' jackets. He knew they were carrying.

'Good morning,' he said, as politely as he could.

The short man stepped forward and offered his hand. 'Good morning,' he said. 'Robin Galbraith. This is my colleague Owen Sharples. Very good of you to wait for us.'

Joe shook his hand and smiled. He decided it wouldn't be a good idea to point out that it wasn't really a question of waiting. He'd been imprisoned in this room all night long. Galbraith smiled back. Sharples, on the other hand, didn't. Joe had the impression that his face was rarely troubled by a smile.

'Sounds like you've been through the mill, old thing,' Galbraith said. 'Wonder if you'd like to talk about it some more.' He looked around. 'We've got somewhere more comfortable we can go. Would you like that?'

'Who are you, exactly?' Joe said. 'If you don't mind me asking?'

'You probably wouldn't mind something to eat, eh? Here . . .' He removed a chocolate bar from his jacket. 'That should tide you over. Till we get there.'

Joe accepted the chocolate bar and read the wrapper, which said 'Snickers'. He was very hungry, but experience had taught him not to gobble food down when it came his way. Much better to ration it properly. He put the chocolate bar in his pocket. 'Thank you,' he said. 'Where is this place?'

'Oh, not far, not far. Shall we go?'

The tall man, Sharples, stepped forward. He grabbed Joe by the arm and Joe understood immediately that although Galbraith's question had sounded like a polite offer, it was anything but. 'I should get that chocolate down you, old thing,' said Galbraith. 'Give you some energy. You never know – you might need it.'

He turned and walked out of the room. Joe followed, with Sharples holding his arm firmly. He thought about pointing out that the man was hurting him, but something told him that would be the wrong thing to do.

★　★　★

Regiment man Duncan Barker stood by a large Christmas tree, its fairy lights twinkling in the grey morning light, in the centre of Parliament Square. He listened to Big Ben striking. 0800 hours. Traffic crawled through the rush hour all around him. From somewhere out of sight, he could hear the ripe tones of a brass band playing Christmas carols. But the constant beeping of car horns told him that not many of the drivers were feeling the festive spirit. And Barker was pretty certain that, in their hurry to get to their destinations, none of them would be noticing anything different about Parliament Square this morning. It took a trained eye to realise that all was not well.

The most obvious sign that a security operation was under way was the lamp posts. At the base of each one was a small lock-able panel – a little door that gave access to the interior of the lamp post. These were obvious places to stash explosives. But now, every one of these panels was wrapped round with a strip of sturdy tape. It would be immediately obvious if anyone tried to tamper with them. A simple preventative measure, but an effective one.

Then there were the down-and-outs. There were at least fifteen of them, dotted around the square, their hair long, their clothes shabby and their faces dirty. Some of them sat begging on the pavement. Others staggered around with tins of Special Brew in their fists. They would be totally invisible to the average man in the street. But Duncan Barker wasn't average. He was Regiment. He'd noticed how the police were not moving the beggars on, and how the Special Brew winos – despite their supposed drunk-enness – were circling the square with a clockwork-like regularity. Because they weren't really down-and-outs – they were security service personnel, fifteen pairs of highly trained eyes keeping careful watch on the vicinity.

Barker knew for sure that none of the pedestrians entering Parliament Square from Millbank to the south would have noticed, as they passed the imposing buildings that lined the side opposite the river, that a series of four ground-floor windows were obscured from the inside by blackout blinds. They'd have no reason to suspect that the Regiment had set up a local operations room at that location, that at this moment it was a hive of urgent activity. And of course, only a trained eye would notice the slight bulge under Barker's black North Face jacket that indicated that he – like every other Regiment man currently on the streets of London – was carrying.

He looked up. Something had caught his eye, high in the towers of the Houses of Parliament. Movement. He kept his gaze fixed on the same location for ten seconds, then saw it again – a distant flash of black. Maybe it was a sniper overlooking the square. Maybe it was a member of the security services checking the tower for any sign of suspicious activity.

To his ten o'clock, taking pride of place in the square, was a statue of Winston Churchill. Barker, who liked a bit of history, couldn't help a grim smile. *Your worst nightmare, mate*, he thought to himself. *Britain's defences are down. The bad guys are already among us. It's not a question of if they hit us, it's a question of when* ...

More movement up above. Two helicopters, one hovering above Parliament Square, one above the river. The sound of their rotors was only just audible above the buzz of the traffic. Choppers were common enough in the London skyline for most people to ignore them. But these choppers didn't contain chirpy radio traffic DJs, or wealthy businessmen getting from A to B. They were military. Merlins. No doubt stuffed full of army personnel. Watching. Waiting.

It was as if there were two versions of London. The normal one, the London of busy pedestrians and impatient drivers. Of wide-eyed tourists and Christmas parties. And then there was the hidden one, the London inhabited by spooks and military personnel – men like Barker, hidden in plain sight. One version of London was carrying on with its life as though nothing was wrong. The other seemed to be holding its breath. It was not a good place to be. Barker was glad he'd warned Danny Black's missus to stay home. He wished he'd told a few more people to do the same.

He looked to his right. He could just see the top of Westminster Abbey, peeking above the smaller edifice of St Margaret's Church.

Not that Barker had known its name before he'd studied a map of this area. His mobile went. He answered it immediately. It was his Regiment-mate Andy Connor.

'Where are you?' Connor asked.

'Just up the road.'

'We need you back here.'

Duncan hung up. He turned his back on the Christmas tree and walked west, across the sluggish traffic and round behind St Margaret's Church. The impressive medieval facade of Westminster Abbey came into view. Barker hardly looked at it. He was more interested in the unmarked white van parked up in a side street to the right of the abbey with a disabled parking permit propped in the front window. He strode up to it and knocked four times on the rear door, which opened immediately. Barker climbed in. Connor was there – tall, shaved head, a couple of days' stubble, civvies – as well as two tech guys. The back of the van was decked out with an impressive array of screens and listening equipment, all manner of black boxes whose function Barker could only guess at. The tech guys had headphones and were examining the screens, which filled the back of the van with a pale electric light.

'The drones are ready,' Connor said. 'We're sending them up now.'

Barker nodded. 'Never thought we'd be doing this in a fucking church,' he said. It was common practice these days to fly cameras attached to small drones over enemy positions. It delivered important tactical information, and if they got shot down, nobody was hurt. Today, though, they had a slightly different purpose. There were parts of the abbey turrets that couldn't be reached without a scaffold. However, enemy drones could easily have delivered explosive devices to these locations under cover of night. Barker and Connor's job this morning was to assist the tech guys in sending their own camera-equipped drones up there. Automated surveillance.

All four men turned their attention to the screens. The tech guy on the right was controlling the drone with two stubby joysticks – one for the drone itself, one for its two cameras. Both cameras were on the bottom. One had a fish-eye lens that gave a 360-degree view of everything beneath the drone. The image from that camera was shown on the left-hand screen. The second was more directional, with a narrower field of view, shown on the right.

The screens showed a retreating patch of grass. From fifteen metres up, they could see lamp posts, surrounding roads and the side elevations of the abbey. From twenty-five metres, the Thames was visible on the left-hand screen. After thirty seconds, the drone was higher than the abbey's two principal towers. The tech guy was clearly very expert at controlling the device. It hovered low over one of the towers, while Barker and Connor examined the footage being beamed down into the surveillance van. They studied the imagery carefully, but there was no getting away from it: all they could see was old stonework, covered in pigeon crap, with semi-composted leaves blown into the corners. No explosive devices. No nothing.

They spent a fruitless half an hour examining the hidden rooftops of the abbey, before the tech guy controlling the drone called a halt to it. 'Battery's running low,' he said. 'We need to recharge if you want to carry on.'

Barker was about to answer when his phone rang again. He answered it immediately.

'Get back here,' said a voice at the other end. 'Both of you. Now.'

Barker hung up immediately. 'We've got to go,' he said.

A minute later, they were striding down Millbank, then into the building that housed the Regiment's temporary London ops centre. The MoD policeman guarding the main door to the room made no attempt to hide his weapon. He checked their IDs before allowing them access.

The ops centre – it was the length of three normal rooms, with a hard wooden floor and ornate plaster ceiling – was humming. Fifteen large, square tables had been set up throughout the room. Each one was a mess of laptops and comms gear. Wires and cables snaked across the floor. There were several screens against one wall, and a huge map of London, dotted with red and blue pins. There were approximately thirty men in here. Barker recognised half of them from Hereford. The rest were from the Firm. There wasn't a single guy who didn't have a grim look of concentration on his face.

'Barker, Connor, over here! Get a bloody move on.'

An older guy on the far side of the room was gesturing to them. Wallace Conlin had been a fixture around Hereford for as long as anyone could remember. As an officer, he didn't command anything like the same respect as Ray Hammond. In fact, Barker couldn't stand him. He was a self-satisfied, Eton type, much more used to giving orders than getting his hands dirty. But this ops room was his. Given the circumstances, there wasn't a man here who wouldn't obey his commands. They hurried up to him immediately. He pointed to a door at the far end of the room and led them through it. Two suits were waiting for them in the room beyond. They stood – there were no chairs in this anteroom.

'Shut the door,' Conlin said, 'and listen up. We've got a lead.' He looked at the suits. 'OK for me to brief, or do you want to do the honours?'

The suits shook their heads in unison. Conlin continued.

'This goes no further than these four walls. GCHQ have just intercepted an American intelligence wire. We think it originates from northern Iraq, but we can't be sure. You need to know that the Yanks have been holding back on intelligence sharing.'

Barker and Connor shared a look. That was unusual news. But they didn't question it.

'The Yanks seem to have a contact embedded with IS. The intelligence wire reports the name of a UK national believed to be involved in an upcoming IS operation in London.'

'Westminster Abbey?'

'Let's find out, shall we? We've got an address for him. We don't want to send the plod in mob-handed in case they screw it up, and we can't afford a song and dance anyway, in case it gets back to the Yanks. Just you two. Lift him quietly. Let's see if we can stop this thing before it happens. Your target's address is 15 Roseberry

Crescent, Walthamstow.' Conlin handed each man a small photograph. 'We lifted these from the passport office records.'

Barker looked at the picture. A nondescript Middle Eastern-looking man. Mid-twenties. Brown eyes, pockmarked face, not a looker.

'His name is Kailash McCaffrey,' Conlin said.

'Weird name,' Barker said. 'What do we know about him?'

Conlin inclined his head. 'You know everything you *need* to know, which is that I've told you to go pick him up. We've got a cell waiting for him at Paddington police station. Let's find out what this little turd knows about our Christmas Day celebrations.' He turned his back on Barker and Connor, then immediately looked over his shoulder. 'Any reason you two are still here?' he said.

In Joe's head, London looked like a postcard. Red buses. Big Ben. Tower Bridge. Buckingham Palace. He was a little bit disappointed to see none of these. Instead, from the back seat of the nondescript Honda that had taken him from Dover to the capital, he saw an ugly, concrete mishmash of roads that he knew, from a signpost, was called the Hanger Lane Gyratory. He wasn't sure how to pronounce that. The silent, moody Sharples with the over-firm grip was driving. When he indicated right off the main road, into a bleak network of three-storey, dark-grey residential blocks, Joe realised that he truly would have to wait a little longer to see the sights of central London.

'Here we are!' Galbraith said brightly as Sharples pulled up on the pavement. 'We have a safe house here.'

'Who's "we"?' Joe asked. It was the first thing he'd said all journey. 'And safe from what?'

'Somewhere we can have a nice little chat,' Galbraith said.

Sharples killed the engine. Both men got out. Joe tried to open his rear door. Locked. He flicked the locking switch. Made no difference. He realised that he'd been child-locked inside the car for the whole journey.

Galbraith opened the door from the outside. Sharples leaned in and grabbed Joe firmly by the arm again, before dragging him out of the car. Joe didn't struggle. He hadn't forgotten about the bulges under the men's jackets. He noticed an old lady with her shopping watching them from about twenty metres away. Was it Joe's imagination, or had Galbraith purposefully put himself in her line of sight so she couldn't see Joe's face, as Sharples dragged him across the road towards the main entrance of one of the residential blocks?

Galbraith unlocked the door and led them into a dark, unfurnished hallway. A flight of steps on the right-hand side led to the upper levels, but to the left was a second door, which Galbraith quickly unlocked. He stepped aside so Sharples could roughly usher Joe in, before locking them all inside again.

It was a cold flat. It smelled damp. Swirly brown carpet, peeling woodchip on all the walls. The curtains of the main room were drawn. It was very dark. The room had a small, dingy kitchenette area to one side. There was no sign of any kitchen equipment. Instead, on the side, was a rather large first aid box with a big green cross on it. Joe felt an uncomfortable pang of anxiety as he looked at it. There was a television in the corner of the room, unplugged, and an old gas fire in the hearth. Not much furniture – four hard-backed chairs, a dusty old standard lamp with a large, wonky shade, and a table tucked into the corner of the room. This was not a place that was well used.

Outside, the sun must have momentarily appeared from behind the clouds. It illuminated the curtains. Behind them, Joe saw the silhouettes of a series of window bars. The brightness disappeared again. Galbraith switched on the light. Joe suppressed another surge of anxiety. He didn't know what was happening.

'What we need,' Galbraith said, rubbing his hands together, 'is a nice cup of tea.' He walked over to the kitchenette and opened the fridge. He said, 'No milk!' without even looking inside. 'I'll just pop out and get some, shall I?' He glanced at Sharples and nodded imperceptibly. Joe knew he wasn't supposed to see the gesture. But he did. 'Won't be a tick,' he said. He left the room. Joe heard the front door to the flat slam closed. He noticed that there was no kettle in the kitchen.

'Sit down,' Sharples said, scraping one of the hard-backed chairs to the middle of the room.

Joe did as he was told. Sharples stood in front of him.

'If I had my way,' Sharples said, 'every single one of you immigrant cunts would be sent straight back to where you came from.'

Joe blinked at him. He didn't know what to say.

'So, we heard what you told that stupid woman back in Dover,' Sharples continued. 'I've heard some pathetic lies in my time, but that—'

'I wasn't lying,' Joe interrupted.

He experienced a sudden, blinding flash of light in front of his eyes, and a burst of pain to his cheek. It was only a second after it happened that he realised Sharples had hit him hard across the side of the face. He touched his cheek and looked at his fingertips. No blood. But the skin throbbed badly.

Sharples walked slowly round the chair. 'So,' he said. 'You're IS's little Internet geek, that's what you want us to believe?'

'I . . . I don't understand what that means—'

The second swipe across the face was even more brutal than the first. Joe gasped in pain.

'You realise we can send you straight back where you came from?' Sharples said. 'You think we give a flying fuck what happens to you? Carry on lying to us, that's what we'll do. The only chance you've got of staying in the UK is to give us hard intel on your terrorist buddies. Intel we can actually use.'

Joe wanted to speak. He wanted to explain that he was going to do that anyway. He wanted to tell the man that terrorists weren't his buddies. They were his enemies, and he'd do anything to compromise them. But he was too scared to speak. And too confused. He'd thought that the UK authorities would welcome him with open arms when he told them who he was and what he knew. He hadn't expected this . . .

And anyway, he could hear the main door opening again, which meant Galbraith was coming back. He sat tight. A few seconds later, the dark iron lever handle of the sitting room door angled downward, and Galbraith walked into the room. He wasn't carrying any milk. He still had that bland smile. He walked up to Joe, bent down and peered at his right cheek. 'Tch, tch,' he said. 'Nasty bruise.' He stood up straight again. 'I'm glad you two have had this little opportunity to get to know each other,' he said. 'I imagine you'd like a little while to mull everything over? We'll leave you alone, shall we?'

The two men wordlessly left the room, leaving Joe sitting, bruised and sore, on the hard-backed chair. He heard the key turn in the lock as the door shut.

Roseberry Crescent, Walthamstow was a dump.

Barker was driving. Their vehicle was a nondescript Ford Focus with a dent on the left wing. The kind of car nobody looks at twice. They drove it slowly down the road, then looped back round and gave it a second pass. No pedestrians. Kerb about a quarter occupied with parked cars. Most of the houses – drab terraces, two up, two down – had the curtains of their ground floors closed. No hint of Christmas decorations anywhere. Litter on the pavement. It was that kind of street.

There was nothing to distinguish number 15 from any other house. The door was a dull brown like all the others. It had wheelie bins out front, like all the others. As they drove past, Barker saw that a first-floor light was switched on. Did that mean someone was in? Possibly. They parked up ten metres beyond the front door. Connor stayed in the vehicle, keeping eyes on the house using the passenger wing mirror. Barker walked to the far end of the street and turned left. He wanted to see if this terrace of houses had any rear alleyways or exits. So far as he could tell, they had back gardens. But at the end of the gardens was a high brick wall. Too high to scale, and with razor wire rolled along the top. It was that kind of neighbourhood.

He walked back past the car. Connor was still there. They didn't make eye contact. But as he walked up to the door of number 15, Barker knew his mate would be watching him carefully, ready to join him at the right moment. Two broad-shouldered, burly guys at the door would look suspicious. One, you could get away with.

He knocked.

Silence.

Then footsteps approaching the door from the other side.

A scratching sound. The person on the other side was engaging the safety chain.

Fine.

The door opened a couple of inches. Barker didn't wait for a voice or even a face. He shoulder-barged the open edge of the door, putting all his weight into it. There was a cracking sound as the safety chain ripped from its fixings. The door crashed inward, against the bulk of whoever was behind it. Barker forced his way in. A musty smell of unwashed clothes hit his senses. It was a man trying to block the door. He could tell by the shouts. And as he muscled his way further in, he saw at a glance that it was Kailash McCaffrey. It was their guy.

Barker forced him face forward against the hallway wall, then yanked his right arm up behind his back, to breaking point. 'Do yourself a favour, mate, and shut the fuck up. Let's try and avoid breaking your arm, eh? Christmas spirit, and all that.'

McCaffrey was trembling. He didn't say anything.

Connor walked through the door and shut it behind him. He had his handgun drawn, and walked past Barker and McCaffrey as if they weren't even there. Barker kept his man tight against the wall, listening carefully to the sound of his mate moving through the house, checking each room to see if there was anyone else here.

'I got friends upstairs,' McCaffrey said. 'Loads of them.'

'Course you have, mate,' Barker said. 'Popular bloke like you.' He tightened McCaffrey's arm a little. His way of telling him to shut up.

Thirty seconds passed. Connor returned, replacing his weapon as he walked back down the hallway. 'Clear,' he said. 'House is empty.'

Barker leaned in so he was speaking a couple of inches from McCaffrey's ear. Very quietly. 'Here's what's going to happen. When I release your arm, you and me are going to walk out of here and into the back of our car which is waiting just outside. If you try to escape, I'll grind your pig-ugly face into the fucking pavement. Then I'll shoot you in the bollocks. Got it?'

The trembling man gave no answer. Barker tweaked the straining arm. He gasped sharply. 'Got it!'

'Awesome,' Barker said. Very slowly he released McCaffrey's arm. McCaffrey exhaled with relief. He turned and looked at the two Regiment men.

Barker knew it was coming. He could tell by the way the young man tensed his body and glanced downward in an attempt to make them think he was not paying attention. He could read the body language. He knew Connor could read it too. Guys like them, it was instinctive. So when McCaffrey raised his right leg, trying to kick Connor in the groin, Connor was more than ready for it. Barker's mate raised his right fist. Then he hit him.

It had always made Barker smile when he heard tough guys talk about right hooks and uppercuts. All that was window dressing. You want to place a proper punch, you hit your guy hard, fast and with all the force you can muster. There was nothing pretty about a punch. It was a short, sharp burst of intense, ugly violence. One step down from a bullet in the face. If you're still conscious after a punch from a guy like Andy Connor, you're doing well.

McCaffrey was not doing well. Problem was, he didn't only have Connor's punch to contend with. He was still standing right in front of the hallway wall and, as Connor's fist connected, McCaffrey's head jarred back and hit it. There was an ominous cracking sound. Barker, who'd heard a few noses go in his time, knew it wasn't that. It was something bigger. A skull, maybe. 'Shit,' he breathed, as the young man crumpled heavily to the floor. '*Shit, shit, shit . . .*'

Barker knelt down over him and felt his neck for a pulse. Nothing.

'We need medics,' he said.

He laid the young man out on his back and started to administer heavy, vigorous chest compressions. He felt the ribcage sinking a good two inches with each one. He knew there was a risk of breaking the breastbone, but that didn't matter, if it got the fucker's heart beating again.

Connor had his phone out. As he pumped, Barker could hear the ringing tone, even though the handset was pressed to his mate's ear. He pinched McCaffrey's nose and leaned over to give him a couple of rescue breaths.

'Boss, it's me, Connor,' he heard his mate say. There was a panicked edge to his voice. 'We've got a problem. You've got to get a medic here ... you've got to get a medic here *now*.'

Trouble was, Barker had been around enough dead bodies to know he was wasting his time.

It hadn't taken Joe long to come to the conclusion that he didn't want to stay in this place, with these people. They'd called it a safe house, but he didn't feel safe at all.

If he was going to do what he needed to do, he had to get away.

He wondered how long they would leave him alone. At least an hour, he thought, if they were trying to play mind games with him. He stood up and walked to the window, where he pulled back the curtains. As he'd expected, there were bars on the other side of the pane. He couldn't get out that way.

He walked into the kitchenette, where he went through the drawers. Maybe he could find a knife. The drawers were empty. So were the cupboards, apart from a few stained mugs. He felt relieved. He wasn't a violent person. He didn't really want to hurt anyone. Except one person, who wasn't here.

Joe looked around the room again. His eyes fell on the dusty standard lamp in the corner of the room. He walked up to it, his head inclined slightly. It was about as tall as Joe himself. An idea formed in his mind. He made some calculations. Voltages. Current. He believed it would work.

He unplugged the lamp. Then he removed the bulb, twisted off the top half of the housing and removed the shade. The dust made him sneeze. Inside what remained of the housing were two small brass screws. He needed something to unscrew them. He cast around the room again and his eyes settled on the first aid kit. He walked over and opened it up. Inside there were sterile bandages, plasters, antiseptic wipes. He stuffed them all in his pocket. Then he found what he was really looking for: a pair of tweezers, and a small pair of scissors for cutting bandages.

It was a moment's work to unscrew the two brass screws and remove the cable from inside the pole of the lamp. Joe was left with a length of cable about two metres long, a plug at one end and two exposed wires at the other. He took it to the other side of the room, and plugged it into the socket nearest the door, taking care not to flick the switch to the 'on' position.

Problem. With the cable fully stretched out, he was still more than a metre from the doorway. He needed to be closer, if he was to get the effect he wanted.

He took the first aid scissors over to the TV and snipped the power cable as close to the unit as possible. He used the tweezers to remove the plug, then carried it over to the new cable. He used the sharp edge of the scissors to strip away the wire at the cut end of the cable. He connected the two cables by twisting together the bare wires at either end. Now he had one cable, long enough to stretch from the plug to the metal handle of the door. He opened up one of the strips of sterile bandage, and used it to wrap the free end of the cable around the door handle, ensuring that the bare wires were in contact with the metal.

He brought one of the hard-backed chairs closer to the door. Then he crouched down by the plug socket, his finger on the switch, and waited.

Joe understood what the men were doing. One of them was being friendly, the other unfriendly. They were trying to confuse him. The more confused he was, the more he would trip up over any lies he was telling them. But their strategy told him something else. They were likely to join him in the room one by one. Alone. Which made Joe's job a little easier.

And if they didn't? At least he would have tried. After everything he'd been through, he was no longer the kind of kid who allowed people to slap him around.

Joe had grown used to measuring the passage of time in his head. All those hours spent stowed away in the backs of trucks. So he knew it was almost exactly thirty minutes later that he heard the footsteps approaching the door.

He held his breath, one finger on the plug switch, the other on the lever door handle.

He heard a key in the lock. Then he saw the handle move.

He flicked the switch.

There was no sound. At first, Joe thought his set-up hadn't worked. But after a couple of seconds, there was a thump in the corridor. The light in the room flickered and faded as he expected it would. He'd blown the fuse board. Jumping to his feet, he grabbed the chair he'd placed near the door and quickly opened the door, holding the chair, legs outward, in case either of the guys tried to rush him.

He needn't have worried. Galbraith was there. He was on the floor, his black hair as crumpled as his suit and tie. The thumping sound must have been him falling. He was clutching his podgy right hand. His eyes were open, but he was clearly dazed. He seemed to be struggling for breath. Joe put the chair down, then hurried up to Galbraith. He ripped his jacket open to reveal the gun in its holster, which he grabbed. Galbraith barely seemed to know what was happening.

He heard shouting from a room off the corridor towards the main entrance. Sharples. 'What the hell's going on? Who turned the fucking lights out?'

Clutching the handgun, Joe felt for Galbraith's wallet. He hastily pulled out a few notes, then ran past the door. He heard a lavatory flushing, and knew what Sharples must have been doing. He'd be out any second. Joe kept moving towards the main door. He reached it.

'Galbraith? What the hell's happening?'

Joe looked over his shoulder. The bathroom door was opening. He fumbled at the latch of the main door. His hands were sweating and he couldn't make it work.

'What the . . .'

He glanced over his shoulder again. Sharples looked up from Galbraith towards Joe. His right hand was moving towards his gun . . .

Joe knew his best chance of getting out of here was to raise the weapon he'd stolen from Galbraith. But somehow, he couldn't. His sweaty hand, still slipping on the latch, got the door open. He slipped breathlessly outside. He ran across the hallway to the main entrance of the residential block. Although he was pumping his legs hard, he seemed to move very slowly. By the time he reached the entrance, he could see Sharples' reflection in the door glass, running out of the apartment, ten metres behind him.

Joe slammed the door open and burst out of the block and into the street. Then he ran. Harder, faster than he'd ever run before. He didn't look back. He didn't need to. He knew Sharples would be following. He'd either catch Joe, or he wouldn't. Joe kept Galbraith's gun hidden under his jumper. He prayed it wouldn't go off.

The main road. Traffic flew by in either direction. Joe hesitated at the kerbside only momentarily, before sprinting across the road. There was a cacophony of car horns, but he made it to the other side, took a left and continued running. Only then did he look back.

Sharples was still on the far side of the road. His lanky frame was leaning over slightly, clearly out of breath. His eyes were tracking Joe. But he wasn't following.

Joe looked straight ahead. He continued to run.

FIFTEEN

Danny was driving. His face prickled with sweat. His head was wrapped in a black and white *shemagh*. It was moist inside from the condensation of his breath. Spud and Caitlin were dressed the same. They hadn't seen any locals yet, but if they did, their white skin would make them stick out like a turd in a swimming pool. So they had covered it.

The terrain was hard going. Their way was strewn with boulders and bushes. Twice they'd had to force their vehicles across shallow waterways, and throughout the morning they'd had to slowly manoeuvre the vehicles up and over stony hillsides, where the ground slipped away beneath them if they attempted anything other than a dead crawl. Occasionally, as they crested a hill, they would see, somewhere off to the east and many tens of miles in the distance, dark smoke billowing up into the otherwise clear blue sky. The oilfields of northern Iraq. Their view of the smoke would disappear as quickly as it had come when their path took them back down into the desolate valleys of the Kurds' back route. Danny knew, from his constant monitoring of the position of the sun, that they were heading relentlessly south.

Now it was mid-afternoon. The air reeked with the stench of goat dung. In the distance, Danny could see a meagre flock of goats on a parched hillside. He knew they ran a risk of being spotted by a goatherd. But Spud, who was in the passenger seat and staring hard at the ridge lines of the hills, was not looking for goatherds. Their little convoy was an easy target, and the hills provided good cover for potential shooters. Danny was as tense as if they were driving through a minefield.

'This is fucking madness,' Spud said for about the fifth time that day. 'Russians, Iraqis, IS, and we're moving cross-country in broad daylight.' He was flapping badly. Danny didn't fully blame him. He too was barely keeping a lid on his tension. You don't eliminate a Spetznaz crew in the field and not expect there to be some comeback. And moving during the day was a serious breach of SOPs. Every time they turned a corner, he half-expected to be driving straight into a contact. But so far, nothing . . .

They were travelling in the stolen grey Russian Hilux, along with Naza. She'd joined them without being told, and without asking. Now she sat in the back with Caitlin. The young girl was obviously numb from the death of her brother, and she'd found someone to look up to. Caitlin had worked that to her advantage. She was as quiet as the girl, though. Occasionally, she glanced down at her, and Danny saw conflict in her eyes. She might be prepared to drag the kid into a battle zone, but that didn't mean she had to like it.

Moreover, Danny sensed that the wound on Caitlin's arm was giving her trouble. He had watched in the rear-view mirror as she had removed her ops waistcoat and peeled back the sleeve of her camouflage jacket to reveal the bite wound on her upper arm. She had carefully swabbed the bite with antiseptic wipes, which soaked up the blood like a sponge. She had chucked them out of the window when she was done with them. Her face impassive, she had then bound the torn skin with Steri-Strips, before binding the whole upper arm in a fresh white bandage. Finally, she had removed an antibiotic jab from her med pack and injected it into the skin just above the wound. She winced a lot as she treated herself. And Danny observed that Naza was watching her with rapt attention. Like a kid watching her big sister.

The other Kurds were in their own vehicle. Pallav was driving, his mate with the shades was in the passenger seat and the third guy was manning the gun. He too had his whole head covered in a black and white *shemagh*. The three Kurds had said it would be slow going. They were right. Since leaving the chaos of the border crossing, Danny's speedometer hadn't edged above 20. He was following their vehicle at a distance of twenty metres, but half the time they weren't even on actual tracks.

'This is too slow,' Caitlin said. 'We'll never make it by nightfall.'

Danny just kept his eyes on the rough terrain ahead.

'Stop,' Spud said suddenly. Danny hit the brakes. Spud peered towards the hill line to their right. 'Nothing,' he muttered. And then: 'This is fucking madness. How do we know these Kurds are taking us the right way?'

'We're still moving south,' Danny said as he moved off again. 'We're heading in the right direction.'

'Yeah, but how long's it going to take us?'

They fell silent again. Danny found himself repeatedly going over their objectives in his head. Approach the IS stronghold. Get eyes on and put in surveillance. Wait for the oil middlemen to arrive at midnight. Work out a strategy to take them out. Then storm the stronghold and lift the IS commander Dhul Faqar. Find out what the fucker knew about the hit on London. And then get the hell out of Dodge.

A long evening's work, even by Regiment standards.

He had to hand it to the Kurds. Their back route was exactly that. They avoided all villages and populations. They only saw their first person at 1630 hours as they were trundling along a rough, dirty path. Sure enough, it was an old guy in dirty grey robes, surrounded by goats, a wooden staff in his hands. He had very dark skin, and a deeply lined, even gnarled face. His piercing blue eyes followed them closely as they passed.

'Should we slot him?' Spud said.

'No. With a bit of luck he'll just assume we're IS. But if we start leaving a trail of dead bodies, someone might take an interest.'

Spud sniffed. 'We should start displaying the IS flags now,' he said. 'We can't be far off.' He frowned. 'But the Russians ...' he reminded himself.

Maybe he was right. Danny waited until they'd left the goat-herd in the distance, then he double flashed his headlamps and came to a halt. The Kurds' Hilux trundled on for a further ten metres, then stopped. Danny and Spud exited their vehicle and walked up to the Kurds. 'How far?' he said.

Pallav looked in the direction they were travelling, then held up two weather-beaten fingers. 'Two kilometres,' he said. 'Uphill. From there, you will be able to see the place.'

'Then we take it from here on foot.'

'A little further by car,' the Kurd countered. 'There is a track that will take you to the main highway if you need it.'

Danny and Spud exchanged a look, nodded, then returned to their vehicle.

They reached the track, which bore to the left, ten minutes later. Danny didn't like it. There was a cliff face to their left, but open ground on the other three sides. Nowhere to hide the vehicles.

They parked up alongside each other and congregated around the pickups. 'Me and Spud are going to do a recce on the stronghold,' Danny said. 'The rest of you stay here, defend the vehicles.' He caught a sharp flash from what was visible of Caitlin's eyes behind her *shemagh*, but she made no comment. Pallav and his mate with the sunglasses instantly moved into defensive positions at either end of the convoy – down on one knee, weapons engaged, pointing either way down the rough path. The guy at the machine gun spun it round on his tripod so he had his back to the cliff face and was covering the remainder of the open ground. Danny was impressed. These guys knew what they were doing. With Caitlin alongside them, they were a strong force. He felt confident that they had his back.

Danny and Spud jogged straight up the hill. It took them five minutes to reach the brow, where they hit the ground and crawled forward. Danny removed his scope and carefully surveyed the terrain ahead.

They were looking out on to a wide, flat basin. The hill was a good hundred metres above it. The level terrain stretched at least six or seven klicks in every other direction. To their nine o'clock was a long, straight supply route. Beyond that, on the horizon, he could make out the smoke curling up into the sky from another oilfield. The sky itself was filled with rolling, boiling clouds. Rain was on its way.

A much narrower road came off the main supply route at right angles. It extended horizontally in front of them, three klicks distant, until it reached a perimeter fence to their two o'clock. The fence was roughly semicircular. Both ends terminated at the edge of a large body of water: the reservoir they had already identified on the satellite mapping. In the centre of the area delineated by the fence and the water's edge was a large compound of squat, whitewashed, single-storey buildings. Dull and functional. Decades old. Like a tiny desert hamlet of plain, squat structures. They looked a bit out of place there, stuck in the middle of the plain. Danny had the impression that they had once been some kind of water utility. It struck him as odd that an IS kingpin would want to hole himself up here. But then he realised that with that high fence and the open ground across the plain, it was a decent defensive position.

Danny counted six individual rectangular buildings. They were arranged in an L-shape at the water's edge, the short base of the L lying closest to Danny and Spud, its long stem stretching away from them. In his head, Danny numbered the buildings from the furthest to the closest, moving left to right: blocks 1 to 6. He tried to identify which one was most likely to house their target, Dhul Faqar. He immediately settled on block 3. It was the largest, and was situated in the middle of the L's stem. That put it closest to the water's edge, but also meant it was the best protected from the road. If Danny wanted comfort and security, he would definitely choose that position.

Between the L and the water's edge was an open area. Two observation towers, like something from a concentration camp, stood about twenty metres apart by the water's edge. Black-clad figures were milling around the open ground. Outside of the L, there was at least 200 metres of open ground surrounding the buildings and the perimeter fence. The open ground was littered with the burned-out chassis of vehicles, some of them quite large. By the part of the perimeter that faced the main supply route, there were three old cherry picker trucks, set about ten metres apart from each other. Their cranes were extended. Each one had a corpse hanging from it by a rope. They were clearly intended as a warning to keep away. Danny reckoned they were doing their job well.

Danny could also see that there were plenty of undamaged vehicles dotted around the compound. Hilux trucks mostly, like the ones the unit was using. Seven that he could see, perhaps more that were obscured by the buildings. They were a good indication that the compound was heavily occupied.

'This is *not* a three-man job,' he heard Spud whisper.

'It is now,' Danny said. He sniffed. 'When we get back, keep an eye on Caitlin. That wound on her arm is worse than she's letting on. If she's going downhill, we need to know.'

'Roger that.'

Danny panned left again, along the line of the road leading to the compound. He picked out two vehicle checkpoints. One was at the point where the road met the perimeter fence. The second was about 500 metres from the main supply route. Each checkpoint consisted of a small building constructed from unrendered concrete blocks. Probably just a single room, though Danny couldn't be sure about that. Vehicles at each. Distance between them: approximately 300 metres.

'Someone's arriving,' Spud breathed.

Danny panned left. A vehicle had turned off the main supply route and was driving towards the first checkpoint. A large four-by-four, in good nick so far as Danny could tell. Someone was arriving who had money, or influence, or both. As it drew closer, Danny focussed in on the checkpoint. Two guys had emerged. Black clothes. Rifles, probably AK-47s, though hard to tell from this distance. The car came to a halt. One of the checkpoint guards approached the driver's window. Danny quickly panned right to the second checkpoint. It didn't look like anyone had emerged. He said as much to Spud. 'Fucking muppets,' Spud breathed. He sounded almost insulted that their SOPs should be lackadaisical. But it was fine by Danny. It gave them options.

Danny considered those options. They could approach covertly. Breach the perimeter fence under cover of night and advance on the compound by foot. It was a possibility, but he didn't like it. They had two objectives – to eliminate the oil middlemen arriving at 0000 hours, and to lift Dhul Faqar. It would be far better to nail the middlemen *before* they got through the checkpoints and entered the compound, because if things went noisy inside the perimeter fence, it would be ten times more difficult to get their hands on Dhul Faqar. And in any case, it would mean crossing open ground that was most likely landmined to hell, in order even to get to the perimeter.

Option two: be more brazen about it. Approach by road. If they were to do that, they needed to be on top of the guards' procedures. As the vehicle cleared the first checkpoint, Danny panned round to the second one. Two guys were emerging from the hut at the perimeter fence. It looked to Danny like someone at the first checkpoint had made a call to advise them that someone was arriving. The vehicle reached checkpoint two. A brief conversation, and it was allowed to pass into the fenced-off area of the compound.

Two-stage security. If the guards at the first checkpoint became suspicious at a new arrival, they could let them through, then attack from behind as the guards at the second checkpoint attacked from the front. It would work well, if the guards were on top of their game. But their visual communication was poor. And that was a weakness Danny could exploit.

He lowered his scope. 'Do you think the guards can see what's happening at each other's checkpoint?' he asked Spud.

'At night?' Spud said. Then he pointed towards the boiling clouds over the plain. 'And in the rain? No. They'll be relying on radio contact. Or mobile phones.'

Danny agreed. 'So if we arrive just before midnight pretending to be the middlemen, we could take out the guards at the first checkpoint, leave a couple of us there to usher the real middlemen through, take out the guards at the second checkpoint, then attack the middlemen from front and behind. If we do it with suppressed weapons, we've got a good chance of taking out the targets and breaching the perimeter without alerting anyone in the compound. Then we can get the Kurds to make a diversion while we advance on the compound itself.'

'Could work,' Spud said. 'So long as the Kurds don't fuck it up. You think they're up to it?'

'The three guys know what they're doing. They took out a Spetznaz unit, remember? Naza's the weak link, but as long as she keeps her head down ...' He checked the time. 1715 hours. At the speed they were travelling, Danny estimated it would take them at least four hours to make it down on to the main supply route – especially as they were going to lose the light in about forty-five minutes. Their plan depended on timing. If it was to work, they needed to get moving.

Five minutes later, they had rejoined the others. Danny explained his plan for checkpoints in more detail. 'But we need to get down to the main supply route before midnight,' he told Pallav. 'Is that possible?'

The Kurd nodded. 'But the closer we get to it, the more chance of Daesh patrols. We should put our flags out now.'

Danny gave it a moment's thought. He looked around, and up. There had been no evidence of Russian drones since they'd left the dead soldiers by the border. The cloud cover was thick, so aerial photography would be difficult, even if the Russians had dared to breach Iraqi airspace. Now it was a question of priorities. A couple of black flags on their vehicles wouldn't get them past a one-on-one with any IS militants. But it might fool them if the convoy was being watched from a distance. And they would certainly help with their approach to the stronghold.

'Let's do it,' Danny said.

Pallav and the two other Kurds began to fix an IS flag to the back of the cab of each Hilux. The sour expression on Naza's face told Danny everything he needed to know about what she thought of those flags. Caitlin spoke quietly to her as the men carried out the job, one arm gently on her shoulder. Danny took paper and pencil from his pack and sketched the layout of the compound from memory, marking each building with the number he had assigned to it. He approached Caitlin and Spud and explained his rationale for believing that Dhul Faqar was most likely to be in building 3.

'Makes sense,' Spud said. 'But we've got to get through the perimeter first.' They re-entered their vehicles and continued along the rough path that forked off to the left.

The going was even slower than before. They found themselves driving down a steep, winding gradient, their brakes squeaking noisily. As the light failed, it became even more difficult to see the track. Danny was totally reliant on following the Kurds' vehicle. Nobody spoke. Spud and Caitlin were scanning the surrounding countryside from their seats. A tense, expectant silence. Danny kept glancing at Caitlin in the rear-view mirror. He could only dimly see her eyes, but he had a nasty feeling that they were glazing over.

2300 hours. The going had been slower than Danny had anticipated. Now, imperceptibly, the track had grown a little broader. There were furrows in it — tyre marks from other vehicles. As the Hilux edged round a bend in the track, and over a substantial bump, Danny caught a brief glimpse of the highway. It was a couple of hundred metres distant, and a little busier than he'd expected, especially in the southbound direction that they would need to take.

The Kurds stopped. Danny too. They congregated between the two vehicles. 'We are twenty minutes from the main road,' Pallav said. 'Once we are on it, it is very dangerous to stop. We should swap over vehicles now.'

Danny nodded, and handed over the keys to the vehicle he'd been driving. He and Spud loosened their Sigs and fitted suppressors to their rifles and handguns. Caitlin did the same. Danny took a GPS reading. The Kurds knew the terrain well, but in the event that the unit had to extract from Dhul Faqar's compound cross-country, they would need a precise method of returning to this spot. 'If and when we need to RV,' he said, 'this is our location. You understand "RV"?'

Pallav nodded. 'I'm trusting you to bring us weapons.'

'You'll have more weapons than you know what to do with.'

Pallav sneered. 'Oh, I'll know what to do with them,' he said.

'Is everyone clear about their roles when we approach the checkpoints?' Danny said as he and Spud fitted their earpieces.

Nods all round. Danny could sense the tension in the air. He looked up. Dark clouds were scudding across the moon. The rain was coming, any minute. That suited them well, as it would cover their approach and camouflage the sound of their suppressed weapons. He and Spud climbed into the back of the Kurds' Hilux. Caitlin took Spud's place in the passenger seat of the vehicle Danny had been driving. They lay on their fronts, one at either edge of the pickup, facing towards the rear of the vehicle. They covered themselves with some dirty old brown sack material that was lying at the foot of the fifty-cal. Danny knew that they would be invisible at a cursory glance. A more detailed examination would uncover them, of course. But by then, if everything went as it should, it wouldn't matter . . .

The vehicle moved off again, with Danny lying in the darkness. Lying on his front, he felt the bumps in the rough track magnified tenfold. After fifteen minutes, the rains came. Heavy. Noisy. Almost immediately the brown sacking was soaked, and so was Danny. He put it from his mind. If he could put up with it on the training fields of Brecon, he could put up with it here. And he'd have to, because right then the road became smooth. He felt the Hilux turning right, then accelerating.

They were advancing to contact.

From the noise of the Hilux's engine, Danny estimated their speed at 70 kph. That gave them just under three minutes to reach the narrower road that came off the main supply route at right angles towards the IS compound. Danny counted down the seconds in his head. Bang on schedule, he felt the vehicle slow down, then turn right.

The road became less smooth again. Distance to the first check-point, 500 metres. About a minute. He gingerly lifted the edge of the brown sacking camouflage. The second Hilux was tailing them closely. Its headlamps blinded him and he cursed himself for looking. Caitlin had obviously seen him. Her voice came across his earpiece. Muffled, because her *shemagh* covered her mouth-piece. '*Two hundred metres to go. Stay covered.*'

Danny unlocked his Sig. The Hilux trundled on.

It was slowing down.

'*Fifty metres,*' said Caitlin. '*You can lose the camo.*'

Danny shuffled off the brown sacking. He half-closed his eyes and avoided direct visual contact with the other pickup's head-lamps. He wormed his soaking body a little further to the back of the Hilux, and was aware of Spud doing the same. He reckoned they were doing no more than 10 kph now.

A moment later, when the Hilux had almost reached a halt, he heard Caitlin's voice again: '*Two hostiles approaching your vehicle. One more standing in the entrance of the checkpoint hut.*' She sounded sharp. '*Make contact when I give the word.*'

A pause. The vehicle was stationary.

'*Now,*' snapped Caitlin.

There wasn't a moment's hesitation. Danny leaned round the back corner of the Hilux and aimed his weapon along the right wing of the vehicle. He knew that Spud would be doing exactly the same thing down the left wing. Sure enough, he saw a drenched but heavily armed guard approaching the driver's door, front on to Danny's line of fire, approximately one metre from the vehicle. Danny didn't have time to ascertain whether the target had seen him or not. It didn't matter either way. He fired three rounds in quick succession, directly at the target's chest. There were three dull thuds from the suppressed Sig – almost entirely camouflaged by the noise of the pelting rain – and a faint, flat, ripping sound as the rounds tore into the target's breastbone. At the same time, Danny heard three equivalent rounds from the opposite side of the vehicle: Spud taking care of his guy.

The target slumped to the ground. Danny threw himself from the vehicle. He caught movement in his peripheral vision as he hit the ground. It was Caitlin. She had jumped from her vehicle and was advancing on the concrete hut, the butt of her suppressed rifle dug hard into her shoulder. Danny braced himself for the sound of gunfire as he advanced to the front of the Hilux, using its chassis as cover. It didn't come. Good. The next ten minutes would be a lot more straightforward if they could keep their third target alive, for a little while at least.

He peered round from the front of the Hilux towards the concrete hut. If there had been someone standing at the entrance, there no longer was. And there was no sign of Caitlin. Naza, however, was striding towards the entrance. 'Stay where you are!' Danny hissed at her. She stopped in her tracks. Still clutching his handgun, Danny emerged from the protection of the Hilux and strode towards the entrance of the hut, aware that Spud was on one knee on the other side of the vehicle, covering him.

Danny raised his weapon, holding it steady with two hands. He scanned towards the second checkpoint and the compound beyond, looking for evidence that their approach had alerted anyone. He saw none, so he entered the hut.

It was bare. There was a small gas lamp in one corner, and a couple of chairs, one of which was on its side. The rain hammered noisily on the corrugated iron roof. In the centre of the room was a young man dressed in standard IS garb. He was on his knees. His eyes bulged. Caitlin stood behind him, the barrel of her rifle resting against the back of his head.

Danny looked back outside. He gestured at Naza to come in out of the rain, then pointed at the body of the guard Spud had nailed, which was lying a metre from the Hilux. 'Bring them both in,' Danny said.

Spud grabbed the corpse by its ankles. As he dragged it through the pouring rain towards the hut, Danny gestured to Pallav, who was still at the wheel of the Hilux, to join them inside the hut. Then he got back in out of the rain.

The IS guard was clearly terrified. He couldn't take his eyes off the corpse as Spud dragged it in, followed by Pallav. Spud left to get the other corpse.

'Translate for me,' Danny said. 'Tell this guy that if he does as he's told, he'll live. But I'm going to show what will happen to him if he doesn't.'

As Pallav translated, Danny removed a knife from his ops waist-coat. He needed to shock this guy into obedience. Their strategy depended on it. He leaned over the corpse and forced its mouth open. It was still warm and malleable. He forced the tip of his knife into the open mouth and, with several quick slashes, cut out the tongue. It didn't bleed too badly – more of a slow ooze – but the tongue itself was still pink and wet. He threw it towards the guard, who took one look at it lying on the floor in front of him before bending over and retching violently. Spud returned with the second corpse, and dumped it next to the first.

Danny wiped his bloody fingers on his clothes, then turned to Pallav.

'Ask him how many guards there are at the next checkpoint.'

Pallav asked the question. The answer came immediately. 'Three.'

'And how many inside the compound, including Dhul Faqar?'

'Seventeen,' Pallav said, having asked the question.

'Ask him where the keys to his vehicle are.'

'In the ignition,' Pallav translated.

'Tell him to get his mobile phone out. He's to send a text to the guys at the next checkpoint to say that some locals have brought them gifts for the guys in the compound. He's driving down to see them in five minutes to deliver them. Check it before it goes.'

Pallav nodded and started speaking in Arabic to the IS guy in quick, urgent tones. The guard nodded fervently, as he under-stood what was being explained to him, his eyes flickering frequently down to the disembodied tongue. He patted himself down and pulled out his mobile phone from his pocket. With trembling hands, he typed a message, which he showed to Pallav. Pallav nodded, and the guard hit send.

One of the other Kurds appeared in the doorway. He said a few short words, which Pallav translated. 'Someone's coming.'

Danny looked at Caitlin. She still had her weapon pointed at the IS guard's head. He nodded briefly. Without hesitation, she squeezed the trigger. There was another dull, suppressed thud. A tiny explosion of blood, bone and brain matter, but by the time the guard had slumped to the floor, Danny had turned and was heading towards the exit. He looked out in the direction of the main supply route. Four sets of headlamps, distorted and hazy through the rain, had turned off on to the smaller road and were moving towards them.

'Is it them?' Spud said from just behind him. 'The middlemen?'

Danny checked the time. 2350 hours. He felt a crunch of urgency in his gut. Either they were ten minutes early, or it was someone else. Either way, they couldn't delay. He swore under his breath. He'd wanted at least some of them to get dressed in the black gear of the IS guards. Now they wouldn't have time.

'Caitlin, Naza, come with us. If they see women at the check-point they'll get suspicious. Pallav, you know what to do?'

Pallav nodded.

'Do what you can to keep everything quiet. There's no sign that anyone in the compound knows what's happening. We need to keep it that way.'

The three unit members strode out with Naza. They moved directly to the IS guards' pickup. It had Arabic writing painted on the side – some kind of IS bullshit, no doubt. But that was good. It meant the guards at the second checkpoint would recognise it easily as it approached. They wouldn't get suspicious until it was too late. Danny got behind the wheel, rested his Sig on his lap and wrapped his *shemagh* round his head. Spud took the passenger seat. The women went in the back. Danny knocked the vehicle into reverse as the others obscured their faces with their *shemaghs*. Then they manoeuvred on to the road and sped forward through the first checkpoint.

He looked in the rear-view mirror. The darkness and the rain made it difficult to judge distances, but he reckoned the approaching convoy was 350 metres from the first checkpoint. He increased his speed a little to 40 kph. 'Twenty seconds to contact,' he said.

There were two clicks from beside him and behind him as Spud and Caitlin prepared their weapons.

'Naza, get down. Stay down, whatever happens.'

'I'm not—'

'*Do it!*' Caitlin barked.

Another rear-view mirror check. Naza was crouching down behind Spud's seat. The convoy was 300 metres from the first checkpoint. Up ahead, a single figure had emerged from the second checkpoint hut. Danny could make out that his weapon was slung over his back. He clearly wasn't suspicious.

Ten seconds to contact. Danny wound down his window, slowing down at the same time.

The vehicle came to a halt. The figure was standing right in front of them. Ten metres from the vehicle. He was squinting, clearly blinded by the vehicle's headlamps. It meant he couldn't see who was inside.

'I'll take him,' Danny said. 'As soon as he's down, we clear the concrete hut.'

He didn't wait for a response. With the headlamps still glaring, he opened the side door. He stepped out into the rain, his hand-gun pointing through the open window.

Two dull thuds. Barely audible over the rain. The guard collapsed. In the same instant that he fell, Spud and Caitlin opened their doors in unison. Danny was already advancing on the open door of the hut. He could sense Caitlin just over his left shoulder.

A figure appeared in the doorway. He probably never even saw the advancing unit. Danny put him down with a single headshot. If the guard at the first checkpoint was to be believed, that meant there was one more target left. They needed to put him down before he had the opportunity to raise the alarm.

Distance to the entrance: five metres. Caitlin drew up alongside him. Both of them had their weapons pointing directly in front of them. As they surged forward, side by side, they alternated rounds, every three seconds, effectively covering the way ahead. At the threshold of the hut, they stepped over the bleeding body of the second guard.

Danny saw his remaining colleague immediately. He was crouched down in the far right-hand corner of the dark hut, the pale glow of a mobile phone in his hand illuminating his frightened face, as he desperately tried to key in a number.

Half a second later, two rounds slammed into his body – one from Danny, one from Caitlin.

Danny rushed forward to check the mobile that had fallen from the dead man's hand. A quick glance told him he hadn't managed to make the call. Which meant he hadn't managed to raise the alarm. The unit's approach on the compound was still covert.

Spud entered. He had the body of the first guard slung over his shoulder. He dumped it on the floor. 'The convoy's come through the first checkpoint,' he said. 'The Kurds are following it. We've got less than a minute.'

Danny started pulling the body in the doorway back into the concrete hut. 'There are three enemy vehicles in the convoy,' he said. 'When they come to a halt, I'll deal with the first, Caitlin with the second, Spud with the third. They'll be sandwiched between our vehicle and the Kurds. Take out the drivers first in case they try to get the vehicles off the road. Then deal with the others.' Danny reloaded his Sig as he spoke. They didn't know how many targets there were in each vehicle. He needed a full clip.

He headed back to the doorway and looked out. The convoy was much closer. Seventy-five metres max. He checked that his *shemagh* was still properly wrapped round his head. When the convoy was thirty metres out, he gave the instruction. 'Go.'

The three members of the unit stepped outside. They walked with a brisk confidence. If the Kurds at the first checkpoint had done their job, nobody in the convoy would know they were driving into a trap. Danny, Spud and Caitlin stood in the road, a metre apart from each other, blocking the way. The air was thick with rain, and the approaching headlamps elongated their shadows behind them. Danny hid his handgun behind the rifle slung across his chest. He only wanted to reveal it when the time came to use it.

The convoy came to a halt. The headlamps burned hard. Nobody emerged from the vehicles. Danny noted that the car in front was a Mercedes. Black. A rich guy's car.

'Go,' he said.

They moved swiftly. Danny waited a few seconds until Spud and Caitlin were alongside the drivers' windows of their vehicles. Through the rain-streaked panes of the Merc he saw the shadows of four passengers – two in the front, two in the back. He rapped three times, hard, on the driver's window.

A pause.

Then the window slid down.

Danny didn't even look at the face of the guy he was about to nail. He simply thrust his handgun in through the open window, up against the driver's head, and squeezed the trigger. There was an immediate spatter of blood, not only over his gun hand but also against the inside of the windscreen. The driver slumped heavily towards the passenger in the front seat. Danny leaned a little lower to get line of sight. It all happened so quickly, the passenger didn't even seem to know what was occurring. He looked towards Danny with an almost comically bemused expression. Middle Eastern. Grey suit. Tie. A fraction of a second later, he was slumped in his seat just like the driver, his face a bleeding mess.

The car started to shake. Panic from the rear passengers as they tried to get the hell out. Danny took a couple of paces along the car so he was alongside the rear passenger door. He fired at the window. It shattered. Shards fell to the ground. He aimed his weapon at the person sitting by it, then hesitated for a moment. It was a woman. He hadn't expected that. She wore a richly embroidered headscarf and heavy make-up. He could tell she was about to scream, and he couldn't risk the noise alerting anyone in the compound. So he didn't hesitate any more. He made the kill with a single shot to the head. The woman slumped forward, her embroidered headscarf blood-spattered. And no scream.

One more guy to go on the other side of the back seat. He was leaving the vehicle. The door on the far side was opening, a figure emerging. In his panic, he didn't even have the sense to keep low as he exited the vehicle. His head was visible above the line of the Mercedes. Danny raised his Sig relentlessly and fired a fifth round. It flew over the top of the Merc and blasted a chunk from the target's skull.

Danny was already looking back towards the others. Caitlin appeared to have killed everyone in the second vehicle. But one of the guys in the third car – Spud's – had escaped from the back seat. He was sprinting from the vehicle. Danny raised his weapon, getting ready to take a shot. No need. Pallav had jumped out from his pickup behind the convoy. He chased the guy for a few seconds, then grabbed him round the neck with one strong arm. They were out of the main beam of the headlamps, but there was enough residual light for Danny to see what happened next. The target was struggling and screaming. The screams were quickly cut short as Pallav brought a knife to the guy's throat. He didn't slice. He simply pulled the broad edge of the blade hard into the target's Adam's apple. The screaming stopped immediately. There was a catastrophic fountain of blood, which subsided after a second and merged with the rain as it drained down the target's soaked business suit. Pallav let him fall.

Objective one achieved: the middlemen were dead.

A sinister, hushed hum filled the air – the sound of the convoy's engines ticking over, coupled with the rain hammering on the car roofs. Caitlin was jogging over to the Hilux. Danny knew she was going to grab Naza and deliver her back to the Kurds. Danny and Spud strode up to Pallav, who was still standing over the butchered corpse of the guy he'd killed. 'You know what to do?' he said.

Pallav nodded. 'We'll give you three minutes to get up to the compound. Then we'll start firing on it to draw them out.'

'Don't fire for more than a minute or so. It's just a diversion, but they'll probably send guys out to chase you. Give yourself the chance to get away in one piece.'

Pallav gave a rare grin, then offered Danny his hand. 'Kill some more Daesh for me?'

'I'll make a point of it.'

Caitlin joined them. She was holding Naza by one arm. Naza was struggling a little. 'I want to stay with you,' she whispered, looking up at Caitlin.

Caitlin thrust the girl towards Pallav. 'Make sure she stays safe,' she said. It sounded like a threat.

Pallav nodded. He grabbed Naza. 'Good luck,' he said, before dragging the girl back towards the Hilux. 'I think you're going to need it.' He thrust her into the back seat, then climbed up to man the fifty-cal as one of his men took the wheel. 'We will meet you at your RV point off the main supply route. If you are not there by dawn, we assume you're dead and we—'

'Quiet,' Danny interrupted him. He cocked his head. He could hear barking in the distance.

'Dogs,' he said. He turned to the others. He was already unwrapping the *shemagh* from round his head so that he could engage his NV. 'We've got three minutes to get to the compound,' he said. 'Our only priority is Dhul Faqar. Once we have him, we can use him as a human shield to fight our way out. Let's move.'

DECEMBER 23

SIXTEEN

Once more, Danny saw the world through the green haze of his NV googles. Hyper-aware of their surroundings, he, Spud and Caitlin passed through the checkpoint in single file. They were now inside the perimeter fence. They skirted clockwise around it for thirty metres, through the heavy rain, so that they were alongside the first cherry picker with its gruesome swinging corpse. He got a whiff of rotten flesh, but from here they could approach the compound to the left of the main track in. But he saw no sign of any militants outside the compound. The rain was doing its job and keeping them inside. He was grateful for it. The elements were keeping them invisible.

Distance to the closest compound building: 200 metres. From his surveillance of the compound earlier that evening, Danny knew that block 3, where he believed Dhul Faqar was most likely to be holed up, was to their eleven o'clock. It was obscured, however, by another long, low building – block 2 – to the right of which was a passageway formed by the left-hand wall of what Danny had dubbed block 4. It was this passageway that they needed to head for. Danny estimated they could make it in forty-five seconds, if they remained unobserved.

He jabbed one finger forward. Spud started running. In his peripheral vision, Danny could see the Kurds' vehicle. They'd killed the headlamps and were moving off the road, heading anti-clockwise around the perimeter.

'Go,' he whispered at Caitlin. She followed Spud, ten metres between them, hands on her rifle, ready to engage it if necessary.

A couple of seconds later, Danny followed.

The NV goggles gave him extra peripheral vision. It meant he could track the movement of the Kurds' vehicle as it drove into position without moving his head. By the time he was halfway across the open ground to the compound, it had come to a halt, having turned to face the compound from its north-westerly position, seventy-five metres from the perimeter fence. Danny estimated they had another minute before the Kurds opened up on the compound. He increased his pace. Spud and Caitlin did the same.

Twenty seconds. He reached the back wall of block 2. It was scrawled with black Arabic graffiti. Spud and Caitlin were in position, both on one knee on either side of the passageway, their rifles pointing down it. Danny positioned himself with his back to the building, and waited.

Ten seconds.

Twenty seconds.

A barking sound. Close. He turned to see the green, hazy forms of two dogs running towards them from across the open ground. He got one of them in his cross hairs. He didn't want to fire until the Kurds had opened up. But the dog was getting closer. Twenty metres. Ten . . .

Thirty seconds.

Gunfire.

The burst from the fifty-cal cut through the noise of the pouring rain, rebounding off the whitewashed walls of the compound buildings. It lasted a full five seconds, and Danny could hear the secondary noise of shrapnel and debris bursting into the air as the heavy-gauge rounds slammed into the buildings on the northern edge of the compound – the short base of the L-shape he'd seen from their vantage position up in the hills.

Danny used the noise camouflage to release a single round on the dog. It was just five metres away, and foaming at the mouth. The suppressed knock of his rifle round put the animal straight down, and he heard Spud releasing a round too, killing the second animal.

Danny forced himself to breathe slowly as he waited for a response to the Kurds' gunfire.

It came almost immediately.

The rain made it difficult to establish exactly where the shouts came from. Numerous locations, Danny sensed, from all around the compound. About ten voices, maybe more. All male. The closest maybe twenty metres away on the other side of the buildings. They died down after a few seconds, but then a second burst from the Kurds reignited them. Danny could tell that the shouting men were moving towards the northern end of the compound. It made perfect sense. They knew they would be protected by the base of the L-shape if they wanted to fire back. What they didn't know was that this would clear the centre of the compound for the unit to make their approach on target.

Danny raised his rifle, and jabbed the butt into his shoulder. He and the weapon were a single entity. Where Danny turned, the weapon would turn. And if a threat appeared in front of him, he would put them down without hesitation.

He swung round from his protected position, into the mouth of the passageway. Distance to the far end, thirty metres. He advanced at pace, past Spud and Caitlin. A flicker in his peripheral vision told him that they'd got to their feet as soon as he'd cleared their position. He knew that as he advanced, one of them would follow, slightly to his left or right. The other would be walking in the same direction, but facing backwards, to keep them covered from both angles.

He had covered ten metres when he heard a third burst of fifty-cal fire from the Kurds. This time it was met not only with shouts, but also with the stuttering, barking noise of return Kalashnikov fire. It sounded relatively puny in comparison to the machine gun. Danny estimated eight weapons, all at the northern edge of the compound. He suddenly found himself thinking of the young girl Naza. Hoping she'd be OK ...

Twenty metres down the passageway. A figure ran across the far end. Danny halted. He had the impression that the man had seen him.

Five seconds passed. The figure reappeared at the end of the passageway. He stepped squarely into Danny's line of fire. Thin. Short beard. Rifle. Danny saw the guy peer in his direction.

No hesitation. Danny squeezed the trigger on his rifle. The single suppressed round flew from the barrel, its dull thud masked by the rain and the continued barking of Kalashnikov fire to the north. It nailed the target full in the chest. He went down without a sound.

The next few seconds were critical. If anyone saw the dead body lying in the mouth of that passageway, they'd realise that a secondary threat was coming in from that direction. He extended his left arm and made a forward jabbing motion with his thumb. Then he fell to one knee, carefully covering the mouth of the passageway, as Spud overtook him at a run. His mate reached the corpse, then bent down to grab its ankles and drag the body into the dark passageway, out of sight of anyone up ahead.

Danny looked behind him. Caitlin was five metres back, also on one knee, covering the passageway behind them. 'Caitlin, keep your position,' he said quietly into his radio. Then he got to his feet and ran to the far end of the passage, his weapon still fixed rigidly in the firing position.

Another burst of fire from the Kurds. The noise had a slightly different quality. Looser. It sounded to Danny as though their vehicle was moving while the machine gun fired. He cursed silently. It was too soon. They hadn't given the unit enough time to penetrate the compound. He surveyed the area beyond the passageway. He was looking out on to a rough triangle of open ground, bounded on the far side by the shore of the reservoir. Distance to the water: twenty-five metres. Precisely to his left was block 3, where he expected to find Dhul Faqar. There were no enemy targets on the open ground, but on the shore of the reservoir were the two observation towers Danny had spotted when recceing the compound from a distance. Twenty metres apart, each one was about five metres high, with corrugated iron cover, and contained a single gunman. It was clear to Danny that the gunmen were positioned to check for anyone trying to approach by water. But of course, with the Kurds' distraction, they were currently looking north. They hadn't seen Danny's unit yet. Their lack of observation was about to prove fatal.

'See them?' Danny breathed to Spud, who had rejoined him at the mouth of the passageway.

'See them,' Spud breathed.

No need to speak any more. Both men knew what to do. Spud was to Danny's left, so he would take the guard in the left-hand observation post. But they needed to take the shots at the same time, and the shots had to be accurate. If only one guy went down, it would give the other a chance to protect himself, or raise the alarm.

Danny aligned his rifle. The thirty-metre shot was not a difficult one, but it needed to be right. He slowed his breathing down, and tried to put the constant barks of gunfire from the north out of his mind.

Five seconds passed.

'Take the shot,' he said.

Danny and Spud fired in unison. He knew instantly that his shot was good, and instantly moved his line of fire towards Spud's guy, in case his mate had made an error. But Spud hadn't. Both observation post guards were down.

'Move towards us,' he told Caitlin over the radio. As she ran down the passageway, Danny tuned his hearing back in to the noises around them. More men were shouting. He heard a couple of vehicle engines start up. This was good. The Kurds' distraction had worked. The IS guards were making chase, taking the heat off Danny and his unit.

But it was impossible to know how long the distraction would last. They had to move quickly.

The door to block 3 – wooden, painted blood red – was five metres to their left. With Spud and Caitlin covering him, Danny moved towards it. He stood by the door, his back to the wall. The noise of the gunfire was a little more distant. He could hear tyres screeching off to the east. The IS guards were definitely chasing the Kurds. Closer by, things were quieter. A strange, unnatural calm covering the centre of the compound, like a thick blanket. Danny could hear his own heartbeat.

It was an inward-opening door. Danny kicked it gently. It creaked as it swung open. A pale, flickering light from inside the room. Firelight. He flicked up his NV goggles. A thick, sweet stench of incense hit him.

He considered utilising a flashbang. It would disorientate anybody waiting for him inside. But the noise could alert others to their presence. He decided against it. Instead, he slowly directed his weapon in through the open door, carefully panning left and right, his finger light on the trigger, ready to eliminate any threats in an instant.

At first, it seemed like there was nobody in there. It was a richly furnished room. Sofas. Embroidered cushions. Expensive rugs on the floor. He'd been right about the firelight – candles were dotted all over the place, filling the room with an attractive, comfortable glow. A closed door at the right-hand end, painted blue.

But no sign of their target. Danny felt a twinge of doubt at his analysis of the compound. Where was he?

'Dhul Faqar?' Danny whispered in a friendly, sing-song voice. '*Dhul Faqar?*'

A distant burst of fifty-cal fire. Rain on the roof. And the soft sound of weeping from the corner of the room. Danny's weapon instantly tracked towards it.

In the far, right-hand corner of the room was a floor-to-ceiling post. Sitting at the bottom of the post, chained to it by a thick metal collar, was a young woman, little more than a girl, her head bowed, her shoulders shaking as she cried.

Danny kept his weapon trained on her as he approached. He saw that she was naked under a gossamer-thin, see-through robe. Her breasts and stomach were badly bruised. There were streaks of blood down her inner thighs. She was starved and thin, her ribs easily visible.

As Danny stood over her, she looked up, slowly, as though terrified to see what horror was in front of her. Her lips were split, her eyes bruised. The skin, however, shone angrily, as though it had been scrubbed too hard. Danny could tell that she'd been beautiful once. But no longer. He remembered Hammond's briefing back on the plane. *Dhul Faqar's a real piece of work, by the sound of it . . . Intelligence suggests that he lets his men rape whichever captured women take their fancy, so long as they leave the choicest specimens for him. You can expect some pretty brutalised sex slaves in the stronghold. Don't start getting chivalrous. Nothing's more important than getting Dhul Faqar alive.*

That might be so. But Danny knew one thing for sure. If there were women here who had been abused by Dhul Faqar, they would want nothing more than to be free of him. Which meant that right now, this poor, molested, maltreated girl was his best ally.

It was too much to hope that she would speak English. Danny whispered, 'Dhul Faqar', then made a slicing gesture at his throat to indicate what might be in store for him. The shadow of fear on the girl's face grew darker, but she couldn't help looking towards the far end of the room, where the closed blue door was. Danny pointed to the door and gave an enquiring look. The girl nodded. Danny put one finger to his lips to make a shushing gesture. Outside, there was a distant burst of gunfire. The girl started violently. Her nerves were obviously shot.

Danny looked back over his shoulder to the main entrance. Caitlin and Spud were there, Caitlin looking in, Spud facing out. Danny pointed sharply at the closed door. Caitlin nodded. Together, they approached it.

A metre from the door, Danny stopped, Caitlin just behind him and to the right. The door didn't look strong. It wouldn't withstand a sturdy boot.

Danny held up three fingers.

Two fingers.

One.

His weapon still pointing straight ahead, Danny booted the door open. It clattered on its hinges in unison with a distant burst of gunfire.

The adjoining room was completely different. Stone floor. Brick walls. A bare light bulb hanging from a cable in the ceiling.

Another door on the far side, inward-opening again and fractionally ajar, a little rainwater dribbling inside. And another solitary woman, crouched in the corner, hugging her knees.

But no Dhul Faqar. *Shit.*

Danny immediately trained his weapon on the woman. She was older than the girl chained to the post, and not so scantily dressed. In fact, she was wearing Western clothes. Jeans. Black shoes. A dark jacket with white stitching. Her face was not beaten and bloodied like the younger girl's. But it was equally terrified. Her lower lip seemed to tremble as she looked directly up at Danny. Danny saw that she was very beautiful. Dark hair. Almond eyes. *Intelligence suggests that he lets his men rape whichever captured women take their fancy, so long as they leave the choicest specimens for him . . .*

'Dhul Faqar?' Danny breathed. And as before, he made the slicing gesture at his throat.

The woman's eyes widened. She looked hopeful and pointed towards the slightly open door.

Danny spoke quietly into his radio. 'Spud, we're heading outside. South end of block one. Meet us there.'

'Roger that.'

As he had with the younger girl, Danny put one finger to his lips to tell this woman to keep quiet. Then he advanced on the door.

'Wait,' Caitlin breathed.

Danny stopped.

'Why is she dressed in Western clothes?' Caitlin said.

Danny suppressed a flicker of annoyance. What did it matter? It was probably just one of Dhul Faqar's little perversions. Dress his sex slaves up like Western women. Caitlin strode up to her. 'What's your name?' she demanded in a hushed, urgent voice.

The woman shook her head. She obviously didn't understand what Caitlin was saying.

'Leave her,' Danny hissed. And when Caitlin hesitated: '*Leave her!*'

He continued advancing towards the door. Half a metre out, he hooked his foot round the edge of the door and dragged it open.

He faced out once more into the rain-soaked night. He glanced down at the muddy ground, hoping to see footprints, but there was rainwater pooling there.

Spud over the radio. *'You're clear to exit.'*

Danny surged forward, flicking down his NV as he did so. He emerged at the southern edge of the compound. Open ground for as far he could see. No buildings ahead of him, and no personnel, except Spud who was fifteen metres to his two o'clock, covering the exit in one direction and the main court-yard of the compound in another, the reservoir behind him. Caitlin joined them. Danny jabbed his thumb left. He figured this was the only direction their target could have taken – they'd have seen him if he'd turned right. Spud ran towards them, but held back a couple of metres as Danny took the lead, flanked by his two unit-mates.

They turned the corner that took them to the rear of the building. From here, they could see back towards the perime-ter fence checkpoint and the road that led up to the main supply route. Several vehicles were speeding up it, both on the road itself and over the open ground to either side. There was a muzzle flash from beyond the vehicles. Half a second later, the sound of the fifty-cal reached Danny. He realised he was watching the Kurds firing as they retreated and headed back to the RV.

He snapped his attention back to his own position. The ground was very soft, but the water wasn't pooling here. He realised his boot had sunk half an inch into the ground. Glancing back, he saw that they had left a trail of stubborn footprints behind them.

But there were no footprints up ahead. Which meant—

'*Shit!*' Caitlin hissed behind him, interrupting Danny's train of thought.

'What is it?'

'Did you see her nails?'

'What are you talking about?' Danny whispered.

'The woman we just left. Her nails were perfect. Western clothes. No bruises.'

A cold, sick feeling grew in Danny's gut as he started to understand what Caitlin was driving at. 'She wasn't a sex slave . . .' he breathed.

'Nothing like,' Caitlin replied.

A pause.

'Guys.' Spud's voice was low and tense. 'We've got a problem. Twelve o'clock, ten metres.'

Danny looked ahead. Then he cursed. How had he not seen it before?

Sitting on the ground ten metres in front of him was an item he had used more times than he could count. A few inches high, slightly curved with the convex edge facing them, and a wire leading from it. It was a Claymore mine, and it was close enough to kill them instantly.

'Back up,' Danny breathed. He had already taken a reverse step. '*Back up now*—'

'I don't think so,' shouted an unfamiliar voice through the rain. Female. Danny heard a series of familiar clicking sounds. He knew that there were armed personnel behind him.

'You are considering your options,' said the female voice in good, clean English, but with a distinct accent. 'But you have only one, which is to do what I say. If you make a single unexpected move, these men – there are eight of them – will shoot you. They enjoy killing the infidel, and especially infidels who have been killing their comrades, so I would be very careful. You will now put all your weapons on the floor.'

Danny didn't move.

Silence, then:

'Do it,' she said.

He unclipped his rifle and put it on the ground in front of him. Unholstered his Sig, and dropped it.

'Remove your waistcoats,' the woman said.

Danny unclipped the straps and let the heavy ops waistcoat fall to the floor.

'Put your hands on your head, then turn round.'

Danny raised his arms, then turned. He saw that Caitlin and Spud had also obeyed the instructions. They had no choice.

Eight armed Islamic State militants were standing in the rain, their Kalashnikovs pointing directly at the unit. And standing among them, her dark hair matted and wet, was the beautiful, almond-eyed woman in Western clothes who they had seen less than a minute ago looking terrified on the stone floor of the last room.

She sneered. 'We are not all pathetic, like that tied-up bitch in the other room.' Her eyes flashed unpleasantly and a brief, triumphant smile flickered across her mouth. 'Lie on the ground,' she instructed. 'Hands behind your back.'

Danny hesitated briefly. His mind was turning over, calculating, evaluating options, looking for exit routes. But they all met the same barrier: the unit was sandwiched between a Claymore mine and a group of armed militants. They would kill them in an instant, given the order. He nodded at the others. They lay down in the very muddy ground. Danny felt his clothes absorbing the wet mud.

She barked a harsh instruction in Arabic. Three of the militants advanced. Danny watched their feet. As one of them stood above him, he considered grabbing his ankles, tussling him down, using him as a human shield. But the risks were too high, the chances of success too small. It would just put Spud and Caitlin in even more danger . . .

He had no more time to think about it. The militant standing above him had removed his rifle. He lifted it above his head, barrel pointing up, butt pointing down. Danny knew what was coming, and prepared himself for the intense crack of pain as the IS guy slammed his weapon down on Danny's skull.

It happened. Danny experienced an intense, blinding flash. Then he blacked out.

When Danny woke, he was still lying on his front. But not in the mud. He was inside, on a hard floor. It was pitch black. Cold. No sound.

He didn't know how much time had passed. Was it dawn yet? If so, they'd missed their RV with the Kurds. But right now Danny had bigger problems than that. His head throbbed where the militant had hit him. He tried to push himself to his feet, and winced. His ribs were bruised. It was painful to breathe. They'd obviously given him a good kicking while he was out. But they hadn't tied him up, which was a mistake. He touched his face. It was sticky with blood. There obviously hadn't been enough time for it to dry; he estimated that he'd been unconscious for less than half an hour.

Once he was on his feet, he started feeling his way around the room. He needed to know how big it was, and where the exit was. But he'd only been groping in the darkness for thirty seconds when the door opened. He winced as light flooded in. A figure stood in the doorway. Tall. Fairly broad shoulders. Probably male. Danny couldn't make out his face because he was in silhouette and seemed to be wearing some kind of hooded top. Distance, three metres.

Danny surged forward. If he could harness the element of surprise, he could knock this figure out of the way. But his move was expected, and Danny was unsteady on his feet. The door slammed shut before he reached it. His sore body whacked against the inside, and although the door shook in its hinges, there was the sound of a bolt closing on the other side.

The room spun. Danny blacked out again.

A bright light woke him. It stabbed the back of his eyeballs. He was on his back. Looking up, he saw that the light source was a halogen-bright torch, being held about a metre from his face. There were figures looking over him, their faces obscured behind the light. He was too woozy to count them accurately – four, maybe five?

An arm appeared in front of the torch. It was holding a camera. There was a fast sequence of clicking sounds as the camera fired off a burst of shots.

The camera disappeared. The torch lowered, leaving multi-coloured dazzle lights on Danny's retinas. There was a scuffling and a commotion. One of the men had what looked like a baseball bat in his fist. Danny registered it just a moment too late to roll away. The baseball bat hit him squarely in the pit of the stomach. He heaved and retched as the wind shot from his lungs. By the time he'd managed to inhale, the men had left and the door was shut.

He was alone in the dark again.

Time passed.

Danny did what he could to keep track of it, mentally ticking off the minutes in the darkness. But he was in a bad state. He kept drifting in and out of consciousness. So he didn't really know how long he'd been in there when the door opened again, casting an oblique rectangle of light across the floor of his cell.

There were three of them. They all had baseball bats this time.

Danny could tell that they were avoiding his face. Instead, they pummelled him hard in the guts and the genitals. They ground their heels into his knees, and they laughed harshly while they did it. Each time Danny tried to fight back, or even to move, he felt another numbing blow in his abdomen. They were beating him to a pulp.

Suddenly it stopped. Danny lay on his side, foetus-like in the recovery position, his breath noisy and strained as he tried to get some air into his system.

A face drew close to his. Just inches away. Danny could smell the stink on his breath and the sweat on his clothes. He was panting slightly, as though the process of beating Danny up had taken it out of him.

Then he spoke. A thick Arabic accent. Almost impenetrable. But not quite.

'Danny Black,' he said.

For a moment, Danny felt like his lungs weren't working.

The man laughed. 'Danny Black,' he repeated.

Danny shook his head. 'I don't know what you're talking about,' he muttered. His voice was dry and hoarse. It was hard to get the words out.

The man stood up. He and his mates left.

241

Danny's skin had turned clammy. His mind rocked with panic. Nobody outside the security services knew he was here. How *could* they? This was a black op. Completely deniable.

Then he remembered: the photograph they had taken of him, before the beatings had started up. But how could they have identified him so quickly?

Get a grip, he told himself. You can't think when you're panicking.

He closed his eyes. Tried to ignore his aching body.

Think, Danny. Fucking *think*—

Suddenly, he took a sharp intake of breath again as a deeper, more sinister fear crept through his body.

These bastards knew his name. And a serving Regiment man's name is a cause for secrecy. Not for his own safety, but for the safety of those closest to him.

Dhul Faqar had men in the UK. That was why Danny was here. And now that his captors knew his identity, they had the ultimate hold over him.

Danny bowed his head, cold dread seeping through his veins. All of a sudden he wasn't thinking about himself. The pain he was in. The danger. He wasn't even thinking about his unit.

He was thinking about a young woman in a tiny flat thousands of miles away, and the baby daughter she was looking after.

SEVENTEEN

Hereford. Dawn.

It had been a bad night.

Rose had woken three times, and it had taken an hour to settle her on each occasion. And when the baby had let her sleep, Clara's dreams were disturbed. They always were, when Danny was away.

She had got up just after five, and crept silently from the bedroom to avoid waking Rose. Made herself a cup of tea, then cradled it in the hallway as she stared at the soft toy Danny had bought, curled round the handle of the pram. She moved to the front room and sat on the sofa, staring at the window that looked out on to the road, absent-mindedly flicking through her phone. Her fingernails, she noticed as the grey dawn became gradually lighter, were sore and chewed.

She sat there for an hour. Her tea grew cold. She knew she should try to sleep again, to give herself a better chance of making it through the day without crying. But she couldn't. She kept thinking of Danny's friend who had turned up unexpectedly the previous day. His words had chilled her. His warning to stay here, and not venture up to London. She'd called her mum and dad to check that they had no plans to visit the capital. And she'd worried about the sort of world she was bringing her little girl up in.

You're safe, she told herself. Rose is safe. And so is Danny. What had his friend said? *Don't worry about him, love. He can take care of himself.* And Clara knew that was true.

It was only when she heard Rose crying in the bedroom that she snapped out of her reverie, spilling some of the cold tea over her hands. She swore, placed the teacup on the floor next to her phone and hurried back to the bedroom. Her baby was lying in her Moses basket. She'd managed to unwrap her swaddling cloth and was all tangled up. Her angry little face softened, though, when she saw her mum standing over her. And Clara's heart melted, as it did ten times a day, when her baby flashed her a tiny, crooked smile.

She lifted Rose out of her Moses basket and held her up against her shoulder, cooing and rocking her very gently. Rose gurgled happily for a moment, but it soon morphed into a cry again. She was hungry. She needed feeding. Clara carried her back into the front room and settled down on the sofa again, with the baby at her breast. She closed her eyes as Rose fed.

It was the sound of footsteps that roused her. Somebody was walking up to the front door. Clara frowned and glanced down at her phone. It was only just gone 6.30 a.m. Who could be calling this early?

The doorbell rang. Clara gently disengaged Rose from her breast and carried her to the front door, gently tapping the baby's back as she went. She was about to open it, but something stopped her. The security chain was hanging loosely. Clara slotted it into position. Then she unlocked the door and opened it the couple of inches that the chain allowed.

There was a man on the doorstep. He wore a woolly hat with a bobble, and was clutching a cardboard box to his chest. In one hand, he had a hand-held electronic scanner. 'Amazon delivery,' he said. He had a distinctly foreign accent.

'I'm not expecting one,' Clara said.

The delivery guy shrugged. 'Christmas present, maybe. Lots of them, this time of year. Need a signature, please.'

Clara nodded. Silently, she wondered if this was something from Danny. Then she told herself not to be stupid. Wherever he was in the world, he wouldn't be sending Amazon parcels. 'One minute, please,' she said. She took Rose back into the front room and laid her on the hearthrug. Then she returned to the front door, closed it, undid the security chain, then opened the door again.

She knew, instantly, that she'd done the wrong thing.

The delivery guy wasn't carrying the parcel or the scanner any more. They were stacked neatly to one side of the door. He was carrying a gun, and the gun was pointing directly at Clara's forehead.

Clara's immediate instinct was to slam the door shut, but the gunman already had one foot over the threshold, blocking it. She staggered back as he forced his way in and closed the door behind him with his foot. He pulled a knife – long, wickedly sharp.

'If you scream,' he said calmly, 'I'll take your baby's eyes out. I have done it before. It takes a few seconds.'

Clara almost choked in horror. 'What do you want?' she whispered. 'My purse is in the bedroom. It's all the money I have. You can take it . . .' Her voice faltered. It wasn't just that the gunman was smiling, as if he found ridiculous the notion that all he wanted was her money. She had noticed something else now that he was no longer clutching the parcel. The man had an angry, ugly scar at his throat, which almost mirrored his smile. It was grotesque, and for a moment Clara couldn't take her eyes off it.

'Where is the child?' the gunman demanded.

Clara shook her head. It was the one question she couldn't bring herself to answer. She didn't need to. Rose started to cry. It was obvious from her thin wail that she was in the front room to the left of the hallway. The gunman twitched his weapon in that direction. Clara understood the gesture. She entered the room. Rose had her angry face on. Her little lungs were bellowing.

'Shut her up,' the gunman said.

'I – I can't. When she starts crying like this she—'

'Fine,' the gunman said. He stepped up to the baby and pressed the tip of his knife against the soft skin under her eye. 'Left one first,' he said. A pinprick of blood appeared.

'*No!*' Clara breathed. She bent down and grabbed her daughter, holding her closely to her chest. 'Quiet . . . quiet baby . . . *please* . . .' She rocked her as gently as her frightened body would allow. To her relief, Rose calmed down, but it still looked as if she was weeping blood from her left eye.

245

'The only reason you're alive is to keep the baby quiet. If you fail to do that, I'll shut her up myself.' He put away his knife. 'Then I'll deal with you.'

'Is this . . . is this to do with Danny?' Clara said.

The gunman swiped her hard round the side of the face. She gasped in pain. 'You don't speak.' He pointed to the window. 'Do you see that van?' he said.

Clara looked and saw a red Parcelforce van parked just outside. She hadn't noticed it arrive. She nodded.

'We're going there now.'

Clara looked down at her clothes. Nightie. Dressing gown. Slippers. 'I – I need to change,' she said.

Another swipe round the face. She felt blood trickle from her nose. Rose grizzled.

'I'm going first with the baby. Then you follow. If you make a noise, or try to run, I'll kill the child. Do you understand?'

Clara stared at him, too afraid to speak.

'Don't make me ask a question twice.'

'I – I understand.'

'Good. Give me the child.'

She couldn't do it. She shrank back from him, cuddling Rose as tightly as she ever had, smearing the trickle of blood on her tiny left cheek. The gunman gave an impatient hiss. He changed the position of his weapon so that he was holding the barrel. Then he stepped forward and struck the pistol handle hard across Clara's rapidly swelling cheek. She gasped in pain, and her knees buckled. The gunman stepped up to her and yanked Rose out of her arms. Immediately, the baby started crying again. Clara lunged at him, and was rewarded with a solid blow to the pit of her stomach. As she collapsed, she was vaguely aware of a spatter of blood streaking across the mirror above the fireplace from the gun swipe. The gunman shoved a rough hand over the baby's mouth and nose to muffle the sound of her crying. Then he bundled her under his coat, like she was an embarrassing package.

'You follow in ten seconds. Otherwise you know what happens.'

He was about to leave the room, but then he saw the phone on the floor. He smashed it violently with his heel, then left. Clara got to her feet. She was dizzy and in pain. She saw the gunman through the window. He was approaching the Parcelforce van. He opened the side door and climbed in. She looked towards the row of terraced houses on the other side of the street, desperately hoping that there might be a neighbour at one of the windows. But all the curtains were shut and the street looked deserted.

Clara felt like she was being ripped apart. To follow this man was suicide. In the back of her mind, she thought about trying to escape. There was a back entrance to the flat. She could make a run for it. Maybe if she'd been alone, she would have done. But he had Rose. There was nothing else she could do. Her legs felt empty with dread at the thought of what this monster might do to her child if she disobeyed him. She left the flat, staggering, tearful, gasping. Icy air hit her as she left the apartment. She looked left and right along the deserted pavement, hoping there might be someone to see what was going on. But there was nobody. The only other person she could see was another man behind the wheel of the van, but she couldn't make out his face. The gunman was sitting by the Transit's door, the grotesque scar on his neck very vivid. She could tell he was still holding Rose under his coat, and felt an almost magnetic pull towards her baby.

Clara took a sharp intake of breath as she entered the Parcelforce van. There was an unpleasant, sickly sweet smell in here. Having worked in war zones and hospitals, she recognised it. Her eyes were drawn to a heap at the back of the van. She saw arms and legs splayed out. A face, etched into a horrific, rictus expression. And a throat, brutally cut, the blood congealing slightly. The dead man had black skin and short hair. He was wearing a red jacket, and Clara could just make out the insignia on the breast, which said: 'Amazon.'

The man uncovered the baby and thrust her into Clara's arms. For a moment, she forgot about the dead body. She forgot about everything except holding her child, whose punctured skin was still bleeding gently.

The gunman jumped out. The side door slid shut. It was pitch black in the back of the van. Clara collapsed in the front corner of the cab, as far away from the corpse as she could be.

She hugged her baby with one arm. Rose wailed. With her other fist Clara thumped against the side of the van. She screamed. 'Let me out! *Let me out of here!*'

The van started to move.

'*For God's sake . . . Let me out of here . . .*'

The vehicle accelerated.

'Danny!' she cried, her words barely audible through the sobs. 'Where are you? Please Danny . . . help us . . . where *are* you?'

They entered Danny's cell on the hour, every hour. Even in his weakened, pummelled state, he knew that.

When they entered for the first time after revealing that they knew his name, Danny had found the strength to go at them with every ounce of aggression he possessed. He'd slammed one guy against the wall, crushing his face into the brick. But then a figure in the doorway had discharged a round into the cell. It sparked against the stone floor just a few inches from Danny's feet. The two remaining guys had laid into him, kicking him hard in the groin and the ribs, and even stamping on his face this time. They weren't good fighters, or even particularly strong. But Danny knew that with a shooter at the doorway, he had no way of over-powering them and escaping. Better to let them have their fun. Appear compliant. Wait for them to make a mistake. To think that they didn't need the backup of a shooter. So he'd absorbed the blows. Sucked up the pain.

On the hour. Every hour.

His kidneys throbbed. His face too. He reckoned he'd managed to avoid a broken nose, but he knew that his skin was swollen, broken and bleeding. He could taste the blood. When the time for each beating approached, he curled himself up into a little ball, protecting his head and his vital organs. Focussing on his slow, steady breathing as the militants beasted him.

On the hour. Every hour.

Sometimes they had a dog. Snarling. Straining on the leash. It would strain even more when they screamed at him in Arabic. Danny didn't know what they were saying. He recognised their shouts for what they were: a psychological exercise, designed to break him down. It was beginning to work. He kept getting flashbacks to the Malinois that had attacked Caitlin. At some point the interrogation proper would start. Then his body – and his mind – would *really* know about it.

During the sixth beating, while the door was open and the gunman stood in the door frame, he thought he heard Spud roar in agony. Maybe he was supposed to hear that. Mind games.

Now nine hours had passed. Nine beatings. Danny reckoned it must be about midday on the twenty-third. He expected the next beating in about five minutes. He crouched down in the far corner of the room, putting the pain in his abdomen out of his mind, and waited.

They arrived just when he expected them to. On the dot. The door slammed open. Danny counted three men entering. He recognised their swagger – it was the same guys who'd been laying into him each time. The same brutal guards who had laughed harshly at him when he offered up no resistance. One of them had even spat a little English at him. 'Big strong soldier, hey? Big strong Danny Black?'

Danny looked past them. The door was still open. There was nobody standing in the door frame. No dog.

Mistake.

Two of the men grabbed him under his armpits and yanked him to his feet. The third stood half a metre in front of him, a lairy shadow whose hot, bad breath Danny could feel on his face. He spat at Danny. As the spittle hit Danny's face, the Regiment man attacked.

He was still being clutched by the two guards on either side. When they felt Danny move, they clutched even harder. It meant that the force of Danny's heel as it connected with the pit of the third man's stomach was even stronger than it might have been.

It was a proper kick. The kind of kick that would have knocked a football out of the stadium. The kind of kick a man like Danny had trained for, and practised, for moments like this. And it had its effect. There was a solid, dull groan as the guard exhaled sharply and, winded, staggered back towards the open door.

The two remaining guards were on either side of Danny, facing him side on. Danny yanked his head to the left, smashing the side of his skull squarely into the face of the first guard. There was a crack as his nose bust. Danny yanked his head to the right. The second guard found his face being sandwiched between Danny's head and the brick wall. Another crack, and the guard slumped, suddenly limp, down to the floor.

Danny quickly turned and grabbed the head of the first guard, who was staggering, dazed, to his left. He thrust his thumbs into the guard's eye sockets, which gave way in a mess of blood and jelly. With a sharp, yanking movement he twisted the man's head. There was a silent twitch as his spine cracked and he slumped to the ground like his buddy.

Which left one more guard. He was still bent over, staggering, winded, gasping for breath. Danny strode up to him, grabbed a clump of his hair and, almost nonchalantly, slammed him against the wall, face first. The guy slumped, but Danny kept hold of him and slammed him against the wall for a second time, then a third. He told himself that he was ensuring his target was dead. In truth, the pent-up anger of the last few hours was boiling out of him. The dead guard had got the brunt of it.

Danny let him fall to the ground. He examined the three bodies to see if any of them were carrying weapons. They weren't. Unarmed, he headed to the door, stopping just short of it to listen carefully for any sounds in the adjoining room. All he could see of it was a concrete floor and breeze-block wall ten metres away.

Silence.

But not for long.

He heard someone burst into the adjoining room. Footsteps. They were moving quickly. Danny hid to one side of the open cell door, hoping that this newcomer would enter the cell quickly and that Danny could attack him as he did so. But the bastard was cuter than that. He stood opposite the door but at a distance from it – Danny could tell from the shadow he cast into the cell. He could also tell from the shape of the shadow that he was armed.

Danny suppressed another surge of anger. His escape attempt was fucked. The newcomer was shouting something. Danny didn't understand what he was saying, but he sensed that the guy was calling to his mates. And when they didn't reply, the shouting got more aggressive, like he was speaking to Danny. He sensibly didn't get any closer – Danny estimated that he was six or seven metres from the cell. Far enough away to take a shot if Danny went for him.

Two options. Stay where he was and hope the gunman would advance. Or show himself, and hope another opportunity to attack arose. After a few seconds he could tell the guy wasn't going to advance, so he chose the latter option.

Danny stepped into the doorway of his cell with his hands up.

He was looking at a windowless room. To his left were two more cells. They weren't enclosed, like Danny's, but had bars at the front, and bars dividing them. Set in the back wall of each cell were two metal rings, about eight feet high. Whatever torture they were intended for, it looked medieval.

To his right, there was a door. It was open, and it led outside.

Straight ahead was the gunman. He looked half scared, half angry. His Kalashnikov was pointing straight at Danny.

Danny took a step forward. A ferocious bark from the man opposite stopped him in his tracks. The gunman made a gesture that Danny understood to mean he should lie down on the ground. Danny gave him a 'be reasonable' look, but that just invited more shouting.

Keep shouting, asshole, Danny thought. The more you keep shouting, the less you're concentrating. He dropped to his knees, then looked stubbornly – arrogantly – at his adversary. The gunman continued shouting at him. His voice was getting hoarse and he took a step closer.

Danny lay on the floor, front down, his head to one side, watching the guard. The guard wasn't shouting quite so much now. But he was still talking. His words – still incomprehensible to

251

Danny – were a constant flow of spitting, bile-ridden invective. He had lowered his gun so that it was still pointing at Danny.

And he was taking another step forward.

Distance, four metres.

Danny knew that the span of one arm was approximately seventy-five centimetres. Another three metres, just over, and he would be within reach.

He was still talking. Danny could see that he was sweating. Did he know his mates were dead? Was he planning to send Danny the same way? He was certainly gesturing forcibly with his weapon.

But he was also getting closer.

Three metres.

Two.

Just a little further, buddy.

Danny kept his arm very still. He didn't want to give the guard any premonition of what he had in mind. But he kept his gaze fixed on the guy's ankles. As soon as he was close, he'd stretch out, hook his arm round whichever ankle was closest, and then . . .

A metre.

He was almost in reach.

His right foot was moving.

Someone entered the room. A female voice spoke harshly. The guard froze.

Another instruction from the woman. He stepped back. Two paces. Three.

Danny felt himself burning up with frustration. He remained very still, but his eyes flickered towards the new arrival. It was the woman who had betrayed them. She stood over Danny at a safe distance of three metres. 'I've told this idiot,' she said, 'that if you move a single muscle without being told, he must shoot you. And please don't imagine he's going to be stupid enough to get that close to you again.'

Danny didn't reply. But there were alarm bells in his mind. Whoever this woman was, she had outfoxed him twice. She showed a load more tactical awareness than Danny would have expected of her. Who the hell was she?

She didn't wait for a reply, but stepped into the cell Danny had just vacated. Ten seconds later, she emerged again. 'I see you've been busy, Danny Black.'

'That's not my name,' Danny said.

'If you insist,' she said. 'Now stand up, very slowly, and put your hands on your head. Dhul Faqar wants to see you. And he doesn't like to be kept waiting.'

EIGHTEEN

It took three gunmen to usher Danny into the elaborately furnished room that he had identified as Dhul Faqar's living quarters. As he stepped out of the cell complex, he realised immediately that he was on the northern edge of the compound. The reservoir was to his right. The two dead guards in the observation tower had been removed and replaced with two of the remaining armed personnel. As Danny passed, they climbed down from their towers and started concerning themselves with a large bundle on the ground – he couldn't see what. The rain had stopped, but it was still cloudy. Danny identified the bright patch in the clouds that indicated where the sun was. His timing had been slightly out of sync. The position of the sun told him that it was mid-afternoon.

It might as well have been midnight in Dhul Faqar's living quarters. The candles still burned and the open fire still smouldered. There was no natural light apart from what came through the open door. The smell of incense was sweeter and thicker than before.

Spud and Caitlin were there. It was clear that they had undergone the same treatment as Danny. Their faces were a mess of bruises, cuts and swellings. They were kneeling on the floor, shoulders hunched. Each of them had an armed guard pointing a rifle directly at their head. Caitlin had been stripped down to her tight grey vest. The wound on her arm was exposed. It looked like the guards had been beating it. It was bleeding, puffed up and pus-filled. Her face was drained white, and she was sweating badly.

Danny clocked the unit's packs and weapons, piled up along the right-hand wall of the room. Next to them, still tied to the post by her metal collar, was the slave girl. She wore the same flimsy clothes, and the same expression of helpless despair. Her eyes flickered towards Danny as he entered, but really all her attention was elsewhere.

Sitting between Spud and Caitlin and the slave girl, in a low, comfortable chair, and wearing a plain white *dishdash* with white socks and comfortable leather sandals, was a short man, slightly plump, with a long black beard that was turning grey at the tips. He had an iPad on his lap, and his face glowed slightly from the light of the screen. He was an unremarkable-looking man, but clearly the boss. Danny instinctively knew that this must be Dhul Faqar. He remembered what Hammond had said about this arsehole not wanting anyone to look him in the eye, and it was true that nobody else in the room seemed to be making eye contact.

Fuck that, he thought, and he stared directly at him.

Dhul Faqar watched with flat, expressionless eyes as Danny was forced to his knees a metre to the right of Spud. Danny felt the hard metal of a Kalashnikov barrel against the back of his head. He stared at Dhul Faqar and waited for him to speak. Dhul Faqar looked at the screen on his lap, then directly at Danny.

'Danny Black,' he said, in stuttering but serviceable English. 'British special forces. Mother deceased. One father, one brother.' He cleared his throat. 'One daughter. Name, Rose Black. Mother's name, Clara Macleod. Place of residence, Hereford.' He pronounced it 'Hear-ford'.

Danny felt his blood turn to liquid fear. It was all he could do to control his breathing. He could feel Spud and Caitlin's eyes on him.

Dhul Faqar looked up and smiled. His lips glistened in the candlelight. The woman with almond eyes stepped up to him and whispered something in his ear. Dhul Faqar nodded gently. 'If he tried to deny it, he is more of a fool than he looks,' Dhul Faqar said. He held up the iPad. 'Your CIA file, Black. It makes *very* interesting reading. You are a hero, although I'm not sure that is quite how *they* see you.'

Danny didn't reply. He was too busy trying to master the dread, so that he could make sense of what Dhul Faqar had just told him. His CIA file? How the hell did an IS kingpin have *that* in his possession?

A memory clicked in his head. Ray Hammond, their ops officer, briefing them before they went after the migrant boat in the Med. *The Yanks seem to think Santa and Rudolph might have terrorist intentions on UK soil, so why they haven't shared this with us is anyone's guess.*

And later, while they were being briefed in the Hercules before their drop into Turkey. *All I know is the Americans are holding back from attacking certain targets.*

'There is something else I want to show you,' Dhul Faqar said. He stood up from his low chair and carried the iPad towards Danny. When he was standing right in front of him, he tapped the screen, then turned the iPad round and held it at the height of Danny's face.

There was some video footage playing. Shaky, close-up of a man's face, Middle Eastern. Hard to make out his features, because the camera was so close. He was talking in Arabic. As he spoke, the footage panned out. Danny saw that this man had a very distinctive scar across the entire width of his throat. The camera panned to the right to show the rest of the room. Danny knew what he was going to see, even before it appeared.

Clara was sitting on a stool. Her eyes were puffy and red. She had clearly been crying. She was wearing a dressing gown and cradling a bundle in her arms. The camera moved closer. A hand appeared and roughly grabbed the blanket that was covering the baby. The child started to cry. Danny saw a glimpse of his daughter. She had a cut under her left eye. It was bleeding. Like she was weeping blood. The camera moved away and returned to the close-up face of the man with the scar at his throat. He continued talking in Arabic.

Dhul Faqar stopped the video footage. He walked back to his chair. Danny followed him with cold, hard eyes. He felt like stone. All he wanted to do was kill the man in front of him. His limbs twitched. But the gun was still pressed hard against the back of his skull. He could do nothing.

'You will all die, of course,' Dhul Faqar said. 'Eventually, and at a time of my own choosing. We will hang you from our cranes as a warning to anyone else who wishes to trespass on our territory. But not before you have served a very useful purpose to us. Three members of the famous British SAS. If we celebrated Christmas, I could not ask for a better gift. After our attack in the UK, this will be ... what is the phrase you use? The icing on the cake. The footage of three soldiers suffering all the humiliations that the Qur'an demands we inflict upon the infidel will be a fitting follow-up to our Christmas celebrations. You will be what I believe they call a "publicity coup".' Dhul Faqar fixed Danny with his piercing gaze again. 'So far you and your Kurdish friends have killed eleven of my men,' he said. 'Not to mention my Turkish business associates whose deaths are, I will admit, a difficulty.'

Danny forced himself to count carefully. The guy at the check-point had said there were seventeen men in the compound, including Dhul Faqar. Eleven down left six. Two guys in the observation tower outside. Three guards in here plus Dhul Faqar. The women were probably extras the guard hadn't taken into account. Dhul Faqar had made a big mistake giving them this information, because now they knew how many hostiles they were dealing with.

'Ordinarily I would expect to exact payment in return,' Dhul Faqar said, oblivious to the calculations whirring in Danny's brain. 'Your child and her mother would seem a good place to start.' He turned to the woman in Western clothes. 'Don't you agree, Malinka my dear?'

'Yes, Dhul Faqar,' Malinka purred. 'It would be a *very* good place to start.' She looked hungry as she walked up to stand beside him, and put one arm round his shoulders. 'The baby first.'

Dhul Faqar raised one hand. 'I am a reasonable man,' he said. 'Your family will remain safe, so long as you do not try to escape. When you are finally dead, Sergeant Black, they will be released.

But if you cause us any trouble . . .' He gave a regretful gesture. 'Our friend Mujahid, he with the . . .' He traced a finger across his neck to indicate the scar of the man in the video. 'He will be very happy to be distracted from his Christmas Day plans to travel west and put an end to your child's life. He will document the process, of course.' An exaggerated shadow fell across Dhul Faqar's face. 'I imagine you would find it a trial to watch such a scene, so I beg you not to force us all into a situation we would rather avoid.'

Danny forced himself to show no emotion. His body was trembling with frustration and fury. He concentrated on calming himself.

'Shall I return them to their cells?' Malinka asked.

'Just one minute, my love,' Dhul Faqar said. 'We have another matter to discuss. Haven't you wondered why these three are here in the first place?' It was strange, the way they spoke to each other in English. Danny could only think that it was for the unit's benefit.

Malinka frowned, but she didn't reply.

'Isn't it clear that the British have found out something about our forthcoming plans? My guess is that they do not know enough to stop it, and so they have sent these soldiers to find me. But how did they know the strategy was mine in the first place? How did they know to find me here?' He looked up, and Danny realised he was staring at the three men who had the individual members of the unit at gunpoint. 'How else,' he said quietly, 'unless we have a traitor among us.'

A thick, nervous silence descended on the room. Dhul Faqar stood again. He turned to Malinka. 'Call the others in, my dear,' he said.

Malinka nodded and left the room. Dhul Faqar walked towards the unit, but his eyes were still on the guards who kept them at gunpoint. Danny looked straight ahead. He didn't want to give any indication of how hard he was concentrating, waiting for the split second of chaos that might occur if Dhul Faqar was foolish enough to reveal one of their guards as a traitor right in front of them.

Malinka returned with the two remaining guards from the observation towers. It was clear that they understood what was happening, because they looked terrified. They took up position on either side of the door.

'Do not look so worried, everybody,' Dhul Faqar said quietly. 'I know which one of you is a traitor. If you have done nothing wrong, you have nothing to worry about.'

Why is he speaking in English, Danny thought. Whose benefit is *that* for?

A tense pause. 'I gave each of you a name,' he said. He pointed to Caitlin's guard. 'You,' he said, 'I gave the name Jacob Hakim.' Spud's guard. 'You, I gave the name Aslan Hossein.' Danny's guard. 'And you, I gave the name Kailash McCaffrey. I told you all that I was giving you the identity of a person who is important to us. I'm afraid I lied. Those three individuals are of no importance to us whatsoever. They are entirely disposable.'

Danny looked at Malinka. She was looking at each guard in turn, her almond eyes narrowed nastily. He wished he could see through those eyes. If one of their guards was a traitor, right now he was their best friend. And if he was nervous, Danny would be able to see it in his face ...

'News has just reached me,' Dhul Faqar said, 'that one of these men has gone missing. He is probably dead at the hands of the British security services. Or he is being tortured.' He waved his hand as though swatting a fly. 'That doesn't matter, of course. He knows nothing, and we all serve Allah in whatever way we can. But the only reason he has been killed is because his identity was passed on by one of you.' Another smile. 'You are probably wondering who it is.' Dhul Faqar looked at Caitlin's guard. 'It was not Jacob Hakim,' he said. 'Jacob is alive and well.'

Malinka's eyes flickered between Spud's guy and Danny's. Danny focussed on the sensation of the gunmetal at the back of his head. Was it wavering? No. It was solid.

Dhul Faqar turned to Spud's guard. 'It was not Aslan Hossein,' he said.

A pause. Dhul Faqar turned to Danny's guard.

'It was McCaffrey. Poor Kailash McCaffrey. I wonder what happened to him.'

Malinka stood up. She pointed towards Danny's guard and looked over at the two men by the door. She barked some instructions in Arabic. One of the door guards strode towards Danny, weapon pointed directly at his head. The other bore down on Danny's guy. There was a scuffle behind him, but Danny couldn't take advantage: he was still at gunpoint.

'And now,' Dhul Faqar announced, 'we shall see what happens to traitors.'

Danny's guy started jabbering in Arabic. Danny didn't understand the words, but he could hear the terror in his voice, and sense the tension among the other guards. Dhul Faqar listened with a bland look on his face. Then he recovered his iPad from where he was sitting. He approached Danny again, tapping the screen. Danny heard the familiar sound of a Skype ringtone. Dhul Faqar turned the iPad so that Danny − and the guards behind him − could see the screen.

The ringtone stopped. Video footage appeared.

There was an old lady in a dark room, strapped to a chair. She was Middle Eastern. Wrinkled, leathery skin. A rag stuffed in her mouth. Unbelievably frail.

Danny's guy let out a gasp. 'His mother,' Dhul Faqar explained pleasantly to Danny. 'I will explain to him that if he does not confess, we shall have to watch her die. You would do well to watch, Danny Black, because this is what your own family can expect, if you cause me any more trouble.' He looked over Danny's head at the guard, and spoke in Arabic. The guard replied. Dhul Faqar inclined his head. Then he raised the iPad slightly and spoke an instruction clearly intended for whoever was at the other end of the Skype call.

The reaction was immediate. A figure in a black balaclava appeared to the side of the old woman and thumped her hard on the side of the face. Danny's guy shouted out again. The old woman's eyes rolled and blood trickled from her nose. The figure struck her again. She started to cry.

Dhul Faqar was staring intently over Danny's head at his suspect. The IS leader had a strange expression all of a sudden. Uncertain.

He spoke another word in Arabic. On the screen, the man in the balaclava stood behind the old lady's chair, grabbed her hair with one hand and pressed a knife against her throat.

'Confess,' Dhul Faqar said quietly, 'and she lives.'

There was a horrible silence in the room, broken only by the frightened mewing of the old lady on the screen.

Dhul Faqar's eyes narrowed. 'Confess,' he repeated.

Danny's guard replied in Arabic. His voice, suddenly, was strangely calm. Danny didn't understand the words he spoke, but he thought he got their meaning. He was denying Dhul Faqar's accusation.

Malinka was at Dhul Faqar's shoulder. She breathed something into his ear, but Dhul Faqar shook his head. He issued an instruction in Arabic. Danny had time to see the man on the screen lower his knife from the old lady's throat before Dhul Faqar turned the iPad round.

'He passes the test,' Dhul Faqar said quietly, his eyes on Danny.

Malinka was looking warily at Danny's guard. 'My love,' she breathed. 'You are in danger.'

'Danger?' Dhul Faqar said. 'Certainly. But not from him.'

'Dhul Faqar, you must be careful—'

'There was another person in the room when I revealed that name to our friend here,' Dhul Faqar interrupted.

Malinka turned to look at the slave girl tied to the post. The girl's eyes were wide and frightened, but she clearly had no idea what was going on.

'Her?' Dhul Faqar said. 'You think I have anything to fear from a pathetic creature like that? No.' He turned to look at Malinka. 'I am talking about you, my dear. *You* are the traitor.'

Danny knew, in an instant, that Dhul Faqar was right. It was the momentary tightening around her eyes, and the way she glanced quickly towards the exit.

It was as if the whole room was holding its breath. Total silence. Total stillness.

Malinka put on a slightly forced smile. 'My love. What are you saying?'

'I think I have been very clear.'

'But my love, I have been by your side for years.'

'Which makes your treachery all the more disappointing.' Dhul Faqar looked towards the guards at the door and clicked his fingers. It was clear what he meant, and it was also clear that the guards took great pleasure in advancing towards Malinka and seizing her by both arms. Dhul Faqar stepped up to her and held her by the chin. 'I think you are either British or American,' he said. 'Not British, now I think about it. If you were British, our guests would have known about you. American, then.' He nodded to himself and murmured, 'Never trust an American.' For the first time, their eyes met. 'I won't kill you yet,' he breathed. 'My men will have their fun first. Then, when you are no more use to them, when you are just an empty, raped husk, *then* I will put you out of your misery, you pig-faced American whore.'

Danny's head was spinning. Everything was moving too quickly. He still felt the debilitating nausea from seeing the footage of Clara and his little girl. He was totally confused about the scene unfolding in front of him. Was Dhul Faqar right? Was Malinka really an American agent? He knew they should take advantage of that confusion, but he couldn't even think straight ...

'You're probably wondering how I came across your CIA file, Danny Black,' Dhul Faqar announced. 'Would it surprise you to learn that it was from the CIA themselves?' His eyes shone with triumph. 'A gift, from one ally to another. But real allies do not spy on each other, as it seems the Americans have been doing. With one hand they give ...' He held up the iPad. 'With the other, they take away ...' He indicated Malinka.

'My love,' Malinka breathed again.

Dhul Faqar took a step towards her. With a sudden, brutal swipe he hit her cheek with the back of his hand. There was a hiss of surprise from the assembled guards, and Danny saw a bead of blood trickle from her right nostril. 'You know what's coming, American whore,' Dhul Faqar said very quietly. 'Do not make it worse for yourself.' He stepped towards the unit members. His face was contorted with hate. 'I have a little something waiting for you, back in the cells. I hope you enjoy it.' He addressed his guards, and now he no longer bothered speaking in English. His instructions were curt and aggressively delivered. The guards acted on them immediately.

The three members of the unit were forced out of the room at gunpoint. So was Malinka. There was no escaping. They were ushered across the open ground by the reservoir back towards the incarceration unit. Danny noticed that the guards were back in their observation towers. The bundle on the ground was no longer there.

At the door to the incarceration unit, they were told to line up in single file. Danny was at the front. He noticed a noise coming from inside that hadn't been there before. A low, constant, monotonous buzzing. The nausea in his gut grew stronger. He knew what that sound was, and what it would mean.

One of the guards barked at him to enter the incarceration unit. Danny stepped in. He saw the source of the buzzing immediately.

A body was strung up at the front of the two cage cells, about a metre off the ground. Its arms were spread wide, so the hands were just above the doors of each cell. The body was female, and naked. The stomach had been split horizontally with a knife, and its contents had spilled out. The buzzing was caused by the hundreds of flies that were crawling over the glistening offal. Blood had dripped on to the ground. And tied to the front of the cells, on a very short rope, was a mongrel dog, licking at the blood.

Danny forced his eyes from the wound to the corpse's face. It was grotesquely contorted. But recognisable. A young girl. Spots on her face. Naza.

A guard opened the doors to the two cage cells. The door to the enclosed cell that had been Danny's was still ajar. Danny noticed as he passed that nobody had bothered to clear out the dead bodies. Not that he cared. His attention was on Caitlin, now walking at gunpoint beside him.

Her eyes were glazed. She hadn't yet recognised the kid.

And then, suddenly, she did.

It was as though someone had flicked a switch. Caitlin suddenly lashed out against the nearest militant, grabbing the barrel of his rifle. 'You cunts!' she shrieked. 'You fucking cunts!'

A second guard ran up to her and thumped the wound on her arm with the butt of his weapon. Caitlin screamed again – but with pain this time.

Danny grabbed her. She was struggling badly. The dog started to bark. Danny held up a conciliatory arm to the gunman – any movement now, he knew, and they would start squeezing triggers. 'It's OK,' he shouted. 'It's OK . . . she's not going to do anything.'

The gunmen were nervous and sweating. They started shouting, and forcing them towards the two cage cells, separated from each other by thick iron bars. Malinka was thrown into the left-hand one, Danny, Spud and Caitlin into the right. Danny understood the logic of separating them like this. These militants wouldn't want anybody killing anybody else before their boss gave the word. It would be more than their own lives were worth. At the same time, they didn't want to use Danny's original cell, because they wanted the psychological effect of Naza's body to do its work.

The doors to the cage cells clanged shut. The militants locked them. With dismissive sneers at their incarcerated prisoners, they left the block. There was silence, broken only by the grotesque buzzing of the flies that swarmed on Naza's body, the sound of Caitlin hyperventilating, and the occasional growl from the dog.

Spud turned immediately to Danny. 'They said they're holding your kid to keep you compliant. But you know that's bullshit? The moment you're dead, they're going to kill Clara and Rose. You *know* that, right?'

Danny barely trusted himself to speak. 'Of course,' he said. He moved to the front of the cage and examined the lock. It was a sturdy mortise bolt, deeply inset. Difficult to pick, even if they had had the right tools.

'We've got five militants plus Dhul Faqar,' Spud said.

'For now,' Danny replied without emotion. 'They'll call for reinforcements.' He was only half aware that Caitlin was utterly silent. She looked like death warmed up. Her wound must be badly infected. No question. It was bringing her down.

He turned towards the other cell. Malinka was in the far corner. She was pale. Frightened eyes. Sweat on her brow. She was staring into the middle distance. One of the flies was crawling across her face, but she didn't appear to notice. Danny couldn't help a creep of revulsion. If Dhul Faqar was right, and this was an American spy, she was in so deep that she was hardly any better than the IS scumbags whose ranks she had infiltrated. She'd been more than happy to sacrifice Danny, Spud and Caitlin. And she had encouraged Dhul Faqar to kill his daughter.

It was almost as if Spud was reading his mind. He put one hand on Danny's arm. 'Easy mucker. We might need her.'

His voice seemed to bring Malinka back to the here and now. She looked sharply towards them. 'We're dead,' she said. 'We're all dead.'

'You stupid bitch,' Danny breathed. 'We could have had you out of here.'

She gave him a contemptuous look. 'You think I was just waiting around for my knight in shining armour? You don't know what I've had to suffer to infiltrate these animals.'

Danny looked towards Naza's body, still hanging at the front of the cage. 'More than her?' he said.

Her eyes steamed with anger. 'You don't understand.' She strode towards the bars. She was suddenly close enough for Danny to reach through, and he felt a bomb of anger blow inside him. He slammed violently against the bars, pushing his hands through to grab her. Malinka jumped away just in time. The dog barked loudly.

'I should fucking kill you right now,' Danny whispered.

'What difference would that make?' she replied, her voice hoarse. 'Look at you, so arrogant. You don't know what's coming, do you? You saw that Yazidi girl, tied to the post? You know how she's spent the last two months. Raped, every day. Vaginally, anally, sometimes twice a day, till she bled like a slaughtered pig. If Dhul Faqar is in the wrong kind of mood, she gets half the life beaten out of her. And when he grows bored of her, which he will very soon . . .' She pointed at the body of the strung-up Kurdish girl. 'You've seen how he and his men get their kicks.'

'Why didn't you help her?' Caitlin asked. Although her voice was distinctly slurred, she still managed to sound threatening.

'Because it would have blown my cover.' Malinka spat. 'But what she went through, that will be *nothing* compared to what's waiting for me.' She paused. 'And for you, it will be even worse.'

'Maybe not,' Caitlin muttered. She sounded weak.

Malinka spat again. Caitlin walked to the front of the cell. Here, Naza's left ankle was tied by a rope to the bars. Caitlin untied it, ignoring the growling dog. Naza's leg fell stiffly away. Holding the half-metre length in her hand, Caitlin turned to Malinka. 'When they come,' she said, 'we can use these to throttle them.' She pointed at the rope tying Naza's right ankle to the front of Malinka's cage. 'I need that one too,' she said, her speech slurred. 'Untie it for me.'

Malinka looked at Danny, who was still by the bars. She clearly didn't want to get anywhere near him. Caitlin turned to him. 'Get away from her,' she said.

What was she doing? These ropes would be no good when they were at gunpoint, and Caitlin surely knew that. She must have something else in mind.

Danny stepped back. Spud too. Caitlin turned again to Malinka. 'They're not going to touch you,' she said. 'Now get me that rope.' She staggered slightly against the bars, and for a moment her eyes glazed over.

Malinka hesitantly advanced towards Naza's body. She was trembling, and kept looking anxiously towards Danny.

'Hurry,' Caitlin hissed. 'They could enter any minute.'

Malinka reached Naza. With clumsy, trembling fingers she loosened the rope.

'Give it to me,' Caitlin said, and she passed her bad arm, which was still carrying her own piece of rope, through the bars.

Still carefully watching Danny, Malinka stepped towards Caitlin.

Caitlin moved like lightning. She thrust her good arm through the bars and quickly hooked it round Malinka's neck. Malinka slammed forward against the bars, which shuddered and clanged. Caitlin swiftly wrapped her rope round Malinka's neck, and pulled the loose ends back through the bars.

'What the hell's she doing?' Spud demanded. 'We might *need* her!' He surged forward to pull Caitlin away, but Danny stopped him. Caitlin might be going downhill fast, but she was still managing to think smart. And Danny reckoned he knew what she had in mind.

'She's buying us a way out of here,' he hissed.

NINETEEN

A sick, throttled sound escaped Malinka's throat as Caitlin twisted the two ends of the rope. Her hands flew up behind her head and she tried to grab hold of Caitlin. Her red-painted nails were chipped, but they were still sharp enough to dig into Caitlin's skin and draw blood.

'Wait,' Danny said. 'Loosen it a bit.'

'We need to do it quickly,' Caitlin mumbled, her dirty hands bleeding. 'These IS – they're going to move us from here any minute – as soon as we're reported missing, this place is a target, and they'll know that.'

She was right. And as soon as they were trussed up and bundled into the back of a vehicle, their options would be severely limited. But Danny needed to get something straight. 'How did he get my CIA file?' he demanded. 'Did *you* give it to him?' When Malinka didn't reply, he strode towards her and whispered in her ear, 'You want to live, you'd better answer me.'

'Why would I have your CIA file? I'd never heard of you before today.'

'Then who—'

'He made contact with Langley while you were in there.' She pointed to the cell in which Danny had been incarcerated. 'He demanded to know why he was under attack by Western forces. Langley denied all knowledge so he emailed your photographs. The other two came back a blank, but the CIA identified you and supplied your file.' She drew a deep breath.

Danny could tell the rope was still tight by the constricted tone of Malinka's voice.

'Why would they do that?' he demanded.

'They're doing a deal,' she croaked. 'The CIA want IS out of northern Iraq and into Syria.'

'Why?'

'To ... to destabilise the Russian-backed Syrian government, and to give America control of the Iraqi oilfields.'

'Jesus,' Danny breathed. He glanced at Spud and Caitlin in turn. They both looked thunderstruck.

'Fucking Yanks,' Spud hissed. 'How many boys do we know who've been killed by IS, and the Americans are getting into bed with them?' He looked sickened. Danny felt the same.

'What do IS get in return?' he demanded. 'What's in it for them?'

'The Americans agree not to target the oilfields they control in Syria – at least that was the plan. Now he knows I've been spying on him for the Americans, things will change ...'

Danny let that sink in for a couple of seconds. His mind was spinning with this new information. *Focus,* he told himself.

'What do you know about my daughter? Where is she? Who's got her?'

Malinka let out a heavy wheeze and then: 'He never shared that kind of information with me.'

Caitlin twisted the rope harder.

'*I swear ...*'

'What about the strike on London?'

'Westminster,' she gasped. 'Christmas Day.' She was trembling.

'Are you the CIA's source for that information?'

'Of course.'

The dog started to bark. Danny glanced nervously at the door. Then he looked at Caitlin and nodded.

Caitlin twisted the rope, a full revolution plus a little more until the rope squeaked. Malinka's neck squeezed hard against the metal bar. A desperate, croaking sound escaped her throat. Her hands shot up to her neck, and she tried to worm her fingers under the rope. Impossible. Caitlin twisted it harder. Her knuckles were as white as her face, and she was sweating badly. The flesh of

Malinka's neck grew thicker, bulging out from the edges of the rope. Her skin turned blotchy and purple. She was flailing her arms now, but weakly.

Caitlin gave the rope a final twist. It only turned a few millimetres, but it was enough. Malinka's arms fell to her side and her body slumped. 'That was for the women,' Caitlin whispered.

'Keep it tight,' Danny warned her. He put his arms through the bars and grabbed Malinka's left wrist, feeling for a pulse. It was weak, but it was there. She wasn't dead yet.

Seconds passed. The buzz of the flies crawling over Naza's body seemed to grow a little quieter. Danny kept his fingers pressed into Malinka's wrist for another ten seconds, until . . .

'She's dead,' he said. 'Ease her down to the ground slowly. She needs to stay close to the bars.'

Caitlin loosened the rope, but did not untie it completely. She kept a grip on it as Malinka's body slumped down the bar, into an awkward heap on the floor. She unwound the rope and staggered back.

'Want to tell me what's going on?' Spud said.

'Dhul Faqar only has five guys left,' Danny replied. 'He's not going to waste more than one guarding us when he knows we're locked up. And whoever's on the other side of that door isn't going to want one of us to snuff it on his watch. When he sees her like that, my money's on him entering the cage to try to revive her. When he does . . .' Danny left it hanging. 'We need to stand away from the body until the right moment. Spud, make some noise.'

Danny and Caitlin moved to the far side of the cage. Spud moved to the front. He pounded his fist against the cage door, which rattled in its frame. It disturbed the flies on Naza's corpse, which swarmed momentarily before settling again. It also disturbed the dog, who went into a frenzy of barking and growling. 'Oi!' Spud called. 'Abdul! You might want to look at this.'

Silence. Spud rattled the door frame again. The flies swarmed for a second time. 'Hey! Get in here!'

The door to the incarceration block opened. One of the militants entered. He wore an irritated frown, and barked something in Arabic. His AK was hanging carelessly across his front. Spud pointed to the crumpled form of Malinka in the adjoining cell. The militant peered over at it. His frown deepened, and he couldn't disguise the look of worry on his face. He closed the door with his heel and ran over to Malinka's cell, opening it quickly with a sturdy key on a chain clipped to his camouflage trousers. He lunged inside, and seconds later was kneeling by Malinka's body, two fingers pressed against her jugular.

Distance to the bars that separated the two cells: four metres. Three paces. Danny was a big man, but he could move fast. He estimated it would take him a second. Then he'd need to get his hand through the bars to grab the militant. Another second. Ordinarily, he wouldn't like his odds. Two seconds was ample time for someone to retreat from Danny's reach, if they saw him coming. But this guy was panicking. Badly. If Danny moved now, he had a chance.

He thundered across the cell. He was practically against the bars by the time the militant looked up. He thrust his right arm through a gap in the bars just as the militant started pushing himself to his feet. The militant was angling backwards, but Danny managed to catch his left wrist in a firm grip.

And that was all he needed.

Danny yanked hard. The militant tripped over Malinka's body as his face crashed against the bars. He shouted out in surprise and pain: that was the last noise he made. Danny thrust his left arm through the bars and hooked it round the back of the militant's neck. Then he released his right arm, pressed the heel of his hand against the man's forehead and gave a sudden, sharp, brutal push. The militant's head snapped back, and there was a crack as the top of his spinal cord split. He went into a crazy spasm, arms and legs flailing, body shuddering. Danny kept his arm crooked firmly round his neck, the face pressed up against the bars as the spasm subsided.

Five seconds later, the militant was still. The tally in Danny's head changed: four guys left. He allowed the corpse to slide down the bars, just as Caitlin had done with Malinka, and carefully released the man's neck at floor level so the body rested at the foot of the bars.

They needed his weapon first. Their captors could notice at any moment that the incarceration unit was unmanned. If that happened, they'd be in here. Danny unclipped the dead man's AK from the sling round his neck, held it vertically and pulled it through the bars. Spud was at his shoulder, ready to accept the firearm. Danny handed it over and was aware, in his peripheral vision, of Spud moving to the front of the cell, kneeling down in the firing position and poking the barrel through the front bars in the direction of the door. Danny himself focussed on the dead man's keys. They were still hanging from a chain in the pocket of his camo trousers. A solid tug and they were away. He moved to the front of the cage. Unlocking the door would be awkward. There was no keyhole on the inside. He had to crook his arm through the bars again and insert it from the opposite side. The dog went crazy: constant, aggressive barking. Anyone who heard it would know something was happening—

The main door opened. A figure entered. His weapon was raised. Danny didn't even glance towards him. He knew Spud had them covered. There was a pause of a fraction of a second as Spud let the guy cross the threshold, then a loud report from the unsup-pressed AK as he released a single round into the newcomer's chest. The militant fell to the ground just as Danny got the cage door open.

The dog continued to strain, growl and bark. Spud turned his weapon towards the animal and silenced it with a single round.

Three militants left, plus Dhul Faqar.

With Spud still covering him, he ran to the bloodied form of the new corpse and helped himself to the man's rifle. Then he looked back at his unit-mates and jabbed a single finger towards the exit, before installing himself in the firing position at the threshold of the door.

Evening had arrived. The light was failing. Danny could hear the engine of a vehicle turning over, somewhere off to his left. Caitlin was right – Dhul Faqar and his men might be preparing to move. They would have decided that this location was heavily compromised. Danny realised there was a chance that the sound of the engine had masked the report of Spud's AK. From the doorway he had line of sight across the open ground towards the two observation posts. They were unmanned. There was no movement anywhere that he could see.

Options. Move out of the incarceration unit. Methodically search the compound until they came across the three remaining militants. Then make a move on Dhul Faqar, who would probably still be in his personal quarters until it was time to leave. He felt his eyes narrowing at that option. Only he and Spud were armed. Caitlin was fading. They couldn't leave her alone, but she'd be a hindrance if they started to comb the area. Option two: stay here. Draw the guards in. Pick them off as they entered the incarceration unit—

The car engine suddenly stopped and a different noise reached him. Screaming: a woman. It could only be the Yazidi slave girl. It sounded to Danny very much like Dhul Faqar was having a final bit of fun before the time came to leave. It meant that for the Yazidi girl, time was running out.

'*Shit* . . .' Spud hissed from behind him. Danny turned just in time to see Caitlin, who was crossing the incarceration unit towards the door, roll her eyes and suddenly collapse.

Spud moved towards her immediately and checked her pulse, but Danny could guess what the problem was: surely a blood infection from her wound.

'Pulse is there,' Spud said. 'But not strong.'

'Move her to the side of the room. Out of sight of anyone entering.'

While Spud did that, Danny dragged the dead guard further to the side of the door. Caitlin's collapse had made his decision for him. With only three guards left, their best bet was to wait until they realised the incarceration unit was open and unmanned, then pick them off individually as they came to investigate. But not with a gun. If the others heard rounds being released, they'd take precautions . . .

Danny took up position by the side of the door frame. Silence descended. It was broken a few seconds later by a distant, inhuman shriek from the Yazidi slave girl. It seemed to echo eerily across the whole compound and it turned Danny's thoughts, which had been momentarily distracted, back to Clara and his daughter. He felt his skin prickling and his blood heating, and an unsuppressed knot of panic in his gut.

Then he heard footsteps. Running. Getting nearer. He tried to estimate the distance. Fifteen metres? Ten? Five?

He recognised the militant who appeared in the doorway as the guy who had held Caitlin at gunpoint in Dhul Faqar's room. The man was slightly out of breath as he entered the incarceration unit. He never even saw his killer. Danny grabbed him from behind, swung him round and smashed his face hard into the wall. There was a smear of blood where flesh met concrete. Danny hooked one arm round the unconscious man's neck and snapped his spine with the same ease with which he'd dispatched his mate minutes before. The body went limp. Danny dragged it over to the rapidly increasing pile of IS corpses, let it fall, then took up his position again.

Two guards left.

More screaming from the Yazidi girl. Danny was sweating badly. He tried to calm himself, but his eyes fell on the eviscerated corpse of Naza. If they'd captured her, they'd probably captured the other Kurdish militants. And most probably killed them – unlike the SAS unit, they were of no publicity value to Dhul Faqar and his men. When – there was no *if* in Danny's mind – the unit got out of here, their ride to the Turkish border was gone. Their extraction plan depended on getting back into Turkey, since Whitehall was so nervous about sending aircraft into northern Iraq. Which meant they were now stuck in the middle of the IS heartland, with no obvious means of escape.

And every second they wasted stuck in the badlands of northern Iraq, the danger to his daughter increased.

Footsteps again. A hoarse voice called something out in Arabic. Danny pressed himself against the wall to the side of the door frame once more, waiting for the footsteps to get nearer. Spud was leaning over the recently dead militant, scavenging the rounds from the magazine of his AK. Danny hissed at him to be silent. Five seconds later, their next guy appeared. This one was not so easy to deal with. He entered warily, his weapon in the firing position, clearly expecting the unexpected. Which was what he got.

As soon as the militant entered the incarceration unit, Danny grabbed the leading barrel of his rifle, fixing his arm so that the weapon's trajectory was clear of him, Spud and Caitlin. The militant fired, and Danny felt the weapon kick back as the round ricocheted dangerously off the front bars of the right-hand cage cell.

Still clutching the weapon, Danny reached out with his free hand to grab the militant's neck. But the militant was strong, and with a ferocious twist of his body he managed to push Danny away, knocking him off his balance and ripping the gun barrel from his grip. Danny cursed. Everything seemed to slow down. The militant was facing him, and the weapon was pointing directly at Danny's chest, the end of the barrel just inches away. A cruel sneer spread across the militant's face as he prepared to take the shot—

Gunfire . . .

For the briefest moment, Danny thought he was hit. But the gunfire had come from behind him. The militant slumped against the wall by the door, half his face blown away and a river of blood gushing from the wound. Looking over his shoulder, he saw Spud with his weapon still engaged, covering the door.

'I make that one to go, plus Dhul Faqar,' Spud said.

'Roger that. But he'll have heard the shot. We can't count on him just walking in here.'

'Then let's go find the fucker. We'll come back for Caitlin.'

Danny engaged his own weapon and turned to face the door.

More shouting. But it wasn't the Yazidi girl this time. Two male voices, perhaps twenty metres distant. One of them sounded like

Dhul Faqar. The second was male. The remaining guard taking instructions from his boss.

'Let's kill two birds with one stone,' he growled.

'Hold your fire on Dhul Faqar, mucker,' Spud reminded him. 'Remember why we're here. We need his intel on the London hit.'

'We need more than that,' Danny muttered, as the iPad footage of Rose and Clara flashed across his consciousness. 'Let's move.'

He stepped out into the half-light of the Iraqi evening, leading with his weapon. The weather had dramatically changed. The sky was very clear, a deep blue. No sign of clouds, and a half moon visible in the sky. He immediately turned ninety degrees anti-clockwise so he was facing towards Dhul Faqar's building. Distance: thirty metres. He could see that the door was open, and as he scoped it, he heard the sound of panicked shouting from the two men again.

Keep panicking guys, he thought to himself. Panic suits me just fine.

He advanced at a fast walk, keeping the weapon fixed precisely at the open door. He knew that if a threat was to come, it would come from there. He was aware of Spud following him. Though he couldn't see his mate, he knew he would be walking backwards, covering left, right and behind, just in case they were making the wrong call about the location of their final target.

But they weren't.

The target appeared in the doorway when Danny was fifteen metres out. Danny didn't fire immediately. He needed to be certain that this was Dhul Faqar's remaining guard, not the man himself. But the image of Dhul Faqar, with his white robe, sandals and greying beard, was burned into Danny's mind. It took a fraction of a second to make the positive ID, and even less time to squeeze the trigger and nail the guy in the doorway. The gunshot echoed across the compound, and a flock of birds rose with a screech from the reservoir to his left. The guard went down. Danny continued to advance implacably on Dhul Faqar's quarters.

Five metres out, he stopped, holding his breath to eliminate any unnecessary noise. The door was open, but it was dim inside and he couldn't see much apart from the shadows cast by a flickering candle. He could hear the sound of desperate whimpering, though. The Yazidi slave girl was still alive. Danny would give almost anything for a flashbang, but their packs had been taken from them. He'd have to make do without.

'Spud, are you with me?' Danny breathed. He didn't look back.

'Roger that.'

'I think he's using the slave girl as a human shield.'

Danny's mate advanced past his left shoulder, weapon engaged, until he was just to the left of the open door. He fired a quick round at the door itself, which splintered and swung open on its hinges. Then he fired two more rounds in quick succession into the room, above the top edge of the door. He nodded at Danny, who advanced carefully through the doorway.

Danny saw immediately that he'd been right. Dhul Faqar was backed into the far corner of the room. Distance: six metres. He had the slave girl in front of him, his left hand clutching her hair, his right hand holding a knife to her throat, which had been released from the metal collar. The blade was long and thin, maybe nine inches, twice the width of the girl's throat. The girl herself was naked. By the dim candlelight and the orange glow of the fire, Danny could see the bruises and welts all over her breasts and abdomen, and blood streaks down her inner thigh. She was shaking. Crying. Danny didn't think he'd ever seen anybody look so terrified.

But Dhul Faqar ran her a close second. His sleazy eyes were wide and alarmed. His knife hand shook. 'If you take another step,' he said, unable to stop the quaver in his voice, 'I slit her throat.'

Danny didn't move. Didn't lower his weapon. He stared directly into Dhul Faqar's eyes. In his peripheral vision, he saw flames licking up from the fire, which had just been smouldering when they were last in here. Something had just been thrown on it. Paper.

But Danny focussed on Dhul Faqar and the girl. 'Go ahead,' he said. 'Kill her. Saves me a job.'

Silence. Danny sensed Spud moving into the room behind him, and saw Dhul Faqar's frightened eyes glance towards his mate, then back to Danny. He licked his lips nervously.

'Drop the girl, mucker,' Spud breathed from behind him. 'He's going to kill her anyway.'

Danny hesitated for just a moment. Then he advanced. He disagreed with Spud. Dhul Faqar *wouldn't* kill this girl. She was all he had, his only negotiating tool. As Danny crossed the room, Dhul Faqar's eyes grew wilder, and his hand shook more violently. But he didn't slice the girl's neck, and within a few seconds, Danny had the barrel of his rifle inches from Dhul Faqar's forehead.

He kept his voice level. Reasonable. 'Drop the knife,' he said. 'I'm not going to kill you. I'm not even going to move you from here. You know I don't want you dead, but you've got to work with me. You have to drop the knife first.'

Dhul Faqar didn't move. His eyes flickered towards the door.

'All your men are dead,' Danny continued. 'You don't have any other option. Drop the knife. You and me, we're going to work this out.'

Dhul Faqar's face twitched. He lowered the knife a couple of inches.

'You've got to drop it, buddy,' Danny said.

Dhul Faqar opened his fingers. The knife fell to the floor. He was still clutching the girl's hair in his other fist.

'Let the girl go,' Danny said.

Dhul Faqar's fist loosened. The slave girl scrambled away from him. Dhul Faqar suddenly shrank further into the corner of the room.

Maybe he'd seen something in Danny's eyes.

Maybe he knew what was coming.

Danny's anger, which he had suppressed so well, burst out. Shooting Dhul Faqar wouldn't be enough. He wanted to hurt him. Badly. So badly that he'd be begging to tell Danny who had his daughter and where she was.

Danny flicked the safety switch on his rifle to the safe position, then advanced suddenly and angrily. He spun his weapon round so that the butt was facing Dhul Faqar, and crashed it hard into the side of his head. There was a nasty crack as the man's nose broke, and a spray of mucus and blood showered across Danny's face and the surrounding walls. He let the weapon fall, grabbed Dhul Faqar by the throat and raised his knee sharply into his groin. Dhul Faqar bent double with an agonised groan, and immediately received Danny's knee on the underside of his jaw. Danny heard teeth go, and a sharp, hissing intake of breath as Dhul Faqar staggered back against the wall, his eyes rolling.

'Don't like people looking at you, you piece of shit? Well how about I gouge your fucking eyes out so you can't tell either way—'

'*Leave him . . .*'

Spud was there, right behind Danny, grabbing him by the shoulders, pulling him back. Danny rounded on his mate and jabbed the heels of his hands into Spud's chest, knocking him back. He knew he was out of control, but he couldn't stop himself. He turned back to Dhul Faqar, and was on the point of moving in again, ready to pummel him with his bare fists, when Spud pulled him back for a second time. Danny's anger swelled. He felt himself burning, ready to go for Spud himself. He was bearing down on his mate, fists clenched, his face set like iron . . .

'You're going to kill him,' Spud hissed. 'What then, Danny? How do you find your kid when he's dead?'

Danny stopped. He was breathing heavily. Sweating.

Spud was right. He needed to get a grip. To control himself—

'*NO!*'

Spud shouted so loudly that Danny was momentarily taken aback. His mate was raising his gun, and Danny suddenly realised that he'd made an unforgivably basic error and turned his back on his opponent. He spun round, fully expecting to see Dhul Faqar coming for him with his knife.

He saw something very different.

The Yazidi girl, naked, bleeding and battered, had a look of animal desperation on her face. She also had Dhul Faqar's knife in her fist. She was crouching to one side of Dhul Faqar, holding it low, the blade pointing upwards, just inches from his midriff.

Danny lunged towards her. But too late. She stabbed the blade hard into the side of her abuser's body, deep into his ribcage. It slid in with atrocious ease – and out again as she stabbed him for a second time before Spud could release his round.

Deafening gunshot resonated round the room. Spud's round slammed into the side of the Yazidi girl's head. She collapsed immediately, leaving the knife buried deep in Dhul Faqar's guts. His white robe was wet with blood. It was pissing from the wound. Dhul Faqar was staring down at himself with a look of mingled horror and astonishment.

Then he tried to breathe.

It was immediately clear to Danny that the long blade had punctured one lung, maybe both. There was a dreadful gurgling, gasping sound as Dhul Faqar collapsed to his knees, trying unsuccessfully to get breath into his damaged lungs. Neither of them looked at the body of the poor Yazidi girl, her head bleeding and shattered. All Danny's attention was on Dhul Faqar as he surged towards his enemy.

Spud was with him. They wordlessly got the IS commander on to his right-hand side in the recovery position, so the wound was facing upwards. Danny pressed his hand hard on to the punctured skin, trying to stem the flow of blood, but it was useless. Thick and sticky, it oozed relentlessly out between his fingers. Danny tried to picture the route the knife had taken through Dhul Faqar's body. It wasn't just the lungs that would be damaged. Stomach. Kidney. Liver. Major organ failure. Without a full med team on hand, there was zero chance of him surviving.

He grabbed Dhul Faqar by the face and twisted his head so they were looking at each other, eye to eye. 'Where's my daughter?' he hissed. 'Who's got her?'

Dhul Faqar didn't reply. A couple of seconds passed. Then a fountain of blood and foam erupted from his mouth as his body went into spasm. Danny rolled him on to his back and started pumping his chest vigorously, one compression per second. The ribcage sank two inches with each pump, and Danny thought he felt the breastbone breaking. But as he tried in vain to keep Dhul Faqar alive, he knew that each chest compression was pushing him closer to the grave as it forced more blood from his wound, each wave less copious than the last.

After ten seconds, he knew he was pumping the chest of a dead man.

'Mucker, he's gone,' Spud said from behind him.

Danny stopped pumping. He stood up and stared at the corpse at his feet, then at his own hands, which were covered in blood, sweat and dirt. The firelight flickered in the room. Danny and Spud were breathing heavily. Danny's anger erupted again. He started kicking the body and head of Dhul Faqar's fresh corpse. Pointless, but the only way he could think of to release his frustration.

He dealt the dead man six solid blows to the head, and only stopped there because Spud dragged him away.

TWENTY

'Did you have to kill the girl?' Danny said bitterly. 'She could have told us something.'

He instantly regretted saying it. Spud had a sickened, haunted look on his face. He had taken the course of action the situation demanded. He'd refused to let emotion get in the way. A bad soldier would have hesitated. That didn't mean he had to like it. And he obviously didn't.

In any case, this was a mess of Danny's making. He'd taken his eye off the ball. He'd done what Spud hadn't, and let emotion cloud his judgement.

'Go check on Caitlin,' Danny said, by way of unspoken apology.

Spud nodded wordlessly, leaving Danny alone in the bloodbath that was Dhul Faqar's quarters. He knew that he, Spud and Caitlin were the only people alive in the compound now. How long for, he couldn't tell. People up on the main supply route could have heard gunshots. Dhul Faqar might have called for reinforcements. Bottom line: they couldn't stay here. It wasn't safe. They needed to extract.

But not yet. Not before Danny had searched Dhul Faqar's quarters.

He looked around and picked out their packs and gear, which had been stashed along the wall. He had to step over the Yazidi girl's body to reach them. He selected his own rifle, which was propped up against the wall, and detached the Surefire torch from its rack. He switched it on and turned back towards the centre of the room. Spud entered, carrying the unconscious

Caitlin. 'Get some meds inside her,' he said, nodding back towards the packs.

'We need to get out of here,' Spud said, laying Caitlin carefully on the ground.

'In a minute.'

'Mucker, we could be overrun by more of these twats any time.'

'I said, in a minute.'

There was a table in the centre of the room. It was littered with books and papers, all in Arabic. Danny shone his torch on it, and shuffled impatiently through the contents, looking for the iPad that Dhul Faqar had used to show him the footage of Clara and Rose. There was no sign of it. He took a step back from the table, and his torch illuminated something on the floor. Black. Rectangular. He bent down to pick it up. It was Dhul Faqar's iPad, but the screen was smashed, like a window with a bullet hole. Danny tried to switch it on, but the device was dead.

He cursed, but kept hold of the iPad. Something else had caught his eye on the table, half hidden under some other documents. It looked like a British Ordnance Survey map. Danny pulled it towards him, and shone his torch at it. The map had been opened up, then refolded to expose four rectangles of terrain. It had clearly been well used, because the mapping was worn away at each crease. Even without examining the place names, Danny recognised London by the shape of the River Thames. One place name in particular, however, had been circled in black marker pen: Westminster Abbey. But there was nothing else that gave Danny any more information about the hit.

Then he remembered the fire. It had been burning brightly, but now the flames had died down. Danny cursed. He should have checked before to see what Dhul Faqar had been so keen to burn.

There was a pile of crisp, black embers on the coals, which Danny realised had been a sheaf of papers. One piece of paper, however, had fallen to the front of the fire and was only half burned. Danny removed it, then examined it carefully.

'Spud,' he breathed. 'Look at this.'

Spud joined him. He was carrying a med pack, ready to minister to Caitlin. He looked at the paper.

It was a printout from a UK weather website. A forecast. Temperature. Cloud cover. And, circled in black pen, and translated into Arabic lettering beneath, wind speed.

Danny double-checked the location for the forecast.

Sandringham, Norfolk.

He glanced back at the map of London on the table. His mind was working quickly, picking out various moments from the past few hours and days. He remembered talking to Malinka, just before Caitlin had killed her, asking her about the strike on London: *Westminster*, she had said. *Christmas Day*.

But as Dhul Faqar had suspected Malinka of being an American agent, he would *never* have let her have that information in the first place, unless it was inaccurate.

And why had he been so eager to burn this slip of paper, while leaving untouched the map of London with Westminster Abbey so clearly marked?

'That's where the Christmas Day strike is,' Danny said quietly. 'He's targeting the royals. It's where they spend Christmas.' He paused. 'Maybe that's why Tony was dispatched to pick up Yellow Seven. Maybe Five heard some whispers and wanted him back in the country.'

A pause. Spud was eyeing him uncertainly. 'I'm hearing a lot of maybes, Danny.'

Danny jabbed the weather report with his forefinger. It left a smear of blood on the paper. 'Wind speed and wind direction, translated into Arabic. What would we use that information for, you and me?'

'Taking sniper shots,' Spud said immediately.

Danny gave him a look that said: got it in one.

'You don't know any of that for sure, mucker,' Spud said carefully.

'Yes I do,' Danny said. Because something else had just clicked in his mind. Something Dhul Faqar had said when they were being held at gunpoint. *Our friend Mujahid ... He will be very happy to be distracted from his Christmas Day plans to travel west and put an end to your child's life.* 'He told us his guy Mujahid would travel west. You'd only say that if you were somewhere east. Sandringham's in Norfolk.'

'I dunno, mate. What about the IS guys on the migrant boats?'

'Patsys,' Danny said. 'Put right into our path to feed us false information. That's how Dhul Faqar operates. He sacrificed one of his people to flush out Malinka. He sacrificed Santa and Rudolph to make us think the strike was going to be in London. But it's not. Think about it. You see it on TV every year – the royals going to church on Christmas morning. And with every military resource focussed on London, it'll be the easiest hit in the world.' He stared at Spud. 'The British royal family, massacred by IS. I can't think of anything those bastards would like better.'

Spud looked unconvinced. 'Hereford are waiting for our communication,' he said. 'Phone all this through. Tell them what you think. Then they can make the call.' He turned his back on Danny and returned to their gear, clearly about to get their satphone from one of the packs.

'No,' Danny said.

Spud stopped. 'What are you talking about?'

'Don't make the call,' Danny said. 'Not until we've worked out what we're going to say.'

'I told you, we just—'

'They've got my daughter, Spud. And Clara too. I've got no leads. No way of finding them.'

'Mate, we—'

'Except one,' Danny said.

A pause.

'What?' Spud asked.

'This guy Mujahid. He knows where they are. And we know where *he's* going to be on Christmas morning. If we let the Regiment know, their first priority will be to shoot him on sight. I can't let that happen.'

Spud's eyes widened slightly as it dawned on him what Danny was suggesting. 'You want to *keep* it from them? Mate, they find out, they'll chuck us in prison and throw away the fucking key.'

Danny stayed silent.

'Just tell them everything you know. Tell them this Mujahid guy has to be taken alive.'

'Right,' Danny said. 'Because we all know what happens to people who need to stay alive, if they get in the way of a Regiment mission objective.' And he looked meaningfully over at the Yazidi girl Spud had shot just minutes previously.

'Jesus,' Spud breathed. He shook his head. 'You haven't got a chance of catching this guy, Danny. If there really is going to be a hit at Sandringham, you've got no way of predicting how it's going to happen, because you don't know what the royals' movements are.'

'Maybe not,' Danny said quietly. 'But we know a guy who does.'

For a moment, Spud looked confused. Then his eyes widened. 'Tony? You've got to be fucking joking. He *hates* you. The cunt wouldn't give you the steam off his piss.'

'We'll see,' Danny said. 'But we've got to get out of here first.' He nodded towards Caitlin. 'If we tell them we got no intel out of Dhul Faqar, Caitlin's a goner. We know how nervous the Firm is about breaching Iraqi airspace at the moment. They won't risk it just for a medical evacuation of a single soldier.'

'It could take us weeks to get to the border,' Spud said.

'Well, we've got hours, not weeks. We need to dangle a carrot. Make them think it's worthwhile getting us picked up.'

Spud pinched the bridge of his nose. 'What have you got in mind, Danny?'

'Are you with me?'

Spud bowed his head. He obviously didn't like any of this. But Spud owed Danny. Big time. Now that it was Danny's turn to call in the favour, he could hardly refuse.

'What do you want me to do?' he said.

'Find us a vehicle we can use. I'm going to make a call. We leave in two minutes, and we'll be home tomorrow. I guarantee it.'

Spud oozed reluctance. But he didn't argue. Danny moved over to the packs, selected his and hurried to the exit. Spud hauled Caitlin over his shoulder again and followed.

Outside, everything was still. Danny strode up to the edge of the reservoir. It was fully dark again, and a cloudy moon reflected on the dark water. Danny removed the satphone from his pack, inserted the battery, switched it on, waited a few moments while it powered up, then speed-dialled their contact number.

It was answered within a single ring. A male voice, very clear. '*Go ahead.*'

'This is Delta Three Tango.'

'*Wait out, Delta Three Tango.*'

A crackly pause of twenty seconds. Then a new voice. '*What do you know?*' Danny recognised the voice immediately – Ray Hammond. He wondered if their ops officer had made it back to the UK.

'Target acquired and eliminated. We have three names.'

'*Please transmit.*'

Danny paused. The success of his plan depended on Hammond not knowing that Clara had been abducted. He couldn't ask him outright – not if he wanted to track down his daughter on his own. So he kept it obscure. 'Do you have anything to tell me?'

Now it was Hammond's turn to pause. '*What are you talking about?*' He sounded genuinely bewildered. That was enough for Danny. '*Transmit the names.*'

'Negative,' Danny said.

Silence. '*Transmit names,*' Hammond repeated.

'You want names, you need to send a pick-up to extract us.'

'*You know that's not possible—*'

'*Make* it possible. We have wounded personnel. They won't survive without a medical evacuation.'

'*Negative, Delta Three Tango. Transmit names immediately.*'

'Take down the following location,' Danny said, and recited the GPS reading that he'd intended to be their RV point with the Kurds. 'We'll be there in one hour.'

He switched off the satphone and pulled out the battery. He knew he'd just dropped a bombshell on the headshed. He knew they'd make him pay for it back in the UK. They'd talk about RTUs. There'd probably even be court martials. Danny didn't care. If the Ruperts thought they'd failed to extract any intelligence out of Dhul Faqar, they'd leave them to find their own way out of Iraq. Danny hadn't been lying when he said Caitlin wouldn't make it. Nor would his daughter . . .

He sensed Spud behind him. His mate had returned to retrieve his and Caitlin's packs.

'You got a vehicle?'

Spud nodded. But suddenly he wasn't looking at Danny. He was staring into the distance, across the reservoir. He pointed. 'What the hell's that?' he breathed.

Danny looked. He immediately saw what Spud was pointing at. Several black shadows, flying low over the water, only visible because they blocked out the stars, and because their down-draught formed white horses on the water, illuminated by the clear half moon.

For a sickening moment, he looked at the satphone in his hands. Had someone been listening in to his conversation? Had the encryption been so easily hacked? Impossible, he told himself. He'd only finished talking a few seconds ago. Nobody could mobilise that quickly . . .

Then he heard the banging sound from the incarceration unit, and he understood.

'Americans,' he hissed. 'Malinka must have not clocked in with her handlers. They know something's gone wrong. They're here to extract her. They're not going to let us leave, knowing what we know.' He turned to Spud. '*Run!*' he hissed.

Spud hoisted the two packs over his shoulders and sprinted. Danny followed him, across the open ground and past the incarceration unit. They could hear the chopper now, the low thrum of its engine and the regular beating of the rotor blades. The Hilux that Spud had selected was parked at an angle on the far side of the incarceration unit. There were several bullet holes in the side, but it was turning over. The left-hand rear passenger door was open, and Danny glimpsed Caitlin lying there, unconscious. The rear window had been shattered, probably by gunfire. Danny and Spud hauled their packs into the back.

Spud sprinted to the driver's seat, Danny to the passenger side, slamming Caitlin's door as he passed. Seconds later, they were moving. No headlamps, so they didn't draw attention to themselves. Spud floored it, the engine screaming as he made his way up the gears, the poorly suspended chassis juddering and bumping over the rough ground. Danny leaned out of the side window, his weapon engaged. Looking back towards the buildings, he could see the threatening form of one of the choppers hovering over the open ground by the side of the reservoir while two others held back over the water, their downdraught kicking up clouds of spray. Figures were fast-roping out of the belly of the chopper that had made landfall.

'American SF!' Danny shouted. '*Faster!*'

The vehicle juddered badly as Spud spun it off the rough ground and on to the narrow road that led to the perimeter fence, past the two checkpoints and up to the main supply route. From the corner of his eye he could see, in silhouette, the corpses still hanging from the cherry pickers along the perimeter fence. Up ahead, the vehicles belonging to the middlemen were still positioned in the road, and nobody had bothered moving the corpses of the men the unit had eliminated on the way in. Ten metres from the perimeter fence checkpoint, a flock of birds rose suddenly from the corpses on which they had obviously been scavenging. Spud didn't slow down. As they hit the checkpoint, there was a bump and a crunch as the wheels of the Hilux steamrollered over one of the bodies in the road. Spud yanked the steering wheel left and swerved sharply out of the way of the middlemen's vehicles, before directing the Hilux back on to the road.

Up ahead, there were the lights of headlamps on the main supply route. It wasn't busy, but they would only be safe once they reached it and could merge into the traffic heading north. He kept the speed up as Danny looked back towards the compound again. The chopper was still hovering. It had been there for about a minute. The troops would have found Malinka's body by now. They'd be expecting to find Danny. What would they do when they discovered he was missing? Danny didn't know the answer to that question. All he knew was that they couldn't hang around to find out.

Fifteen seconds later, they reached the checkpoint nearest the main supply route. Spud burst through it. Distance to the road: 500 metres. The speedometer was tipping 120 kph. It would take fifteen seconds to cover it. Looking back, Danny saw the chopper rising. The flight crew had switched on a searchlight.

'I got it,' Spud breathed, before Danny could point it out.

The searchlight was panning across the compound, obviously looking for something.

Obviously looking for them . . .

Two hundred metres. The chopper was rising higher. Danny's gut went cold. The higher it was, the greater its field of view, and the better its chance of seeing them.

A hundred metres.

Fifty.

There was a groaning sound from the back. Caitlin stirred, but then closed her eyes again.

Spud didn't slow down until they were twenty metres from the main supply route. Nor did he switch on the headlamps. Danny gripped his seat hard. An articulated lorry was trundling along the main road at a stately 60 kph. For a horrific moment, he thought they were going to collide. There was a loud klaxon sound – the lorry driver was clearly thinking the same thing. But Spud's skills were good. At the last moment, he hit the brake. The Hilux decelerated just in time for them to swing on to the road, less than two metres behind the lorry. Spud quickly switched on the headlamps and allowed the Hilux to fall back. Suddenly, they were just another vehicle on the road.

Danny looked back towards the compound. The chopper had killed its lights. It obviously hadn't found what it was looking for, and seemed to be banking back towards the reservoir. He allowed himself a moment of relief as the Hilux headed north.

'I told them to pick us up at the RV point we identified with the Kurds,' Danny said.

Spud nodded. 'It could take a long time for them to get a pick-up to us, mucker. You know that, right? They were jumpy as fuck about breaching Iraqi airspace when we inserted.'

'They've got stealth choppers. And they think we've got the key to stopping a major hit on the capital. Something tells me they'll work it out pretty quick.'

He looked straight ahead. The tarmac of the main supply route flew past as Spud headed towards the RV point.

Danny was right.

It took them just shy of an hour to make their way up the rough track into the mountains that the Kurds had shown them, to the RV location. When they stopped, Danny double-checked that their GPS coordinates matched those he'd given over the satphone. They did. Now they just had to wait. They drove the Hilux off the track, hiding it behind a rounded, weathered boulder that was twice the size of the vehicle. There was a freshwater stream about thirty paces to the west. Danny and Spud carefully carried the unconscious Caitlin to it. Danny removed her top and did his best to wash the wound. It was in a very bad state. The flesh was mushy and bloodied, and it oozed with the telltale white pus of infection. Her body temperature was high, her breathing shallow. They tried to make her comfortable and safe by lying her back in the vehicle. But she needed serious medicine, and fast.

Danny and Spud took up covert defensive positions: Danny in the shadow of the same boulder that hid Caitlin and the Hilux, Spud on the other side of the track, belly-down amid some thick gorse bush. Danny was bone tired, and sore from the beatings he had endured at the compound. Covered in blood and sweat and dirt. Maybe a couple of broken ribs. It certainly hurt to breathe.

He put the pain from his mind. The call he'd made on the satphone hadn't lasted longer than thirty seconds, but he'd been obliged to transmit the coordinates of their RV location. It was unlikely that the Americans had intercepted that call, but if they had, he and Spud needed to be prepared for company.

But their only company, as two hours passed and then three, was the occasional scratching of unseen wild animals in the vicinity and, just before midnight, the ominous thunder of a fighter jet somewhere off to the south.

The noise they were waiting for – hoping for – arrived twenty minutes after that. It seemed to come from nowhere. One minute there was silence, the next there was a subdued hum, close yet somehow distant, like the ghost of a chopper. The ghost itself appeared in the sky moments after that. It was not the first time Danny had seen the sleek, angular contours of a stealth Black Hawk. The very existence of this aircraft was routinely denied by the MoD, but the sight of it, with its downward-pointing rotors designed to reduce noise and radar splash, was like a balm to Danny. He didn't move, however, or make any attempt to show himself, as the bird touched down. Spud lay low, too. It was only when the side door opened and a figure in camouflage fatigues appeared, whose top clearly displayed a 1Para flash, that Spud emerged from his gorse bush and ran, with full pack and rifle, towards the soldier.

Danny started to extract Caitlin from the Hilux, and within twenty seconds he had help – Spud and two others were there. Together they carried Caitlin and all their remaining gear from the vehicle towards the strangely quiet chopper. A medic was waiting for them inside, saline drip at the ready. He instantly took over Caitlin's care, while the loadie – a severe-looking man with a shock of ginger hair – closed up the door and gave the all-clear to the pilot. As the Black Hawk rose effortlessly from the ground, the loadie turned to Danny holding a headset and boom mike. 'Hereford HQ,' he said.

Danny felt Spud's eyes on him as he accepted and donned the headset. 'Go ahead,' he said.

'*Give me the names, Black.*' Ray Hammond, sounding angrier than Danny had ever heard him.

Danny caught Spud's anxious glance. 'You get the names when Caitlin's on British soil, boss,' he said.

'*For Christ's sake, Black, we haven't got time for this.*'

'Then get us home quick.'

He ripped off the headphones, handed them back to the loadie and looked out of the dark window at the mountains of northern Iraq, a fast-moving, moonlit blur below.

DECEMBER 24

TWENTY-ONE

Joe didn't think of it as stealing. He thought of it as survival.

He was slowly chewing a chicken sandwich that he had taken from a branch of Pret A Manger during the morning rush hour. Even though he had a little money, courtesy of Galbraith's wallet, he knew it had to last. The less he spent, the better. He had waited until now – nearly midnight – when his hunger pangs were unbearable, to eat the sandwich. He had no way of knowing where his next meal was coming from, and it had been risky taking it. He had thought, as he left the shop, that one of the staff had shouted out after him. He'd run away without looking back.

The expensive laptop whose screen he was staring at had, iron-ically, been easier to steal than the sandwich. He'd walked into a public library, found someone working at a machine that would suit his purpose, and waited for the owner to go and find a book from a nearby shelf. It took five silent seconds to close the laptop and swipe it. Nobody had even looked at him as he left the library. Outside, he had checked the battery charge. Thirty-eight per cent. Not good, and he had no charger, so he had to work fast.

Which was what he was now doing. He sat in an all-night cafe somewhere in the middle of London – he didn't know where he was exactly. There were a few feeble lengths of silver tinsel along the counter, and the radio softly played the same Christmas songs that Joe had heard relentlessly since his escape from Galbraith and Sharples. The guy behind the counter was whistling along tunelessly.

Earlier that day, Joe had overheard someone say that they didn't feel all that 'Christmassy'. He wasn't quite sure what they meant.

But he had decided that whatever 'Christmassy' did mean, it wasn't a good description for how Joe himself was feeling. He felt like there was a policeman on every corner. As though Galbraith – or even worse, Sharples – would put one hand on his shoulder at any moment. Galbraith's handgun felt heavy and leaden in the inside pocket of his coat. He didn't like carrying it. He couldn't shake the feeling that everyone knew it was there, and was staring at him. But he had decided it was necessary to hold on to it.

He had bought himself a small coffee using Galbraith's money, not because he wanted the drink but because he needed to use the cafe's Internet connection. It would have been possible to hack in to a random Wi-Fi network elsewhere, of course, but that would have taken time. And with only thirty-eight per cent battery, he didn't *have* the time.

'Did you buy that here?'

Joe looked up. The guy from the counter was standing by his table, pointing at his Pret A Manger sandwich. 'You can't eat what you didn't buy here, son.'

Joe frowned and nodded. He carefully packed up the remains of his sandwich and put it in the pocket of his red hooded top, then took a sip from his coffee.

'What you doing here this late anyway?' the man said. 'You're not one of them immigrants, are you?'

The real reason for the lateness of the hour was that the emptier the cafe, the more bandwidth on the Wi-Fi. But Joe didn't say that. He just muttered, 'College work.' It seemed to satisfy the man, who returned to his place behind the counter.

Joe had several windows open on the laptop. Two of them had black backgrounds and were running lines of the code that Joe was using to hack into certain servers by brute force. He could see his face reflected in them. A third window had open what looked like a Facebook page, filled with Arabic. It was in fact a dark-web equivalent of Facebook, open in the Tor browser. Highly encrypted. Available only to those who knew the relevant ciphers and passwords. It lurked on a corner of the dark net that was almost impossible to access if you didn't know how. Inaccessible to security services and curious individuals alike. Joe knew all this because he'd put it there for his Daesh controllers. The fourth window showed a Google map of the UK. A blue dot pulsed on Joe's position in central London.

He scanned the Arabic text on the Facebook clone, his jaw set as he did so. He was reading a conversation between a person he knew, and that person's boss. Nobody would be so foolish as to put a picture of themselves on this site, nor to use their real name. But having been forced, on pain of death or worse, to set up these networks and modes of communication, Joe knew quite well that the real name of the user who had given himself the handle that translated roughly as 'God's Truth' was Mujahid. That he had a scar that spanned the full width of his neck like a gruesome smile. That this was the same man who had stripped his father naked, hooded him and hung him from a tree. That he had raped Joe's mother in front of him, before killing her.

A memory flashed in his mind. He had just got off the train that had smuggled him into the UK. An aggressive soldier had said, *Here for the handouts, are you?*

A grim look crossed Joe's face. If only the soldier had known how far off the mark he was. Joe wasn't here for the handouts. He hadn't made that journey, and risked so much, for a few pounds a week.

Mujahid's messages were obscure. Joe knew that his correspondent, who styled himself 'Warrior King', was an IS commander by the name of Dhul Faqar. They always gave themselves names like that. Joe had never met this guy – he had been based over the border from Syria in northern Iraq – but it had been Mujahid's habit to use that name as a threat. Do as we say, or you will have Dhul Faqar to answer to.

As Joe scanned hurriedly through their conversation, he tried to piece together what they were talking about. There was talk of an event. It was to take place on 25 December. Christmas Day. His eyes passed over a string of numbers that meant nothing to him. And there was talk of a man named Black. A soldier. The conversation suggested that Dhul Faqar would be sending details of this man to Mujahid on a separate private network. One sentence caught his eye and made his stomach turn. He read it slowly. 'Take the child,' Dhul Faqar had instructed Mujahid. 'Keep her safe, for now.'

He was still wondering what those words could mean when the lines of code running on the windows with black backgrounds suddenly stopped scrolling: an indication that his brute-force hacking was complete. Joe's eyes flicked away from the conversation and became fixed on the Google map. The laptop's hard drive whirred. A few seconds later a number of red pins appeared on the map.

Joe experienced a moment of great satisfaction. This was the information he *really* wanted.

He knew, of course, that most smartphones tracked the location data of the user on a continuous basis. And he knew that Daesh used this facility to keep track of their agents abroad. What he had not been so sure of was his ability to access that data on a stolen computer in the scant time he had available.

He needn't have worried.

Mujahid had been busy. There were several pins dotted around London. As Joe hovered the cursor over them, a date and time popped up on each. The Daesh militant had been moving constantly around the capital during the past week. Joe's eyes were drawn to a lone pin a good distance to the north-west of London – a town called Hereford. It appeared that Mujahid had been there that very morning. From Hereford, it appeared he had moved north-east, to a city called Birmingham, where he had been at 1 p.m. After Birmingham, he had moved a few miles south . . .

But then the trail died away. Joe experienced a moment of bitter disappointment. Perhaps Mujahid had destroyed his phone, or removed the battery in case he was being tracked. He wondered what could have happened to make him suddenly nervous. But it didn't matter. The trail had gone cold.

Joe glanced at the battery indicator. It had diminished quickly to six per cent. His eyes returned to the Tor browser, and the conversation between Mujahid and Dhul Faqar. He scanned the conversation again, searching for anything that might be of use to him. He googled 'Soldier Black', but that returned nothing of any interest. Then his eyes fell on the seemingly meaningless string of numbers that he had all but ignored so far. Hardly expecting much, he keyed those numbers into his web browser. And he took an involuntary intake of breath when he realised that they were not meaningless at all. They were very specific. They were coordinates.

His search had returned a link to a new Google map. Joe clicked it. Another pin appeared on the map of the UK. It was superimposed on the symbol of a cross, which Joe understood to represent a place of worship.

The laptop screen went black. The battery had died. But Joe continued to stare at it. He knew, with absolute clarity, where Mujahid – the man he hated more than any other in the world – would be on Christmas Day. And he had a pretty good idea what he intended to do when he got there.

Should he tell someone? Alert the authorities? His mind turned to the memory of Galbraith and Sharples. After his encounter with them, it was more likely that Joe would be locked up than listened to. His fingers edged towards the heavy handgun in his inside pocket. They traced its outline. Suddenly, the weapon did not feel so cumbersome.

He closed the laptop and slid it into his shoulder bag. His coffee was still full, and slightly warm. He gulped it down, because it was a cold night out there. As he drank, another customer entered the cafe. He took off his heavy Puffa jacket and draped it over a seat near the entrance, before putting his phone and keys on the table. He then walked up to the counter and started to talk to the guy.

Joe was almost on autopilot now. He stood up and headed to the exit. As he passed the newcomer's table, he swiped the phone and dropped it in his pocket. Then he left.

You sleep only when it's safe. That was a lesson Danny had learned well over his years of active service. He was as safe as could be expected in the confines of the stealth Black Hawk. He forced himself to rest as it hummed quietly along the Turkish–Syrian border towards the eastern Mediterranean coast. Not easy. The footage of Clara and Rose kept replaying itself in his head. Constantly repeating, until he fell into a disturbed sleep, haunted by a nightmare of a little girl with a tiny tear of blood.

He woke as they hit the Med. The medic was no longer fussing over Caitlin, who was laid out on a stretcher bed with a saline drip above her, its surface tension vibrating with the movement of the aircraft. Twenty-five minutes later, they were touching down at the British military base in Cyprus.

The unit weren't on the ground for more than five minutes. A Hercules was waiting for them as they landed. The Paras on the Black Hawk carried Caitlin off the chopper and up the tailgate into the belly of the plane. Danny and Spud followed, carrying packs and weapons. They didn't speak. Danny could tell Spud didn't like what they were doing. That he was worried about the reception they'd get when they touched down in Blighty.

Flight time to RAF Brize Norton: three hours fifteen minutes. Danny found it harder to rest on this leg of the journey. He was burning with adrenaline and anxiety. What if he was wrong? What if he was making a bad call? What if, by going it alone, he failed to save Clara and his daughter? What if Mujahid, the man with the evil scar on his throat, had already killed them?

He pushed those thoughts from his head. They had no place there. He would not consider the possibility of failure.

0900 hours. The aircraft had been losing height for at least ten minutes. Danny looked through the window. It was light. England looked as vividly green as it always did on his return from an overseas job. Three minutes later they were touching down. As the aircraft screeched along the tarmac, Danny caught a glimpse of flashing lights. An ambulance, but also several police cars, waiting for them.

And Ray Hammond. As Danny and Spud followed Caitlin's stretcher bed down the tailgate into the cold morning air, he was standing there, arms crossed, his face more thunderously angry than Danny had ever seen it. The black rings under his eyes looked like they'd been painted on. A few metres beyond him, six police officers in hi-vis. Armed. Hammond glanced momentarily at Caitlin and nodded to the soldiers carrying her. They hurried her towards the ambulance, which was waiting with its rear doors open. Hammond turned to Danny.

'You don't make it easy for me to stick up for you, Black,' he said. 'Give me the names, now.'

A beat.

'There are no names,' Danny told him. 'Dhul Faqar died before we could get anything out of him.'

Hammond said nothing. A vein pumped in his neck.

'Once we realised the mission was a dud,' Danny said, 'my first priority was the safety of my team. Caitlin needed a medic.'

'You've had medical training, damn it,' Hammond spat.

'She wouldn't have made it,' Danny persisted.

'Have you got any *fucking* idea, the risks we ran getting you out of there?' Hammond turned to the police officers standing behind them. 'Relieve these gentlemen of their weapons,' he instructed. And as they approached, he turned back to Danny. 'I'd have some Regiment personnel here to deal with you, but every fucking man jack of them is in London, working on this job, standing by to pick up these people whose names we *thought* you were going to give us. These police officers are going to escort you back to Hereford. You'll be debriefed there. You'd better hope to hell I can call off the MoD's lawyers between now and then.' He started to walk away, but then turned back almost immediately. He pointed at the armed officers, then at Danny and Spud. 'Don't even fucking *think* about it,' he told them.

Danny understood what he meant.

They were in the back of a white Transit van, sitting on benches along either side, facing each other. Their packs and personal weapons were being transported in a separate vehicle. Two of the armed police officers sat by the rear door. The remaining four sat either side of Danny and Spud. Danny estimated their speed at 95 kph. At this rate, it would take them another two hours to reach Hereford.

The police officers had been tense at first. Like they were escorting two dangerous weapons. Which, in a way, they were. But Spud and Danny had offered no resistance, and now the officers seemed more relaxed. They'd stopped staring curiously at their bruised, beaten, dirty faces. One of them even had his head leaning back against the side of the van and was staring aimlessly at the ceiling.

Spud gave Danny a questioning look – a raised eyebrow, a slight incline of the head. He glanced towards the rear door, then back at Danny.

Almost imperceptibly, Danny shook his head. Sure, they could overpower these police officers in a matter of seconds. But then they'd be wanted men. Hunted men.

No. Hereford first.

Hammond was waiting for them in the yard at RAF Credenhill. One look told Danny that he'd regained none of his good humour. Danny felt disorientated. It was midday. Twenty-four hours previously, he'd been at the mercy of Dhul Faqar's men, being badly beaten in that dark cell. Now he was in the familiar surroundings of SAS headquarters.

Danny strode up to Hammond and jabbed his thumb back to indicate the armed police, who were following him uncertainly. 'You can lose them, boss,' Danny said. 'Me and Spud aren't going anywhere. We're not stupid.'

Hammond seemed to consider that for a moment. Then he looked towards the police officers. 'Get back to London,' he said. 'You're needed there.' He pointed at Danny and Spud. 'You two, with me.'

Credenhill was clearly being manned only by support staff. Danny, Spud and Hammond's footsteps echoed down the empty corridor as their ops officer led them towards his office. Once there, he silently pointed at two chairs on the other side of his desk. He sat down, pressed his fingers together and looked severely over them at his two soldiers. 'Caitlin will be fine,' he said. And then, rather grudgingly: 'It looks like you might have had a point. The medics said it was touch and go.' He sniffed. 'You two look like shit. Especially you, Black.'

Danny inclined his head.

'Talk,' Hammond told them.

Danny drew a deep breath, willing Spud to keep quiet. He reckoned he had his story sorted. With the practised skill of an operative who had been in more debriefs than he could count, he explained the events of the past forty-eight hours. The HALO insertion. The border crossing with the Kurds. The Spetznaz contact. The assault on Dhul Faqar's compound. Malinka. The Yazidi girl. Their capture and escape. Hammond listened quietly and intently. Only when Danny explained the CIA's involvement with Dhul Faqar, and the arrival of American special forces to extract their mole, did he ask Danny to repeat himself. Danny understood why. For the security services, intel like this was solid gold. And it might just buy him and Spud out of a court martial.

'The CIA were brokering a deal with IS,' Danny said. 'It's why they were holding back on supplying any information on the London hit. The Americans wanted to persuade him to move his forces out of northern Iraq and into Syria, to help destabilise the Syrian regime. If the Firm want more intel on Westminster Abbey, they should turn the screw on the Americans. They know more than they're letting on.'

Hammond nodded. 'What else?' he said.

'That's all,' Danny said. He sensed Spud give him an anxious look. Hammond looked from one man to the other. It seemed that he was trying to decide whether or not to believe them. Danny stayed silent. There was certain information he wasn't prepared to share. His daughter's abduction. His belief that the London strike was a red herring. Because he knew that as soon as he offered up *that* intelligence, the one man who could lead him to his daughter would have the cross hairs of 22 SAS aimed firmly at his skull. And that story was only going to end one way.

'I want you both to return home,' Hammond said. 'You don't leave your houses.'

Danny nodded. Silently, he told himself that Hammond wouldn't have given that instruction if he knew anything about Clara and Rose being abducted. Good.

'You've left me a fucking mess to sort out,' the ops officer continued. 'If the security services like your information there's a chance – a *chance*, mind you – that you'll have a job after Christmas. If not . . .' He left it hanging. 'Now get out of here.'

Danny and Spud stood up.

'Black,' Hammond said. 'Is there anything you're not telling me?'

Danny paused.

'No, boss,' he said.

'Spud?'

'Nothing, boss.'

They made to leave the room. But as Danny's fingers touched the doorknob, he stopped and turned.

'Boss?'

'What is it?'

'Any news of Tony?'

Hammond gave him an impassive stare. 'What is he, your best buddy all of a sudden?'

'I just need to know what to expect, next time I see him.'

Hammond stood up. 'Looks like there's some kind of love-in between him and Yellow Seven. The palace have requested that Tony be assigned to his CT team. I'm fighting it – we don't have the resources – but for now he's cosying up with the royals.'

'Sandringham?' Danny asked.

'What is it, Black, you thinking of sending him a Christmas card?' And when Danny didn't reply: 'Yes, Sandringham. Now get the fuck out of here, I've got work to do.'

Danny and Spud left, closing the door quietly behind them.

'What now?' Spud hissed as they walked back along the corridor, their footsteps echoing as they went. 'We go home like Hammond said? Sit and play with our dicks all Christmas?'

'Of course not.'

'Then what do we do? Where are we going?'

'To the armoury.'

Spud closed his eyes. 'Jesus Christ, Danny,' he breathed.

Dusk was falling as they crossed to the separate building that was the Regiment armoury. With Credenhill all but empty, Danny knew there was little chance that the armourer would be there. Having taken a detour to their bunk room to change into the civvies they'd left here before leaving for the op on the migrant boat, and to fetch a sturdy sports bag, he and Spud loitered in the shadow of B Squadron hangar all the same, keeping eyes on the armoury building for a full five minutes to check there was no movement of personnel in and out of it before making their approach.

Access to the armoury required a six-digit code on a numerical keypad by the main door. Danny tapped it in, and the heavy door clicked open. They entered quietly.

The familiar smell of gun grease and cordite hit Danny's senses. He moved quickly to the rack that ordinarily housed his personal rifle. The weapon had been returned since they got to Credenhill. Danny made to take it, but then stopped before his fingers touched the gunmetal. If anyone noticed that his and Spud's personal weapons were missing, questions would be asked. Better to take a couple of anonymous rifles. They would have the opportunity to zero the sights before the weapons were needed.

That was not all they took. Suppressors. Handguns. Ammunition. Laser sights. Covert radio equipment. Danny had a very specific shopping list, and he packed it all carefully into the sports bag, first stripping down the rifles into their constituent parts so they would fit. The chances of any of this stuff being missed this side of Christmas were slim. Spud hung at the doorway, nervously scoping the exterior for any sign of movement.

'We should go back to Hammond,' he said finally, as Danny zipped up the bag and lifted it easily, despite its weight. 'Tell him everything. Mucker, if the hit's going to be on the royals on

307

Christmas morning, they'll need a whole bunch of shooters. The chances of just two of us stopping them are tiny. It'll be a fucking JFK moment.'

'I don't care about the royals,' Danny said, his voice sounding bleak even to himself. 'I just care about my kid. If you don't want to come, say the word, I'll go it alone.'

For a moment, Danny thought Spud was going to take him up on the offer. But Spud shook his head. 'Let's get out of here,' he said.

Danny's BMW was one of the few vehicles parked up in the Credenhill car park. It beeped loudly as Danny pressed the button on his key fob, and its hazard lights flashed, illuminating the two SAS men as they approached. Danny stowed the sports bag carefully in the boot. A minute later, the MoD policeman at the camp entrance was waving them out of base. Danny floored the accelerator, and could sense Spud's eyes on the speedo. 'Take it easy, eh?' Spud said. 'Let's not get pulled over tonight.'

Danny barely heard him. 'I'm going to drop you off at a car hire place,' he said. 'Get a vehicle, meet back at mine. I don't want to use this car.'

'Why not?'

'If they find out we've gone AWOL, they'll try to track us using this numberplate. I don't want anyone to know where we've gone.'

Spud nodded, and stared straight ahead.

Danny walked alone from room to gloomy room in his ground-floor flat. He was wearing a long coat. It was a suitable garment for hiding an assault rifle. He felt like he was reading the story of Clara and Rose's abduction. In his bedroom, the bed was unmade. There was still an indentation in the pillow on the side where Clara slept. On the same side of the bed was Rose's Moses basket. The blanket Clara used to swaddle the baby was still there. In the sitting room, a cup lay on its side on the carpet, next to the stain its contents had made as it spilled. There was Clara's phone, smashed. On the mirror above the fireplace, a narrow spatter of blood.

Almost on autopilot he opened a wooden box on the mantelpiece and removed a wad of notes – an emergency fund he always kept there – and shoved them in his back pocket. Then he stood in silence. He expected to feel anger. Determination. But he felt something else. Sickness. Dizziness. That damn image of his daughter, with her bleeding eye, kept playing in his head. Making him lose his focus. He looked at his hand. It was shaking, and for a moment he thought he might vomit.

He mastered it. Tried to quell the frustration. He wanted to act now, this very minute. But he needed patience.

He closed his eyes and drew a deep, tremulous breath. How long since he'd slept? Apart from a couple of hours' shut-eye on the flight back from Iraq, days. He couldn't let Spud – or anyone – see him like this.

He had an old laptop. It was in its usual place, shoved under the sofa. He powered it up and got online. Then he navigated to the website for the Sandringham Estate. One more click and he was looking at a colourfully drawn plan of the estate, clearly designed for tourists. The North Garden. The West Lawns. The Visitor Centre. Not that the public would be allowed on to the estate at this time of year, when the royals were in residence. He noted the position of the main gates on the northern edge of the estate, and another set on the south-eastern perimeter. He tried to identify which part of the estate would be set aside for Tony and any other security personnel. Either the eastern wing of the main building, or the separate group of buildings by the south-eastern gate. Either way, that gate would be closest to where Tony would be sleeping, if he was on the estate. A strategy began to form in Danny's mind. He shut down the computer and gathered up the power cable, the map already burned indelibly on his mind.

The doorbell rang. It was Spud. 'Christ, mate, you look like death warmed up.'

Danny didn't answer, or ask him in. He just put his laptop and cable into the sports bag containing the hardware they'd taken from the armoury, picked it up and stepped outside into the cool night.

'You get the motor?'

Spud nodded and pointed to a black Honda Civic parked up in front of the flat.

'Good,' Danny said. 'Let's go.'

TWENTY-TWO

Yellow Seven had told Tony there was nowhere more boring than Sandringham. In the forty-eight hours that he'd been here, Tony hadn't seen much to make him disagree.

The Regiment man had been assigned quarters in a small house fifty metres to the east of the main residence. This was where all the security personnel were housed, but Yellow Seven had pulled some strings to get Tony a pad to himself. Not that it was any great shakes. It looked swanky and ornate from the outside, all red brick and manicured gardens. Inside, it was shabby. Moth-eaten furniture that couldn't have been less than fifty years old. Dusty hunting prints hanging crooked on the wall. A smell of age and neglect.

At least there was a TV. Tony was sprawled on a lumpy old sofa in front of it, a glass of Scotch at his side. Decent stuff. Yellow Seven had pressed it on him when they'd arrived at Sandringham, and it was already half gone. Tony flicked through the channels with a bored, glazed look. One moment there was a rerun of some twat dancing the tango, the next there was footage of hungry Syrian civilians starving in some town under siege by government forces. Tony found them both equally tedious.

He thought about leaving. Truth to tell, he'd thought about leaving since the moment he'd arrived and delivered a shaken-up Yellow Seven to the royal family's CP team. But each moment he was on the point of jacking it and heading back home to Hereford, he reminded himself why he was here. Proximity to the royal family was an asset that a man like Tony could use to his advantage. Fuck the army. Fuck the Regiment. If Yellow Seven wanted

Tony by his side, and if Tony had enough dirt on his new royal friend to bury him – which he already did – he reckoned he could name his price.

So he'd made the best of it. He'd got in with all the royal protection officers on site, and all the minor security personnel. To a man, they were pissed off that they'd be spending their Christmas keeping tabs on this bunch of overprivileged twats. It hadn't taken much to cosy up to them. A few well-chosen comments about the royals and they were putty in Tony's hands. Half of them were in the grounds now, supposedly combing the place for intruders, more likely loitering out of sight and smoking cigarettes to make the evening pass quicker. Talk about a crappy way to spend Christmas Eve.

He flicked the TV off and drained his Scotch. He thought about calling his missus, but decided against it. Stupid bitch had played hide the zucchini with Spud Glover, for Christ's sake. She could sit by herself all fucking Christmas, as far as Tony was concerned. Yellow Seven had asked that Tony accompany him on a clay pigeon shoot on Boxing Day. Should be good for a laugh, watching those inbred cunts trying to handle a shotgun.

His phone rang. Tony glanced at it. At the sight of the name on the screen, he felt a wave of dislike so powerful it made him sit up.

Danny Black.

What did that piece of shit want?

He let the call ring out.

Tony felt his pulse rising. What was it about Black that did that to him?

Ten seconds' silence. Then the phone rang again.

This time he picked it up.

'What?' he spat.

The connection cut in and out. Crappy signal in this part of Norfolk.

'*You still in Sandringham?*' Black's voice sounded different to usual. No expression. Tense.

'What the fuck difference does it make to you?'

'*We need to talk,*' Black said.

Tony frowned. He could only think of one thing that Black would want to talk to him about, and that was the events on the migrant boat four nights ago, the little fracas between him and Spud. And Tony had a pretty good idea how *that* conversation would go.

'You'll have to come to me,' Tony said.

'*We already did.*'

Tony's eyes panned across the room. His sidearm, holstered up, was hanging on the back of an old dining chair on the far side of the room. 'Where are you?' he asked carefully.

'*Sandringham Estate, north entrance. Come alone, and don't tell anyone. There's something in it for you.*'

Sure, Tony thought. Like, one behind the ear.

'Tempting, Black,' Tony said. 'But I think I'll take a rain check.'

'*That's your call,*' Black said. '*But then you won't find out why everyone was so jumpy about getting Yellow Seven back to the UK. Laters, Tony.*'

'Wait,' Tony said. He paused. If Black was waiting at the north entrance, it would take him three to four minutes to get to the south-eastern entrance, whereas it would take Tony forty-five seconds. He could get there first, rather than walk into some clumsy trap of Danny Black's. 'There's an entrance at the south-eastern perimeter. I'll be there in five.'

He hung up and hurried to grab his sidearm. Seconds later he was outside. Mist had descended, thick and freezing. Tony sprinted through it towards the south-eastern gate, keeping to the cover of the trees by the side of the road that led up to it. He knew that the estate grounds were being patrolled by security personnel. He'd been introduced to them, and they knew his face. But he didn't want any of those muppets stopping for a chat, slowing him down, so he kept hidden and moved quietly.

The gates were a good twelve feet tall, impressively constructed from black wrought iron, and incredibly ornate. They were covered with a thin film of frost. The CCTV camera covering the gates was situated atop a post a couple of metres inside the perimeter – no attempt to conceal it. Beyond the gates, a road, but the visibility was so poor that it was impossible to see as far as the forest on the far side. There was a smaller pedestrian gate to the left, electronically locked and with a video intercom. Tony approached the intercom and pressed the button. Security was high tonight, so he needed to buzz out as well as buzz in. A few seconds later, a voice came from the speaker. 'What's up, Tony?'

Tony recognised the voice. He'd been introduced to its owner earlier in the day. Youngish bloke with a beard to make him look older. He'd looked like he might jizz his pants when he found out Tony was Regiment. 'Alright Matt,' Tony said, remembering his name just in time. 'Let us out, would you? Got a bird waiting for me down the road, if she fucking shows up in this weather.'

Matt chuckled. 'Give her one from me,' he said. There was a buzzing sound. Tony pushed the gate open, scurried ten metres to the left to get himself out of the range of the CCTV camera, and quickly started looking for a place to conceal himself before Black arrived. Now he could just make out the trees on the opposite side of the road. Distance, twenty metres. They would afford him enough cover. He moved towards them.

Then he stopped.

The red pinprick of a laser mark was dancing squarely on his chest. Its beam cut a faint red line through the mist.

Tony drew a deep breath. He even smiled, though not pleasantly, as he realised that Black had lied about which gate he was waiting at. The silhouette of a figure appeared, emerging from the misty tree cover on the other side of the road, breath condensing in billows around his head. Tony couldn't make out a face, but he didn't need to.

'You were there all the time,' he called. It wasn't a question.

The figure kept walking. The laser dot stayed on Tony's chest.

'You're a devious cunt, Black. I'll give you that.'

The figure was crossing the road. Ten metres. Danny Black's dark features became visible. He walked right up to Tony, dead-eyed. 'Takes one to know one, Tony.'

'What the fuck's happened to you? You look like a corpse.'

'Give me your gun, Tony.'

'What makes you think I'm carrying?'

'Give me your gun.'

A pause. Tony put his hand to his holster, pulled the sidearm and handed it to Black, handle first. Black took it, then raised one hand. The laser sight disappeared from Tony's chest, but he wasn't stupid enough to think he wasn't still a target. He peered towards the trees. 'Spud?' he said.

Black nodded. He looked towards the Sandringham grounds. 'Security?'

'Of course.'

'Get to the trees. Don't worry about Spud. He won't be squeezing triggers unless you do something stupid. So try to break the habit of a lifetime, huh?'

Tony walked.

Danny followed. They reached the cover of the trees in ten seconds. Spud was visible five metres back, the butt of his rifle pressed into his shoulder, mist curling around him like dry ice. Danny gestured at him to lower it. 'It's OK,' he said. 'Tony's going to try very hard not to be a dickhead. Plus, I've got his gun.'

Spud lowered the rifle. He and Tony glowered at each other. 'I see you brought the work experience,' Tony said. 'He'd probably miss if he tried, but since I'm still breathing I take it you're not here to nail me.'

'We can help you,' Danny said, 'and you can help us. Simple as that.'

'You can help me do what?' Tony said. He sounded like the idea was ridiculous.

'I know how you think, Tony. You're always trying to work out how to turn a situation to your advantage. You didn't want to go babysit Yellow Seven, but now you're with him, you're thinking: what's in it for you. Am I wrong?'

Tony sniffed, but didn't answer.

'The security services think there's going to be a hit at Westminster Abbey on Christmas morning. They're wrong.'

'Like you'd know,' Tony snarled.

'The hit's going to be here, at Sandringham, on the royal family, while everyone's attention is on London. At least one sniper, probably more. We're going to stop it. You're going to take the glory. I'm going to take the shooter. Simple as that.'

'Nothing's as simple as that. Why don't you inform the head-shed? They'll put a stop to it in a second.'

'There are reasons,' Danny said.

'Yeah? Well unless you tell me what they are, you can fuck off.' He turned and made to leave.

Danny paused. He felt the skin round his eyes tightening. 'Because one of the guys involved in the hit has my daughter,' he said. As he spoke, he had to suppress the nausea again.

A pause. If Tony was concerned, or shocked, he didn't show it.

'How d'you work that out?' Tony said.

'It's not the sort of thing I'd make up.'

Tony seemed to accept that.

'Are you in?' Danny said.

'Maybe.'

'Maybe's no good to me.'

'Best you're going to get,' Tony said.

Danny paused. 'Talk me through the security arrangements around the grounds,' he said.

Tony gave a dismissive hiss. 'Piss poor,' he said. 'These royal protection officers need a kick up the arse.'

'The security arrangements, Tony.'

'The perimeter's fairly secure,' Tony said. 'High fencing all around, CCTV on the weak spots. There's a security room in the south wing of the main house where the camera monitors are, but just one guy watching them.'

'The public are allowed into the church on Christmas morning, right?'

'Right,' said Tony.

'Security checks?'

'Of course. Handbag searches and metal detector sweeps.'

'So none of the public can get a weapon through the perimeter.'

'A ceramic knife, maybe. But no firearms.'

Danny thought for a moment. 'How long have the royals been in residence?' he asked.

'About a week. That's the thing – when they're not here, the security isn't even ten per cent of what it is now.'

'So,' Danny said, 'if you were going to take out a hit on Christmas morning, you could get your hardware on site weeks beforehand?'

Tony nodded. 'Months, even,' he said. 'And there are plenty of places to hide it. It's all fucking trees and lakes.'

It was a strange thing. The animosity between them seemed to have fallen away as they spoke. It was as if the Regiment men were suddenly on autopilot, forgetting their differences for a moment, as they focussed on what they did best.

'I checked out the map,' Danny said. 'The route from the house to the church is direct, right?'

'Right. Along the northern edge of the West Lawns. Distance, about 400 metres. The old ones drive most of the way. The younger ones tend to walk it.'

'From what I saw,' Danny said, 'there's tree cover on either side of the road for about 150 metres, halfway along the route.'

'About that,' Tony said. His eyes were fixed on Danny, and it looked as if he'd just come to the same realisation that Danny had. 'So if you were going to take a shot, that would be your best place to take cover.'

'What about the church itself?' Danny said. 'There are trees in the vicinity, and it's closer to the exit when you need to get away.'

'Maybe,' Tony agreed. 'But the armed security will be heavier there, because it's where the oldies will get out of their vehicles. If you were going to take out a hit, you'd definitely want to do it before you got to the church.'

Danny nodded. There was a long silence as he considered his options. 'Can you get us into the grounds now?' he asked.

'Of course.'

'Are there security personnel in the grounds at the moment?'

'Yep.'

'Me and Spud are going to do a recce. Try to find any positions the shooters have set up. You need to keep the security personnel off our backs. If we locate the firing positions, it means we'll be able to put our hands on the shooters when they take their positions in the morning. I get the information I need out of my guy while you keep the other security away from us, then I hand the fucker over to you and you can do what you want with him. Nail him for all I care. Stand back and bask in the glory.'

Danny could tell Tony liked the idea of being a national hero, though he was doing a good job of not letting it show in his face.

'I'll do what I can to keep security off your back,' Tony said. 'But if anyone finds you, far as I'm concerned you're a couple of creeps trying to break into the old girl's bedroom.' He looked at his watch. 'I'm going back in,' he said. 'Give me exactly five minutes. I'll get you forty-five seconds to scale the gate. Be careful, it's icy. Be a fucking shame if you were to fall.'

Danny and Tony raised their watches, set the timers for five minutes and simultaneously started them. Without another word, Tony turned and ran back across the road to the gates. They watched his shadowy figure through the mist, speaking into the intercom. The side gate clicked open and he disappeared into the grounds.

'Do you trust him?' Spud breathed.

'If there was nothing in it for him? Of course not. But there is. He'll be the royals' golden boy. Man like Tony could make a career out of that.'

'He's a bad soldier,' Spud muttered. 'We shouldn't have anything to do with the fucker.'

'No,' Danny said. 'He's a good soldier. He's just a bad man.' He checked his watch. 'Four minutes,' he said.

'Whaddya know, Matt,' Tony said. 'Stupid cow didn't even show up.'

'Can't trust these Norfolk lasses,' said the voice at the other end of the intercom. 'Her father's probably her brother, and all.'

318

The gate buzzed and Tony opened it. But he carried on talking to Matt. 'I've got a bottle of Scotch at my place,' he said. 'Fancy a Christmas sharpener?'

'Can't leave my post,' Matt said, the regret in his voice very plain to hear.

'I'll come to you,' Tony said. 'Give me a couple of minutes.'

Once he was inside the perimeter, Tony kept behind the treeline again. Knowing that he was out of sight of anyone patrolling the ground, he sprinted back to his house. The mist felt even thicker now, like it was clinging to him. He was there in less than a minute. He grabbed the half-finished bottle of Scotch and checked his watch. Two minutes fifty to go. He left his digs again and hurried towards the main house. He knew where Matt would be – in the monitor room in the south wing. Ninety seconds later he was outside the door. Time check: one minute twenty to go. He knocked softly on the door, and entered.

Matt was sitting in front of a bank of eight screens, lounging on a swivel chair. He spun round casually as Tony entered. His eyes lit up at the sight of the bottle of Scotch. 'Not really s'posed to be drinking on the job,' he said.

'Quick nip never hurt anyone,' Tony said. 'Especially in weather like this. Freeze the bollocks off a brass monkey out there.' He looked around, found a couple of coffee mugs and drained their contents into the pot plant in the corner of the room, before pouring a good slug of Scotch into each. Matt still had his back to the screens. Tony quickly examined them as he handed him his drink. Of the eight screens, five were constantly changing camera. The remaining three showed clear footage of the northern gate, the western gate and – crucially – the south-eastern gate, shrouded in mist but perfectly visible, that Danny and Spud would be scaling.

Matt took a sip of his drink. 'Compliments of the season,' he said. 'Look, I'd better keep one eye on these sodding screens.'

'Course,' Tony said, as Matt turned to face the bank of monitors. He glanced at his watch. Twenty seconds till the five minutes was up. He looked at the screen that showed the gate. No movement. But in fifteen seconds . . . ten seconds . . .

'Hey,' Tony said suddenly, 'check this out.'

Matt turned again on his swivel chair as Tony pulled his phone from his pocket.

'So I was outside the main house a couple of hours ago,' he said, 'just doing a security sweep, and I was by the window to one of the small rooms next to the ballroom, and I heard the sound of a bird panting.'

His eyes flickered to the screen. Movement: two figures running towards the gate.

'So I had a little shufti, and it's only Violet Two giving it to his missus under that big fuck-off Christmas tree.'

Matt grinned. 'Dirty bastard,' he said.

The two figures were scaling the gates. One of them had a bag over his shoulder and was moving a bit less quickly than the other.

'So I recorded it on my phone. Want to listen?'

Matt's grin grew a bit wider. 'Yeah, course.'

Tony swiped his phone and navigated to his voice memos. On the screen, both figures were descending the other side of the gates. Tony frowned. 'Fucking phone,' he said. 'It was here a minute ago.'

The figures were on the ground, disappearing out of the camera's field of view.

'Must've deleted it,' he said. 'Stupid bloody machines.'

'Bet she's a right screamer,' Matt said.

'Too right, buddy.' Tony chuckled. They clunked their cups together and drained their Scotch.

'Look, I'd better get back ...' Matt pointed at his screens again.

'Course, mate. I should get some shut-eye myself. Got to take the kiddies to church in the morning. Better be bright-eyed and bushy-tailed.'

'More than you can say for Violet Two.'

Tony forced himself to laugh. He pointed at the Scotch. 'Keep that, if you want,' he said.

'You're a gentleman.'

Tony winked at him, then left the room. 'Fucking muppet,' he muttered to himself as he closed the door behind him.

Danny and Spud stood stock-still in the dark cover of the trees just to the right of the gate, mist curling around them. Danny was sweating hard, but he kept his breathing steady as they waited.

Three minutes passed. A car drove along the road outside the Sandringham perimeter fence. It made their shadows, and those of the surrounding trees, longer as it passed. The sound of its engine faded into the distance.

'So you made it in,' a voice said from a distance of about five metres. Tony stepped out from behind a tree.

'Keep your voice down,' Danny said.

'If you want to recce that bit of the route from the house to the church where the trees are,' Tony cut across him, 'you don't want to take the direct route. Too much open ground – you'll be seen. Better to follow the perimeter fence. It's got tree cover all along. Just don't get too close to the fence itself – CCTV.'

'What about you?' Spud said.

Tony feigned a look of surprise. 'It talks!' he said. And before Spud could respond, he continued: 'I'll follow the same route as you, but I'll stay outside the treeline. Keep an eye on me. If we come across any security personnel, I'll head them off in a different direction.' He pointed north. 'That way,' he said, before turning his back on them and moving out of the trees.

'I don't trust him,' Spud hissed. 'Since when was Tony Wiseman so fucking helpful?'

'Since there was something in it for him,' Danny murmured.

'I still don't like it. We're AWOL, we're in the grounds of Sandringham and we've stolen half the Hereford armoury. That cunt decides to shop us, we're fucked.'

'He won't. Not so long as he gets a chance to act the hero.'

It was impossible to move completely noiselessly – too many twigs underfoot, which kept cracking. But they kept the sound to the bare minimum. It was a skill Danny had learned on the training fields of Salisbury Plain, and used all over the world. But he'd never expected to find it useful in the heart of Norfolk. They were little more than shadows, skirting the perimeter of the grounds. Grey men. Invisible. Danny kept glancing left, trying to spot Tony in the open ground towards the treeline. The night was too dark, however, the mist too thick. It was only when he heard the sound of someone whistling – 'God Rest Ye Merry Gentlemen', or some tuneless version of it – maybe fifteen metres to their left, that he was sure their Regiment colleague was nearby.

They had been carefully picking their way through the trees for five minutes, however, when the whistling stopped. Danny instinctively held up one hand. He and Spud halted. Danny found himself holding his breath to avoid the clouds of condensation, and listening hard. Silence. Then Tony's voice, filled with what Danny instantly recognised as a false bonhomie. 'Jerry! Fucking hell, mate, didn't see you there.'

A pause. 'Tony?' The second voice sounded a little uncertain. 'Is that you?'

'Yeah.' Danny heard Tony sniff. 'Fucking typical, eh? Their royal highnesses get to sleep off their Christmas Eve brandies, we get to freeze our nads off out here.'

'I thought I heard something, in the trees.'

'Probably just me, mate,' Tony said. 'Needed a slash. Dick feels like an icicle now. Nearly snapped it off. You look fucking freezing and all.'

'Roger that.'

'You know Matt, in the CCTV room? He's got a bottle of Scotch on the go. You should go join him. No point both of us freezing. I'm on it out here.'

A pause.

'You sure?'

'Yeah, of course. Have one for me.'

There was a moment's silence. Then Tony's whistling started up again, and the sound continued to move round the perimeter. Danny and Spud followed.

They reached the north gate five minutes later. Here, they crossed twenty metres of open ground, keeping well clear of the gate and its CCTV camera, before regaining the treeline and continuing to skirt the perimeter. They advanced for another hundred metres. The whistling stopped again. This time, however, Tony appeared in front of them ten seconds later. He pointed south. 'That way,' he said quietly. 'You'll cross one open path, then enter another copse. Then you hit the road to the church. I'll take up position on the road itself. You two can search the trees on either side.'

Danny nodded his agreement. He and Spud followed Tony, across the first path, into the copse and up to the road that interested them. Tony stepped on to the road and started walking east, fading slightly into the mist, towards the main house. 'We'll check this side first,' Danny said.

They were looking for a firing position. It was unlikely that a sniper would already be in position – Danny expected them to arrive on Christmas morning when members of the public were let into the grounds. But there would be a limited number of positions from which they could take a shot on the royals. Danny expected such a position to be raised from the ground, and to offer a direct line of sight on to the road where the royal convoy would be passing. It also needed to offer a place to hide weapons for a period of weeks. It meant their assassins really had only one option.

'We're searching the trees, right?' Spud breathed. He'd clearly come to the same conclusion.

Danny nodded. 'Every tree that's easy to climb, and which forms a natural platform where the main branches diverge.'

Spud nodded his understanding. He moved west, while Danny headed east, examining each tree that lined the road. They either had long, smooth trunks with no notches below a height of three metres, or the branches formed a dense knot where they spread out from the trunk – impossible for a kid to sit down on, let alone for a fully grown sniper to establish a firing position. As Danny rejected each tree along the path, he found himself having to suppress a mess of panic in his gut. He had felt so sure they were on the right track. But now, what had seemed so obvious a few hours ago began to feel improbable.

It was instantly clear, when he rejoined Spud, that his mate was having the same thoughts. He spoke carefully, as though not wanting to antagonise Danny. 'Nothing, mate. They're just . . . I don't know, the wrong kind of tree.'

Danny pointed towards the road. 'Other side,' he said.

Tony was walking back towards them now. When he saw them waiting on the edge of the treeline, he nodded. They ran across the road and into the trees on the southern side. Danny headed east again, Spud west. Danny rejected the first three trees he passed. But the fourth one made him stop.

He knew, at a glance, that he could climb it in seconds, to a height of at least five metres. More importantly, there was a natural platform where the branches diverged. Danny felt a small surge of adrenaline. He ran back to Spud, brought him back to the tree and dumped his bag of hardware at his mate's feet. 'Watch that,' he said quietly, before grabbing one of the lower branches, finding himself a foothold and launching himself easily up the tree.

He was clambering on to the platform within seconds. It was covered in a thin frosting of ice crystals. Leaves had gathered in the hollows, and turned into a fungal-smelling compost, now frozen hard. Danny felt and looked all around him, convinced that his fingers would at any moment touch the cold, hard steel of a rifle strapped to one of the branches, or locate an ammo stash in one of those leafy hollows.

He found nothing.

Tony's whistling grew nearer. Danny looked down to see him five metres from the base of the tree, looking up. His expression was almost amused, as if he was watching a child.

Danny drew a deep breath and climbed back down the tree.

'Mate . . .' Spud started to say, but Danny stormed away from him, examining the remaining trees on this side of the road. But none of them were suitable as firing positions.

Disappointment crashed in on him.

He returned to Spud. A moment later, Tony joined them. He had a characteristic sneer on his face. 'Let me guess,' he said.

'Nothing doing. Surprise fucking surprise.' He seemed to have forgotten that twenty minutes ago, he'd been agreeing with Danny that this was the obvious location for an ambush.

Spud glowered at Tony, then turned to Danny. 'Mate, this was always a long shot. We've got no real evidence there's going to be a hit here anyway. We should get the hell back to Hereford. Tell the headshed the truth about your kid. They can put out a search—'

'No,' Danny said. He closed his eyes. '*No.*' He opened his eyes again. 'They must have stored their hardware somewhere else in the grounds. Where do you—'

'Nah, fuck this,' Tony interrupted. He was looking at Danny like he was crazy. 'Never thought I'd ever say this, but Spud's right. I've had enough of this shit. You two twats want to play boy soldiers, you can do it without my help.'

He turned his back on them. Danny grabbed him. It was almost like an electric bolt had been forced through Tony's body. He spun round and fronted violently up to Danny, their faces inches apart. 'Get your fucking hands off me,' he hissed.

Danny loosened his grip.

'You're an arrogant cunt, Black. You think you're the king of the fucking Regiment, don't you? Well, one word from me and you know what you are? A sad twat on civvie street.'

And with a nasty, vicious glance at Spud, he tore away, disappearing into the mist without looking back.

Silence.

'Danny, you've got to listen to me,' Spud said. 'We have to get out of here. We can't trust Tony. He'd love to screw us over.'

'No.'

'Mate, we've got it wrong. The hit's in London. The security services are all over it. You're *never* going to find your daughter like this. It's not going to happen.'

'Fine,' Danny said. 'Leave.'

'*Mate*—'

'When they let the public in tomorrow morning,' Danny cut in, 'one of them is going to be the shooter. Maybe even Mujahid himself. We have to have eyes on. Till then, we hunker down.'

'For fuck's sake, Danny, you're clutching at straws.'

They stared at each other.

'Look buddy,' Spud said, 'I can't pretend to know what you're feeling at the moment, with your kid missing and everything. But you've got to see sense. The hit's in London. You *know* it is. There's nothing we can do here, and Tony Wiseman is a danger to us. We've *got* to leave.'

Danny blinked. He stared at Spud.

'Mate, are you OK?' Spud said, his voice suddenly full of concern. 'You don't look good. Look, we've only had a few hours' kip in the last three days—'

'I'm fine.' But he wasn't. Nausea was coursing through him. For a horrible moment, it was all Danny could do to keep standing.

'It's a bad plan, mate,' Spud was saying. 'It stinks.'

'I know,' Danny replied. He was feeling dizzy. Overwhelmed with exhaustion. His voice sounded slurred. 'I *know* it's a bad plan. But it's the only one I've got . . .' He snapped himself out of his nausea. 'You don't have to stay,' he said.

He turned his back on his mate, and walked away.

DECEMBER 25

TWENTY-THREE

London. Dawn.

From somewhere on the other side of the river, a solitary bell was ringing. Happy fucking Christmas, Barker thought to himself.

He was standing on the south side of Millbank, watching the mist curl lazily over the Thames. Apart from that bell, London was almost silent. It was as if the old city was holding its breath.

He turned his back on the river, crossed the deserted road and headed up towards Westminster Abbey. This whole situation was ludicrous. They should be cancelling the Christmas morning service. Cordoning off the whole area. There couldn't be a terror attack on an event that wasn't even happening.

But word was that the PM had put his foot down. The service would go ahead as usual. He and his family *would* attend. To consider anything else would be to hand a victory to the forces of terror that wanted to threaten our way of life – or whatever politician's bullshit he'd come out with. Barker couldn't help wondering how he'd feel about his way of life if his teenage daughter was massacred on Christmas morning by some Islamic State scumbag.

The front of the church had been cordoned off into various approaches: one for the public, one for the VIPs and anyone requiring extra security. The exterior was crawling with police in hi-vis jackets, perhaps thirty of them. But there were also an equivalent number of plain-clothes guys. Guys like Barker. He saw his mate Andy Connor talking into a covert microphone on the lapel of his jacket up by the west door. Barker and Connor

329

were in the doghouse after the fuck-up with Kailash McCaffrey, but the general situation was too serious for anyone to be truly out in the cold. The security services needed all available personnel present.

Though what they were supposed to do, Barker wasn't sure. The abbey had been cased more times than he could count. There wasn't a square inch of that building that hadn't been searched for IEDs, chemical weapons, biological agents, ammo caches, weapons stashes. MI6 drones had examined and photographed every last spire and turret. Sniffer dogs were in constant attendance. There had been background checks run on every single member of the clergy or support staff who would be present for the Christmas service. By 8 a.m., there would be Regiment snipers in the rooftops of the buildings surrounding the abbey, and armed guys inside. Barker would be one of them. His position would be at the end of the front pew, five places along from the PM himself – not that the PM would know him from Adam. While the congregation were praying, or singing 'Oh Come All Ye fucking Faithful', Barker would be constantly scanning the interior of the abbey, picking out faces, searching for that suspicious activity, that telltale movement, that could precede an attack. The gesture that you couldn't predict, but which you'd know when you saw it.

And if you didn't see it?

Barker was trained to think positive. Difficult, on a day like today.

He heard a noise overhead. A chopper had hovered into view against the grey dawn sky. Barker figured he'd be seeing a few more of those before the morning was out. He knew why it was there. It was an unspoken warning to the people behind the attack: we're expecting you, and we're ready. A show of force. Barker didn't have much faith in it. Sure, there would be bag checks as the congregation entered the church, and as many members of the public as possible would be scanned with handheld metal detectors. And though the thought left a bad taste in Barker's mouth, the reality was that those with darker skin would be more thoroughly searched than others. But there was a hole in every net. The security services knew full well that there were IS sympathisers with white skin. And if a terrorist was willing to lose their own life to make their deadly, bloody point, the possible countermeasures were limited.

A voice from behind him. 'What are you, Barker, a fucking sightseer?' He recognised the voice of his boss, Wallace Conlin. Barker was *not* in Conlin's good books. If ever there was a time to tread softly, now was it.

'Just trying to think what we've missed, boss,' Barker said.

'Yeah, well leave the thinking to those who can do it. The PM's CP team will be here in twenty minutes to review the arrangements. I want all our guys in position. That means you.'

Barker knew better than to argue. He hurried up towards the front entrance of the abbey. The armed police officer monitoring entry into and out of the building recognised him and allowed him to pass. It was warmer inside than out, though only slightly. A clergyman in a white frock was lighting huge candles on the altar, and there was a lingering smell of incense. Barker's footsteps echoed as he walked up the aisle towards the front of the church. His eyes flickered up, left and right, and he caught sight of several faces he recognised: armed Regiment men, preparing their positions overlooking the main congregation. Ready to take a shot with the advantage of height, if the situation demanded it. And as he took his place on the front pew, he retrieved his own weapon from the holster under his jacket. Sig 9mm. It felt a hell of a sight better in his hand than it did in its holster.

'Excuse *me*!'

Barker looked up to see the clergyman who had been lighting the candles. The guy was standing right over him. He had jowly features, rimless round glasses and a film of sweat on his upper lip.

'This is a holy place. Please put that thing away.'

Barker stood up and looked meaningfully around him. 'Won't be the only holey thing round here,' he said, 'you fellas don't let us do our job.' He holstered the Sig.

The clergyman gave a complacent smile. 'The Lord will protect us,' he said.

'Course he will,' Barker replied. 'That's why he got us on board.'

From the corner of his eye he saw five broad-shouldered men in suits walking up the aisle. The PM's security, without a doubt. He turned his back on the clergyman and went to meet them.

Time check: 0700 hours.

The rising sun failed to burn the mist from the grounds of Sandringham. It clung to everything. To the ground. To the buildings. To the trees. And to the two soldiers, hunkered down among thick, thorny bushes, thirty metres from the west gate.

They'd been scouring the grounds since Tony had left them. Or, more accurately, *Danny* had been scouring the grounds. Spud had been on edge. Jumpy. He didn't trust Tony not to raise the alarm. Intruders in the grounds. So while Danny had searched every bush, ditch and outbuilding in the vicinity of the road leading from Sandringham House to the church, Spud had stood guard, peering into the mist, checking for security personnel. At one point, just after 0400 hours, he'd heard footsteps along the road. He and Danny had gone to ground, keeping eyes on. Two figures, warmly wrapped in black jackets, gloves and hats, had sauntered past. Danny could tell from their body language that they weren't looking for anyone in particular. But their presence only served to put Spud even more on edge.

As the hours passed, Danny's search for weaponry remained fruitless. Each time he saw a mound of thick foliage through the dark and the mist, he experienced a surge of hope. And each time that hope faded it was replaced by a new knot of panic. Spud had stopped telling him that they'd made the wrong call. He didn't need to. It was becoming increasingly obvious.

Now, as daylight arrived, they had no choice but to stay hidden. The hard, frosty ground had sapped all warmth from them. Danny's body felt numb. So did his mind. His eyes kept rolling with tiredness. Then, on the verge of sleep, his mind kept replaying Dhul Faqar's video of Mujahid, Clara and their daughter, snapping him back to reality . . .

He had to keep awake.

From their OP in the patch of thick evergreen bushes almost as tall as Danny and several times as deep, they had line of sight towards the little church where the Christmas morning service would take place. Distance: 100 metres to their ten o'clock, across a well-kept lawn and a narrow road. Through the mist, he could make out the silhouettes of three figures in the vicinity of the church. Royal protection officers, performing a quick security check. His mind turned to London. He wondered how many of his colleagues would be in situ at Westminster Abbey at this very moment.

He wondered if he should be there with them.

His eyes rolled again.

Stay awake . . .

The weapons from the armoury were laid out in front of them, fully assembled. Suppressed rifles. Sidearms. The works. 'Any of these security guys find us with all this gear, they'll take a shot, mucker,' Spud had warned him. 'You know that, right?'

Yeah. Danny knew that. He looked to his two o'clock. At a distance of seventy-five metres was the western gate where the public would be entering. Danny estimated that security would open it in two hours' time, at 0900 hours. That would give the public an hour before the royals arrived at the church. He reckoned the royals themselves would leave Sandringham House at 0945 hours.

'If anyone's going to take a shot at them, they'll want to be in position by 0930 hours,' he muttered to Spud. Spud didn't reply. He looked as exhausted as Danny. 'So I think our man Mujahid will walk through that gate between 0900 and 0930.'

'Yeah,' Spud said. 'Either that, or we're in a prime spot to watch all the old ladies of Norfolk waddle past on their Zimmer frames.' His voice trembled somewhat as he spoke. He was obviously as cold as Danny.

Danny didn't bother answering. He panned between the church and the gate. Watching. Waiting. Forcing himself to keep alert.

★ ★ ★

Big Ben struck 0900 hours.

Barker hardly heard the nine solemn echoes. His covert earpiece was a buzz of activity. Stressed, serious voices. Some he recognised, some he didn't.

– All units, this is unit base. We have secure transport waiting outside Number 10. The PM and his family will be leaving at 0940, estimated arrival 0955.

From his position at the front of the abbey, he looked back along the aisle. The place was already a quarter full. Well-heeled Londoners in heavy winter coats. A low chatter emanating from the pews.

– All units, this is sniper team red commander. We have all personnel in position. Repeat all personnel in position.

He wondered how many of the public now filtering in for their Christmas morning worship realised that the front of the abbey was being covered by the most highly trained snipers in the world.

– All units, this is sniper team blue commander. Target interior is covered, repeat, target interior is covered.

He glanced up. The balcony was closed to the public. But there were people there – grim-faced men conducting constant, unflinching surveillance. Would any of the congregation twig who they were or why they were there?

– This is SCO19 command. We have armed personnel covering all entrances . . .

Barker's mate Andy Connor walked up to him. Dark bags under his eyes. Concern etched on his forehead. 'Get the impression someone's panicking?'

'Too right,' Barker said.

Connor looked around. 'What have we missed?' he muttered.

Barker was thinking the same thing. It didn't matter that Westminster Abbey was currently the best-defended location in the entire country. He couldn't shake the sneaking suspicion that something was being overlooked.

'There are no IEDs,' Barker said. 'The headshed's sure of that. They're scanning every member of the congregation as they come in. The only person not getting fleeced is the PM.'

But Connor's gaze had drifted up towards the altar. 'No,' he murmured. 'Not just the PM.' He was eyeing the clergyman Barker had spoken to earlier that morning. He was standing at the altar, wiping an ornate golden chalice with a crisp white cloth.

Barker stared. 'You can't be serious,' he said.

Connor looked deadly serious. 'Check out the robes,' he said. 'You could hide enough C5 under those to take out half the abbey.'

'He's a fucking vicar, mate . . .'

As Barker spoke, the clergyman looked up and saw them staring at him. He looked suddenly flustered. He put the chalice down rather clumsily, then turned and shuffled hurriedly away from the altar towards the oak-panelled vestry at one side.

Barker and Connor looked at each other. Then towards the clergyman.

They followed him.

The organ started to play. Gentle music filled the cavernous space of the abbey. It barely registered with Barker. Suddenly all his attention was on the sweaty clergyman now disappearing into the vestry, ten metres from their position.

'Barker, Connor, what the hell are you doing?' The men stopped. The voice was behind them, but Barker recognised it well enough. Wallace Conlin, when Barker turned to face him, had a face like a thundercloud. 'I thought I told you I wanted you in position.'

Barker and Connor exchanged a sidelong glance. A glance that said: should we tell him what we think?

Barker stepped forward. 'Boss,' he said quietly. 'We've found a weak spot.'

'What are you talking about?'

'The priests. They need to be searched. They could be hiding anything under those . . .'

His voice trailed away as he saw the expression on Conlin's face.

'The priests,' Conlin said, 'are as white as you or me.'

'Boss, we *know* there are white IS sympathisers. It's not just about skin colour—'

335

'I thought I told you,' Conlin interrupted, and his voice was dangerous, 'to leave the thinking to the people who know how to do it.'

'Boss, I'm just saying ...' He blinked. What *was* he saying? A thought crystallised very clearly in his mind. 'Boss, the people who are most likely to bring a device into the abbey are the people who've had access to it for weeks, months.' He looked back towards the entrance. 'No member of the public's going to get an IED in here today. Not with all this security.'

'All this security?' Conlin cut in. He waved one finger around, vaguely indicating the security personnel all around the abbey. 'You know *why* there's all this security, Barker? Because of you. We had a direct lead to a UK-based IS cell, and you two idiots killed the fucker with a badly placed fist. Now you seem to think you have a better handle on what's going on here than the combined brainpower of the UK security forces? I promise you, gentlemen, that you don't. So do us all a favour, leave the fucking vicars to fondle the choirboys and get the hell back to your positions before I have you both RTU'd.'

Barker and Connor both glanced towards the vestry.

'*Now!*' Conlin said.

They didn't have a choice. Barker returned to his place in the front pew. Connor took up position on the other side of the aisle.

Time check: 0925.

T minus thirty-five minutes.

Time check: 0927.

Danny and Spud had watched members of the public entering the grounds without exchanging a word. Danny estimated that there were just shy of 100 people. The visibility was appalling: mist as thick as soup made it hard to discern individual figures. Nevertheless, he had used the rifle scope from his bag of gear to focus in on every member of the public as they passed through the west gates. Old ladies, mostly. A few younger couples with kids. A handful of toddlers. Several babies in prams. Woollen hats and heavy coats.

Danny's vision went blurred. All the faces merged into one. He shook his head. Snapped out of it. Focussed in on individual faces again.

Not a single face that looked remotely Middle Eastern. Not a single person who Danny could even begin to think might be the animal who had his daughter.

Until now.

He was a tall man. Broad-shouldered. Dark skin. He wore a black beanie hat. Black gloves. A navy Puffa jacket. But it was the man's scarf that jumped out at Danny. He could just make it out, despite the mist. The man was not wearing it in any of the usual ways: two tails hanging down, or knotted under the Adam's apple. The thick woollen material was very precisely wrapped. Swaddling the neck. As though it were hiding something.

'That's him,' he hissed.

Spud inhaled sharply. 'Are you sure?'

Danny cursed. His hands had gone shaky. Probably just the cold. He realigned his sights so they were fixed on this new target, who had raised his arms and was being scanned by the security guys at the gate. The guy held out a rucksack, which one of the security guys looked through.

'He had a scar on his neck,' Danny muttered to himself, still watching. 'A bad one . . . He'd want to hide it . . .'

'Mucker, what are you talking about?'

Danny let out a low hiss. 'Watch – he's not following the others to the church. He's heading in this direction . . .'

And he was. The guy was looking over his left shoulder, checking that he wasn't being observed by the security guys on the gate. They were too busy searching a few new arrivals, however, and the guy easily slipped towards the treeline and out of Danny's sight.

He lowered his scope. 'I'm going to find him,' he said. But his voice suddenly sounded slurred, and Spud was looking at him in a curious way.

'Mate, I'm not fucking with you . . . You don't look—'

'Just keep eyes on the latecomers, check for anyone suspicious.'

Danny backed carefully out of the clump of bushes that formed his OP, rifle in hand, the freezing cold metal almost burning his skin. At least, he thought to himself, the mist was also obscuring him and Spud. Standing up, he hid the suppressed weapon under his long coat. And once he was fully clear of the bushes, he stood very still. Here, among the trees, his sense of hearing would be just as important as his vision. His target had entered the treeline fifty metres north of their position, at a bearing of approximately thirty-five degrees. Danny estimated that he'd cross his line of sight in approximately one minute, before heading north to meet the road that led from Sandringham House to the church. Camouflaged by the thick trunk of an old oak tree, he waited for the telltale sound of footsteps shuffling through the forest.

They didn't come.

He peered out from behind the tree trunk and immediately discerned movement, thirty metres distant. The mist meant he couldn't quite make out the figure, but he had a sense of someone picking their way east, but slowly. Like a pro. Danny moved swiftly, cutting noiselessly from tree to tree, stopping behind each one to check he wasn't observed. His target was moving well, but Danny was moving better, closing the gap quickly. When it had closed to fifteen metres, he removed his rifle, pressed the butt hard into his shoulder and aimed it directly at the moving target . . .

The target stopped with his back to Danny. Distance, ten metres. Danny could see clouds of the man's breath condensing in the cold air. He showed no sign of knowing he was being followed. He pulled his rucksack off his back, knelt down and started removing unseen objects from the bag. Danny heard the gentle click and clunk of items being slotted together. A sound he knew well . . .

Very calmly, and quietly, he spoke.

'Hands in the air, you piece of shit.'

The target froze. He didn't raise his arms, but looked over his shoulder. Dark, hooded eyes widened. Then his arms shot up into the air.

'I'm approaching,' Danny said. 'Don't make a fucking mistake.'

'I wanted to find the best place for a shot,' the target muttered.

I bet you did, you piece of shit, Danny thought as he took a couple of paces forward. But all he said was: 'Take your scarf off.'

The target hesitated.

'Take it off,' Danny repeated.

The target slowly lowered his arms. His hands were trembling. He slowly started to loosen the scarf. Three winds, and it was off.

'Drop it. Then put your hands on your head and stand up.'

The scarf coiled to the floor. The target followed his instructions and got to his feet.

'Turn round.'

He turned.

'Let me see your neck.'

Danny knew immediately, from his target's expression of confusion, that he'd made a bad mistake. The guy loosened the top of his coat and raised his chin to display his neck. There was no marking. Just a little downy stubble. Danny looked at the ground. The gear that he'd been clicking together was camera equipment.

'Who are you?' Danny growled.

'Ph – photographer,' the guy stuttered. 'P – paparazzi. I just wanted to . . . Look, I can leave now . . .' He stepped back.

Instinct took over. Danny surged forward, lowering his weapon as he moved. This guy obviously thought Danny was part of the royal security team. If he twigged that he wasn't, all hell could break loose. Danny needed to silence him. Quickly.

One hit was all it took. A solid, sharp blow to the neck. Not enough to kill him, or even to cause permanent harm. But enough to put him down, unconscious.

The guy crumpled heavily to the ground. Danny was suddenly sweating badly. Breathing heavily. He looked around, checking for threats. He was suddenly dizzy.

Exhaustion. Cold. Panic. It was all catching up with him. He staggered towards a tree trunk and supported himself against it.

The same nausea he'd experienced the night before came rushing back on him, only twice as bad this time.

His knees weakened. He crouched down.

Maybe if he just closed his eyes for ten seconds . . .

No—

He opened them again. But everything became a blur: bare, wintry trees . . . dark evergreen bushes . . . and were there figures, moving at a distance through the forest?

Danny's eyes rolled. He felt his head against the tree trunk. Everything was dark.

He saw a motorcade trundling slowly along the road. Two black cars. Eight or nine people walking alongside. Shrouded in mist. Yellow Seven was there. And Violets One, Two and Three. And Tony. Suddenly, from the far side of the road, five figures appeared. They wore camouflage fatigues, balaclavas, black and white *shemaghs*. They brandished rifles. They looked like they had walked straight out of the badlands of Iraq, not emerged from the forests of Sandringham.

One of them was holding a baby. It was screaming. A shrill, desperate scream that pierced everything. Nobody seemed to pay it any attention. Danny didn't understand it. *Why was nobody helping the child? It was weeping blood . . .*

The militants opened up. A choking thunder of automatic rifle fire. The motorcade windscreens shattered. The rounds ripped twisted holes into the metal. Blood spattered over the tarmac as the walkers hit the ground . . .

There were more screams. More automatic fire. But above it all, the constant, horrible, desolate wailing of the baby . . .

Danny's whole body started. He was still crouched down by the tree. The mist was surrounding him like a blanket.

He forced himself to his feet. Mastered the exhaustion again. He looked over to check that the photographer was still down. He was.

Then he realised he could hear something. A car engine. Maybe more than one. Quiet. Moving slowly. North-east of here. Hard to tell the distance, because the mist and the trees were messing with the sound.

Time check. 0946 hours.

Shit. The royals' motorcade.

He picked up his weapon. Inhaled deeply. Checked his surroundings. No sign of movement.

The road was thirty metres through the trees. Danny crashed through the forest, cold sweat dripping into his eyes, breath billowing all around him. He reached the edge of the treeline ten seconds later. Kept himself hidden behind a thick tree trunk again. A grey figure in the all-encompassing mist, he knew he would be invisible to those not looking for him. And from here he finally had eyes on the royals.

The motorcade was thirty metres from Danny's position, and it was moving very slowly. Almost like a funeral procession. In his hallucination there had been three vehicles. In reality there were two, one behind the other. He predicted that the front vehicle would be security. The senior royals would be in the car behind. At the front of the motorcade was a TV camera guy, walking backwards with a camera on his shoulder, filming the convoy. Trailing the second car were all those who had decided to get to the church on foot. Danny instantly picked out Violet Two and his missus. Violets One and Three were walking in a little group on the far side of the vehicle. There were three CP guys – the unnecessary sunglasses gave them away. And Yellow Seven, trailing at the back, with Tony beside him. Tony was the only security guy not wearing shades. He appeared to be in deep, flamboyant conversation with his new royal buddy, but Danny – who had been trained to notice such things, and who now zeroed in on him with his scope – observed that even though he was making a show of paying attention to Yellow Seven, his eyes were darting all over the place. Into the trees on the left and right. Up, down, straight ahead. And while he gestured with his left hand, his right was constantly resting by the buttons of his suit jacket. He was ready to grab his sidearm if the situation called for it.

Tony was on high alert. No question.

Danny too. The weakness he had felt since arriving in the UK had fallen away. Everything seemed crystal clear. He had failed to locate the terrorists' shooting position. Now he only had one choice.

Wait for them to shoot. Then follow the line of fire.

He turned his attention from the motorcade towards the trees on the other side of the road. They were dark, gnarled shapes in the mist. Easy to hide in. Difficult to penetrate. If there was a shooter waiting, or more than one, Danny was still sure that they would be using the tree cover by the side of the route to hide.

Motorcade distance, twenty-five metres. Danny lowered his scope and turned to peer through the woods on his side of the road. Nothing moved. Back to the motorcade. Yellow Seven was talking at Tony nineteen to the dozen. Tony was nodding vaguely, but Danny could see that really he was trying to look through the treeline on both sides.

Twenty metres.

Danny's heart was thumping. There were no militants on this side of the road, he decided. He would have seen them by now – or they would have seen him. He decided to concentrate on the trees at the far side. With their mist-shrouded, gnarled shapes, some of them even looked like people. Spotting a shooter at this distance, in these conditions, was a massive ask.

But when the motorcade was fifteen metres distant, he spotted *something*.

It moved. A grey silhouette. The height of a man. Danny trained his rifle, zoning out the thick knot of mist and trees, focussing on that moving silhouette. His finger rested carefully on the trigger.

His eyes tightened.

The figure had stopped.

Danny had a decision to make. Should he fire? A suppressed round would be all but inaudible. He wouldn't give away his presence. He could stop an imminent attack.

But he'd also lose the chance of getting a lead to his daughter. And what if this figure in the trees was entirely innocent, like the photographer he'd just put to the ground?

Danny took his eye from the scope and checked the position of the motorcade. It was now almost adjacent to his position. Distance, ten metres. Yellow Seven was laughing loudly. Tony was grinning, but also looking left and right, his gun hand still at the ready.

He suddenly locked gazes with Danny. He had clearly picked him out behind the treeline – the only one of the royal CP team who had done so. Tony raised an eyebrow. It was a sly, arrogant expression, but Tony couldn't hide his anxiousness: the slight twitch around the eyes, the way he momentarily bit his lower lip.

But he did nothing to reveal Danny's location. Danny himself looked back through his scope. The motorcade passed in front of it. The black vehicles dominated Danny's field of view. He had to pull away again and watch the royals pass with his naked eye. Tony glanced in his direction once more, then to the left.

Danny's heart thumped. He was waiting for the shot . . .

Waiting for one of them to go down . . .

Waiting for the bastard militant who could lead him to his daughter to reveal himself . . .

He could hear Yellow Seven's braying voice barking a boorish laugh. Tony was still smiling. Still glancing occasionally towards Danny.

And now, the motorcade had passed his position.

Danny moved through the trees, keeping adjacent to the vehicles, every sense on high alert. The motorcade had another thirty metres to travel before it cleared the tree cover on either side of the road. He took a moment to scan the trees on the other side through his scope. Again, the gnarled, mist-shrouded trunks came into focus. Again, he thought he saw a figure, mirroring Danny's own movement alongside the vehicles.

The figure increased its speed, so now it was in position just ahead of the motorcade. Danny kept up . . . stopping when the figure stopped . . . raising his weapon . . . trying to see the face through his scope . . .

The mist cleared momentarily. His target's features flashed across the scope's field of view.

White skin. Headset. Boom mike.

This was no shooter. It was a member of the royal CP team.

Danny lowered his weapon. He was sucking in lungfuls of air. The motorcade cleared the treeline. The CP guy emerged from the trees on the other side of the road.

Tony looked back over his shoulder, sneering dismissively at Danny.

The motorcade entered the cordoned-off area in front of the church.

The royals peeled off to shake hands with their adoring public.

They were completely unharmed.

TWENTY-FOUR

London. 0958 hours.
– All units, this is unit base. The PM has arrived. Repeat, the PM has arrived.

Barker stood up and looked back down the aisle of the abbey. He could see the Prime Minister's entourage, rather than the PM himself. A huddle of approximately ten people entering the building. Three CP guys at the front. Two girls – the PM's daughters. His wife. The PM was in there somewhere but Barker couldn't see him. More CP guys at the back. Everyone in the congregation – it was full now, and buzzing – had turned their heads to take a look.

Barker turned his attention elsewhere. The podgy clergyman with the sweaty upper lip had taken his place up at the altar. His ornate communion chalice was right in front of him. To either side, set slightly back, were two more clergymen. And behind them, in the facing choir pews, fifty or sixty young choristers. All boys.

Barker's eyes shot back to the clergymen. Was it his imagination, or did they look nervous?

He glanced over at his mate Connor who was standing by a column on the other side of the abbey. He was watching the clergyman too. Watching him very closely . . .

'Move.'

Barker started. The PM's entourage had reached him. One of the CP guys was nudging him. Barker stepped to one side, allowing the security guys, then the PM, then the girls, then the PM's wife, to take their seats. Barker took his own position in the same row, in the seat next to the aisle. He had barely glanced at the famous face of the Prime Minister, which he was seeing in the flesh for the first time.

The organ music swelled. Then stopped.

Silence in the abbey. Someone coughed. It echoed around the vaults.

Silence again.

The clergyman at the altar raised his hands, palms outward.

'My brothers and sisters,' he announced. His voice, picked up by the small microphone on his lapel, echoed over the loudspeakers. 'In the name of Christ, I—'

Feedback squeaked over the loudspeakers. The sweating priest hesitated. He lowered his hands and moved them to his belt area, hidden by the altar.

It was pure instinct that made Barker move his hand to his own holster. And from the corner of his eye he saw Connor taking several steps forward from his position in the wings. Just as Barker was feeling for his sidearm, however, his earpiece burst into life again. Barker recognised Conlin's withering voice.

— *Relax, everyone. He's adjusting his microphone pack.*

Barker let his hand fall to his side. The priest cleared his throat and tried again. 'In the name of Christ I welcome you! We have come together to . . .'

Barker zoned out as the clergyman droned on. Hyper-aware, he sensed movement up on the side balcony, but a quick glance told him it was a Regiment shooter shifting position.

Movement to the right. It was just one of the PM's kids fidgeting.

'. . . through scripture and silence, prayer and song . . .'

Movement behind the altar.

Barker caught his breath. Everything went into slow motion. Because he had suddenly realised, beyond question, where the threat lay.

All of the choristers standing in the pews behind the altar were under sixteen, some of them much younger than that. All white. Except one. He stood out, not just on account of his dark skin and black hair among the blue-eyed, blond angels surrounding him, but also because he was the only one moving. As the priest droned on, he had bent down, looking nervously from left to right, and was now holding a navy-blue rucksack in front of him.

One of the adjacent choirboys looked at his companion. Confused. A bit irritated. He clearly hadn't been expecting this to happen. It was more than high jinks. It was unusual . . .

It was as if everything else in the abbey had become a blur. The only person on whom Barker was focussed was the dark-skinned chorister. Barker stepped out into the aisle. He strode up towards the altar. Somewhere on the edge of his perception, he sensed that the priest had stopped talking. He pulled his sidearm, unlocking it as he picked up pace towards the altar.

Voices in his ear.

– *Barker, what the hell are you doing?*

– *Stand down! Repeat, stand down!*

Barker did not stand down. He continued past the altar, running now, his weapon raised and held in two hands, the choirboy firmly in his sights.

Someone screamed. Several people. There was shouting all around. As Barker homed in on his target, the other choirboys fell to the ground like wilting flowers. His target, however, remained standing, clutching the rucksack close to his chest like it was the most precious thing in the world.

Distance: ten metres.

'DROP THE BAG!' Barker shouted, and his voice echoed dramatically around the abbey. '*I SAID, DROP THE BAG!*'

The kid didn't drop it.

He clutched it.

His face was suddenly twisted in an expression of humiliation and anger. Barker had seen that expression before. The look of a bad guy who knew he'd been thwarted.

– *Barker, stand down! That's an order!*

'*DROP THE FUCKING BAG!*'

The kid still didn't drop it. In fact, he seemed to be trying to open the zip.

Barker's reaction was immediate and instinctive. He released a single round. The report echoed around the vaults of the abbey as the round slammed hard into the choirboy's left shoulder.

Screaming. Everywhere. Confusion behind him. The congregation rushing into the aisle. Barker's earpiece was a sudden burst of such confused shouting that he couldn't make out a single word.

His target seemed to spin on his heels with the impact of the round. His white choir robe was suddenly splashed red. The rucksack flew into the air as the kid crumpled in a heap, down on to his chorister companions.

Barker lunged towards the rucksack, catching it a fraction of a second before it hit the ground. It was heavy. He held it to his chest as his own body thumped to the hard stone floor.

He could hear sirens outside, above all the shouting in the abbey. The fierce barking of his Regiment-mates as they closed in on the altar area, screaming at everyone to hit the ground.

He was breathing heavily. Sweating. He closed his ears to the anguished shrieks of the chorister he'd just hit, and who was now writhing in agony just a couple of metres away. He ripped open the zip of the rucksack and carefully, gingerly, looked inside.

There was an iPad. Its screen was shattered. There were bags of sweets: Haribos, Maltesers. There was a hymn book and a phone.

But there were no weapons. No explosives.

He looked up. He was surrounded by armed Regiment men, weapons drawn, faces fierce. But none so fierce as that of his boss, Wallace Conlin, whose jugular was pumping, and whose every expression and body movement told Barker he'd just made his last mistake as a Regiment man.

Danny Black was numb.

He stared from his covert position behind the treeline. Thirty metres away, the younger royals were at the cordon, shaking hands with the members of the public crowded round to see them.

Smiling. Laughing. The older royals were exiting their vehicle, royal protection officers loitering nearby. A priest was standing in the door of the church. White robes. Prayer book in hand. A gentle smile as he surveyed the scene.

Danny hardly saw any of it.

He'd failed. He'd thrown the dice and lost. He should have listened to Spud. Told the authorities what he knew and enlisted their help in finding his daughter, rather than coming here and clutching at straws. The old nausea washed over him. He felt himself starting to shake. As if all his strength had been drained out of him.

The younger royals turned from the members of the public. Still joking with each other, they turned towards the church.

Danny collapsed to his knees. He put his head in his hands. Anger was suddenly burning through his veins. He thumped a clenched fist against the bark of a tree, and didn't even wince when he felt his skin scraping away. There was a strange ringing sound on the edge of his hearing. It seemed to come from inside his skull. With his face clenched, he shook his head to get rid of it.

The sound didn't go. It was high-pitched. Needling. Distant.

He suddenly took a sharp intake of breath. His eyes shot open. He looked up.

The sound was not inside his head. It was airborne.

He blinked. A memory crystallised in his mind: the half-burned weather report he'd found in Dhul Faqar's fire.

Wind speeds.

Danny had been so sure that piece of paper had indicated a sniper attack. He'd been wrong. Because it wasn't just bullets that were affected by wind.

He shifted into the firing position. One knee down. He raised his rifle and looked through the sight. All the while, he forced himself to focus on the distant whining sound. Trying to discern the direction it was coming from. He couldn't.

There were footsteps, crashing through the trees behind him. He quickly glanced over his shoulder. Spud was there, running towards him, face sweating, eyes wild.

'It's a—'

'. . . drone strike,' Danny finished the sentence for him, getting his eyes back through the sights. 'That's what the wind report was for.'

He focussed in on the royals and their CP. Particularly on Tony. He showed no sign that he had noticed the sound. 'It must be coming from our direction,' Danny said quickly. 'Tony can't hear it.'

The high-pitched sound was getting louder.

'It's close,' Spud stated.

Danny stood up.

'Mate,' Spud hissed, 'you can't put yourself out there. Those CP guys see you with a rifle, they'll open up immediately. It'll be a fucking firefight, ten against one.'

Spud was right. Danny raised his rifle, so he was covering the airspace above the crowd outside the church. Field of view was too narrow. He lowered the sight slightly to watch the airspace with his naked eye. 'Keep eyes on Tony,' Danny breathed. 'Tell me when he notices the sound.'

'Roger that.'

The whining noise sounded like it was very close. Grating. Threatening. Danny forced himself to take slow, deep breaths. To reduce his heart rate. He could feel the blood thumping in his head. When, if, the time came to take a shot, he needed to time it between those thumps, to give himself the best chance of landing his round.

'How do you think it's weaponised?' Spud said.

'Could be anything,' Danny said without taking his eyes off the airspace. 'IED. Big lump of C5. We're about to find out.'

A pause. The whining noise was directly overhead.

'I didn't believe you,' said Spud. 'My bad.'

'Just keep your eyes on Tony.'

Almost immediately, Spud responded. 'He's got it. He's looking up.'

And even as Spud spoke, Danny saw it.

The drone looked black against the sky. Spider-like. It was about two metres in diameter, with four small rotor blades on the top, a circular, spinning blur. On the underside were two landing skids, which made it look like a miniature helicopter. Height above the ground, approximately fifty feet. It moved at maybe ten miles an hour in a zigzag formation. Danny's response was almost robotic. He raised his rifle and directed his sight at the patch of airspace through which the drone was speeding. It was a sixty-metre shot. Tough, not only because of the distance, but also because of the erratic movement. It flashed across his field of view, too quickly for him to take the shot. But it was enough for him to identify a Go-Pro camera fitted to the base of the drone, and also a second item suspended between the landing skids: a curved bar of metal, chunky and dull-coloured, the convex side pointing towards the earth. Danny immediately recognised it for what it was. He had seen one very recently, in an IS compound in northern Iraq.

'Claymore mine,' he said tersely.

'What about the detonation clackers?'

'It must be modified. Remote detonation.'

'If you hit it, the fucking thing'll blow! It'll take out everyone in the vicinity.'

Danny didn't need telling. The shot had to be right. It had to hit the drone, not the Claymore, and he had to do it before the mine was detonated remotely. He panned his sights across the sky. The fast-moving drone crossed his field of view for a second time. His trigger finger twitched, but he didn't take the shot. The drone had moved out of sight again.

'It's twenty metres from the crowd,' Spud hissed urgently. *'They're in the kill zone already!'*

Danny followed the drone. His heart rate was increasing. He could hear shouting from the direction of the crowd. *'Get down ... GET DOWN!'* No screaming yet – the public didn't know what was happening, what danger they were in ...

'Tony's raised his weapon. He's going to try to take the shot!'

To take out a drone like that, at distance, with a handgun? Good luck with that. It needed a harder-hitting round. It needed Danny's rifle shot ...

The drone came into view again. It was yawing somewhat in mid-air. The Claymore mine wobbled precariously. Danny caressed the trigger.

Heartbeat.

He knew he only had one go. The drone was practically above the crowd. It would detonate any second.

But the shot had to be right . . .

Heartbeat.

'*Take the shot!*' Spud hissed. '*Take the fucking shot, Danny!*'

Heartbeat.

Danny fired.

Heartbeat.

His suppressed weapon made nothing but a dull knocking sound as Danny expertly absorbed the recoil into his body. At exactly the same time, there was the much louder report of an unsuppressed handgun from the direction of the crowd. Danny knew instinctively that Tony had fired on the drone simultaneously with him. He was in no doubt, however, as to whose round had hit its mark.

His.

He lowered his weapon, breath held. The whining of the drone had suddenly become even more high-pitched. The rotors were failing. The drone itself was rocking from side to side. Struggling to keep height. Forty metres. Thirty. Danny's eyes were fixed on the distant curved shape of the Claymore mine as it swung like a pendulum, one second pointing at the crowd – who were now all crouching on the ground as the royal CP team started bundling their charges towards the safety of the church – the next second pointing clear of them, before swinging back to the crowd.

And then away from them again.

The motor cut out. The whining stopped. The drone dropped like a stone, the Claymore pointing momentarily towards safety. But it still had the momentum of its last swing. As it hurtled to the ground, it started skewing back towards the crowd.

The drone was twenty feet in the air when the Claymore detonated.

There was a massive crack that reverberated across the Sandringham grounds, as the hundreds of tiny shrapnel beads inside the Claymore sprayed down towards the earth at sickening velocity. The force of the blast knocked the drone up and sideways a couple of metres, while the shrapnel itself made a sound not unlike machine gun fire as it blistered into the metal and glass of the two black vehicles parked in front of the church.

There was a moment of silence, then the drone hit the earth with a distinct crash.

The royals were still being bundled into the church. The public were on the ground. More security guys were running towards them from the direction of the west gates. Danny couldn't tell at first if any of the crowd had been hit by the Claymore shrapnel. His question was answered in seconds. There was sudden screaming – three people, maybe four. Danny had heard the screams of the wounded enough times to know that he was listening to them now.

'Those CP dorks are only interested in the fucking royals,' Spud said, his voice slightly wild and highly strung. 'We should get to the wounded.'

Danny turned. 'No. We need to find the fuckers who were controlling that drone.'

A shadow fell across Spud's face. 'They could be anywhere,' he said hoarsely. 'Those drones have a range of, what? Two miles? We can't—'

'I said we need to find the—'

He was cut short by the sound of gunfire. It came from the west. A single shot that echoed across the misty morning. There was another surge of screams from the crowd. Danny barely heard them. He started sprinting through the trees towards the perimeter of the grounds. He gave no thought to silence or subtlety now. He crashed through the mist and the undergrowth, vaguely aware of Spud following just behind, his only objective to find the source of that gunshot. Perhaps someone had caught up with whoever had been controlling the drone. That thought was all he had now. His only lead to Mujahid, and to his family.

They hit the perimeter fence in less than a minute, about twenty-five metres from the west gate. They could hear shouting and chaos from the direction of the church. The gate itself, however, was unmanned.

'We can't use the gate,' Spud said immediately. 'There'll be cameras. People will know we've been on site.'

Danny sniffed. He raised his rifle, looked through the sight and in a matter of seconds had located the position of the security camera overlooking the entrance. A simple shot. He released a single suppressed round and immediately saw the camera shatter and fall limply to one side. 'Move,' he told Spud.

They ran along the perimeter fence. When they hit the gate, Danny briefly glanced left. He could see the church fifty metres away. The crowd back on their feet. Chaos. Shouting. A good moment to slip away. They ran through the gates and across the road. There was a visitor centre here. It was closed, naturally, the environs deserted. Danny and Spud thundered past the little collection of buildings to find a car park beyond them. Maybe fifty cars, obviously belonging to the Sandringham visitors. And surrounding the car park, shrouded in heavy mist, was thick forest.

Danny sprinted north to the far end of the car park. This was the direction from which the gunshot had come. He burst into the trees again, Spud close behind. Visibility through the trees and the mist, ten metres max. He forged twenty metres beyond the treeline.

A dead body was slumped against the foot of a gnarled old tree. The man was clearly freshly shot, straight in the face. His features were unrecognisable, and the blood was flowing freely. He was still clutching something: a hand-held screen in a tough, rugged case, which was covered in spatters of gore. The corpse's hands told Danny that he was dark-skinned.

Danny's stomach turned to ice. Was this Mujahid? Had he been killed before he could give Danny the information he needed?

'Is that him?' Spud asked.

Danny stepped up to the corpse. He put his hand underneath the sticky, dripping chin, lifted the head and, with his free hand, wiped more blood away from the neck.

There was no scar.

'No,' Danny said, letting the chin drop heavily to the corpse's chest again. 'Not him.'

'Drone that size,' Spud said, 'needs two operators. One to watch the camera footage and navigate, the other to operate the controls.'

Danny stood up straight and looked around. His sharp eyes immediately picked something out. There was a tree sucker, six paces to the north, with several sharp thorns sprouting from the side. Hanging from one of these thorns was a thread of red fibre. Someone had brushed against it as they passed.

'Someone must have been on to them,' Danny said. 'If they killed this guy, they'll be trying to kill Mujahid too . . .'

Danny couldn't let that happen.

They started running through the forest again. The trees grew thicker all around, but there was a clear animal trail through them. The path of least resistance, which anyone running in this direction would have followed. Thirty metres from the corpse, Danny noticed that a tree branch crossing the trail had half snapped – the lesion was fresh – so it was pointing in the direction he was running. Confirmation that he was heading the right way.

More confirmation came thirty seconds later, in the form of another gunshot.

It was loud and close. And it was immediately followed by the sound of a scream, which faded away into a pained whimper. The sounds stopped Danny in his tracks. He stared, breathing heavily, through the thick trees. The mist was thick. Like smoke. Barely five metres' visibility now. But there was no doubt about it. The pained sound was coming from straight ahead. Danny's best estimate was that whoever it came from was twenty metres from their position.

He prepped his weapon. Safety off. Butt into the shoulder. Spud did the same. 'If it's Mujahid, we need him alive,' Danny reminded his mate under his breath.

'Shame,' Spud replied.

They advanced, stepping more carefully now, keeping footfall to a minimum. He didn't know what he was about to stumble across, but he knew he had to be prepared to fight. So, once more, his weapon was an extension of his body. If Danny turned, the weapon would turn. And whoever got in his way would be the half inch of a trigger squeeze from death.

Figures emerged hazily from the mist. Just silhouettes. No faces. Distance: fifteen metres.

There were two people. One was on the ground, leaning against the tree as the previous corpse had been. The other was standing a couple of metres in front of him. One arm stretched out straight, at right angles to Danny's trajectory. A handgun in his fist. Danny could tell, at a glance, that the person holding the gun was not a pro. The arm was locked and shaking, and Danny could tell from his stance that the recoil would knock him backwards. That didn't make him any less dangerous, though, so Danny trained his own weapon directly on the figure, while he tried to work out what the hell was going on here. If the corpse they'd already encountered was anything to go by, the guy on the floor – who had just started moaning again – was dark-skinned and probably connected with the drone. Mujahid? Maybe. But who was the guy with the gun? Security services? Police? No way. He was holding that thing like he was scared of it . . .

Distance: ten metres.

'Drop your weapon!' Danny shouted. He kept his own rifle firmly trained on its target.

The gunman didn't move. He just kept the weapon pointing straight ahead of him.

Danny stepped forward. 'I said, drop the weapon.' As he spoke, the gunman's face, almost in profile, became a little clearer. Those features made him hesitate. They confused him. The gunman had dark skin. Was this Mujahid? It couldn't be. He was too young. Fifteen? Sixteen at a push. He wore very ordinary clothes – jeans, trainers, an old red hooded top. His dark hair fell in a centre parting. He had on a pair of glasses with thick rims. Sideways on, Danny could just make out that those glasses were being held together by Sellotape. He looked like a nerdy kid.

Danny moved his gaze to the kid's target on the ground. He instantly felt himself burning up with hatred. This guy had obviously taken a round to the left shoulder and was clutching it with his right hand, but blood was seeping through his fingers. His body shook badly. He was wearing black clothes – a warm waterproof jacket, sturdy boots. Lying to the side of him was a drone control unit with a long silver antenna.

Danny focussed in on the target's face. He didn't even need to see this bastard's neck. He immediately recognised those features from the video clip he'd seen back at the IS compound in Iraq. He knew it was Mujahid.

And it was very obvious that the kid with the gun wanted him dead.

Danny took another step closer. He saw that the kid was crying. Shoulders shaking. Tears running down his cheek.

'You need to listen to me very carefully,' Danny said in as neutral a voice as he could muster. 'You have to put that gun down. If you don't, I'll have no option but to fire, and trust me, I don't want to do that.'

There was a pause. The gunman glanced in Danny's direction. 'Are you the police?' His sobbing voice trembled.

'No. Not the police. But you still have to drop that weapon.'

The kid was breathing heavily. He didn't move the gun. 'You know what he did?' he said. 'You know what he did to my mother and father? He hung my father from a tree. He raped my mother and killed her, and made me watch. I have tracked him all the way from Syria. It has taken me months. And you think I'm going to let him go now?' He gave a humourless, tear-filled laugh.

Danny moved forward again, two paces. He was only five metres from the gunman, and he spoke with a sudden, quiet urgency. 'Let him go? I promise you, my friend, that's the last thing I'm going to let happen to this man. By the time I've finished with him, he's going to wish you'd emptied every round in that weapon straight into his skull. That bullet in the shoulder? It'll be the least of his problems.'

Another step forward. Three metres. The kid didn't shift position. His body shook even worse than before. 'I can't trust you,' he whispered. 'I can't trust anyone here.'

'What's your name?' Danny said.

'Joe.'

'That your real name?'

'No.'

'Doesn't matter to me. You know those things this guy did to your family?'

The kid nodded hesitantly.

'He's going to do all those things to my family too. If you kill him now, I'll never find them.' Danny narrowed his eyes and then, knowing that Spud would have him covered, he took a gamble. He lowered his weapon. 'You're a clever kid, Joe. I can tell that. You know what to do.'

Joe blinked at him, his eyes still heavy with tears. Then, slowly, hesitantly, he let his gun arm fall to his side.

The reaction from the kid's target was immediate. Still clutching the wound on his shoulder, he made a sudden and frenzied attempt to scramble to his feet. But Danny was there before he could even stand up. With all the force he could muster, he jabbed the heel of his right foot directly into the gun wound in the militant's shoulder. The guy inhaled sharply with the sudden pain, and was clearly about to shout out again when Danny directed a second kick hard into the pit of his stomach, winding him so badly that Danny knew he wouldn't be able to shout out for at least thirty seconds.

Danny bent down, grabbed a chunk of the target's hair and yanked his head back. There, clearly visible, was a scar the shape of a smile that spanned the entire width of his neck.

'Hello Mujahid,' he breathed. He leaned in closer so that his lips were just an inch from his target's ear. 'My name's Danny Black. Maybe it rings a bell.'

The effect of his name was immediate. Mujahid started to writhe and struggle, desperately trying to get away. It was a useless attempt. Still clutching his hair, Danny simply slammed his face against the rough bark of the tree. Soft enough to keep the bastard conscious, hard enough to hurt. Badly. Then he leaned in again.

'I think you've got something that belongs to me,' he said.

TWENTY-FIVE

'What was it? What the bloody hell was it?'

Yellow Seven was stammering. His hands shaking. The rest of the royals were at the altar end of the church, surrounded by a ring of close protection officers. Yellow Seven had somehow broken free of them. None of the public had been allowed inside, of course. Too great a security risk. Tony could hear their panicked commotion outside as he stood near the church's entrance, with Yellow Seven tugging at his arm.

'I said, what the bloody hell was it?'

'Remotely controlled drone,' Tony said. 'Modified Claymore mine.'

'Someone was trying to kill us?'

Tony gave him a withering look. 'Yes, your Grace. Someone was trying to kill you. If that drone had been a few metres higher when it blew, it would've butchered all of us.'

'And you ... you shot that thing down?'

Tony kept his poker face. 'Yes,' he lied.

Yellow Seven blinked. 'There's an honour in this for you, Tony. I'm going to see to it that there's a—'

'You need to get with the other CP guys. The threat could be ongoing.'

'Where are you going?'

Tony sniffed. 'Hunting for bad guys,' he said.

He left Yellow Seven standing there and walked out of the church.

It was bedlam. Half the crowd were still crouching on the ground, ghostly amid the heavy mist. Mothers were clutching their children and crying. Everybody was avoiding the twisted form of the downed drone, but it was impossible to get away from the stench of cordite in the air, a remnant of the Claymore's explosion. A couple of security guys were tending to the wounded with the help of two men who looked like they might be doctors. A body was lying aside from the others, its face covered with someone's jacket. It looked small, probably a kid.

Tony wasn't here to mourn the dead. He was here to find Danny Black. After all the work he'd put in on Yellow Seven and his inbred family, Tony was fucked if he was going to let Black take the glory. He gave the treelines surrounding the area a cursory scan, but he knew he wouldn't see Danny or Spud there. Because even if everyone else, in the chaotic aftermath of the drone strike, had missed the sound of gunshots to the north, Tony hadn't. He knew that Danny Black would be following that sound.

He started moving clear of the crowd, past the vehicles peppered with Claymore shrapnel, putting the screams of the injured from his head. After only a few seconds, he sensed someone at his shoulder. He turned to see Matt, the whisky-loving kid from the CCTV room. 'Where you going, Tony?' he asked breathlessly.

'Checking the perimeter.'

'I'll come with you.'

Like hell you will, Tony thought.

'Mate,' he said, 'you need to do me a solid. Get into the church, keep an eye on Yellow Seven. Don't let him get a bad case of stupid and leave the church before we get the all-clear.'

Matt's face became doubly serious. He nodded and ran back to the church, leaving Tony to start jogging towards the exit.

He picked up pace as he drew clear of the crowd, knowing that he would be fading from their view as he headed off into the mist. It had been three minutes since the strike. Another ten minutes, this place would be crawling with armed response units and buzzing with helicopters. He needed to catch up with Black before that happened. Make it clear to him who was running this show.

He sprinted through the gates at full pelt. His instinct told him that the gunfire had come from the direction beyond the visitors' centre on the far side of the perimeter road. He shot through the collection of small buildings to the car park on the other side. He hesitated here for a moment. The car park was surrounded by trees. Where now?

His directions came in the form of a second gunshot. Directly north, beyond the far end of the car park. Tony didn't know what the hell the gunshot meant, but he followed it anyway. He burst through the trees into the forest, his breath steaming in the mist as he ran.

Twenty metres on, he came across proof that he was heading in the right direction: a corpse, slumped against a tree, a close-quarter bullet wound to its face, a smashed-up navigation screen in its fist. Tony gave it only the briefest of glances. He scanned the area to the north. His eyes instantly zoomed in on a tree sucker, springing up from the ground, with a red thread of clothing hanging from one of its thorns.

He followed the direction that the marker indicated, surging along an animal trail that showed signs of having been recently followed – bent-back branches and the occasional footprint in the softer patches of earth.

After forty-five seconds, he stopped.

There were figures in the mist up ahead. Twenty metres. Four of them. They were just silhouettes, but Tony could make out the squat form of Spud Glover with his back to him. Another figure was slumped up against a tree, and the remaining two were close to each other, apparently talking. Muffled voices drifted through the mist towards Tony, but he couldn't hear them clearly.

He drew his weapon and stepped forward. Slowly. Silently.

Sudden movement up ahead. One of the figures – Tony could see now that it was Black – had rushed over to the person slumped at the base of the tree. Black had grabbed the figure's hair and was slamming his face against the trunk. Bending over to whisper in his ear.

Tony was ten metres from them now, and only five from Spud. He saw that the fourth figure was a Middle Eastern-looking kid with thick-rimmed glasses and a shabby red hoodie, awkwardly carrying a handgun.

Tony gave himself a moment to take in this scene, to get straight in his head what he thought was happening. Then he cleared his throat.

Spud spun round. Instant dislike spread across his face, but that didn't bother Tony. The kid with glasses shrank back a little – he looked like he was thinking of running. Fine. Let the fucker run. Black was the only one Tony was interested in.

And as Tony stood there, Black turned towards him, still holding the figure by his hair. Even Tony was surprised by the appearance of his Regiment-mate. His eyes were bloodshot, his bruised face as pale as death. And when he spoke, his cracked voice was hoarse.

'Get out of here, Tony.'

Tony gave a bleak smile. He stepped forward. Spud stood in his way, weapon raised.

'You never were one of life's thinkers, Glover,' Tony said. 'But even you're not that stupid.'

With a contemptuous flick of his hand, he brushed Spud's weapon away. Spud didn't stop him as he paced towards Black.

'So,' Tony continued coolly. 'Looks like you got your man. Has he given you the location of little baby Black yet?'

'This is nothing to do with you,' Black said. 'Take my advice and fuck off out of here. You can tell your new friends it was you who stopped the hit, let them puncture your chest with medals.'

'I already have, Black, you don't need to worry about that. Of course, that doesn't mean there isn't a bit of unfinished business.'

Black yanked his prisoner to his feet. The guy's face was scraped bloody, and he looked like he was going to piss himself with fear. 'I haven't got time for this,' Black said. He looked over at Spud. 'Let's move,' he said, and he nodded at the young kid with the glasses too. 'Come with me,' he said. 'We need to get you away from the police.'

Black gave Tony a look of contempt before turning his back on him and facing further into the forest.

Tony moved fast while he still had the opportunity, and to stop that moron Spud Glover doing anything stupid. He raised his handgun and fired.

There was no question of missing. Not at a range of five metres. Not for Tony. The 9mm round from his handgun slammed straight into the back of Danny Black's prisoner. Tony knew that the round would enter his heart from behind, and kill him instantly.

The sound of Tony's weapon resounded through the forest. Mujahid collapsed.

Danny jumped back as he fell.

The world seemed to spin.

He fell to his knees, preparing to administer CPR, to try to keep his prisoner alive. But it was totally obvious that Mujahid was dead already. No breathing. No pulse. Blood seeping from his back.

Danny got to his feet again.

Deadly slow.

He turned to Tony.

Spud looked genuinely panicked, like he didn't know what to do. For a moment, Danny thought he saw a twinge of fear in Tony's face. Like the sight of Danny walking slowly towards him had got him thinking he'd maybe gone too far. But the expression died quickly, and was replaced with Tony's regular arrogant swagger.

A sudden scuffle. Spud had kicked Tony behind the knee. It was impossible for Tony to remain standing. He collapsed. A moment later, Danny and Spud were standing over him, weapons pointing down at him.

'What the – what the hell—' Danny could hardly talk. He felt like he was hyperventilating. 'That man – my daughter – you *knew*—'

Tony slowly got to his feet. 'Poor Danny Black,' he said, as insultingly as possible. 'But let's look on the bright side. Not only did I shoot down the drone that was going to take out, what, a hundred and fifty people? I also just stuck a round in the heart of the fucker responsible. That's got to be worth a bit of a celebration. For me at least. I'd say this is turning into my day.'

Danny pressed the barrel of his rifle into Tony's chest. 'Maybe,' he breathed, 'your day's about to take a turn for the worse.'

Tony looked meaningfully at the two weapons pointing at him. Then he smiled again, this time as though he was genuinely amused. 'You're not going to shoot me,' he said quietly. 'Nor's your monkey. You're too cute for that, Black. Give it a few minutes, this place is going to be crawling. Security. Armed response. Military. Do you really want to explain to them why they found me with a round from your stolen Regiment weapon embedded in my chest? Who's going to save your darling little daughter when they've stuffed you in a prison cell?'

Silence. Nobody moved.

'I'm leaving now, fellas,' Tony said. 'Do yourselves a favour and don't try to stop me.' He stepped backwards. Neither Danny nor Spud lowered their weapons. But they didn't fire them either.

As Tony continued to move backwards, there was a new sound. A helicopter, somewhere overhead. Clearly heading towards the attack site.

'Here comes the cavalry,' Tony said. 'Get the hell out of here now and I won't tell anyone you've been sniffing around Sandringham, or that you knew about the hit and failed to warn anyone. It can be our little secret, right?'

He turned his back on them. A deliberate gesture. And a brave one. Danny was burning with rage. He was on the point of releasing a round. But Tony's words had rung true. There was no turning back from shooting a Regiment-mate in cold blood.

'Hold your fire,' he breathed to Spud.

They lowered their weapons.

The chopper was louder. Almost directly overhead. A searchlight cut through the canopy and the mist. Tony stopped. He let the chopper pass. Then he turned again.

'Word of advice, fellas,' he called. 'Next time you want to screw me over, like you did after that op in the Med, think twice, yeah?'

Tony cocked his head as though listening to something. Danny heard it too. Voices. Many. From the direction of the Sandringham Estate. Moving this way. A self-satisfied smile spread across Tony's face. 'I'd get out of here, Danny Black,' he said.

He jogged away, and disappeared into the mist.

TWENTY-SIX

'Danny!'

Spud's voice was little more than a low, urgent hiss. Danny barely heard it. He was still in shock.

'*Mate!* We've got to get out of here. We can't let them find us. If they—'

'You!' Danny said. He had turned to look at the young man with the glasses and the red hoodie. The kid who'd called himself Joe was still holding his gun, but he was now staggering backwards into the forest, his eyes wild.

'I'm not going to hurt you,' Danny said.

Spud stepped even closer to Danny. 'Fuck's sake, mucker. Let him go. If we get our collars felt, we're going to—'

Danny shrugged him off. The voices in the forest were getting nearer. He didn't care. He stepped towards Joe. 'How did you get here?' he said.

Joe blinked heavily, but didn't answer.

Danny pointed towards Mujahid's bleeding corpse. 'You knew where to find him,' he said. 'How?'

'Danny!' Spud hissed. 'If we don't go now, we're fucked.'

Spud was right. The voices were loud now. Close. Thirty metres. Maybe less. He nodded. Together they jogged past the corpse towards Joe. 'Stick with us,' Danny told him, 'and you'll be OK.'

Joe nodded nervously. He let Danny take his weapon. Danny made the handgun safe, then grabbed Joe's arm. 'Run,' he said.

The trio sprinted off in a north-westerly direction, into the penetrating mist of the forest. Danny and Spud made almost no noise as their boots skimmed over the forest floor. The kid was more of a problem. He was gangly and awkward. Dead branches crunched heavily under his feet, and he was out of breath within thirty seconds. Danny didn't let go of him. He couldn't let him drag behind. He couldn't lose him.

They ran for two minutes, then stopped. 'What are we—' Joe started to ask, but Danny silenced him. He listened carefully. The sound of voices had disappeared. He looked enquiringly at Spud.

'Nothing,' Spud breathed.

'Tony will be telling them that he caught up with and shot the target,' Danny said.

'They're still going to scour the area for accomplices,' Spud pointed out. 'We're going to be compromised in the next ten minutes. We've got to keep moving.'

Danny consulted his mental map. 'By my reckoning, our vehicle's about a klick north-east of here,' he said. 'Agreed?'

'Agreed,' Spud said. They'd parked it in a road siding, well clear of the Sandringham Estate.

'We can make it in five.'

'I can't run—' Joe gasped. 'I have to rest . . .'

Danny turned to him. 'You're a Muslim kid in the vicinity of a terror attack. Trust me. You can't rest yet.'

'We need to get our bearings first,' Spud said. Danny watched as his mate hurried up to a tree trunk. He circled it, examining it to see which part of the trunk had the most moss. That would tell them which way was south. After a couple of seconds Spud nodded and pointed off at an angle. 'That way,' he said.

Danny still didn't let go of Joe as they changed trajectory. The mist swirled and curled around them. Occasionally, a voice drifted through the trees towards them. Hard to determine the direction from which it came. They had no option but to keep running and to hope they had their own direction right.

Six minutes. They hit a road. Joe was gasping for air. Danny looked to the right. The rented Honda was just visible by the side of the road, fifteen metres distant. Their bearings had been spot on. He was about to lead the others towards it, when the sound of a siren hit their ears – distant, but approaching. He yanked Joe back into the cover of the trees. Twenty seconds later, two police cars screamed past. Their sirens faded. Danny, Spud and Joe remained statue-still. The only noise was Joe's heavy breathing.

But now there was a new sound. Another chopper overhead. Danny looked up. Through the bare canopy of the forest he suddenly saw the charcoal-grey silhouette of a military helicopter about a hundred feet up, its edges blurred and ill-defined because of the mist. It was moving fast and south, towards the Sandringham Estate.

'Let it pass,' Danny breathed.

Thirty seconds later it was out of earshot.

Joe had regained his breath. Now the only sound was the persistent dripping of condensation from tree branches all around them.

'Get to the vehicle,' Danny said. 'Now.'

They sprinted across the road. Once they were at the Honda, Danny threw the keys to Spud. 'Drive,' he said. He turned to Joe. 'You – in the back with me.'

Joe looked scared. His patched-up glasses had slipped down his face, which was sweating and dirty. He seemed very unsure that he should do what Danny said.

'Unless you get in the car with us,' Danny told him, 'you're *going* to be picked up by the security services. Do you think they're not going to shoot the only Muslim in the vicinity of a major terrorist event?'

His words obviously hit home. Joe's face twitched. Spud pressed the key fob to unlock the car doors. Joe clambered into the back. Danny opened the boot. He and Spud carefully placed their weapons inside, then he climbed into the back while Spud took the wheel.

There were no tyre screeches. No revving of the engine. Spud clearly understood that if they were to get out of here they needed to keep under the radar. He switched on the headlamps to burn through the mist, and trundled carefully on to the road.

Danny turned to Joe. 'How did you know where to find him?'

Joe was digging his nails into his palms. 'Are you sure I'm not in trouble?'

'You're in a world of trouble, Joe. Unless you stick with me. But you've got to tell me: how did you know where to find him?'

Joe drew a deep breath. 'I tracked him,' he said.

Danny shook his head. 'I don't get it,' he said. 'How?'

'I – I was forced to work for Daesh in Syria. After he ... after Mujahid killed my mum and dad.'

'What sort of work?'

'Computer systems, social media – they wanted me because I'm ...' He searched around for the right phrase. 'Because I'm good at it,' he finished a bit feebly. 'I told your security services this. They tried to threaten me. I ran away.'

'How did you track him, Joe?'

'Through his communications with Daesh. And through his phone.'

Danny stared at him. 'How long have you been doing that for?' he asked. His heart was pumping hard.

'A couple of days,' Joe said.

Danny was almost too scared to ask the question. 'So you know where he's been?' he breathed.

Joe nodded.

'*Exactly* where he's been?'

'Of course.'

'Can you show me?'

The kid looked at the rucksack on his lap. 'I need a lead for my laptop,' he said. 'And power.'

Danny's mouth was suddenly dry. He tasted something almost – but not quite – like excitement.

'You got it,' he said.

Guy Thackeray, director of MI6, looked sick.

It seemed that with every minute that passed, a new piece of information, each one worse than the last, reached his ears. An innocent choirboy shot in Westminster Abbey in full view of the PM by an out-of-control SAS man. A terrorist strike at Sandringham. Three casualties, including one child.

If Thackeray still had a job by Boxing Day, it would be a miracle.

But that wasn't the worst of it. The news out of Iraq had left him dumbstruck. The CIA negotiating with Islamic State. The Americans withholding intelligence from the British because they planned to strike a deal with IS just like they'd cosied up to the mujahideen in the eighties.

No wonder Langley was avoiding his calls.

But they couldn't avoid him for ever. And now, the secure phone in his office overlooking the London skyline on this brutal Christmas Day was ringing. He picked it up.

'Thackeray,' he said.

'Guy. It's Al.'

Al Scott, his counterpart at Langley.

'I have to tell you, Guy, we got some pretty pissed individuals here at the agency, and in Washington.'

Thackeray didn't trust himself to speak. So he didn't.

'It seems your guy Danny Black had every opportunity to help our mole escape out there in Iraq, but didn't. Blew her cover instead. One of our deepest agents, too. Plenty of folk this side of the water want to have a word with him, Guy. Plenty of people.'

Silence on the line. Thackeray breathed deeply.

'Listen carefully, Al,' he said, very quietly. 'Wars have been started for less than this. I recommend you think about that very carefully.'

'Back up there, Thackeray, we will *not* be—'

'And one other thing, Al. If it comes to my attention that Danny Black, or any of my guys involved in that operation, so much as trip up in the street and graze their knee, you're going to find that your agents in London start meeting with accidents.'

Silence.

The door opened. Alice Cracknell walked in. Her face was haunted. 'It's the PM,' she mouthed. 'He wants to see you now.'

'I hope I've made myself clear, Al,' Thackeray said, and he put down the phone. He looked at Alice. 'Where is he?' he demanded.

'We don't know,' she said. 'He's just . . .' She spread her hands. 'He's just disappeared.'

Thackeray stepped out from behind his desk. 'He's in danger,' he said. 'Find him.'

'But sir—'

'*Find Danny Black!*' Thackeray shouted, and he stormed out of the office.

Christmas Day. Nothing was open. Spud drove carefully through the wide, flat Norfolk scenery. Past closed-up roadside burger vans, and through sleepy towns with fairy lights twinkling in the windows, and no pedestrians on the streets. The only indication that this Christmas Day was different to any other was the police presence. They passed countless police cars heading in the opposite direction, their neon lights flashing but their sirens switched off. They saw five choppers speeding back the way they'd come, including a Chinook. They passed several military trucks, heavy and khaki-coloured, carrying troops to the strike area.

Each one made Danny's pulse race. They couldn't risk being stopped. It wasn't that he cared about anyone finding the weapons stashed carelessly in the boot of this rented vehicle. It wasn't that they were AWOL. It wasn't that they had a wanted former IS associate in the back of the car.

It was simply this: the clock was ticking. And with every second that passed, Clara and Rose's chances of survival diminished.

1147 hours. Spud slowed down as they approached a roundabout. There was a Little Chef off the second exit. Five or six cars were parked out front. It looked open.

'Pull over here,' Danny instructed.

'Who has their fucking Christmas lunch at a Little Chef?' Spud murmured as he drove towards the restaurant and parked up.

Two dirty, tired, grizzled Regiment men. A scared Muslim kid in tow. Danny knew they looked like an unusual trio as they entered the restaurant, which stank of grease and bad coffee. He didn't care. He told the spotty teenage waitress that they needed a seat by a power socket. They were led to one with bad grace. They asked for the Wi-Fi code and ordered black coffee. Danny and Spud watched as the kid plugged in his laptop, using Danny's lead.

'It will take a couple of minutes to power up,' he said.

Danny nodded. He looked around. There were four other parties in here. All of them were eyeing the kid with barely concealed mistrust. On the far wall a TV was on. BBC News. The sound was down, but that didn't matter to Danny. He recognised the aerial shots of Sandringham House and grounds. Stills of the church, and of Yellow Seven and the other royals. Danny thought he caught a glimpse of Tony standing there behind them.

The footage cut to Westminster Abbey. Crowds. A high police presence. A part of his mind wondered what had been happening there. But he was too focussed on other things to care deeply.

'It's on,' Joe said.

His fingers flew across the keyboard, opening up windows that displayed lines of impenetrable code. Then, after thirty seconds, a map appeared. Joe tapped on the screen, and Danny examined it.

There were pins placed in the map, many of them, at approximately five-millimetre intervals. They described a journey. It started in London. Moved along the roads Danny knew so well to Hereford. From Hereford it moved north-east, to Birmingham.

From Birmingham, the trail disappeared. But then there were more pins on the north Norfolk coast. Joe pointed at the gap between the two. 'He must have removed the battery from his phone between here and here,' he said.

'How long was he in Birmingham?'

Joe hovered over the pins. 'About two hours,' he said. 'On the morning of the twenty-third.'

'Can you give me an address?'

Joe swallowed hard. He typed a few more lines of code. Cross-referenced a GPS location. 'Yes,' he said. 'I can.'

'Danny,' Spud said quietly. He glanced towards the counter at the front of the restaurant. The spotty waitress was on the phone.

She had one hand over the mouthpiece, as though talking secretly. She was looking at the three of them, and occasionally glancing towards the TV screen.

Danny pulled out a twenty-pound note and left it on the table. 'Pack up,' he said.

The kid blinked at him, then shut down the lid on his computer and quickly stuffed it into his rucksack. By that time Danny and Spud were already on their feet. They strode to the exit, Joe scurrying behind them. The waitress slammed her phone down, guilt written all over her face.

Back at the vehicle, they took their usual seats. Danny turned to Joe. 'The address,' he said. 'Give it to me.'

'Milton Road,' he said. 'I'm sorry, I can't tell you the number.'

That didn't matter. For Danny Black, it was information enough.

Ray Hammond's landline was ringing, and so was his mobile. He ignored them both and stared at the member of Regiment support staff standing nervously at the other side of his desk.

'What?' he snapped.

'They've been sweeping the ground at Sandringham. They found a box of ammo in the bushes near the strike area. They came from the Regiment armoury. We've just checked it. There are several items missing. Two assault rifles, two handguns, sights, radio equipment, ammo—'

'Yeah, I get the fucking picture,' Hammond spat. 'Did you call Danny Black and Spud Glover in?'

'We tried to, boss.'

'What do you mean, you tried to?'

'They're not at home. We called, sent people round . . .'

Hammond covered his eyes with his hands. 'Find him,' he said.

'Boss, he's gone AWOL.'

'Don't give me fucking excuses!' Hammond roared.

The guy swallowed hard. 'We've had a report of two men answering their description in a Little Chef about eighty miles from Sandringham,' he stuttered. 'But I don't think it can be them.

They had a Middle Eastern kid with them. I mean, surely he's not—'

'Just find him!' Hammond shouted. 'Just find Danny Black!'

Night had fallen.

Milton Road was an unpleasant street on the northern edge of Birmingham. Houses along one side. Lock-ups along the other. There were no Christmas lights here. It wasn't that kind of area.

The mist had stuck around all day. Now the temperature had dropped and the fog seemed to freeze against everything. The windows. The tarmac. The metal of Danny and Spud's weapons.

The car was parked at the top of the street. Danny, Spud and Joe were standing on the opposite side of the road, next to a lock-up whose grey garage door was fastened with a huge padlock.

'You can stay,' Danny said. 'We'll find a place for you.'

Joe shook his head. 'I want to disappear. It shouldn't be too hard. I've been learning how to be invisible.'

Danny inclined his head. He put his hand in his pocket and pulled out a thick wad of notes, which he handed over to Joe. The kid looked hesitant. 'Take it,' Danny said. 'Find somewhere warm to stay. You ever need me, get a message to RAF Credenhill. Can you remember that?'

'RAF Credenhill.' He took the money and gave Danny a grateful look.

'If you're going to go,' Danny said, 'it's best you go now.'

Joe glanced up the road. 'Are you going to kill them?' he asked.

Danny sniffed. 'What's your real name, Joe?'

'Yusuf,' the kid said.

Danny nodded. 'It's best you go now, Yusuf,' he said.

The kid stuffed the money into his trousers and stuck his hands in the pockets of his hoodie. He nodded at Danny and Spud, then turned his back on them and walked away into the freezing mist.

Danny and Spud watched until his grey silhouette disappeared.

'Good kid, that,' Spud said. Then, as they both turned to look the other way: 'Ready?'

Danny looked down at himself. He was filthy. Covered in blood, sweat and mud. He removed his Sig from its holster, cocked the weapon and then made it safe. When he looked back at Spud, he saw that his mate had done the same. 'Ready,' he said.

They walked calmly and silently down the street. They heard music coming from one of the houses. Distinctively Arabic. They passed that house, and three others, before stopping.

They were outside house number nine. It looked just like all the others. With one small difference. Just to the side of the front door was a pram. Danny recognised it. Recognised the multi-coloured toy tied to the handle that he had bought for his daughter just six days ago.

In the front window was hung a thick net curtain. Behind that curtain was the silhouette of a woman holding a child. She was pacing the room, swaying from side to side, clearly trying to comfort the baby.

Spud turned to Danny. 'Shall we go get them?' he said.

Danny nodded. He flicked off the safety catch of his weapon. Then he and Spud advanced towards the house.

You have to **survive it**
To **write it**

NEVER MISS OUT AGAIN
ON ALL THE LATEST NEWS FROM

CHRIS RYAN

Be the first to find out about new releases

Find out about events with Chris near you

Exclusive competitions

And much, much more ...